FATES DIVINE

FATE

OF

SMOKE AND ASH

BOOKS BY SHANIA SCICHILONE

The Fates Divine Series

A Fate of Smoke and Ash

READERS DISCRETION

A note for readers,

A FATE OF SMOKE AND ASH is a Young Adult novel; however, it should only be read by mature readers. This book contains sensitive content, and it is advised to review the list of potential Trigger/Content Warnings provided. You can find the list on the author's website at www.shaniascichilone.com under the tab "MORE: TW - Fates Divine Series". Readers discretion is advised.

CHARACTERS

- Shivalri Acadia Grimsbane-Gray (Shih-v-all-rEE Ah-kay-dEE-ah Grim-s-b-ay-n Gur-ay)
- Raidan Grimsbane-Gray (R-eye-den)
- Eden Grimsbane-Gray (EE-d-in)
- Archer Gray (Arch-er)
- Diego (DEE-y-egg-oh)
- Satyra Grimsbane-Duke (S-ah-tEEr-ah D-ooh-k)
- Enya Grimsbane-Duke (Ehn-Yah)
- Olliver/Olly Duke (All-ih-v-er/All-EE)
- Sabine Grimsbane-Cormier (S-ah-b-EE-n K-or-mEE-ay)
- Nathan (N-ay-th-uh-n)
- Avery (Ay-vrEE)
- Mr. Lane (L-ay-n)
- Gladys O'Donnell (Glad-ih-s Oh-d-on-l)
- Moira Darkmore (Moy-r-ah Dark-more)
- Sora Fujin (S-or-ah Fyoo-jEE-uhn)
- Ember Blackwood (EM-ber Bl-æ-k-w-UU-d)
- Damek Lagunov (Dah-mek L-ah-g-uh-n-aw-v)
- Nesrin Mehra (Neh-z-r-in M-ay-r-ah)

- Baaz Mehra (B-ah-z)
- Pyre Malum (P-eye-er M-ah-l-uhm)
- Alriq (All-r-ih-k)
- Nor (N-or)
- Drakovyr (D-r—ay-k-oh-v-EE-r)
- Ombrose (Aw-m-b-r-oh-s)

To the readers who live in the pages with me,
To my husband for the support and never-ending belief in my book,
To my cousins, who never cease to keep magic alive,
And to my grandmother, who instilled storytelling into my soul the
moment I was about to weave words.

CONTENTS

Salem
Witch House
Salem
Proctor's Ledge
House of
Enchantment

Grimsbane
Manor
Essex
Fishing Dock

1

———

DARK

I was floating in darkness, lulled by the pull of the wind caressing me. A thrum beneath the corner of my jaw thumped in tune with my heartbeat as the breeze rocked me tenderly from side to side. My body felt calm, but my mind wouldn't rest. I could feel it then, the unforgiving sensation of the wind clawing at my skin, fooling me into thinking it was comfort. I knew nothing that came from the dark was ever comfort.

I opened my eyes to a blaze of red flame, but it vanished instantly, leaving me in complete obscurity, suspended in the never-ending swelter. I could touch nothing in this oblivion and saw no one as I hung in midair. There was no weight to my body as the darkness hugged me, pressing in, pretending to be gentle love, when it was only trying to snuff me out. I started to panic, trying to shake myself from its grasp. A chill ran down my neck as I felt the claws tighten around me. It would never let me go.

"A dream..." a voice soothed from a far-off distance.

"Who's there?" I croaked, voice dry.

"It is only a dream...."

The darkness around me loosened at the revelation. Still, I hung in its grasp, but no longer did I fight. My eyes stung as the light came forward, surrounding me and illuminating the night sky in which I floated. I could feel my pulse settling now. When I breathed in a long, deep breath, my ribs shuddered from the release. The tension in my neck eased as I looked around. There were no monsters here—only myself.

OMEN

I am exhausted.

I'm eighteen years old, and still, my night terrors frighten me through to morning. They've dramatically increased since leaving Massachusetts and moving to North Carolina. I'm only five weeks into my twelfth-grade school year in this new state and already tired of being away from the Grimsbane family home. Everything was always better there.

In school, I am one year older than most of my classmates. I was born at midnight on New Year's Eve, and I started school late, meaning I'll be nineteen and a half years old when I graduate. The students were quick to point attention to that oddity. Not only does my age make me stand out, but naturally, my hair is a dark ginger tone, and my facial features are all fairly large—big blue and yellow-ringed eyes, big lips, big persistent personality. Before moving, my mom reluctantly agreed to pay to have my hair bleached blonde to avoid starting this new school with similar victimizations. I stand out like a sore thumb with red hair. Blonde is pretty and soft. Red has always felt like a statement that never felt like me. All the women in my family had red hair, and it was weird to part with it, but it felt right.

My brother got the lucky end of the stick, sharing traits with my dad and grandfather. Clean, sharp facial features from my dad's French heritage, and thick, dark hair and bronzed skin like my Acadian grandfather. The unbelievable height and broad shoulders were also from Pépère.

Raidan was the preferred child all around. He had my mother wrapped around his finger from birth. This morning, I'd opened his bedroom door and peeked in to see if he was awake before heading to the bus stop. To no surprise, Raidan was snoring like a sleeping giant, feet hanging off the edge of his too-small bed. I'd flicked his light on, and he rolled onto his stomach, hiding his eyes from the striking light. Diego, our dog, mimicked the movements as he slept peacefully with my brother. Yet again, Mom would be driving Raidan to school while I suffered riding the bus.

My school looked woeful as I walked across the field toward the entrance. The building was gray beneath the rain and did not fit with the beautiful fall colours. A few weeks of this wet weather had taken over my mornings, but I couldn't complain. Though I was drenched from head to toe, and my rheumatoid arthritis was acting up, it was still my favorite time of year. The leaves were so full of animation. I loved how the sun perfectly hit the shades of ruby, mauve, and gold, creating an art-like glimmer atop the soil.

A large raven cawed from a nearby tree, and we watched each other through the mist. It stared at me knowingly as I admired its brilliant feathers. As the bird flew away, I looked back to the ground, appreciating the beauty of the leaves. I found that the dew on the grass had seeped through my beige pants, leaving stains of water along the cuffs. The cool, crisp air felt wet and dry at the same time. I could almost taste the season through my breath. I sent up a silent prayer of thanks to Mother Nature for creating such a wonder. I had always appreciated the outdoors. It was the one thing in this world that eternally changed yet remained unchanged. Beautiful.

OCTOBER

We don't have assigned seating in Mr. Lane's class. Just assigned instructions:

- Do not sit next to someone who will distract you.
- Do not sit next to someone you would like to distract.
- No gum.

Avery, the friend I'd made at this new school, sat at a desk at the back of the classroom, and I plopped right next to him. He was not surprised, rather impassive, and handed me a pen, knowing I had forgotten one.

"You are truly a lifesaver," I said, pretending to wipe the invisible tear from my arid face.

"Truly," he agreed, placing a delicate hand on his heart.

Mr. Lane came through the door, and everyone simultaneously covered their ears in repulsion, knowing he liked to begin the day with torture. He approached the chalkboard and ground his nails, creating the vilest noise of all. I twitched and wrinkled my nose. I would never understand why my history teacher felt the need to commence my day like this every single morning.

"*Bon dia! Kaliméra. Guten Morgen! Bonjour!* Good morning to you all. Welcome to my class. As you all know, I am Mr. Lane. Feel free to call me Mr. Lane," he offered. "I am here to teach you history, and history is what I shall teach. Sit back, buckle up and get ready to hit the road maps." He pulled down the map of Europe stowed away in a roll above the chalkboard and began his lesson.

Unfortunately, I couldn't pay attention. That nightmare from last night kept playing in my mind. I couldn't shake the feeling that there was something more to it. My thoughts circled about my head, mixing into slosh.

"Shivalri, when was World War Two?" I heard from afar. "Shivalri?" It grew louder. "Miss Grimsbane-Gray?"

"What?" I snapped my head up from my desk; eyes peeled wide open. Mr. Lane was looking straight at me, along with the rest of my snickering classmates. In front of me, Nathan sat turned to sketch on my notepad at my desk, his mind elsewhere. Gladys O'Donnell, next to him, sat with her shoulders hunched forward and her nose in her books, a true history buff and teacher's pet. Quickly, she turned around to look at me. It was the first time I'd ever closely seen her face at this embarrassing moment. Her eyes shone beautifully when she made contact. I didn't know the answer to the question, which seemed almost to frustrate her.

"September first, 1939, to September first, 1945," she whispered and quickly turned back. Her face was utterly freckled, and her eyes dark, but she had a bold emerald green on the rim of her left eye. She was entirely enchanting.

"Well?" Mr. Lane prompted.

"Uh... September to September," I scrambled, feeling the heat rush to my cheeks. "Thirty-nine to forty-five," I added.

"Good," he praised. "You're brilliant, Miss O'Donnell, but don't give the answer away so quickly next time." He winked at Gladys. I couldn't imagine how someone with such beauty recoiled from notice, but she slumped, outwardly embarrassed to be in the spotlight.

"Thank you," she muttered. Mr. Lane turned to face me now.

"I'll get you next time," he said, rubbing his hands together and letting out an evil cackle. I rolled my eyes at his over-the-top laugh and copious hand friction and looked down at my note-free notepad.

"What are you drawing, Nathan?" I probed, grabbing my notepad from his pencil-stained hands.

"Don't! It's not done yet," he groaned.

"An eyeball?" I asked as I did a three-sixty of his drawing with my finger on a corner of the notepad.

"It's not done. I'll finish it for you tomorrow," Nathan began to say as the notepad slid from under my thumb and onto the floor.

It landed directly in front of Mr. Lane in the middle of the room in plain sight. I watched as he bent over, snatched it up with his gritty eager hands, and began to read.

"OMG, isn't he like the coolest and most intelligent teacher in the world? Couldn't you just, like, die?" he said in the most annoying, girly voice imaginable. The class was roaring with laughter, and I could feel my face turn into lava.

"I did not write that! You're ridiculous!" I shouted, pointing my finger in his direction.

"OMG, totally! He's like a young Tony Stark," he continued.

"Ha!" I sneered. "I don't even know who Tony Stark is, so there!" I lied.

"Gasp! You are a disgrace." He sighed and clutched his chest. "Come get your notepad before I turn this into a novella," he said, irritably waving my book in the air. I walked over to him, grabbed the book, and with the back of my hand on my forehead, I looked him dead in the eye.

"Please, not a novella," I mocked. The students snickered at the distraction from class. The bell rang as I got to my seat, so I grabbed my stuff and got the hell out of there before becoming the lead character of Mr. Lane's fictional girl-world tale.

Fumbling with Avery's lock, I tried to get into his locker. I decided to opt out of having one of my own since I had never used them. When I brought extra things to school, Avery let me stack whatever I needed on his top shelf. The downfall was that I could never remember his lock combination, and I needed to change my clothes for my gym period after the twenty-minute break. I preferred getting my stuff out beforehand since I often went to the school's auditorium to listen to music or read during my free time. I didn't want to be late for class, so I always took care of getting my things beforehand.

"One, three, two, four. How can you not remember that?" Avery was behind me now, sighing in disapproval. He shoved me aside with his elbow and grabbed ahold of the lock.

"I swear I tried that! It just doesn't like me." I rolled my eyes in disbelief as he unlocked his locker with implausible ease. "I am incapable of being."

"You're welcome," he chided and approached my face with his to rub in the victory.

"Your breath smells like feet," I derided. He blew his breath over me, and I coughed overdramatically, passing him some gum. It didn't actually smell, but we'd grown accustomed to teasing each other whenever the opportunity arose.

"Sorry, I just finished my snack," he said, lifting his gym shoes. Leave it to him to be ready with a prop for his retort.

"Next time, perhaps a granola bar would suffice." I laughed. He popped a piece of gum in his mouth and returned the pack to the locker.

"Thanks for the gum," he said.

"Tame that dragon," I demanded, grabbing my stuff from the locker. He slammed it shut in amused distaste.

"Careful. I bite."

THE AUDITORIUM at this school was large and very old, holding an ominous feel, like many ghosts were floating about, watching from above. Goosebumps pricked my arms as I sensed their presence. It was similar to walking through a graveyard or entering an old abandoned house. Unseen eyes were watching me, but I did not mind their company so long as the lights stayed on.

On either side of the stage, scene houses, cherub-carved statues, and religious paintings covered the ceiling. I felt like I was in a whole other world when I came here, especially when alone. I got to envelop myself in the moment and my surroundings completely. There was never anyone else in the auditorium during the break, and it was completely soundproof. I could play my music as loudly as I wanted, and no one would hear a sound. I always set my alarm on my phone to vibrate in my pocket for the exact instant the school bell rings. Avery told me that the PA system and speakers in the auditorium have been dysfunctional for years now, and it doesn't seem to be within the school's budget to fix it.

After waking from a somewhat restless night this morning, I decided to give myself a moment of relief. I resorted to music to release almost all of my problems and stress. Not only do lyrics carry thousands of stories, but scoring and instrumentation convey feeling and every emotion thinkable. As I listened to the sounds of dark pop reverberating through the echoey room, I started to sway, moving to the rhythm. Flickers of the darkness from my nightmares swarmed my mind, but as the chorus erupted, my movements became less solid, and my body flowed with the lyrics rather than the counts. Spinning throughout the stage, I let my feet guide me into a story of music, and the nightmare washed away. Enveloped in music was the only time elegance ever found me. With no one to hear me, I sang from the top of my lungs, exhilarated by the freedom.

My phone buzzed in my pocket after my allotted time had passed, interrupting my bliss. I rubbed at my knees, sore from the movement, grabbed my books off the floor, and crept up the staircase, shutting the light off behind me.

The students rushed about in a haze, loud in discussions. It almost felt like they were shouting at one another. Noisy, unruly hums boomed from left and right. I turned the corner to head toward the school's front end, where I would find my English class. The voices kept getting louder, frantic. As I looked from student to student, I noted sickness on their faces. A young girl to my right was crying into a friend's shoulder. Flustered, I started to walk a little faster. As I heard the sirens, I bolted to the end of the hall and burst through the school entry. When I made it to the source of turmoil, I lost my breath in one short instance.

"Get her out of here!" I heard from afar. Fast-paced bodies

were rushing all around me, speaking in hushed tones. It all became a blur. Dizziness flooded my head as I realized I had stopped breathing. All I could see was black. Why did I see black? I couldn't see... As soon as I could sense my legs weakening beneath me, I felt two solid arms fold behind my backbone. Those arms then settled my wilted form onto something hard and cold, and I drifted off into space.

4

———

KINDLE

It was so dark; black didn't even begin to describe it. I hated not being able to see my surroundings. Trying with all my ability to force my eyes open, I could feel my entire face straining to see. Suddenly I realized—my eyes were open.

How on Earth was it so dark? Closing my eyes, I blinked forcefully, only to open my eyes and have absolutely nothing change. Where was I?

I could feel a tingling sensation all over my body, as if I had been lying down for centuries, and I felt the urge to move. I started to focus on my vision again. I hated that I couldn't see what was causing my pain, and I didn't want to experience this any longer. The dark was my worst enemy. I opened my eyes as wide as possible, and this time, I felt my eyelashes brush against something. I swiftly grabbed at my face and felt what was evidently a blindfold. As I drove it up to my forehead, the elastic band in the back sprung upward to the top of my head, and the bright white wall in front of me stung my eyes.

I was standing next to a gurney. I did a ninety-degree turn on my heels and realized I was in the teacher's lounge, and no one else was with me. I shook my head in attempt to remove my confusion.

I started to walk toward the door and tried to peer out its tinted window, but I could barely make out what was on the other side. I took a deep breath, twisted the knob, and opened the door. Mr. Lane, my history teacher was standing just outside.

"Are you keeping guard?" I cleared my throat. I could hardly hear myself. Mr. Lane started making gestures in front of my face. "What?" He lunged toward me, and I backed away, startled. He raised his hands, pointed to each of his ears, and repeated something without making sounds. I gave him a dirty look. He reached for my right ear, and before I could say anything, I felt him pull something out of my ear, and I could finally hear again.

"Earplugs," he said, showing me the orange foam he pulled from my ear. I flushed and quickly twisted the other from my left ear. I instantly felt the volume balance itself throughout my head. My vision and hearing restored themselves, though the confusion was unresolved.

"Uh, why was I on a gurney? What's going on?" I asked.

"You don't remember?" he questioned. His brows tilted upward at the inner corners, and his crow's feet worsened. He looked uneasy as if it concerned him that I was disordered.

"I just remember seeing black and being cold. Then I woke up and realized I had been sleeping in the teacher's lounge. What's going on? Am I sick?" My hand flew to my mouth, embarrassment washing over me. "Did I pass out?" I asked as fear rushed through me.

"It's not like that. You did pass out, but you're... You're going to be okay," he muttered, looking at his feet.

"Are you going to tell me what all of this is about?" I was getting impatient. I had had an IV stuck in my arm and was unconscious at school, with little to no explanation. Mr. Lane looked me in the eye, and for the first time, I saw him become sincere rather than the sarcastic man I was used to seeing.

"Shivalri, your brother and your mom... They've been in an accident." *Oh.*

The room started to spin, and my head became full, all in one instant as I remembered.

The memory of what I had seen earlier at the school entrance began to flood my brain. The sirens replayed in my head as I felt a wave of heat roll throughout my body. My face was on fire, and my tears were cold against my skin. I could see it all as if it were right in front of me, staring me in the face.

The front of a silver car crushed against the brick building, glass shattered everywhere, and my brother, Raidan, was drenched in blood on the pavement next to the dismantled car door. I shook my head, horrified by the image of my mother, limp, with her head against the steering wheel. My mom... Holy Gods.

"No..." I scrambled, unaware of my heaviness, as my entire frame seized in place. "No, no, no!" I screamed as grief surged forward, swallowing me whole as the image played over in my mind. Everything in me boiled; my gut wrenched as I cried, shriller than conceivable. An unforgiving shriek tore from my throat, so raw and bloodcurdling that stars blurred my vision. A crack like thunder erupted all around us, rumbling as it came from my chest. My shrieking shattered me, and the blood in my throat slapped my tonsils as I collapsed to the ground. The entire floor was trembling in tune with my despair. The tiles began to lift, and the earthquake became extreme. Still screaming, I covered my head, and Mr. Lane dove on top of me, shielding me from disaster.

It was excruciating. I could feel my vocal cords burning in boiling blood, and I instantly knew that my lungs and heart had stopped working. All I felt was raging, stinging pain all over. The images of the car and my brother covered in blood played repeatedly. My mother looked lifeless. The desolation came over me like my own personal cloud raining hellfire, burning through my flesh and straight into my heart.

Mr. Lane grabbed my shoulders and shook me. He forced me to face him, and suddenly, I had no more noise left to expel. The trembling stopped, and we purely watched each other for a moment, staring, neither one of us saying a word.

"You're okay," he held me, soft-spoken, his chin trembling. Immediately, my mind shut down, and my body returned to function. The sweat from the heat became very cold against my skin. My clothing felt uncomfortably stuck to my body, and my lungs finally began to wheeze. My organs started to work again, and the blood flowed naturally through my veins. My heart, however, was undoubtedly altered.

"I need to go," I rasped.

"We just had an earthquake, Shivalri. I don't know if it's safe."

"I don't care!" I boomed, pulling away from his grip. He looked me over, hesitating.

"I can take you to the hospital if you want to go see them." He inhaled sharply.

"Yes. Yes, please," I stammered, gathering my thoughts. I smeared the moisture from my face to my sleeve and scrambled to my feet. I was so light-headed.

We started to walk through the halls, and all eyes were on us. People were huddled in doorways, whispering to one another. They all wore their backpacks, meaning I must've been out for hours. I heard my name several times but flinched when someone uttered my brother's. Mr. Lane put his arm around my shoulders and turned me into his side, and I hid my face. We got to the school entrance, and he pushed the door open for us. It was so dark outside. The sky was an unfathomable, murky shade of red and the clouds were their darkest shade of grey. We walked past the demolished car, avoiding the puddled blood and shattered glass around us. I couldn't bring myself to scan the vehicle. I was too frightened to distinguish the specifics of the accident. I heard a car honk and jumped, my heart racing unnaturally fast.

"It's okay. It's just my truck," he reassured, pointing his keys toward his blinking vehicle. I eyed it, contemplating how I could possibly get into it when I just saw my family car destroyed. I held my breath and opened his passenger door. I pulled myself up by clutching onto the seat. My five-foot-five frame was too short for the elevated build. I fastened my seat belt and watched the sky throughout the drive, in all its ambiguity. We were both silent for the entire trip, and for that, I was thankful.

5

BY A THREAD

We finally arrived at the hospital and parked in front of the emergency area. My stomach lurched at the discontinued movement. I thanked Mr. Lane with a nod and then backed away, shutting the door before me. I hesitated before getting the courage to turn toward the emergency lobby. I could do this. I had to. I clenched my fists and started toward the automatic doors.

Dad rushed toward me, panic in his eyes as he pulled me into his arms. I shut my eyes against his chest. He let go of me, then took my hand.

"Dad," I murmured, afraid that if I opened my eyes, I'd see the accident all over again.

"Shiv, we need to go." I reluctantly looked back at him and let him guide me through the halls.

"Do you know where we're going?" I asked, chin trembling as I searched each room we passed, hoping to see Mom and Raidan.

"Yes, we're going upstairs where Raidan is being operated on."

"What?" I spun on him, forcing him to slow his pace. "Dad, tell me what's going on!"

"Come on, Shivalri. We don't have time for this. We have to go."

"Dad. Is he going to be all right?" He only nodded and pulled me faster through the hospital until we reached the ICU. "Dad!" I tugged at his arm, panic-stricken.

"What, Shivalri? Do you want me to tell you I don't know if he'll be all right? Do you want me to tell you that your brother looked just as dead as your mother when I got here?" *Dead.*

"No," I said, in but a whisper. "No." My voice broke. "No!" I cried, falling to the floor.

"I—I'm so sorry. I didn't mean to..."

"Oh, Gods..." I heaved, vomit splattering at my feet. My mother was... *No.* I couldn't handle this, couldn't contain my emotions. My dad took my face in both hands and forced me to look at him. I shut my eyes.

"I know," he said, but he didn't understand. How could he be so calm if he understood?

"Are you sure?" I managed to ask, hoping this were all a nightmare I would soon wake from.

"Yes, Shivi." Dad nodded solemnly.

"She's... She's dead!" I sobbed.

"I—I know...." Dad's eyes wavered, and then he fell apart, collapsing beside me. "Oh, no... Eden..." He sobbed and pulled me into the tightest hold I had ever felt.

We sat there for a while in disbelief. All this grief was too much to handle. I didn't know what to do with myself. My mom was dead. What about my brother? How could this happen in such a short moment? My world turned upside down in the blink of an eye. I was still sobbing, but there were no longer tears to shed. Abruptly, I closed my mouth and wiped my face dry. My eyes were heavy and swollen. I stared at the pool of vomit in front of my feet. After what seemed to be a very long time of silent weeping, I mustered the nerve to stand up. My dad stayed on the floor, still sobbing. I grabbed at his sweater.

"Dad, we have to go find Raidan," I insisted. He wouldn't budge, though I tugged at his sweater harder. "Dad, he's alone, and he was hurt. He needs us." I pushed. I started to pace back and forth beside my dad. He sat still, never once looking up. "Dad, you have to be brave. For Raidan." I bent down to meet his gaze. "Let's go," I demanded.

Gradually, he rose to his feet, stumbling to a standing position. He did not look at me. Instead, his eyes locked onto a nurse who seemed to recognize my father.

"Is he all right?" My father asked the nurse.

"Is Raidan okay?" My eyes burned as I waited for the answer.

"I believe he will be," he said, giving me a reassuring smile. "Come. I'll show you to his room."

We followed the nurse down the hallway until we reached Raidan's room. Beside the door was a sign on the wall for room F21—ICU.

"Um, before we go in, I should mention a few things to better prepare you for what you will see," the nurse began. I looked to him for more. "He's still sleeping, so you won't see any movement. He is healing, and the surgery was a success. They stopped the bleeding in his brain, and he is wearing an upper-body brace to keep him immobile. He's hooked up to a ventilating system, so he'll have a tube taped to his mouth to help him breathe. The machine controls his breathing because he physically cannot do it on his own after the force of the accident," he explained.

"His brain was bleeding?" I asked, my mind running a mile per minute. "It was a success? He's going to be all right?"

"Yes. He is going to be fine now. We have the best of the best taking good care of him," he assured. "I'll leave you alone to see him now."

"Thanks," I said, opened the door, and let myself in, Dad following behind. A sizeable beige curtain hung from the ceiling and spread across the room. I pulled the side away from the wall, creating a space to pass through. My heart thundered as I searched for my brother.

There he was, just as the nurse had said. It was uncomfortable to see him this way. He had tubes running through his arms and face. Shades of indigo, mauve, yellow, and olive tainted his body. The bruising clashed with his skin; the contrast of the dark bruises made his usually tan skin seem pale. I cringed at the thought of his pain, but he was alive, and I couldn't be more grateful. I tried to touch his hand, but I was quivering, visibly shaky. A shock like lightning lit through my fingers, and I shook them frantically, overwhelmed by the sensation. Like a lit match, a tiny spark lifted from my fingers, and I stopped, confused, and turned my hand over. *There had been a glow like fire.* I stilled my outrageous thoughts and decided it had only been static. I moved away from my brother, though. I didn't want to hurt him any more than he already was. I backed away, observing his quiet, wounded body.

"My son," Dad exclaimed, propelling himself onto his bedside. "Thank God," he praised, resting his head on the side of the bed.

Hours passed as the room became darker. I could still see the red woven between the clouds above. It cast an eerie light through the window onto Raidan's bed and danced upon his bruises. I watched as the sun faded into the night, thinking of this morning when I had been internally complaining about having to take the school bus. I'd thought about how lucky and spoiled my brother was for always getting a drive with my mom to school. It was clear now that he was in no way fortunate. I felt like the cruelest person for having ever poorly thought about their daily morning drives to school. Now they would never do that again.

My mouth tasted sour as I reflected. Had I jinxed them? Was my complaining a curse that I had unknowingly placed upon them? I couldn't help but feel I was to blame for this. This morbid new life I'd have to adjust to.

I wished desperately for this not to be real. It didn't feel real—a senseless distortion. My mind and body felt like they no longer belonged to one another. My family had been torn from my very hands. Life as I knew it had been completely altered in a matter of seconds. I couldn't grasp the reality of it. What were we going to do?

As visiting hours ended, my heart felt empty for leaving my brother at the hospital. Walking with Dad through the hospital lobby, I tried to imagine what my house would feel like once we arrived with my brother and without my mom. Would the furniture vanish, along with the memories? Would the paint go from its lively golden color to cold, impassive taupe like all vacant houses were? Would my dog, Diego, even know something was amiss? How would it feel to lie in my bed knowing that my brother's bedroom was directly across the hall or that my parents' room was just a few steps next to mine? Where would my dad sleep? Would he brave the bed without Mom or use the couch? Would he even sleep at all?

6

RUBY GLOOM

Last night, I cried myself to sleep. I knew this because I woke with tears still seeping into the pockets of my swollen eyes. I dreamt of night skies filled with weeping stars—the perfect representation of how I felt. I started to remember yesterday. The images ran through my head so vividly—the people in the hallways, the smashed car, and my brother on the ground. Realizing my mom was *gone*. I vividly recalled seeing Raidan entirely dependent on tubes and machines. I pictured him lying so still and bruised to the brim. My father was utterly destroyed and so incredibly silent. It was all too much to bear.

My body felt numb this morning in place of my usual aches. I struggled to get up from my bed, then quickly remembered that the nurse had told us that the visiting hours in the hospital began promptly at seven AM. My dog huffed and moved his head to lie on my legs. The small gesture was a comfort, one that I was desperate for. Diego stirred and sighed heavily as I gave him a loving pat on the head and hurried over to my phone to check the time. It was only a quarter after five in the morning, and I had no messages. I wasn't surprised, as I hadn't made any real friends, and I didn't use social media. My family was all I'd ever cared about. None of them live close by, and I imagined the news hadn't gotten to them yet, especially with the Grimsbanes never having functional phones.

I put my phone back on the dresser and took a deep breath. I needed to find something to busy my mind for a while. I hadn't worn pyjamas last night, so I was still wearing yesterday's clothing. I started sifting through my clean items and pulled out a grey knit sweater and some black jeans. I dug through my underwear drawer, grabbed what I needed, and headed for the bathroom, leaving my dog to snore peacefully.

I tiptoed down the hall, ensuring Dad didn't hear me. Closing the door, I took a deep breath and undressed. As I looked in the mirror, the yellow-tinted lights made my typically blue eyes turn a pale green, highlighting the ring of yellow around my pupil. I leaned in closer, finding they were almost gold. The lightness of my eyes was in deep contrast with the dark circles beneath them. My hair was tangled, a mess of curls from the night before, and my freckles were starting to fade along with the life in my cheeks. I no longer looked like myself.

Kicking the pile of dirty laundry toward the bottom of the door to mute the noise, I turned on the shower and waited for the room to steam before getting in. I felt lightheaded in the heat of the room. I held on to the bar of the shower wall, looked up at the water, and submerged myself in it, feeling every single drop of water beat on my skin. It was searing against my frostiness, but it was a good kind of icy burn.

I stood there with my hair drenched and draped over my face and shoulders. I could almost swear that the scorching waters came straight from my eyes as I soaked in the moment. A whirlwind of emotion struck me hard, and I was suddenly engulfed in far too much steam. A dizzy spell hit me like a wave, and the water wrapped around me, stealing the breath from my lungs. It poured down like a jet, throwing me against the wall. I couldn't breathe, and the water stole my vision. I tried to scream, but all the came forth was gurgling sounds. I hastily reached for the handle, turned the water from hot to cold, and the pressure of the heat released me. I wrapped my arms around my shoulders.

What the hell was that?

I felt the heaviness in my chest force my body's weight further against the shower wall, and the shower bar dug into my shoulder blade. I didn't care enough to move. Snot slipped down my chin and onto the tub floor as I sobbed. I just watched, disgusted and frozen.

After wasting a lot of time underneath the cold water, I brushed my teeth, dressed, and headed for the living room. Diego was sitting at the back door, wagging his tail and whining.

"Hey, baby Dee. Who's a good boy? You need out?" I asked, petting him behind the ear. He answered with a deep groan, his tongue halfway out of his smile. I buckled his leash onto his collar and let him out to do his business. My stomach growled when I realized I hadn't eaten in at least twenty-four hours. I rapidly began salivating. I was famished. I headed to the kitchen, grabbed a slightly browned banana from the fruit basket, placed it on the counter, and opened the fridge. I pulled out what was left of a loaf of bread, took out two slices, popped them in the toaster, and grabbed a plate and knife from the cupboards. The peanut butter was left out yesterday, so I made a peanut butter and banana sandwich, something my grandmother used to make me as a child.

I sat on the couch and turned the TV on with my sandwich in hand. I thought to watch cartoons to lighten my mood, as I usually did, but instantly felt guilty for wanting to.

Choosing to watch the local news channel, I ate my sandwich and mindlessly watched as the news anchors told tragic stories about robberies and cats stuck in trees. Diego barked, so I got up to let him back in. As I unbuckled his leash, I heard the news switching to the weather segment. I could hear them discussing an earthquake. My memory flashed back to the trembling I felt at the school with Mr. Lane. That must have been the earthquake we had felt. My interest was piqued as I heard them describe the disaster it caused. I sat on the couch again, and Diego joined me, curling his body into my legs.

The weather segment shared videos from the witnesses in the nearby region. The video clips were shaky handheld visuals that filled the screen, and several people were talking over one another in muffled tones. The videos kept rolling in, now showing clips from worldwide. The earthquake had made its way through every country imaginable. The same ruby gloom that covered the entirety of my window was now spreading vastly worldwide. Many people saw the same blackened clouds and red spewing out from them. The news anchor began to read from her prompter:

"Yesterday, the world experienced a catastrophic earthquake that affected all areas of our planet. People describe the view as ungodly, dark, and red. This is truly the sight of a nightmare," the reporter said. "Although the effects were universal, the earthquake had little to no destruction below. Our atmosphere, on the other hand, has its troubles. Described as being split in two, we can see from several videos that the sky has physically separated. The rain is falling from the sector above, and the sky's final anticipated splitting location has yet to be determined; it just keeps extending. As for now, the red skies have been seen in all of North America and South America and are working their way through parts of Antarctica. NASA says there have been no abnormal activities outside our globe, and we should not panic until we find answers. Further investigations will continue throughout the week. We will have more details in the coming days. Stay tuned for more information about this extraordinary occurrence."

The news anchor signed off, and the screen returned to playing clips from around the world. It was indescribable. It looked like a scene from a sci-fi movie. My eyes fixated on the screen, now involuntarily permitting my mind to imagine hideous aliens running amuck and invading our planet. I pictured cows airborne and spaceships zooming by. My staring became so unbreakable that the TV grew into a blur. A sudden flash of fire and broken trees invaded my imagination, my heart thundering rapidly. Dark, black shadow enveloped me until I could no longer breathe. I shook my head rapidly, removing the vision from my head. Diego shot up, watching me, completely puzzled. It seemed my nightmares were bleeding into daydreams. I calmed my breathing, and Diego scoffed, spraying a thick mist of sneeze across my thighs. I rolled my eyes and slicked the goop from my legs to the couch. It would dry.

I had had enough folly for one day and had only been awake for about an hour. It was time to stop watching television. I grabbed the remote, hit the power button, and sat quietly, crouched in the couch corner with my big, sleepy dog. I watched his belly move in and out while he breathed peacefully. He had no idea that anything was out of the ordinary. He was just a dog. He slept, ate, and craved love and attention. He didn't care if the sky was cracked in two. He had a roof over his head and a lifetime of cuddles.

"You were watching TV?" I jumped, hearing a voice directly behind me.

"Dad," I began, but he interrupted.

"You want to go to the hospital?" he asked. With much effort, he was able to look at me this morning. I looked him in the eye and nodded. His eyes were puffed and swollen, and his hair was a mess. He must not have slept much last night, as I presumed. How could he? I had been haunted by night terrors, replaying the horrific events.

"I didn't hear you get out of bed," I murmured, almost to myself, trying to shake off the memory.

"I fell asleep in the garage last night," he said, combing his fingers through his dark, ragged mane. He smelled like beer and misery, looking even worse. *He was drinking again.*

"Do you want to jump in the shower before we go?" I asked, trying not to insult him completely.

"I think the hospital has seen worse, Shiv. I'm fine," he asserted himself. "Let's go," he demanded and left my doorway. I grabbed my phone and followed. I trudged down the hallway, past sleeping Diego, moved down the five-step staircase, and shoved my feet into my shoes again. I picked up my purse from where I had thrown it carelessly the night before and locked the door behind me.

7

———

LOST

At the hospital, a nurse led us to find Raidan. I followed promptly behind, my heart thudding with every step. Through the bedroom, there was a door connected to an adjoined room. She fiddled with the doorknob and let me in. This room was really, very dark. I could hardly determine where the furniture was. I saw something move, barely, and suddenly an arm lighted a bedside lamp.

"Sir, no lights," snapped the nurse.

"I know, I know." *That was my brother's voice.* "It's just so dark," he said.

"Raidan," Dad exhaled. "He's talking." He looked at the nurse in disbelief.

"You're okay," I gasped, rushing to see my brother.

"Of course I am. I'm stronger than you think." He brushed a hand through his black hair. It was strange to see him in this position. Though younger than me, he was tall and built like a tank. He was always the protector between us, but here, lying in this bed, he looked like a little boy again.

"I can hardly believe it." I laughed, voice wavering. He took my hand and squeezed. I returned the gesture, only more carefully.

"What about Mom? Is she okay?" he asked. "She's probably a wreck," he trailed. I fidgeted with the hem of my sweater, avoiding his gaze. That was the wrong thing to do because by avoiding my brother's, I met with my dad's. He looked empty and shell-shocked. I looked away quickly, blinking out the image.

"Uh, yeah. I'm just glad you're okay. You don't even look sick anymore." I gawked, studying his appearance. Just last night, he was beaten by contusions from head to toe. Now he just looked tired with gauze around his head. "Rai, you looked like absolute shit yesterday. I don't know how, but you look so much better already. There's such a difference." A single tear trailed down my cheek. "How do you feel?" I prodded, looking him over. The swelling had gone down, but most of the bruises did remain blue.

"Yes, how are you feeling, Raidan?" Dad added to the sentiment.

"It feels like a massive headache," he replied, frowning slightly. "The nurse said I can leave in two weeks if I stay steady." He pointed to the brace that held his chest and neck. "I don't think I have a choice in that matter." He laughed. I grimaced at the brace, trying not to imagine what lay beneath it. Was his chest covered in the same kinds of bruises?

"He's recovering rapidly," the nurse said, checking his vitals. "We just need to keep him under observation to ensure it stays that way. The operation was a success, and now we'll watch him and ensure he behaves." She pointed her finger at him, then shut the lamp off.

"Behave," I said pointedly with a teasing tone. He rolled his eyes at me.

"He can watch TV for thirty minutes in the morning and

another thirty in the evening. We have a dim setting on the television which he must not remove. Aside from the allotted hour, he should be kept in the dark. Bright lights could make things worse for him, but since he's doing so well, we won't completely deprive him. We'll keep an eye out for swelling or infections, but he seems to be doing very well so far," she explained.

"This is the day after surgery. Shouldn't he just be sleeping?" I asked, baffled.

"You just don't want to deal with me," Raidan chimed.

"Or maybe I don't want you dead." Dad snapped his eyes at me, and I stopped my words, shuddering. My head started feeling light, but my body was burning with rage. I couldn't tell him about Mom yet. This was not how he should find out. Not now, while he needed to focus on healing himself.

"I'm not dead. I'm tough," he assured me with a thumbs up.

"Tough doesn't begin to describe it," the nurse interjected. "He's healed incredibly well overnight. His vitals are strong. The way his health has reacted to his experience is amazing, to say the least. It's as if he had come in here simply for a mild concussion," she explained.

"How can this be? Is this usual?" Dad asked.

"Not in the slightest," the nurse answered, her expression bewildered.

"That's incredible," I answered. "Looks like you're hard-headed after all, Raidan," I teased, making a knocking motion to my head.

"That's what she said." He coughed under his breath. I rolled my eyes playfully. He was doubtlessly feeling like himself.

"Raidan." Dad scoffed, shaking his head. My brother and I looked at each other, cheeks puffed, trying our best not to laugh. The nurse left the room to the three of us, and I sat on the chair, carefully moving the brown bloodstained pillow to the floor.

I couldn't help but wonder what was going on with my brother. There was nothing ordinary about what had happened. I witnessed my mother and brother crash their car into my school. My mother didn't survive, and my brother was here as if nothing had occurred. My mom *died*. I found it difficult to wrap my mind around that fact. I needed to focus on the positive. My brother was okay. He was going to be okay, and he would come home. But then, of course, we would have to break the news to him. As I watched the sun from the crack of the curtain go from light to dark, I knew it was time to go home again, welcomed only by its door and Diego, oblivious to the chaos.

* * *

I didn't know what to do with myself, my family, or my life. Everything felt dim whenever trapped inside my house. I could see that in the forefront of the red skies, the clouds were still a dark, gross, rainy gray outside my bedroom window. Sometimes I wondered if maybe I had brought this upon myself. I'd internally complained about my brother being favored, getting drives to school from Mom. What if I had fought harder to make Raidan take the bus with me? Had I forced him to go on the bus with me and dragged him out of bed, Mom wouldn't have had to drive him to school; therefore, there would've been no crash. Did I believe the collision would've been avoided or was it all inevitable?

I had always believed that everything that happens was meant to happen, and there was no avoiding what was meant to be. Knowing that sounds morbid, twisted, and cruel, I still genuinely felt that was how life worked. That was what my grandmother would say to me whenever anything went amiss.

Sometimes, shit happens. Then again, my beliefs may be morbid and twisted and cruel. Perhaps it was the fault of my belief system—the one Gram taught me, which inescapably caused the shit.

Gram is faithful to her Gods and taught me that everything that happens to us is supposed to work according to their plan. Maybe that is precisely the problem. If there verily were Gods, they were supposed to be good and whole, forgiving and loving. Why would they send me this life? Why would they kill my mom? I didn't ask for this. No one would ask for this. I tried not to cry again, but my eyes deceived me as the tears trickled down.

ALTERED

After an unusually minimal amount of time, Raidan finally left the hospital and came home. The two weeks of recovery were baffling. He had nothing to show of the accident. The incisions from the surgery had already flattened against his cranium. The only proof of his misfortune was the slightest pink pigmentation scratched along the front and back of his head. He even grew back his then-missing patches of hair the doctor had shorn off.

"You look like a million bucks," I said, watching him examine the minor scars on his forehead. He pulled the mirror closer.

"Million and one," he added.

"Looking for treasure in there?" I asked, trying to lighten the mood.

"Yeah, I struck gold," he replied casually, still looking for the scars that hardly appeared.

I wanted to keep a calm presence. I had been roiling in all that had happened during these weeks, with lots of time to process. Raidan, on the other hand, hadn't had the tiniest fraction of time to process his accident or the loss of Mom. I figured if I could keep my words and actions the same as they usually were before it all happened, perhaps he'd be able to grieve a little lighter. I would do all that I could to make home and family life as close to what it had been before our world came crashing down. It would be hard sometimes but well worth it if I could help my brother in some small way.

When we told Raidan about Mom, Dad couldn't get the words out. I had to be the one to tell him. He took it much harder than I did, and seeing him in so much pain broke my heart. Of course, Raidan got along well with Mom. They were always together, whereas I was always in my own little world. Regret sank in as I understood that I had missed so many opportunities to spend time with my mother. I supposed my brother lost a more profound relationship than I did because of it, so he was more upset than I was. He had lost so much more. I was devastated at the loss of Mom. But my brother... He was strong, but I was unsure if he would ever heal from this.

Dad was still in a slump. His routine had become familiar. He would wake up by noon, drag his blanket down the hallway, grab a beer and a box of soda crackers from the kitchen, lay on the couch, eat half a cracker, feed Diego the other half, and doze off on the sofa. I had never seen anyone behave like this in my life. This was what depression looked like in its many forms.

"Does he do this every day?" Raidan asked, handing me the mirror he had taken from my dresser. We could hear our father snoring from the couch.

"Yup. For the last few weeks." I shrugged, not wanting to go into too many details.

"Do you know when he'll return to work?" he questioned, looking to me for answers we both knew I didn't have. Sluggishly, despite my knees' protestations, I got up from the bed and moved to where he stood. I took a hair elastic from the dresser and shoved my hair in a bun. I immediately felt the tight pull of hair on my head, screaming to be let down. I ignored it.

"I don't know if he can, Rai. He's not doing too well."

"Seriously, Shivi. Are you going to say something to him?" Raidan scoffed, crossing his arms.

"And say what? Hey Dad, sorry your wife is dead, but could you please pretend it never happened and go to work?"

"Are you defending him?" He scowled at me now.

"I would never condone this kind of behavior, and you know that. But I am not his boss. I am his child. I don't get a say in what he does while grieving," I tried to explain.

"He's intoxicated," he spat. "I get it. I'm hurting too." His lips started to quiver, and my heart sank. "He got a letter in the mail yesterday. Did you know that? His bereavement pay is gone. There's no more money coming in. We need money for food—for our house. He's spent every dime on liquor," he finished. His voice became weaker, but he cleared his throat. I could see the anger replacing the sadness as it throbbed from his temples.

"I don't know what to tell you. I could drop out of school and work, but that'll only be half of Dad's income, if even, at minimum wage." I scrambled for a solution. When my dad got into drinking again, there was no stopping him until he hit rock bottom.

"No, this is ridiculous. You're eighteen. He can be sad and still be responsible."

"This is different," I tried. Before, when our father drank, it was over petty things and rooted in addiction. *This*, his depressive state, was a new thing to behold. Internally, I fought between pity and shame, anger and understanding as I considered the hole my father had fallen back into after several years of sobriety.

"Dad is drinking all of our money away. He's gone too far for too long," he said, enunciating every word before turning on his heel toward the door.

"What are you doing?" I asked, chasing after him. The nerves started to buzz up my arms.

"What you should've done while I was gone," he replied, marching toward the living room. My eyes widened.

"Raidan, stop. He's going through a rough time." I couldn't intercept. He was already halfway down the hallway. Whatever he needed to say had to come out. I cowered from behind, waiting for Dad's reaction. Dad looked up hazily, his brown eyes still sleeping off his misery.

"Stop your yelling," he mumbled groggily. "You're so loud that the neighbors could hear you." He hiccupped, then groaned.

"Yeah, and you wouldn't like that, would you?" Raidan retorted. Dad waved a hand to shoo him away and pulled his blanket closer to him. Raidan knelt before the couch, stopping only inches away from Dad's face. Tightly, he closed his eyes and inhaled. Raidan grabbed Dad's shoulders and exhaled, backing Dad into the cushions. "Stop. Stop whatever this is. Just stop it. You are supposed to be the adult taking care of things around here. Shivi's been cleaning, getting groceries at the gas station, and keeping up with school homework; on top of that, she was the one checking in on me at the hospital. The nurses told me everything. How you were acting, and how Shivalri called in twice a day to see how I was whenever she couldn't get to the hospital to see me. You visited me once while I was stuck in the infirmary. What have you been doing this whole time?" he questioned, looking him dead in the eye.

Dad's face wore utter shock. My brother's eyes flickered, filling with sorrow.

"I, uh—" Dad mumbled.

"Be who you're supposed to be. Be our dad," Raidan begged, gripping his shoulders even harder.

There was a long silence before Dad looked down into his lap and played meaningfully with his wedding ring. Tears splattered against the blanket he held tightly to his chest. He shuddered before looking back to Raidan; his face was smooth this time—a clean, blank slate.

"I'm sorry. I will be better," he replied calmly. Raidan gulped, wiping the sweat from his brow on the back of his hand. He blinked and backed away slowly. The minute Raidan removed himself, Dad got up without a word and headed straight for the bathroom, shaking his head. The shower turned on, and that was that. It was as if he hadn't been drinking at all.

"There is a time for everything, and a season for every activity under the Heavens: a time to be born and a time to die, a time to plant and a time to uproot, a time to kill and a time to heal, a time to tear down and a time to build, a time to weep and a time to laugh, a time to mourn and a time to dance..."
Ecclesiastes 3:1-4

9

COLD

We all wore black this Sunday.

Under the red, gloomy sky, the rain was soaking through everyone's clothing as the funeral parlor's men lowered my mother's casket into its resting place. A few of my mother's family members and friends came to say their goodbyes; however, most of them lived too far to have come all this way in the rainstorm. The dirt under my feet came to be mud rather promptly. I couldn't take my eyes off the ground. The rain was as cold as ice—almost as cold as my heart felt.

I heard a tin-like thwack and looked up from my murky feet. It was the sound of shovels clanging together as one of the men passed them around. With each pile of dirt thrown onto my mother's casket, I felt farther away from the world. We all wore black today. I understood why.

The unrelenting thud of dirt landing atop my mother's casket built immense unease in my chest. I felt compelled to look down and fidget with my hands. Against the darkness of my dress and shawl, the wedding ring my mother left for me shone brightly on my right hand. I rotated it around my ring finger for good measure. I was happy to have a small piece of her with me.

I saw a figure dressed in black making its way to the grave from the corner of my eye. *Gram.* She had made it here despite the rainstorm. A limited amount of relief stung my ribs, and I exhaled the breath I didn't realize I had been holding in. She looked up at me, our eyes meeting, and a wave of emotions hit me at once. The darkness that had crept too near washed away the closer my grandmother got—a light in the dark.

"Gram..." I sniffed. The sting of my tears was hot, and I blinked them away as my grandmother approached.

"Come here," she motioned, gesturing for me to go to her. She was warm and steady. "I'm so sorry, my dear," she said, holding me close. "She is resting now. She will have made her way to the other side. Rest assured, the Gods will take care of her well," she reassured, patting my wet hair. It had stopped down-pouring, and a light, hazy mist filled the air. I rested for a moment in her arms, then backed out, wiping away at my face. Her white, blown-out hair had caught on my sticky cheek.

"I..." My words faltered.

"I know," she simply answered and squeezed my hand. "Are you ready to come in now?" she asked. Surprised, I looked up to meet her gaze. She looked back at me. The confusion interrupted her stare, compelling me to look behind my shoulder. I turned abruptly to see that there were no longer people surrounding the burial area. It was just the two of us—and Mom.

"I didn't realize we were alone," I said. As if my words had summoned it, a wash of fog as tall as the trees began pooling into the cemetery from the forest.

"Oh, but we aren't, are we?" Gram replied. A wash of unease lifted the hair on my arms and legs as my body grew colder. *No, we most certainly weren't alone.* "Shall we go now, Shivalri? Are you ready?" Gram asked again.

"I don't know," I responded, my words like verbal diarrhea. I didn't have to think about it. I just knew, and the words flew out. "I don't think I'm ready for any of this. I don't think anyone could ever be. What do I do, Gram?" I asked, desperate for advice.

"All you can do is take it one step at a time. Believe it or not, you are much stronger than you think you are. You are a Grimsbane. You are stronger than most," she said matter-of-factly. I shrugged half-heartedly. "You're strong like your Gram," she continued. "We will get through this, my granddaughter. This I know," she said with certainty. I attempted a laugh.

"Yes, yes. You know everything." I managed a grin. She smiled back, face relaxed.

"Yes, dear. I'm glad you know it." She nodded. She looked up from my face, watching the clouds. "The sky is quite gloomy this afternoon, isn't it?" I nodded, still uneasy about the redness of the sky above us.

"It makes me uncomfortable," I answered truthfully. Though fascinating, earthquakes and all things disastrous gave me the creeps when it was close to home. Especially when it so vividly reminded me of my nightmares.

"Let's get you inside," she instructed.

"Do we have to go in there?" I questioned, sulking.

"I am sure they are waiting to pay their respects to us, Raidan and your father," she responded as we headed toward the service hall. "Though it will not be easy, it comes with the act of holding a funeral service. Consider that we celebrate your mother's life rather than mourn her death. That's how my Eden would want us to look at it." She smiled, small but purposeful.

"Are you going to be okay, Gram?" I asked.

"*We* are," she answered, and I nodded, lips tight.

When we entered the building, the buzzing of voices startled me. It had been so hushed outside, aside from the rain, that I had forgotten how noisy these people were. Gram and I walked to our assigned seats next to Dad and Raidan, and the room continued to buzz. Family and friends made their rounds to speak with us, mostly recalling good memories and sending their thoughts and prayers to our family. Dad looked grossly pale, and Raidan sat quiet, eyes welded to his phone.

"I feel so awkward," I said to Gram, shifting in my seat. "I feel like I'm supposed to do something or say something to make these people feel better."

"You don't have to do anything you don't want to, my dear. They are here to mourn your mother and pay their respects," she replied.

"I know. It just feels weird," I said under my breath as family members walked past, offering grim smiles. I flexed my hands, trying the ease the swelling in my joints. The more upset I become, the more my bones grow angry.

"Understandably." Gram nodded.

"Satyra couldn't come?" I asked, frowning. I'd expected her to be here. I'd needed my best friend.

"No, I'm afraid your cousin couldn't get away from work. She's been so busy these days. That management position she took has taken up a lot of her time. She sends her regards and best wishes." I slumped in my chair. It would have been nice to have Satyra here during this time, but I knew it must have been important if she didn't make it out to my mother's funeral. She was always there for me when I needed her.

"Do you think she'll come to visit sometime soon?" I wondered aloud.

"Perhaps when the busy season settles," Gram answered,

offering a small smile. "You know how October gets to be in our neck of the woods."

"That's true," I said. I missed being there with them. Having grown up with my grandparents and my cousin, all those years had become habitual. "Gram?"

"Yes, dear?"

"Will you come to visit again sometime soon?" I asked, hopeful.

"I couldn't miss my daughter's funeral," she said, voice low. "However, my dear, it's a very long drive for me to make. I am growing elderly." She chuckled. "I won't be doing this drive again anytime soon. But you know you are always welcome to come back home, any time, and for as long as you'd like."

"Yeah, thanks," I mumbled. "If I get a chance, I'll come by." It was wishful thinking. I knew I wouldn't be able to. I didn't have my own car, and I couldn't take Dad's. Gram lived too far away to take the car for that long. Maybe I could take the train...

AS THE NIGHT ENDED, we thanked our family members with passive courtesy and eventually ended the evening with just Raidan, Dad, Gram, and me. I didn't want my grandmother to go back home. I hadn't realized how much I needed her until I had seen her walking toward me just hours ago in the cemetery.

"Do you really have to go back to Massachusetts? It's already quite late in the afternoon," I said, trying to reason with her.

"You know very well I am at my best in the night." She winked. Raidan came forward and hugged her.

"The night-time knitter. What a thing to brag about." He laughed, patting her on the head like a dog.

"You laugh now, but wait until you see your Christmas gift," she chimed in. "Perfect for the winter solstice."

"Great," he answered, frowning at her.

"Seriously, though," I started again. "It's like ten hours of driving."

"Eleven," she corrected. "I'll be fine, my dear. Don't worry." She pulled me in for a hug, and I soaked it in, slumping my shoulders. No one could convince my grandmother to do anything she didn't want to. Once she set her mind, that was it.

"Goodbye, Archer." Gram spoke with the softest tone I'd heard all day. She took Dad by the hands and did her usual squeeze. He looked pitiful.

"Thanks for coming, Sabine. I know it's a long drive, but I am glad you made it," he said, then paused for a moment. "Though the unknown road is your inevitable fate...." He pulled his hands from Gram's and wiped at his eyes.

She pulled him in for a hug and whispered, "You will find your way home, for I am your anchor, your weight." That was my mom's line.

I felt so much sadness in the pit of my stomach, and my heart ached like never before. It was time to say goodbye to Gram—time to say goodbye to Mom. I watched as Gram stepped into her car, silver hair whipping in the wind, as she waved us all goodbye.

10

UNCHANGED

Three days had passed since Mom's funeral and over a week since my brother left the hospital. Nothing had changed. My dad was still depressed, I was still indifferent, and my brother's head still hurt. I hadn't returned to school yet, and I was certainly not looking forward to it.

I felt very lost and isolated. I was tired and sometimes barely felt anything at all. That's when it hit me the worst. If I didn't feel anything, I was angry and hated myself because I was supposed to feel something. I was supposed to feel angry and sad and maybe somewhat ashamed. I mostly felt guilt.

I could hear *Family Guy* playing from Raidan's room, meaning he must've been awake. Dad texted me from the garage to ask if I'd check on him to see how he was doing, but instead, I decided to drown out the Griffins with a bit of my music. Raidan was undoubtedly awake. If he needed something, he could shout out to me. I disconnected the Wi-Fi from my phone, put my earphones in, and drowned myself in what I loved. A little bit of Ariana Grande never hurt anybody. I started singing the lyrics, drifting away in the sound embrace of music.

My favourite song began to play when my door suddenly swung open, struck the wall, and recoiled. My earphones fell out as I shot up, finding my father, inebriated and angry as ever, coming toward me.

"Are you kidding me?" he slurred, face red with anger. "You have a fucking nerve to be singing right now as if you're happy. You better shut the hell up right now, or so help me!" he spat at me, clenching a fist. I was in absolute shock. I had never seen him so angry. I also had never seen him so unwell in my entire life. The veins in his neck protruded, and his scruff was covered in spit. I could feel the warmth swelling in my eyes. *Don't cry, don't cry, don't cry. Don't show him you're vulnerable.* He was so terrifying like this, and I didn't trust him. He was invariably the person I relied on for everything and anything, and now I was scared of him. I was scared of my father. What had my family become? This devastation had destroyed us.

My father slammed my door shut and stumbled away, a beer bottle in hand. I sat up on my bed, wiped the tear glistening down my cheek, and looked out the window to find rain. Rain understood my pain.

I felt my phone vibrate from under my pillow. Tears staining my vision, I shoved my hand under, feeling for it. I pulled it out from under me and wiped at my misted glasses.

Raidan: Hey, are you okay? You probably don't want me to see you, but just text me if you do.

Me: I'm fine. He's not. I'm fucking tired of this bullshit.

Raidan: We're his kids!

Me: Yeah.

Raidan: We could leave.

I thought about that for a moment. *We* couldn't. But maybe *I* could. My brother was still healing, whether he wanted to admit it or not. On the other hand, I could go to Gram's house for a while to get my head straight. She was very spiritual, and I always felt better around her. My grandmother was always full of answers. She practiced the art of tea leaf reading and has predicted more than I'd like to admit on more than one occasion. She always knew what to do and say to guide me on a better path. Whether I believed in tea leaf reading or not, I did believe in Gram. Maybe her wisdom was just what I needed.

I turned back to my phone as it buzzed in my hand.

Raidan: You there?

Me: I'm not sure you can leave, Rai… We'll figure something out.

Raidan: I can do what I want. I want to leave.

Me: As I said, we will figure something out. Goodnight, and thanks for checking in.

Raidan: Always, Sis. I've got your back. Night.

I tucked my phone back under my pillow and began to devise a plan. I had about two thousand dollars saved up from my summer job at the local library. I knew that my grandmother lived in another state, so traveling to and from would be expensive. I could take a cab to the train station and board the train for the rest of my commute. It would empty my pockets; nevertheless, it was worth it.

I had a gut feeling that I needed to be with my grandmother. She always made things better, and I couldn't talk to her unless I went straight to her house, the home I grew up in. Gram has many strange beliefs, one of them being that phones are dangerous tools. Her superstitions get the best of her, leaving me unable to call her.

Poor Satyra. She lost both of her parents at age twelve, so she's lived with our grandmother and her curious ways ever since. Satyra is my only cousin on my mother's side, and the only one I keep in touch with. If we could have it our way, we'd have been sisters. Our mothers were twins, making their bond very strong. I like to think that Satyra and I are soul twins cut from a very similar cloth. Now, as I thought about fond memories of Gram, Satyra, and me, I decided a reunion at the Grimsbane house would be a lovely idea. A good dose of Gram and Satyra was precisely what I needed—my grandmother to be a clear-headed, consoling, and gentle adult and Satyra to help me through something I had helped her with all those years ago.

I had always felt guilty for moving away from the pair. If I had had it my way, my family would have lived in the Grimsbane house right into our old age. Saty and Gram were both grieving in the worst of ways, and we had left them to manage their pain on their own. Now having lost my mother, I felt even worse.

I sighed heavily, rolling onto my side. Shivering, I tucked my feet into a lumpy mass of blanket and clothes that I had dumped onto my bed. I could care less about the clutter. I scanned the bed for something cozy and spotted my oversized hoodie. Offhandedly, I grabbed it, tucking it closely in my arms for comfort. Tomorrow was a new day. I closed my eyes and drifted off to sleep.

11

GO

Today I woke yet again with a sopping wet pillow, though the stars of my dreams did not cry beside me. Feeling woozy, I sat up in my bed. I rubbed at my eyes, removing the crusted tears from my lashes. My head was so heavy. Enough was enough. It was time I got out of this hellhole. There was nothing left for me to do but wallow in sadness when I was home, and my dad did the same thing every single day. What was I supposed to do? Was I meant to sit around waiting for something to feel okay again? I felt the rush of heat swarm my body, and I knew that today was the day I made a run for it. I got up in a hurry, dizzy, as I determinedly jumped off my bed: clothes—money—and the will to move forward beyond those doors. I quickly started to pack my suitcase as quietly as possible, undoing the zippers as silently as a mouse.

I grabbed everything I could fit into my suitcase, swaying unsteadily from a weak night's sleep. I began shoving socks, underwear, shirts, and jeans into my luggage. That should do. I was getting more and more anxious as the minutes ticked by, preparing myself to go through with running away. My skin was crawling with cold flashes of gooseflesh. I was nervous about embarking on my first solo trip but also worried for my brother. My dad was a lost cause, and my job was not to clean up his act. Here, I was stuck in a loop. Forever hollow, trapped in my room, waiting for my dad to act up, incessantly falling from grace. With every fiber of my being, I knew I needed to go to Gram's house.

I grabbed my hair tie, pulled my hair up into the messiest disaster of a bun I'd never seen, and started to walk for the door. The floor beneath me creaked, and I cursed in protest.

"Dammit." I stiffened and waited to hear if anyone had gotten up—dead silence. I started for the doorknob and twisted slowly and quietly. I listened intently to ensure the coast was clear, switched my light off and sent a thought of goodbyes, vowing to return as soon as possible. As I turned to step through my doorway, I was dumbfounded to find my brother standing there watching me, arms crossed.

"And just where do you think you're going, dear sister?" Frantic, I quickly threw my hand over his mouth to cover the noise he'd been making.

"Shh," I hushed irritably. "Don't make a sound." I grabbed him by the scruff of his shirt and pulled him into my room.

"What are you doing?" he asked quietly.

"I have to get out of here," I explained, voice still low. He was about to offer a rebuttal when I cut him off. "No," I started. "You can't talk me out of it." I wouldn't falter.

"I'm not trying to talk you out of it," he whispered loudly, giving me an exasperated look. "I'm coming with you." He squared his shoulders, his eyes mirroring mine.

"You just got out of the hospital," I huffed, stating the obvious. "You are in no shape to go anywhere, especially where I'm headed. It's too far away."

"In case you haven't noticed, I'm completely healed. We've

been over this. I'm not asking for permission," he said, crossing his arms. "I'm going." I suppose he did seem better, and perhaps leaving him here with Dad would only be worse. I hadn't thought of it like that until this very moment. Leaving Raidan with Dad would only make things more difficult for him.

In a moment of weakness, I answered hesitantly.

"Then you'd better get packing." He was shocked but didn't question my judgment. The truth was, I didn't really want to leave him behind. It may be selfish to have him tag along, but at least this way, I wouldn't have to worry about him being alone with Dad.

I grabbed my suitcase and pushed him out into the hallway. Quietly, we snuck into his room so that he could pack a bag. Quickly, he grabbed his schoolbag and dumped its contents onto the bed.

"Where am I packing for?" he asked.

"Gram's," I said softly. He looked at me, eyes wide. It was a long drive to visit our grandmother's place. We rarely made the trip. However, I don't know why he would've assumed I was headed elsewhere. It was the only place to go.

"All right," he agreed and let out a sigh. He grabbed the needed clothes while I scanned his room for items to bring when I noticed his schoolbooks sprawled on the floor. Reaching for his dresser drawer, he slowly slid it out, not letting so much as a creak slip out.

"I'll write a note." I decided as I lifted pen to paper.

Dad,
Raidan & I are going to Gram's house.
We have our phones & I have money saved up

from the summer job at the library. We're fine,
but we needed a breather. I think you need
one too.
    We'll let you know when we get there.
    We'll be back after Halloween.
    Don't be mad,
    Shiv

"There. Good to go," I whispered, shoving the pen into my purse.

"Cool."

"Ready?" I asked, the nerves heating my hands.

He grabbed his wallet and shoved it into his pocket. Before I could second-guess myself, he nodded and looked me in the eye. We gave each other silent acknowledgment, knowing the dangers ahead, and solidified our agreement without a word. We were leaving without the permission of our inebriated father.

Scurrying down the hall, I couldn't help but peek into Dad's room to see if he was awake. To my surprise, he wasn't there. I felt a sudden moment of panic creep up my throat. If he were up, he would never let us leave. I looked at my brother and mouthed my worry.

"He's not in there." His eyes widened, but we continued down the hallway.

As we rounded the corner and entered the living area, I saw that Dad had fallen asleep on the couch. Diego whined as we entered the living room. I felt a wave of sorrow wash over me as I looked at the pair. My innocent, saddened family members I was about to leave behind. I gulped. No time for second-guessing, I decided. My brother had already made it to the door and carefully slid his shoes on. I quickly and quietly poured food and water into Diego's dishes and left the bag on the counter so Dad could grab and refill it easily. At least, that was one thing he'd been taking care of. I knew my dog would be safe and fed while I was gone.

Diego started to get up, and dread shook me as I worried he'd wake up Dad. Of course, Dad was passed out, and Diego had no problem making his way to us, begging us not to leave with his puppy dog eyes. After shoving my shoes on, I leaned down to kiss him on the head and scratched him behind his ears. I whispered, just for him to hear.

"I love you, baby Dee. I'll be back soon... You'll see." Raidan leaned over to pat Diego's head, and we exited the door.

I took out my phone and started to dial for a taxicab when my brother grabbed the phone out of my hands and hung up.

"What are you doing?" I asked, frustratedly trying to grab my phone from his hands.

"I've kind of been hiding a secret," he said, shrugging his shoulders and turning away.

"What do you mean?" I asked, starting to get worried. He headed toward the shed we never used and took out his keys. I needed clarification. What had he been hiding in our shed?

"I've got something in here you might like to see," he said.

"Listen, if you tell me you're hiding a body in there, I want nothing to do with it."

He turned around, rolling his eyes at me. "Oh, come on. Where's your sense of adventure?"

I crossed my arms at him. Once I heard the lock click as he started to open the door, I looked inside. I couldn't believe my eyes."

Are you kidding me?" I asked, bewildered. "What the hell is a car doing in there?"

"It's Pépère's," he replied. "Gram gave it to me after he passed away. Satyra drove it up, following Gram's car, and I've been keeping it in the shed ever since. She told me to keep it to myself because if I told Mom and Dad that she gave it to me, she would get in trouble." He ruffled his hair instinctively. "I didn't want that to happen, and since I haven't gotten around to getting my license yet, I haven't had a use for it." He threw the keys at me, and I caught them in disbelief. I didn't know what to say.

"You're telling me you've been hiding a car here all this time?" I was baffled. How was this even possible? "I guess it's good that Mom and Dad never use the shed. I can't believe they never found it."

"Well, I haven't been caught yet." He grinned. "If we don't leave soon, my luck may run out."

"Enough said." I laughed in disbelief, grabbing my luggage and heading toward the shed. I couldn't believe it. It had been here all this time, and none of us had known. "Let's get this show on the road. It's going to be a long drive."

12

THE WINDING ROAD

I gave up battling my brother over the aux cord because I knew letting him choose the music rather than fight over it was easier. Due to my giving up, I had a splitting headache from all the ridiculous music he had been playing. It was a mixture of indie, screamo and parody wrapped up into one long playlist.

"Who in the world listens to this stuff?" I grumbled in distaste. This music was irritating. It felt like we'd been driving for days.

"Listen, I'm telling you. This music is pure genius," he exclaimed. I rolled my eyes and scoffed. "You have to take it all in." He grinned.

"It's total and utter bullshit, and you know it." I scowled. Laughing, he turned up the volume. I gave him a stern look, and he turned it back down, crossing his arms. "What's the GPS say for time?" I asked, afraid I wouldn't be too fond of the answer. "We must be getting close. We passed the sign for Boston not too long ago, and I don't think Essex is all that much further." He tapped his phone screen, and the light lit the car like a disco ball.

"Sorry," he grumbled.

"Gods, that's harsh," I griped. "You know, I need to see the road to drive." I pointed, frustrated. The light was piercingly bright.

"I didn't know it was going to be that bright. Calm down." He huffed and turned the setting down.

"Thank you," I blew out, calming myself, though I didn't enjoy being told what to do.

"It says we have twenty-seven minutes to go. We passed Salem, so we're close," he told me.

"Half an hour." I sighed. "Better than the last time I asked."

"Yeah, this drive felt like it took ten days," he muttered, not paying much attention. He had been playing a new Pokémon game on his Nintendo Switch that he had bought with his birthday money. I didn't know how he could play those games while in the car. I'd have been too dizzy, especially after recently enduring head trauma.

"Yes!" he exclaimed, shifting in his seat. "Oh, hell yeah! I got him!" I laughed at his enthusiasm.

"You're not dizzy looking at that screen all day?" I asked, making casual conversation.

"No, but I'm glad we're almost at Gram's." He exhaled. "I just finished the whole game." He put the gaming console in the side door storage compartment and stretched out his legs. He was so tall that he barely had room to sit in this tiny car. "I caught the shiny one I wanted."

"I don't know what that means, but I'm happy for you." I laughed.

"It means I can now train, evolve, and make it ready for battle."

"Ah-ha..." I mumbled, more focused on the road ahead.

"Like, this one had two regular abilities and one hidden ability. I needed one of the regular ones, but I got the wrong one," he explained. "But it's all good because I can use an ability capsule to change it to the other ability I need."

"Oh, okay. I get it," I said. I did understand the basics of the game, but all the details you'd need to grasp it fully were not something my memory kept in storage.

"Do you?" He sneered knowingly.

"I understand as much as I need to," I said, rolling my eyes. He interjected an "mm-hmm" and took his phone out again.

"It's starting to get dark out," Raidan noted.

"What's the GPS say now?" I was tired of our repeated map conversations, but the time started making me anxious again.

"It says in two miles to take exit nineteen A," he informed me.

"Finally." I exhaled, stretching my arms, still holding the steering wheel. "It's already six, and I hate driving when it's pitch-black," I admitted, thankful to have avoided that situation.

"Good timing," he offered casually.

"Can you use your data to message Satyra to let her know we're almost there?" I asked.

"She didn't even answer when we said we were going over there in the first place. She probably won't see it."

"Just, please try," I said firmly. "Hopefully, they're home. It's so annoying when Gram doesn't have a phone."

"First of all, they're always home. Secondly, she never does."

"Just send a message in case we manage to get through to her." I was getting impatient. "You have nothing better to do, and it just takes two seconds." His unwillingness to send a text was getting on my nerves.

"'Kay," he finished, slouching in annoyance. The GPS rang through my Bluetooth in the car and told me where to get off for Essex, Massachusetts, and I flicked my signal light on. I was so glad to be done with this driving excursion.

"She didn't answer," Raidan chimed as we started to pull into our grandmother's driveway. She lived in a wooded subdivision, and yes, she technically had neighbors, but you couldn't see them from her house. The time it took from the beginning of her driveway to the end was quite literally a five-minute drive.

I looked through my windows and felt an eerie chill crawl up my spine, nesting at the tip of my neck. The woods, in general, freaked me out. The woods at night were a whole other kind of creepy. I turned down the music to properly focus on driving down the winding road.

"This just got creepy," Raidan blanched, finally looking up from his phone. "Did it always look like this?" he wondered aloud. The chill along my neck spread across my shoulders and down my arms. I shivered.

"Are the doors locked?" I asked, feeling the sting of panic pinch my skin.

"Yes, we're driving. They're always locked when we're driving," he said. "Why?" His voice started to match my level of panic.

"I swear on the Gods I saw something move up there, and we have to pass it to get to Gram's," I answered, mind alert.

"What the fuck?" His eyes widened. "Are you serious?" I only nodded. I pushed my glasses up the bridge of my nose and braced my arms, gripping the steering wheel with as much courage as I could muster. The realization sank in coldly.

"I don't think it was an animal," I said, steadying my eyes. The sweat surfaced on my brow.

"Are you fucking serious? A person is lurking in the woods?" Raidan asked, quickly going on high alert.

"I think so," I said blankly. "Keep your eyes peeled on the road. I have my bright lights on. If you see something, say something," I demanded. He nodded, and I let the heaviness of my foot lean harder on the gas pedal. It felt like the distance between the house and our car grew further away. Had it become darker in a matter of minutes?

"Holy shit!" Raidan screamed at the top of his lungs.

I saw the figure step out directly in front of the vehicle in a flash. My first instinct was to step on the gas and close my eyes. I stopped myself from making things worse and jammed on the brakes instead.

"Gram?" My heart was pounding a mile a minute. My senseless grandmother stood directly in front of the car, hair whipping in the wind. She casually waved at us as if she hadn't just appeared out of nowhere. I could feel my heart thudding in my throat and remembered to take a breath. I rolled down my window and shouted out to her.

"I almost murdered you! What are you doing out here in the middle of the woods at night?" I shrieked. She had the nerve to answer with the simplest of shrugs. Raidan was still clinging to the side of the door, bracing himself.

"Are you okay?" I asked him, still catching my breath.

"Yup," he exhaled slowly. "Just coming down from the thought of getting into a car crash—again," he said, slowly removing his hands from the door.

"Are you going to offer me a ride home?"

"Ah!" I screamed.

"Oh, come, now. It wasn't that bad," Gram said, her head sticking through my window. I hadn't noticed her slink over to the side of the vehicle.

"Jesus Christ, Gram. Are you done scaring the shit out of me?" I asked, now unlocking the door for her to get in the back. She climbed in as if nothing had happened and smiled at me in my rear-view mirror.

"My dear, I will never be done scaring you," she answered sweetly.

13

THE GRIMSBANES

The rest of the drive through the Grimsbane woods was both unnerving and inviting all in one. My blood felt like it was singing, but the chant was frightening and fast-paced. The Grimsbane woods was named after my family because my ancestors had lived on the property for many centuries. Grimsbane is my grandmother's maiden name, and we've all kept that name, hyphenating if a Grimsbane maiden married. My grandfather even hyphenated his name when he married Gram, making him forever Joseph Grimsbane-Cormier. He was proud of his Acadian heritage and proud of Gram and all she was. He had taught me that there was so much meaning in a name and that I should always take care to honor it. I carry pride in the name Shivalri Acadia Grimsbane-Gray. It makes me feel whole and comforted.

The forest, however, did not bring me comfort. It always freaked me out. I knew that monsters and creatures of the night were just a bunch of folklore, but my mind always jumped to hideous beasts and phantoms lurking about, unseen but felt through the shivers sent all over my body. I don't believe in monsters. I do, however, believe in ghosts.

Gram and Pépère's house would be what most call a mansion. There are three floors and one loft above ground, and of course, the basement. They have a two-car garage attached to the house, and the guest house connects to the garage from the backyard. The backyard is where my grandmother plants her gardens and tends to her greenhouse. Some of my favorite memories are of watering the crops and eating fresh beans straight from the stalk, dirt and all. I was born here, and I lived here all my life. That is until Mom got a promotional transfer to a rehabilitation center in Andrews, and we left our roots to live in North Carolina.

Here, at my grandparents' house, I had had my fair share of run-ins with otherworldly phenomena—far too many to rule out the possibility of spirits on Earth altogether. According to my grandmother, I used to chat with spirits in the night. My parents say I was just full of imagination. I say it makes no sense for a small child to be playing patty-cake with the air in the middle of the night.

It was more than the things I couldn't remember, though. I had an excellent memory—and an early one. I can remember many pieces of the events that impacted me most during my childhood. I could remember when I'd first been diagnosed with juvenile rheumatoid arthritis. At just four years old, I'd had to go through physical torture during therapy as I learned how to walk again, forcing my knees to move in ways they refused to. I remember having chicken pox at five years old, and the first time I was stung by a bee on the ankle when I was six. My mom had been putting clothes out on the clothesline, and I, barefoot, had been walking amongst dozens of bees, smashing their flowers with my tiny, monstrous feet.

Of course, there were good memories too. Those of

playing with my cousin catching imaginary fairies in the back-yard. Those of playing Super Mario games with my little brother. I especially loved my time retelling stories with my grandmother, running away from her as she pretended to be the Big Bad Wolf.

I also remembered when I saw a pair of eyes staring at me through the blinds in my window, my cousin also bearing witness to this. I remember objects, such as pencils and my eyeglasses, suddenly moving from place to place. I recalled having my door shut completely and seeing the doorknob twist itself open, with no hand attached to said door. I was twelve years old. I knew I hadn't imagined these things.

It seemed as though the older I got, the more frequently I became able to sense the presence of someone—or rather, something—in just about every place I entered. In North Carolina, the library and school auditorium seemed to have the heaviest presence. These woods, the Grimsbane woods, were made up of the loudest silence I had ever experienced. I could only describe it as an internal buzzing meant only for me to sense. I felt the wind calling my name the minute we pulled up to the house. *Home.*

The front porch of the manor was made up of vinery and dark-stained wood. There were pumpkins placed along each extremity, lighting the walkway and the entrance to the house. The glow was iridescent, casting dark, smoky orange shadows on the ground and up the building. Bright light curled around the ribbed skin of the gourds, allowing my eyes to make out fumes flowing gently. I watched and savored the sight as the vapor spread into the night sky.

We got our bags out of the car and headed toward the house. I inhaled the fragrance of dusk and savored the scene my heart had been missing so much.

"You've got a lot of pumpkins out," Raidan said, gesturing to the passage.

"I always do around this time of year. You can never have too much protection," she said matter-of-factly. "Best to ward off evil when it's most likely to strike. It is, after all, almost Hallow's Eve."

"Rational thinking, Gram," I joined in on their conversation. She was very superstitious, but we were used to it. We had been raised with rather different beliefs—the kind that would haunt any soul.

14

WARM WELCOME

I had forgotten what it was like to be here in the night. The house was alive, with candles lit throughout. The only part of the house lit by lamps was the living room. There were table lamps and reading lamps alongside the couch and chaises on either side of the massive fireplace.

"Wow... I forgot how dark you keep this place," I muttered, taking it all in.

"No need for the fancy things in life. We're good as we are here," she said, hanging her coat. I shook my shoes off one by one and adjusted my glasses up the bridge of my nose. The lenses wore a film of fog.

"Where's Satyra?" I asked, eager to finally see my cousin. With our busy work lives in the summer, we could only see each other once. She had invited a few of her friends and me over for her wizard-themed nineteenth birthday party. I had never been to a themed birthday event before, but let me tell you—I was glad to have taken a weekend off to be there. My grandmother's house and my cousin's decorating made for the most dreamlike setup I had ever experienced. With her love for magic and my love of fantastical books, we'd had a blast pretending to be wizards, wearing long gray beards while singing karaoke and dancing with her friends.

"She's here," Gram answered as I heard the footsteps coming down the stairs.

"Saty!" I beamed, running to meet her.

"Oh, my Gods! What are you guys doing here?" she asked, running down the staircase. Her hair bobbed up and down, causing her shiny red locks to wave about. The floral print of her dress flowed after her with each step.

"Spur of the moment, road trip," I called, now meeting her at the bottom of the stairs. Cheerfully, she hugged me and laughed. We had almost half a foot's difference in height, forcing me to bend a little to meet her halfway.

"You've never been one for adventure in the night. How'd you get here? Is your dad coming in?" she asked, peering behind me.

"About that..."

"He's not here," said Gram. I flushed, trying to think up an excuse for his absence.

"He's not here, and he's not coming," Raidan spat. "He probably still hasn't woken up from having drunk all night," Raidan added with a sneer, throwing his bag to the floor. I needed to intervene. Nobody needed to know Dad's business when he was at his lowest.

"Drank all night?" Satyra questioned, mouth gawped.

"Now, now. We do not insult the wounded while they are down," Gram said, head held high, face wise beyond her years. Thankful for her interruption, I gave her a meaningful look. She bowed her head slightly, acknowledging my thanks. I caught Satyra giving my brother a big-eyed look and knew she wouldn't drop the subject altogether. She'd just bring it back up when our grandmother left the room.

I always felt immeasurably awkward when it came to

family dilemmas and just about anything personal. I didn't enjoy talking about my feelings, and I had never once appreciated being embarrassed. I felt ashamed of my dad's misbehavior. Even though it shouldn't, his actions affected how I perceived myself.

"I'm so sorry about Aunt Eden, guys," Satyra said quietly. My eyes started to tear up, and I stiffened my shoulders. I didn't want to get into this yet. It was still fresh, and my mind wasn't ready to delve into it after such a long drive.

"Thank you," I answered, looking away.

"I wish I could've been there for you at the funeral, but I couldn't get time off work," she explained.

"They wouldn't let you take time off?" Raidan asked. "For your aunt's funeral?"

"No, they wouldn't. I tried explaining that it was a close family member, but there was no getting through to my boss," she breathed discontentedly. "We're understaffed right now during the busy season, and I couldn't afford to lose my job." She looked down at her feet. "I tried calling you guys, you know." She looked back up anxiously.

"I didn't get any missed calls," said Raidan. His response was short, causing Satyra to shrink under his tone.

"I swear I did! Almost every morning, right before my shift at the docks, I called from work. That's the only time I have any signal." She was scrambling now, trying to convince us of her efforts. I knew my cousin well. If she said she tried to call, she did.

"You must've had some bad signal there, too, because I didn't get any calls." Raidan shrugged, looking at me now.

"Actually, Rai, I got a few missed calls. It was marked as an unknown caller. I never thought to call back," I explained.

"New phone," Satyra said, shrugging.

"Oh, that makes sense," I realized.

"That's why you weren't getting my messages earlier!" Raidan exclaimed, frustration apparent.

"That, and there's hardly any signal here." She gestured to the house. "Nonetheless, I didn't get any messages."

"Thank you for calling," I said to Satyra and hugged her again. "Even though I didn't get the call, it's nice to know you tried."

"Of course, I did, Shivalri." She sighed. "I will always be there for you guys. Even if I live far away."

"Us too," I matched her promise.

"Always," said Raidan, and he put a hand on Satyra's shoulder.

"Oh, come on, Cuz. Give me a hug!" she exclaimed, laughing in an embrace. I shook my head at her, enjoying my brother's torment as my cousin squeezed him half to death. She hadn't changed one bit.

"Tea?" Gram interrupted. I felt a pang in my sides. I knew precisely what tea could lead to in this house. I looked to my grandmother, who had already started making her way to the kitchen, and panic rose up my throat, resting in the cave of my mouth. I hadn't expected to get into the heaviness so soon into our visit, but it had been a big part of the reason I had wanted to come here.

"Okay," I murmured inaudibly. I felt the heavy thud of my heart punch the roof of my mouth. Nervously, I grabbed my purse and hung it with the coats, leaving my phone zipped inside. Dad hadn't called us yet. If he tried to call now, he could wait. I supposed he deserved a moment of panic. The guilt and grudge were battling each other in my brain at that thought. I was constantly in an internal quarrel with all my thoughts and emotions.

On the one hand, I felt bad for my father. I could empathize with him on a level I wished I couldn't reach. On the other hand, I was angry with him and ashamed of his behavior. I wanted to both hug him and reprimand him at once.

"You coming, Shivi?" Satyra shouted from the kitchen.

"Coming," I answered. I gulped and took a moment for myself.

A tea leaf reading from Gram could mean so many things. I'd typically given in, undoubtedly, to her readings, eager to find out what my lifeline held. However, this time, I was afraid to hear anything about the spirit world, what with Mom's passing. I was scared to have anything come up that may confirm my innermost awful assumptions, the thoughts that consumed my dreams—that the car crash was my fault. Yet come what may, I knew I wasn't getting out of this reading. Though I was apprehensive, it was a part of why I came here in the first place. I needed guidance. This was the best way Gram knew how to give it.

The kitchen was well-lit with candelabras on the counters and on the main dining table. Gram had set four chairs in place and four mugs on the tabletop. I had come to expect Gram's usual spread of twelve chairs and placements lining the long table. The four places already made up caught me off guard.

"How'd you know we were coming?" I asked, confused. "Saty, you said you didn't get Rai's messages, right?" I looked at her. She shook her head and pulled out her phone, hazel eyes darting back up to meet my waiting gaze.

"No bars here these days," she answered, shrugging her shoulders. Raidan, sitting next to her, took her phone and examined the screen.

"No bars at all?" he whined. "How do you live here?" He

then took out his phone to check if he had also lost service. He grumbled, his disappointment distinct. "Mine are gone too." He huffed a sigh and shoved his phone back into his jeans pockets. My grandmother laughed aloud, shooing his misery away with a wave of her hands.

"I had an inkling that I'd be expecting visitors this eve," she said, pulling us out from our complaints. "I was happy to find it was my two dear grandchildren, though I must say I was surprised."

"Thanks for the warm welcome." I laughed. "You almost gave us a heart attack out there."

"What happened?" My cousin grinned, waiting on a story.

"I simply met them outside." Gram shrugged in innocence. "Nothing out of the ordinary."

"You popped out of the woods, and we almost ran you over," Raidan scoffed, shaking his head.

"Oh my gosh!" Satyra exclaimed, laughter filling her voice. "Gram!"

"So dramatic." Gram sniggered.

"Well, we're here, and we're all alive. Not that you helped with that whatsoever, Gram." I gave her a stern look. "How'd you know someone was coming?"

"Just a hunch." She looked out the window. "Although, I would have never guessed it was the two of you. It seems the rebellion has rubbed off on you after all." She winked. The kettle on the stove whistled aloud, and I jumped in my seat at the sound.

"I think you're the one who's been doing the rebelling, Gram. Do you mind explaining how you managed to keep Pépère's car in our shed?" I pointed. "Our little driving excursion seems mild compared to your keeping a whole car at our place without anyone knowing. You realize that if Mom had seen... Mom would've been so—" I stopped myself.

"Never your mind about the car." She turned and patted me on the head like a dog. "You made it here safely, and I'm glad for that. It is quite a long drive for you two young ones," she said, bringing the boiling water to the table. In silence, we three grandchildren watched as she poured the steaming water into our teacups. The room lit up as our grandmother took her seat.

"You know the drill," she said. "It will not burn you, for it is made with love." She placed one hand over her heart and closed her eyes briefly. We knew this was her moment to say a small prayer. "Light, purity, strength, and protection. *Cognitionis. Vita. Spiritus. Vide quod tibi necessarium.*" Gram held out her hands, and we all joined in, connecting the space between us. We all took a deep breath and closed our eyes. Here, we were taught that we must only think of light and goodness. We kept our calm and allowed our minds to be quiet.

"*Vide quod tibi necessarium,*" we chanted. "See what you need." An unexpected jolt of lightning ran through my fingertips, eliciting a yelp from both Gram and me.

"*Fulgur...*" she whispered and took a minute to gather herself. "Shivalri, you shocked me." She drew her hand out from mine, rubbing at her palm.

"That was a sharp one." I exhaled, shaking my hand. I looked at my fingers and twitched them nervously. Another jolt surprised me and singed my mother's ring. I gasped, feeling frantic. My grandmother drew her hand rapidly to her mouth. She looked at me with enormous, stunned eyes.

"Can it be?" Gram mumbled to herself. "Show me your hand," she insisted. "Are you hurt?" she asked, grabbing my hand again. She held it tightly, and my mouth dropped. I felt it again, that pulse of electricity, only now it was stronger.

"Gram, it's static!" I said, backing into my chair. "Leave it be, and it will settle." I took my hand back from her, and she shook her head no in bewilderment.

"I saw a glow!" Satyra beamed, releasing Raidan's hand to reach for mine. I yanked it away from the table.

"Don't, Satyra! It hurt." I groaned, massaging my palms.

"I heard it, Shivalri," Raidan said, looking at me now, worrying away at his lip. He shook his head, perplexed. "I heard a zap." I looked at him, then at Satyra, and then back to Gram.

"It's nothing," I insisted. It was obviously just a static charge; only it hurt much worse than I'd ever experienced before. It felt like a fiery crackle spreading through my skin. I looked to my brother now, who was all too pale. Raidan's eyes were wide. "What?"

"I'm not sure how or why, but something about this feels like déjà vu." He shook his head in confusion. "I don't think that that was my first time hearing something like that," he said, now looking down into his lap. I looked at him, scared and entirely confused. He had never looked so grim.

"What's wrong, Rai?" I asked, reaching for his hand, but hesitated at the thought of the earlier bite.

"The sound of that static," he mumbled. "It's like a ringing I've heard in a dream or something. I swear, I've heard it some-where before."

"You heard it the day we all heard it, my dear," Gram affirmed. "Only, of course, it was much louder. I, for one, felt it in my bones." She quieted, reaching over and forcing my hand back into hers again.

"I know exactly what you're talking about," Satyra said, skittish in her seat.

"What is it?" I asked.

"I don't know what it is, but I heard it too," she rushed. "I thought I was losing my mind. I thought that I had caused it."

She was visibly shaking. Inhaling sharply, she sat upright, her ribs protruding, displaying the deep breath she held. She looked like she'd been dying to get a secret out. She was teetering on the edge of her seat, breath still caged.

"Satyra?" I prompted. My fingers were trembling. My family had never acted like this during a tea leaf reading. Seeing them all on edge over a little bit of static was weird.

"What is it, my sweet?" Gram eyed her. Saty's breath loosed in one big heave as she clung to the table's ledge.

"I see things," she breathed and threw her hands in the air as if that was any explanation.

"So do we all," I said slowly, gesturing to the four of us.

"No, you don't understand," she huffed in annoyance. "I sometimes have dreams where I see this man, and he shows me things that are going to happen, and then they do."

"I'm sorry, what?" I stared. Had she lost her mind?

"It's true!" she exclaimed. She looked around the table and cocked her copper head forward in emphasis. "I know I sound ridiculous. Trust me. I thought I was irrational. I thought I was alone, but I know that I am not."

"What are you talking about?" She ignored my question and looked to our grandmother instead. Was this some sort of game to her? What was she trying to get at, and what did that have to do with my static reaction?

"Gram, I know you've been hiding things from us, but I feel like now would be a really good time to fess up." She urged her with her gaze. This was nonsense. I watched my grandmother grow uncomfortable under her watch.

"My dear," she started, but Satyra shook her head, exasperated.

"The day Aunt Eden and Raidan were in a car crash, I was outside in the greenhouse, and I heard a loud-sounding zap—

like a thunderclap." I flinched at her mention of my mom and the accident.

"What do you mean, a zap?" I questioned.

"I don't know how else to describe it other than it was something like a much louder version of your zap." She paused to look at me. "It sounded the same. I don't understand tuning like you do, Shiv, but what I'm trying to say is that it sounded the same, only louder. Like, the same note."

"Okay, go on," I suggested. She took another breath, then began to spew words out.

"Immediately after hearing the zap, I practically jumped out of my skin and fell on my ass. It took me a minute to realize that I had cut myself on a pair of shears, so I ran outside to get Gram for help." She took another breath, trying to get a hold of herself. "It hurt so bad; I was crying! My eyes were blurry, but I swear to you, when I opened the door to go into the backyard, the sky was splitting right before my eyes."

"What?" My stomach sank at her words.

"I thought the world was ending, Shiv." Darkness tipped her face. "It was so, so red. I know right now it's reddish, but I'm talking like the red you'd imagine Hell might be. That's when I ran into the house to find Gram," she explained. "She didn't know I was home since I was supposed to be working out at the harbor." I could see Gram's face filling with concern, her eyebrows creasing. She kept her gaze on my cousin.

"Satyra," Gram began, but her words quieted when my cousin pressed on.

"Gram was in the basement, and I called out to her, but she didn't hear me." She looked up at Gram now, squaring her shoulders and drawing a breath. "I know we're not supposed to go in the basement, but you had left it unlocked, so I went down to find you. I could hear you yelling in your old tongue from the top of the steps. I thought maybe something was wrong. You never yell." She pointed, face flushed.

"Satyra," Gram said more impudently now. My cousin cut her with a glance.

"When I got to the bottom of the stairs, everything I've ever known ceased to exist as I watched you hovering in place." She shivered visibly.

"Oh, come on, Saty." I rolled my eyes, looking to my grandmother for some sort of explanation. My cousin enjoyed telling her fair share of stories, but this was entirely absurd. "That's enough."

"Look at me," she demanded. I watched her in dismay. "Do I look like I'm in the mood to be joking right now?" I snorted implausibly. This was getting way out of hand.

"You can't expect me to believe this one, Cuz," I scoffed. "I'm happy to give you the benefit of the doubt in almost all cases. This," I held my ground, "is not funny."

"I'm not lying, Shivalri. Gram was literally in the air doing a séance or some shit!" She slammed her hands down on the table. "I see things before they happen; Gram floats in the air, and does Gods know what." She pointed at our grandmother. "Tell them, Gram. We're witches, aren't we?" she barked, now leaving all the attention on our grandmother.

"Oh, come on." Raidan choked out a laugh. I was just about to do the same when the look of worry on my grandmother's face suddenly grew stronger. Something about the seriousness of both Saty and Gram told me that there might be some truth to her outpouring. Perhaps my cousin had hurt herself on the shears. Maybe she had seen the red skies and ran to Gram, only to injure herself further. Head trauma could lead to delusions. When I looked at the two of them now, I saw that this was not a laughing matter. I waited to hear an explanation for this burst of absurdity.

Gram didn't say a word. Taking her teacup in both of her hands, we watched in silence as she began to drink, swallowing every last drop. She exhaled, and steam swept over her lips. She looked down into her cup, examining the tea leaves that remained at the bottom.

"*Pythonissam haereditatem.*"

15

AWAKENING

"It is your birthright to know the absolute truth. *Pythonissam haereditatem*—your witch heritage," said Gram, looking aged and worn. I couldn't think straight. I couldn't even speak. I just stared up at her, feeling confused and senseless. "We are the Grimsbanes, daughters of enchanted; daughters of Earth. We were born from hellfire, untainted waters, unspoiled air, bottomless earth, and best of all, spirit of spirit before us." I dizzied at her words.

"You've got to be kidding me," Raidan said, crossing his arms in disbelief. "This is ridiculous."

"My grandson, have I ever lied to you?"

"You must have," he spat. "You two have snapped if you think that I would believe any of this for one second."

"You have not answered my question," Gram held.

"Well, Gram, you've been lying to us all if even a grain of this is true. Either you're lying to us now, or you've lied to us all our lives. Which is it?" he stipulated, tightening his cross-armed stance.

"Do you think I am lying now?" she asked. I couldn't help

myself. Something in me urged an answer forward, and somehow, I knew it to be true.

"No," I whispered, wonderment rattling my chest. Gram tipped her head.

"Seriously?" Raidan choked. "Witches? You don't seriously believe in magic."

"I do," Satyra jumped in. Her face lit up in awe. It was clear that she had been hoping for this.

"How... How can this be?" I stammered. "How could this be true of us, and I not know of it?"

"It is not simple, but it is a fact. We are taught that our gifts only come to us once we've reached adulthood. When we are grown, we are more careful with the use of magic. Naturally, our power only comes to us when we are ready to use it wisely," she explained. "You didn't know because your magic was dormant until now." Raidan scoffed at Gram's words, rolling his eyes in protest.

"If you want me to believe in this crap, you'll have to prove it," he huffed and tilted a brow. Gram raised her brow at him and smirked. "Well? What are you waiting for?"

"What would you like me to do, Raidan?" she questioned. "Take the fire out from the candles?" She twirled her hand in a circular motion, the slightest breeze picking up around us. I couldn't stop my mouth from gaping as I watched my grandmother eliminate the candlelight in front of us. The room was darker now, but I could still make out the smoke drifting up to the ceiling. Raidan's eyes were wide in astonishment. Satyra was grinning from ear to ear.

"Do more, Gram," she cheered. Gram only nodded and held out a hand toward the fireplace.

A tiny spark, small as a grain of rice, floated out from the crackling fire and into the air above our heads. We watched as it danced, slowly lowering itself toward the candles still smoking around us. The spark lit the wicks in an instant, and the candlelight glowed once more. It was incredible. It was terrifying and unbelievable. "Why didn't you tell us?" I shook my head. My heart strangely understood, but my mind still didn't fully acknowledge that any of this was true.

"It is the duty of the mother to tell her daughter. My mother told me when I reached the ripe age of eighteen. She noticed unusual behavior and realized that my magic was trying to come forth. The first time she recalled was having come into my room, waking me up, and asking me to get dressed and ready for the day. She closed my door, and I opened it a split second after leaving. I was fully dressed; my hair was coiffed, and I was ready for my day. To me, I had spent at least thirty minutes in my room. My mother swears it took me just one second. She deemed the situation my first weaving of time. I was able to manipulate time, spinning my own version of it, only affecting the phase that I was in. My mother knew my power was surfacing, so she told me every-thing I suppose I will now tell you." We were all quiet for a moment.

"This is all way too much, Gram," I started.

"It is all too little," she quieted me. "You do not know a thing at all, Pumpkin." She pushed my teacup toward me. "Drink up," she ordered, now pushing Raidan's and Satyra's cups into their hands. Hesitantly, we all began to drink. It was still hot, but it did not burn.

"My tea leaves will tell me all that I need to know," our grandmother told us matter-of-factly. "Shivalri, I do not ques-tion that you have power. If what I believe is to be true, I do not recall ever having met anyone with the power you hold. It is said to be impossible to wield lightning. It is one of the powers never to have been replicated by anyone other than its true creator." I shivered. Me? Power? How could any of this be?

Something within me nudged my mind to be open to the possibility of magic—a stirring premonition came over me, like veins in the earth allowing life to flow to sleeping seeds. Though my mind fought to defend realism, my body bloomed as if awakening at the mention of power.

"What about me, Gram?" Satyra asked. She didn't look scared at all, and her thrill unsettled me. I suppose she had had her suspicions for a while now. After seeing Gram in the basement, she had some time to wrap her mind around it. I, on the other hand, was dumbfounded; my brother even more so.

"Give me your cup, and I will tell you all that I know. The spirits will guide us to see the truth," Gram said.

"Here," Satyra said, shoving the cup into Gram's hands. She let out a nervous titter as we watched our grandmother take a deep breath and close her eyes.

"*Vide quod tibi necessarium,*" she blew into the cup. I could smell the sweet scent of her home-grown green and black tea waft through the air and sweep into my nose. A recognizable smell and a familiar sensation pricked my face.

"And?" Satyra prodded impatiently. Gram was silent for a moment, watching as I trembled in my seat.

"It seems as though I have not kept my eyes as open as I thought. Satyra, you have a clear gift." She regarded the cup intensely. "You are a seer. With the spirit affinity, you have the natural ability to see clearly, and you have incredible intuition. You said earlier that you had odd dreams... I believe that these are not dreams but, perhaps, visions. I am surprised to find that you have been using this magic for quite some time, though, my sweet. I'm sorry I didn't notice sooner." Gram adjusted her posture, facing my cousin.

"What do you mean?" my cousin asked. I, too, was confused.

"You have a blockage," Gram explained. "You have built a wall around your mind as a way to cope with the loss of your parents. This I have known for some time now. However, I did not realize that you had been using this barricade as a form of keeping my magic out. You kept me from seeing that your powers were manifesting."

"I didn't know I was doing anything at all!" she protested.

"No, of course not, sweetie. That is because of your foolish grandmother," she answered, lowering her voice gravely. "I did not consider that the loss of your parents would force you into growing up early. I did not stop to think of the effects on a young witch. I should have known; should have looked further," Gram said solemnly, passing Satyra her teacup to show her the leaves. She pointed into it, revealing an image. "What do you see?"

"I see people, I think." Satyra examined the cup more closely.

"Those are your parents. Over here, in the top left corner, I see your heart broken into two parts. This represents you, your mother, and your father's separation. Each piece represents the people you love most who have passed on." Satyra began to cry, and I could feel the sympathy tears surfacing in my own eyes.

"I don't feel broken anymore, though... They left us a long time ago. It's been years...." She trailed off. Our grandmother nodded.

"This does not mean that you are broken; rather, that you and your parents were split apart. That hurt will never go away, and I, too, still grieve for the loss of my daughter and your father," she said. "Now I have lost all of my daughters, and I also bare the broken heart in my tea leaves." She pushed her cup toward the center of the table, and Satyra took it right away.

"We match," she revealed, wiping away a tear. "But Gram, your heart is broken in four." Our grandmother nodded and took Raidan's and my cup to read them.

"It seems as though we all match," she said solemnly. "We all have the symbol of *Familia Dolor*. We are a family of pain." By this time, we all had been wiping tears and stifling our sobs into our sleeves. Gram cleared her throat, pulling our attention to her.

"I miss them," I breathed.

"Me too," Satyra added. Raidan coughed and sniffed to hide his impending tears.

"I miss them terribly," Gram told us. "My daughters no longer walk the Earth with us. Though they would much rather be here, holding your hands, know that they are with you in spirit."

"Yeah..." Raidan mumbled and grabbed Gram's hand. She sat up quickly and offered a cheerful grin. She didn't say a word, her face growing stranger by the minute.

"Uh, Gram?" I urged. Raidan pulled his hand back, unease creeping in. Gram's eyes were blank.

"What in the world?" Satyra gawked, snapping her fingers in front of our grandmother's eyes. "Gram? Hello?" Gram's body suddenly slumped, and her smile went from wide to casual. She looked around the table.

"What—What happened? Did I miss something?" she asked, looking completely dazed.

"You were acting weird," Raidan said cautiously, clearly just as confused as all of us.

"That's funny... I was just thinking about how full my heart is now. Seeing you three together with me in my home. I must've gotten carried away." She still looked confused as she rubbed her temple.

"Are you trying to convince us, or you?" I wondered, feeling unsettled.

"Let me see that cup of yours, Raidan," she requested, beckoning with her hands. He gave it back to her and leaned over the table in anticipation.

"Oh my... Oh my! Eden, you are a genius!" she exclaimed and kissed the teacup. "Sweet soul..."

"What are you talking about?" Raidan asked, stirring in his seat.

"Oh, if you only knew," she sang and kissed the teacup again before setting it down.

"Gram, spit it out," I begged, the impatience harsh on my tongue. I couldn't stand not knowing. Especially now. She looked over at my brother and offered a compassionate smile.

"During the car crash, your mother must've used the rest of her strength to save you. I thought it strange when the reports said that your side of the vehicle was worse in damage, yet she did not survive.... The only way this would work is by her giving her life to you. There is no magic that can do this, apart from sacrifice." Raidan's face looked traumatized. She stopped herself and cleared her throat. "You will not feel guilt over this. Your mother made a choice and saved your life with full intent. In doing so, she used the rest of her life's energy and transferred it over to you. You see, your mother was a *Medica*, a healer, and this was her greatest gift of all." I was sobbing aloud now, and Raidan matched my cries with sniffling.

"What?" he asked, voice cracking.

"Mom saved him?" I asked, sniffling.

"That she did, and so much more." She grabbed Raidan's hand and squeezed. "She transferred her power to you. My grandson, my blood... You are now a Grimsbane witch." His eyes bulged, and my heart dropped into my stomach at her proclamation.

"Are you serious?" he asked, blinking the tears away.

"How?" I wondered aloud. My mom saved my brother's life, and in doing so, she gave him her powers. This was unbelievable—incredible. My mom was magnificent, even in her last moments on this Earth.

"When your mother transferred her life's energy, her love for you was so strong that she transferred her power into your soul," Gram explained, carefully stroking the top of his hands. "When you took my hand, what were you thinking?" she asked excitedly. He sniffled.

"I just wanted to make you feel better," he said, voice gravelly.

"And you did. You were sending me happy thoughts to heal my mind." The realization hit me like a truck. "You lifted the pain and replaced it with love."

"Oh, my Gods, Raidan! Do you remember when you approached Dad on the couch? You grabbed him by the shoulders, shook him, and he listened to you. He acted like he'd gotten instantly sober." He looked at me in disbelief. "You must've been healing his mind then too!"

"I wish I could do that. You're incredible," Satyra whispered.

"Healing magic can not bring forth sobriety, and it does not truly remove sadness. Rather, the healer can focus their energy on good thoughts, and those will be felt most."

"Still very cool," Satyra chimed.

"Not only that, my dear," our grandmother started. We all looked at her. How could there be more?

"What's most impressive is how well and fast Eden's life energy took over Raidan's. He healed tremendously well after the car crash. He has hardly a mark of proof of the accident," she said, folding her hands over the cup.

"I..." Raidan searched, tracing the discreetly raised scar atop his head.

"It's true, Rai," I confirmed. "It was as if one day you were attached to tubes that were feeding you life, and the next you were complaining about your TV allowance. It was all so shocking, but I was relieved to see you doing well. I didn't think about it enough to have questioned the logic." I shook my head in bewilderment. "I was just happy that you were going to be okay."

"My grandson, a *Medicus*," Gram breathed. "Your mother would be so happy to know you've become a healer just like her." I could sense the pride in Gram's words as she spoke them. I felt it too.

16

POTESTATES

Everything hit me like a wave in the sea, pulling me under and swallowing me whole. I couldn't breathe. The room began to spin, and the lights went out in a flash. My grandmother's words and the acceptance of this new information were too much to bear. All I could see was red. Red like the gloomy sky that worried me. I felt as if I were gasping for air, but there was none to spare for my taking. How could this be? This was imaginary. This was make-believe. Witches weren't real. Magic wasn't real. The feeling of no longer having anything definite to hold on to consumed me.

The most fearsome blow stung my entire body, and the wind returned to my lungs like fire. The lights were dim, but they were there. I tried to focus on my surroundings, but everything was a blur. I saw dust fluttering in front of my face, and an urge to cough was begging for my strength. I tried to clear my throat, but it burned my esophagus. I tried to cry out, but my mouth was too dry. I felt another thump across my chest, which released the cough I'd been holding in as my vision began to clear.

The lights were much brighter now, and the room smelled of ash. I could see my brother and Satyra waving their hands in front of me. I tried to ask them what was wrong but stopped when I looked down at my body to see that I was covered in a blanket and lying on the floor. What the hell?

"What's happening? Why am I cocooned?" I asked, trying to peel it off of me. My voice was harsh and full of gravel. I pulled the top corner of the blanket down to reveal an almost naked chest. I could see bits and pieces of my bra. "Uh, what the fuck?" I shrieked, now pulling it up to my neck.

"Stop, drop and roll," Raidan said, shoving his hands into his pockets.

"What?"

"You were on fire," Satyra marveled, face full of enthusiasm. She laughed cheerily, clinging to her chest. "I can't believe what I just saw!" She drew her phone out and snapped a flash, blazing my eyes.

"Satyra!" I screamed, scrunching my face.

"I need to capture this moment," she declared, satisfied with the photo and shoving her cell phone back into her pocket. I suddenly remembered somebody was missing from the group.

"Where's Gram?" I asked, terrified. "Is she hurt?"

"I'm just over here, dear," I heard her voice carrying through the house as she came down the stairs. I looked around and realized my family members had dragged me into the living room.

"I thought you could use a change of clothes," she said, shrugging and handing me one of her sweaters I used to sleep in when I was a little girl.

"Gram, what happened?" My head felt woozy. I grabbed the sweater, pulled it over my head, and slipped the blanket out from beneath.

"You happened," said Satyra, holding her hand out. I took it and let her help me up. I felt so weak, my knees buckling under me.

"Woah…" I muffled, steadying myself.

"I think it's time we study you now, Shivalri. Will you be able to calm yourself?" my grandmother asked me, her face concerned. I felt nausea rushing back and shuddered. She looked so severe. "This is very, very important. Satyra, I will need you to take this seriously as well. This is not a laughing matter." Saty swallowed her chuckle and nodded in agreement.

"Totally serious," she settled.

"This is all too much to take in, Gram." I groaned at the discomfort. My head was pounding.

"It is not easy to face ascendency, but you are not alone in this. We are with you. Your family spirits are with you too."

"Ascendency?" I repeated slowly, still feeling the effects of my light-headedness.

"Ascendency is all about rising into your higher self," she explained. "You are all ascending into your witchhood. As you grow, little bits of your magic develop within you. When you are ready to accept your gifts, you enter full ascendency."

"This is so weird," Raidan said, nudging me. My dizziness got the best of me, and I leaned even harder into my cousin's hold. "Whoops," he sniggered, holding my shoulders so as not to knock Satyra to the ground.

"I'm dizzy." I groaned, holding my head.

"I've got you, Cuz." She laughed, helping Raidan to straighten me upright.

"Let us sit you down at the table," Gram suggested.

"Are you going to study me now?" I asked with protest heavy in my voice.

"It is urgent that we do," she insisted. "I will guide you

through this, but before we begin, we must all be in agreement to dive into your soul. This requires pure intentions, strength, and, most of all, your consent. Your magic is growing stronger and stronger within your soul, and it is crucial that we have some understanding. We must be ready for what is to come. We must help you prepare for what you are made of." Dread crept up my throat at the thought of it all. My brother and my cousin already knew what power they had. What was my fortune going to tell? I couldn't fathom how I had seen past all of this for my entire life. My grandmother had always given us tea leaf readings. She had taught us that it was for guidance and help on our life's path. I had never questioned it, calling her intuition an internal piece of luck she held. All this time, she truly did see into our future. She read our life like a book made of herbs, dusted along the bottom of a teacup.

Gram extended a hand to me, and hesitantly, I nodded, my head feeling woozy.

"I'll do what I need to do, Gram," I agreed, taking her hand. "Where do we start?"

"First, we should start by keeping the fire extinguisher close at all times," Raidan said, removing his hoodie and tossing it to me. One of his sleeves was completely toasted, but the rest remained untouched. He was laughing, but I was not.

"When you say I was on fire, what exactly does that imply?"

"It's as I said. Your hands were on the table, and suddenly you were holding flames," he answered. I examined my hands, flipping from palms to backs. They were in perfect shape—no sign of flame or burns.

"Are you sure it was my hands? It could've been a candle close by," I tried to find a more realistic justification.

"Your eyes rolled to the back of your head," he replied, the tease gone in his voice.

"My eyes?" Abruptly, I remembered seeing nothing but the red that reminded me so much of the sky, and the unease crept back into my mind.

"I tried to grab your arm," Raidan started, interrupting my train of thought, "but the fire spread up my sleeve."

"I..."

"It's not your fault," Gram said, clasping her hands together.

"I'm the one who put it out," Satyra blurted, looking guilty but audibly proud. "The fire in your hands, I mean."

"Thank you."

"You're welcome," she chirped. She chewed on her fingernails, then added, "I kind of threw the rest of the hot kettle water on your hands."

"What?" I shouted.

"Yeah, and some help that was!" Raidan boomed. "I told you not to, and you did it anyway!" He turned to me now. "The hot water made you scream, and the water suddenly lifted off of you, and you flung yourself onto the floor. Your screams were deafening. I thought you might pass out from that, but then your whole head caught fire! Your hair, even," Raidan said, panic rising in his voice.

"My hair!" I grabbed at my head, happy to feel my hair still attached, though it was no longer in my bun. I blew out relief.

"Your hair is fine. The fire just burned your clothes; nothing else. It didn't burn you at all, from the looks of it," Satyra said. "The water didn't burn you either." When I looked at her, I could almost sense a tinge of jealousy wrapped in her body language. I shrugged the thought away.

"How'd you guys put the fire out?" I asked. Our grandmother looked at me now and smiled, her composure smoothing the creases in her forehead.

"When you fell into unconsciousness, most of the fire went

out on its own. I threw a blanket over your head, but you fell to the floor." I felt the pain now, throbbing up my elbow and into my jaw. I grabbed my arm and flinched. That was going to bruise.

"You smothered me?" I scoffed. Satyra snickered at my irritability.

"What else would you have me do?" Gram asked. "I didn't have a firehose at hand." She shrugged.

"You seemed to be getting better by that point, Shivi," my cousin added.

"Yeah, and then we dragged you out here," Raidan continued. "Gram said to get you to the living room since there is more breathing space here. Whatever that means."

"It means that the fire Shivalri expelled was eliminating her oxygen. I could see it pouring out of her. I knew that once she woke, she would feel—" She paused. "Claustrophobic," Gram explained.

"I did," I said, clearing my throat. "I felt like I couldn't breathe. I thought I was just having an anxiety attack." I frowned. "Wait— You could see the oxygen?"

"I can see more than you could ever imagine, my dear."

17

THE BASEMENT

I was still feeling a little light-headed with all this new information. A new sense of identity brewed in the back of my mind, and I didn't quite know what to make of it. I had always felt slightly off. As implausible as it may seem, being a witch cleared up many of my latest occurrences.

I should have known sooner. The signs in Gram's behavior and spirit were undeniable. Somehow, I just hadn't clued in. I had known Gram to be a bit strange, what with her religious beliefs and tea leaf shenanigans, but living with her obscured me considerably. I spent so much time with her that I had gotten used to all her quirks. It felt natural. Now realizing what her unusual behavior truly meant, I could see just how unconventional she had been all of those years we'd spent together.

"I have so many questions," I realized, finally surfacing from my thoughts.

"I have so much to teach you all," Gram said. "Come now." She gestured for us to follow her.

"Where are we going?" I asked, tugging on the sleeves of

the sweater my grandmother gave me. I eagerly curled my fingers into its warmth.

"To the basement, of course," she replied, dangling the keys for all to see.

"You're going to let us go into the basement?" I questioned. I had no idea what she kept in it, only that I was never permitted to descend.

"Wait till you see what's down there!" Satyra said excitedly, grinning from ear to ear.

"Is it the Bogeyman?" Raidan chuckled.

"Oh, Raidan," Gram's voice was dark. "Do not joke of such a creature. He is most certainly not good company to keep."

"Wait—the Bogeyman is real? No way!" His face wore skepticism but mostly interest. I could imagine this new world being quite fascinating for Satyra and Raidan. Satyra had always loved her fairy tales, and Raidan was fanatical about monsters all throughout childhood. I had had too many night-mares to consider folklore a good thing. If it were up to me, the tales would stay in books, where I could remain safe behind the pages.

"The Bogeyman exists, my dear, but that is not his real name." She turned back and looked at us all. "Let's go down now. My grimoire collection is full of stories to tell. I'll explain as much as I can, and I will not spare any information."

She spun on her heel and started toward the entrance of the basement. Through the living room and down the hall, we all followed Gram to her always-locked basement door. She paused in front of it and stood tall with pride.

"I don't think I've ever seen what's down there," Raidan said, looking at me. I shrugged.

"I never have. It's always locked."

"For good reason. Magic in the wrong hands or the hands

of those unprepared is perilous," my grandmother warned, turning the skeleton key in the carved keyhole.

"Makes sense," I agreed. Gram smiled and opened the door. The hinges sounded a rusted creak, revealing how old the house was. Gram took the first step onto the wooden staircase with a hissing sound and gestured for us to follow, but it was pitch black, and I couldn't see anything. Gram started down the stairs, and I lost sight of her completely. I began to feel for a railing but was met with nothing but air.

"Gram, it's too dark down here." I shivered, a cold prickle rushing up the back of my neck. When she didn't reply, I almost panicked, but the sound of crackling and sizzling caught me off guard. In an instant, the walls lit with golden hues of fire—flames in the haze of the loveliest cavern I had ever seen.

The smell hit me at once, awakening all of my senses. It was a scent I knew, like the back of my hand. One that always puts me in a good mood. It smelled like books. The further we got down the stairs, the more pungent the odor became, and the more it mixed with the smell of freshly lit torches, dirt, and herbs of every kind imaginable.

"Gram, this is incredible." I reached up to caress a healthy plant of lavender that hung above my head. An extensive collection of glorious books, withered and worn, caught my eye, and I practically floated from excitement. Books were everything to me. They were the perfect learning tool, a crutch during social gatherings, and my source of escape when I craved a life other than my own.

"Told you," Satyra said, coming down the last few steps. "It's a secret underground world we never even knew about."

"This doesn't make any sense," Raidan said, looking around the cave. He bent to pluck what looked like a mint leaf and held it to his nose before taking a bite. "How is this possible?" he asked as we marveled at the sight. A click of a tongue caught all of our attention, and Gram poked her head from behind the large boulder she'd been hiding behind.

"This way," she motioned. "I want you to see my favorite room before we get into the nitty-gritty."

I was the first to start walking her way. I couldn't wait to pass by the shelves upon shelves of tomes that sat along the walls. They were beautiful in every way. I felt the dirt soak into my socks as I passed through the cave. Leaning on a dust-covered shelf, I quickly bent over, removing them and shoving them in my back pocket.

"Good idea," Raidan said as he and Satyra followed suit.

The flames along the walls washed over me and toasted the air I breathed. I felt the most extraordinary sensation of intimate comfort. I let it circle me and drank it in. I swiped my finger down the spine of a book and felt a pang so vital it tempted me to steal it. It was so timeworn, however; I couldn't fathom removing it from its shelf. Reluctantly, I resisted the urge and walked away.

As I got closer to the boulder that Gram had stood behind, a sudden and very faint trickling sound echoed in my ears. Rounding the thick rock wall, I could hear the sound begin to take over the entire space. Could it be that there was water down here? It was possible. This house was ancient, and I could imagine that the expertise of construction workers at the time wasn't as advanced as today. Perhaps there had been a flood or a leak of sorts. I was about to ask if there was a leak in a pipe somewhere when Gram grabbed my wrist and tugged me back. My footing came to a dead stop as the water went from a trickling sound to a downright gushing.

"My goodness, Shivalri. Would you please learn to walk with your eyes open?" She jerked me further into the corner she stood in.

"Your house is sitting on top of a fucking waterfall?" I couldn't believe my eyes.

"Watch your tongue, little witch. Or I'll cut it out and feed it to the fish," she scolded me, only she couldn't help but let out a smile while doing so. I grinned as wide as could be. This was a sight only seen in paradise. It was dark and damp, but the cavern walls glowed with more torches, giving the cave a luminosity like none other. I looked over the edge and felt my heart sink into my gut. It was so deep, so far down. Something about the cave and waters felt like vivacity and mortality to me. A strange mix that didn't seem far off from my past experiences. The water danced, shimmering like a dream, but my goosebumps warned me not to get too close. There was something strange about these waters. Otherworldly, like a phantom energy I couldn't see. The sensory overload sent chills down my arms. Though I knew not to lean too closely to the edge, I peered down in awe. I had never felt so blissfully elated in my life.

"Am I hearing water?" Satyra called to us, her voice echoing through the cave. "I never got this far into the basement."

"Hurry up! You have to see this!" I yelled back to her, voice echoing, just as Raidan peered around the corner.

"Holy shit!" he boomed, his laugh carrying his thrill.

"What's over there?" Satyra asked, sounding closer than she had before. I stepped a little closer, eying the edge of the rocks. Small pebbles crumbled lightly under my feet and fell into the water below me. My heart skipped as I waited to hear the splash of the stone plunging into its demise.

"Be careful, my curious, curious grandchildren," Gram warned as Satyra skirted around the corner, barely dodging the big, chunky stones that formed the wall we stood behind.

"A waterfall?" she gasped. Her smile lit up her rosy cheeks. "This is unbelievable! How in the world...." She trailed off.

"Why, with a little bit of magic, of course." Gram stood proud and dusted off her hands.

"I can't believe this is all real. I'm standing in a basement-turned-underground cave with a waterfall. How did I manage to live here for most of my life and never find out about this?" I contemplated, looking at my family with a whole new perspective on life and who we are. A shiver ran up my spine, and I shuddered in place. "How is this possible?"

"Allow me to teach you." Gram beamed, nodding to herself. "We shall go back to the central chamber."

"But we just got here," Saty complained.

"We will have lots of time for play," Gram promised. "Now that you've seen my mausoleum, it is time to educate you on your witchhood."

"Mausoleum?" I gasped. "This is a crypt?"

"Of sorts," she answered, and it all made sense. I had felt the tingling of ghostly presence when I peered into the water. I just hadn't recognized it for what it was.

"That does not make me feel comfortable," Raidan said, eyes wide.

"Are there dead people down here, Gram?" My cousin looked to be wrung out of her skin.

"There aren't any dead bodies down here if that's what you're implying," she assured us.

"What are you implying, Gram?" I questioned uneasily. She sighed, exhaling heavily before gesturing to the waterfall behind us.

"This is a safe haven for the souls of our family. It is resting grounds for those who are lost and a safe space for those who would simply like to visit."

"Are you telling us that ghosts are living down here?" I asked, bewilderment striking me hard.

"Not living," she corrected. "But yes, many spirits are roaming about these walls."

"That's creepy," Satyra said, rubbing at her goosebumps.

"Not at all, my dear," Gram encouraged. "Those surrounding us are family. They are loved ones who only mean kindness. Don't worry about these spirits. They are harmless." At the mention of the spirits resting in my grandmother's basement, I wondered who might be down here.

"Do we know any of the ghosts down here?" I asked, suddenly realizing that my mom, grandfather, uncle, and aunt Enya could be here.

"No, I'm afraid not," she said quietly. "The ones you know do not come here freely."

"Can they?" Raidan asked. I could tell he was thinking of our mom just by looking at his face.

"Sure, they can," she replied. "But we would not wish for that. We want them to find peace in the Heavens. Here, it is like being stuck. It is only a means of making the melancholy of being lost a little more comfortable for our family members. My grandmother created this safe space while my mother was pregnant with me, and I keep it safe for those who have use for it."

"Are they sad?" Satyra asked.

"Do they understand that they are lost souls?" I wondered, chewing at my nails.

"Some of them are sad, but most are in a state of confusion. There is always something left undone or unsaid with the lost, and what makes it difficult is not knowing the problem."

"Do they ever get to leave?" Raidan asked. I couldn't imagine being stuck like that.

"Because they do not fully understand, it takes a very long time to piece things together. It could take several lifetimes to leave for the other realms."

"Other realms?" I gulped.

"I think it's time we head back to the sanctuary now so that I can teach you all about it," Gram said. I exhaled deeply, more than happy to leave the resting grounds of the lost souls.

"Are we going to look at the books?" I asked, eager to learn everything and anything they could provide me. Not only did I want to leave the creepy waterfall, but I was also happy to get a better look at the old books we had passed. There was something special about reading and experiencing others' works of writing.

"Why, of course." She chuckled, patting my back. "Come along now," she insisted, and we followed her like shadows, eager in the night.

18

COMPELLING TOMES

When we all reached the main room again, excitement crashed into me. There were just so many books. I had to read them all. I forgot about the eery vibe from earlier, and without much thought, I immediately headed for the bookshelf I had encountered.

"Is there a book calling your name?" Gram questioned. Confusion flooded my mind, causing my forehead to crease. Gram took a step in my direction.

"What?" I asked, keeping my eye on the shelves in front of me.

"Close your eyes and take a deep breath. Let your hand flow over the shelves and focus your energy," she insisted. "All of you," she spoke louder, now addressing us all. "Take a walk amongst the room, sweep past the books, and steady yourself where you feel the strongest connection." I didn't need to make a move. I was already in position, eyes closed. I could hear Satyra and Raidan making their way around the room, their feet scampering in the dryer parts of the soil.

"I think I'm good here," Satyra declared.

"I don't know where I'm supposed to go." Raidan exhaled, sounding frustrated. "This doesn't make any sense to me."

"Raidan, just relax and don't think. Just do it," I said, understanding the lesson. His feet made a fuss, and he came to a halt.

"Okay, sensei," he mocked. "I'll go here. But I can't promise this is the right spot," he gave in.

"Good, good," Gram chimed. "Now, as I said, close your eyes and lift your hand to the stacks. Imagine your hand like a magnet, the pull strengthening when you find what your magnet wishes to attract. This act is called compelling." I focused on her words, clearing my mind and only inviting the thought of my magnet guiding my hand.

"It's not doing anything," Satyra huffed in frustration.

"You don't feel that?" I asked. "You don't feel the tug, like your hand wants to reach out and grab a book?" I could sense it immediately. Then again, it could just be my eagerness to get my hands on any one of these books.

"No, but I'm trying." She blew out a breath, exasperated.

"That's it. Clear, conscious dedication to your hand's will," Gram pressed on, governing us from the room's core. Just as I was about to lift my hand, I felt a heaviness in the air, a pressure against my palm, and I experienced a frigid breeze brushing against my skin. I opened my eyes in time to see a gush of wind pull a book from its slot and drag it directly into my expectant grip.

"Gram, did you see that?" I marveled, wholly exhilarated by the touch of magic. My hair still blew in the wind around me.

"I felt it, my dear," she answered gently. I turned to look at her with a wide smile.

"I did it," I huffed, primarily to myself, as I looked down at the book which rested in my grasp. It was filthy and chockful of dust. I noted the clean line swiped down the spine's middle as I turned it over. Instinctively I knew it was the book I had initially touched when I crossed paths with the bookshelf. I focused on the phenomenon I held in my very hands, gently turning it over to see its cover. I couldn't make out the title, but it looked to be of ancient origin. It was so fragile. I made my way to my grandmother, who stood patiently waiting for Satyra and Raidan to retrieve their books too.

"Gram, I don't know if it means anything, but—" She stopped me.

"Shh, lower your voice. They need to focus," she whispered, pointing to the pair. They still had their eyes closed, flailing their hands in the air.

"Okay, sorry," I murmured.

"What is it that you were going to tell me?"

"Well, I can hardly believe it." I flipped the book over in my hands. "Before following you into the mausoleum, I stopped at that same shelf and touched this book. This specific book. Isn't that strange?" I probed, curiosity peaking at the end of my phrase. "Look." I pointed to the spine. "That's my fingerprint." I moved it closer to show her.

"Then it is your book," she answered simply. Still, she observed the other two, but I knew that she was aware of my excitement. Though she did not look at me, she put a firm hand on my shoulder. That gave me a moment of gratitude I hadn't been anticipating. I wasn't sure how or when the change happened, but a sense of rightness washed over me now as I stood next to my grandmother. Having successfully compelled my tome made me feel like maybe I could be a witch. Though I had had a shocking outpouring of fire during the tea leaf reading, perhaps I would grow to control my power. It was weird to think that I had any semblance of power within me, but it felt right.

"I wish they'd figure out how to compel their books, too," I said, growing impatient as I watched my brother and cousin boil with frustration. Instantaneously, a heavy wind came up from behind me in a gust. My hair flipped over my head and into my face, pushing past where Gram and I stood. I brushed my hair, gasping for breath, and watched the wind whirl around the pair. It whooshed up into their shirts, and I heard them both wailing, raspy-voiced, their lungs declaring deprivation.

"What is this?" Satyra cried out, her arm coming to a stiff stop. Raidan froze entirely, aside from the wind that twirled the ends of his shirt. A sliver of movement permitted his hair to lift from its roots. He looked petrified.

"Gram!" I screeched, grasping at my throat. It felt like I had stuck a vacuum to my mouth in an attempt to disconnect from oxygen.

"Shivalri, listen to me carefully." Gram grabbed me hard, digging her nails into my arms. I freaked, scraping at my collar. "Inhale as hard as you can. You have to take your air back." Her eyes darted across my face.

"But I can't...." I really couldn't.

"You must!" She struck me in the chest, and I curled into myself, expelling the rest of my lungs' air. I closed my eyes and clenched my fists. My chest felt hollow, a bottomless aching that wouldn't relent. I had to breathe. I opened my mouth and began to inhale. It stung my lungs, and I coughed it all back out. I couldn't keep the air I took. Spots covered my vision as I grated, clutching at my throat.

"Help," I croaked.

"Shivalri, now!" Gram screamed, twisting forward and holding her abdomen. She looked like she was about to croak. Bracing myself, I set my jaw and squeezed my book with two hands, tightening, and then with all of my might, I drew the gust back to me. The burn was icy and prickled my insides. My eyes were leaking, and it took everything in me not to start coughing again. Still, I held my stance and took back all my air. I focused on my family and wanting to keep them safe.

Cool wetness tickled my feet, and I looked down just in time to see tiny chamomile flowers growing between my toes and around my ankles. The wind around us began to settle, and my head felt high like the clouds. After a moment of intense silence, my ears started ringing, and nausea dominated me. The walls around me began to spin, and my vision blurred.

"Shivalri," Satyra choked out. I saw her thrice. "You don't look very well."

"I think I just need to sit for a sec," I replied, tongue dry and sticking to the roof of my mouth. I was already lowering myself down to the damp soil beneath my feet. I watched as three Satyras walked toward me and sat, crossing their legs in front of me. They coughed, clearing their throats.

"Can you tell me how many fingers I'm holding up?" they asked, holding up three fingers on three hands. That didn't make any sense. I shook my head and felt the world tilt along with it.

"Woah..." I murmured, blinking away the fog. "I'm fine. I just needed a minute to sit." I patted the ground and raked the dirt with my fingers. I began forming little lumps of earth that emptied between the cracks of my fingers. Then I plucked a small flower from the ground and blew out a long, hard breath. So confused and so dizzy.

"You're doing what your body is telling you to do," Gram spoke nonchalantly. "Take a moment to ground yourself. The soil will help."

"Well, that was one way to get our books." Raidan choked on a laugh. He waved his book in display. It was newer-looking and fortified in a green and gold hardcover. The spine's foiling glinted in the cave's lighting.

"Mine didn't come to me," Satyra grunted, folding her arms in disapproval. It was odd seeing this reaction from her. She had never been the jealous type, but envy was written all over her face at this moment. I imagined the reason behind it was to do with her knowing about this for much longer than Raidan and I. She had had time to process and question it all. She seemed excited about the news of us being witches. She'd practically jumped out of her seat when she spilled the beans about her espionage and discovery. I felt for her now, considering this. She wanted this to be true. She wanted to be a witch.

"Yours fell to your feet before Shivalri sent the air your way," Gram assured her, pointing in its direction. Saty's frown flourished to a smile when she saw that she did call her book. A warmth grew in my chest at that. "Don't fret," Gram added, picking it up and bringing it to the table in the middle of the room.

"What's my book about?" she wondered, excitement washing over her.

"Come take a look-see," said Gram, gesturing for us to go to her. Gram took a seat at the perfectly round slab of marble that took up the middle of the room. Satyra looked at me now with worry in her eyes. She took my hands in hers and huffed.

"All right, Cuz. Let's get you up," she ordered, and I groaned in aversion. I still felt shaky from the dizzying spell. We got to our knees and pushed ourselves up. Halfway there, I wobbled, and she steadied me, pulling me the rest of the way.

"Helping me up twice in one day," I muttered. "Thanks." I gave her hand a squeeze. That was Satyra, always there to lend a hand.

"All good. Let's go read some books; you personified windmill." She giggled, still holding onto me. I let out a weak, diminutive laugh and followed her to Gram and Raidan, who were waiting for us in silence. They matched Saty and me perfectly in complexion. Lethargy and exhaustion wore us all down. How many more times would my magic get the best of me, unruly as ever? Would these books have the answers to taming it? Would Gram?

When we got to the table, I positioned my book at my spot and placed my hands on the table to boost myself up onto the chair. The marble was cool to the touch as my weight put pressure on it. The chairs were of timeworn wood and steel, crafted together to make medieval-looking thrones that sat just as tall as the table. My legs dangled below me as I sat down, and I couldn't help but feel small.

Once we all settled, ogling the three books sitting at the table with us, my grandmother reached out to hold our hands, just as she always did before a tea leaf reading. I panicked and nervously shifted away from her.

"We're not doing another reading, are we? Because I don't think I can handle that right now," I stammered, my head feeling muddled again as I remembered the smell of scorched misfortune upstairs. I looked around at the torches of fire that lit the room, and I quivered.

"No, no, dear. We are just connecting. That is all." My grandmother reached out again, and I eased up and gave her my hand this time. One by one, we took each other's hands and closed our eyes, as per usual. Gram to my left, Raidan to my right, and Satyra facing me; we all took a deep breath. I felt Gram release, and in turn, I let go of Raidan's hand as I opened my eyes. I sighed.

"What have we gotten ourselves into?" I wondered aloud, meeting the eyes around the table. This felt like an all-too-real dream. One that, if I had the choice to wake up from, I would.

"Can we open our books now?" Satyra begged, grabbing for her own that faced our grandmother. Gram stopped her reach before she could get to it.

"Ah, ah, ah. Please have patience, Satyra. You can take it, but I would ask you not to open it just yet. I have a little explaining to do before we dive into these tomes." Satyra rolled her eyes. It was typical of Gram to speak to us like we were still five, but in this situation, I could understand. Gram pushed the book in Satyra's direction, and my cousin slid it in front of her. I could feel her restraining herself from taking a peek under the cover. I stared at mine as it lay face down on the table.

"You've got the floor, Gram. Explain away." Satyra motioned with the flow of a hand.

"All right." She grinned. "Where else to begin but at the beginning?"

19

———

FABLE

"Legend says that the discovery of witches commenced during the fifteenth century," Gram said and looked at each of us, making sure we all paid attention. "Of course, this is just regular humans' discovery, not that of our kind, who have known who we are for centuries and centuries, BCE."

"Witches existed before Christ?" I gasped. "I would've never thought...."

"A magical being created the world. It is not so far-fetched," Gram held. That was true. If I could believe that a powerful, almighty God created the world, why couldn't I believe in witches? I had never considered such a notion.

"Amazing." Satyra sighed, clear awe ringing in her tone. This was all so surreal.

"Tell us about the discovery," I prodded. My mind wanted to wander through all of my what-ifs. I needed to know the story. I needed the facts.

"When you say the discovery of witches, are you talking about the witch trials?" Raidan questioned. I hadn't even begun to think about that horrible history. It hadn't crossed my mind at all.

"It does play a part," said Gram. "The trials closest to us were in Salem. The Salem witch trials were during the seventeenth century, but the awareness of witches and their witchcraft rose among humans during the fifteenth. That's where most of our troubles began. The witch hunts were launched in Europe and made their way to us.

"The first thing you need to know is that we used to be called wise women. For a long time, there was no such thing as a witch. There were just healers, nurturers, and midwives," Gram continued. "We were women who knew instinctively, deep in our bones, how to help those in need of helping."

"Only women?" Raidan interjected.

"During this time, that was presumed," Gram answered.

"So, what happened that these women turned from healers into witches suddenly?" I wondered.

"First, you need to understand that any sort of magic was forbidden to show among the humans. We had to hide it for ourselves."

"I heard about that before in legends," Raidan said.

"How did people find out about the magic?" I wondered.

"They never did! That is what frustrates me to this day." Gram sighed.

"What do you mean?" Satyra asked.

"We were once praised for our cunning and kindness. They used to call it a gift." She blew out a breath, shaking her head. "The trouble only came when evil, most often that of man, blamed us for things that were not of our control, such as a woman perishing during childbirth or accidentally selling a rotten piece of fruit to an unsuspecting customer. The famous Salem trials were utter chaos. Most of the time, the people accused weren't even witches."

"That's terrible!" Satyra exclaimed, hand over her mouth. "They murdered people who weren't even real witches?"

"They did, but they also killed many of witch-kind too, do not forget," she reminded us.

"Unbelievable," I remarked.

"The worst of it all was being deemed a whore when we would not comply with the wants of greedy, cruel men," she spat. My back went upright at her profanity. I had never heard my very proper grandmother swear like that in my eighteen years of living.

"They what?" I choked. Raidan and Saty snickered, knowing well that they would never hear our grandmother repeat that word ever again.

"They cursed our names and renounced us all, claiming that we were evil. For the most part, we were not guilty of evil doing. The scared folk turned us into the image through word of mouth."

"That's awful," Satyra said to Gram. I was busy chewing at my nails.

"It was," Gram agreed. "Now, I must confess, there were wise women who dabbled in darkness. There were absolutely some of us that did horrible, evil things. That, however, is something that witches learned to hide very, very well," Gram said solemnly. My nails tasted bitter as I continued chewing anxiously. Her words heeded a warning.

"How does this explain magic? How did the witches dabble in darkness?" I pressed, pulling my fingers from my mouth.

"That is a story that strikes me to this day," Gram replied. She looked almost nervous, but she kept her voice calm. "Long, long ago, angels and demons roamed Earth."

"What?" I gasped, eyes bulging out. "Angels and demons? They're real?"

"As real as you and me," she answered, a bead of sweat glinting above her lip.

"Holy hell," Raidan muttered.

"Holy hell, indeed." Gram laughed, but I knew it was just for our peace of mind. This was not a laughing matter.

"Okay, so where are they now?" I asked, focusing on the reality of things.

"Let me explain," she insisted, sounding touchy.

"Full attention," I answered. Gram cleared her throat.

"I cannot say for certain what truly happened, as stories have changed time and time again. But I will teach you what my mother taught me in hopes that these stories will help you all along the way," she told us, and we all leaned in, listening intently. "As I said, angels and demons used to roam Earth. They were the children of Mother Earth; the creation of divinity."

"That's who you always pray to," I stuttered, remembering my grandmother's teachings from my childhood. I, too, learned to pray to her from a young age.

"Yes, she is one of the Gods I praise," she said. "I honor Earth for all that it is and all we are."

"So, what did the angels and demons do on Earth?" Raidan asked, eager to understand. "I thought they were in Heaven and Hell."

"There was never use for Heaven and Hell during the creation of our world. It was only when war struck that they were divided."

"I know about this," Satyra said, cutting in. "There was Lucifer, right? The fallen angel. The devil was sent to Hell."

"A devil is not a real creature, my dear. Not that I know of. I was taught the stories my family passed down, so I can only tell you what knowledge they imparted to me. We come from a long line of witches, and we believe we are descendants of our Mother Earth. As far as Hell and devils, there are so many religions depicting so many different deities that it is hard to decipher which is true and which is artificial. Lucifer is the story of a fallen angel, yes. He was one of many angels who fell from their reign. I don't know for certain what his name was. Some say Lucifer. The Egyptians have Anubis. We will never know their true names as we were not there to witness the world's birth, but I do know that he is real. As I always say, all of the stories are true."

"What happened to him and the others who fell?" Raidan questioned.

"When the corrupt fell, they were cursed and deemed to be demons. They, and their demon children, preside in the other realm. Some rule over it, some exist there after death, and others are tortured for eternity."

"They all descended into Hell," I whispered, terrified at the thought.

"*Hell* is only a word for mortals. We do not know what Hell is truly called until we arrive at the other side of the Gates." A chill ran over my arms at Gram's words. I couldn't even begin to imagine such a thing.

"So let me get this straight," Raidan started. I studied his concentrated regard. "Demons are all in Hell right now? Before then, all beings lived in the same place, right?"

"Exactly," said Gram. "Every being imaginable used to live together. This worked well for many, many years until humans were created. From what I am told, that's when chaos erupted."

"Humans?" I interjected.

"Yes," she declared. "Everything began with Gods, and Gods created everything. When humans were made, they were powerless and fearful. The Gods promised the humans whatever they wanted, so long as they worshipped them, as

Gods were prone to seeking influence and command. There is so much that even I do not fully understand, but I believe this to be true."

"Wow..." I mumbled to myself.

"Tell us about the humans," Saty urged. "What were they like?"

"They had a rather difficult life, relying on the divine for everything. When the Gods decided to add humans to the mix, their world and rules became even more complicated than before."

"That sucks," Saty murmured. It was strange to consider all of these possibilities. Now that I knew magic existed, I had no reason not to trust that some of this might be real. I could understand that there was a Heaven and a Hell. I had grown up believing so, even before knowing about magic. What I still did not understand was how my family, *humans*, had magic.

"Gram?" I looked at her.

"Yes, dear?"

"If we are humans, how do we have magic? You said that the humans didn't have any power, but we do."

"Oh, pumpkin. Don't you see?" She sighed. "We are not simply human."

"What?" Raidan choked. I couldn't help myself from gawking at my grandmother.

"What do you mean?" Satyra asked, eyes wide.

"We are semi-divine."

"Oh, my Gods! What?" Satyra exclaimed, her face lit with enthusiasm. "That's so cool!"

"What does that even mean?" I asked, bewilderment harsh on my lips.

"We are both human and divine," she explained. "You must remember, it takes two to procreate. Our lineage is that of magic." She paused and exhaled. "Humans often became consorts to the divine when the world was one. They made children with angels, and many, many demons." I could feel the tension in the room. This was an unbearably horrendous new territory.

"How do we know which part we're made of?" Satyra asked, her smile turning to a frown.

"That answer is the same for all of our family—We are human due to man's blood, but we are also very different due to the company they consorted with. Those made up of divine angel DNA and human blood are called Nephilim. The Nephilim possess angelic energies."

"Like what?" I asked.

"Like superior health, intelligence, beauty, and pure hearts. Some of the Nephilim have the ability to detect those of other supernatural forces. They were witch hunters long ago, though I believe the practice of hunting demons has died down substantially over the centuries," Gram replied. Her words rang in my head.

"So, are you saying we're Nephilim?" Raidan asked, shock apparent in his tone.

"No," I whispered. "She just said that witch hunters hunted demons...." Shock bore through me at my realization.

"We are not Nephilim, my dear grandson. We, the Grimsbanes, all share the DNA of a mighty, magical deity and their human mates. We are made up of demon's magic." Panic skewered my gut.

"Are... Are you sure?" I stuttered. My eyes began to sting as the salt from my tears surfaced.

"I am." She rested her hand on mine. "We are the descendants of magic, life, and everything in between."

"That's freaky," Satyra mumbled, examining her hands. I started to imagine the demon blood that ran through my veins. *My blood.*

"It is extremely frightening," Gram replied, "but only if you do not fully understand it. That is why we begin today. I promise you; you will know everything you need to know, so long as I am around to teach you," our grandmother assured us and patted Satyra on the head. She jumped in response.

"So, do you know which demon deity we are related to? Or does that matter?" Raidan asked, now more severe than ever.

"That information was lost to us long ago. I do know that not all demons were created to be evil, just like not all angels turned out to be good. Most demons were troubled souls who were given hard lessons to face. Some certainly tried to become a better version of themselves. My mother told me of a time when most of the world was peaceful, though I do not know what is true and what is not, as I was not there to witness it."

"Okay, so witches exist because of a demon and their children. And there's also a hybrid called Nephilim, another group of offspring created. What worries me most is the whereabouts of the angels and, more specifically, the demons. They're not still on Earth, are they?" I pleaded for an answer. I started thinking about all the what-ifs. If we witches were here, were our creators also roaming the Earth?

"No, they are no longer on Earth. After the chaos of war, Mother Earth decided to leave Earth to the humans and sent the angels and demons to their separate realms where they could not interfere with their opposing species' affairs. The Triple Goddess of the universe came to existence by the will of Mother Earth herself to ensure the realms stayed intact."

"So, Heaven and Hell—They're both real?" Raidan asked. "I'm having a hard time wrapping my head around it."

"From what I believe, yes," Gram declared.

"If the demons and angels went to Heaven and Hell, why didn't we?" I wondered aloud.

"Because we are human, and our souls are not complete until death."

"What do you mean?" I prodded.

"When we die, and the human in us dies, our divine souls will travel to the other realms to rest."

"God, that's freaky," Saty muttered.

"Wait, are we going to Hell?" I gasped. I could feel my heartbeat thrumming at the base of my neck.

"I guess we will see." Gram shrugged.

"What?"

"Oh, Shivalri. Do not fret about death. Whether we would like to accept it, it will come for us one way or another. There is no use in worrying about the afterlife."

"Um, yes, there is!" I burst. "I don't want to go to Hell!"

She sighed heavily and put a hand on my shoulder. "Focus on life, my dear. If you don't appreciate the now, you will regret it in the then." I couldn't believe her. I could not understand how my grandmother could think this way. *Does she not understand the gravity of the situation? Does she not comprehend what she's told us? She's cursed us with this knowledge and expects us to stand by and accept it. I cannot. I will not.*

"I don't want this life," I whispered, feeling the heat rise to my face.

"Shivi," Saty said, turning my attention to her. I hadn't looked at my cousin or brother too often during this conversation. I could see it now, the worry and dread that filled their hearts. This was just as difficult for them to swallow. They were not arguing. They didn't so much as grunt a complaint. As I looked at Satyra, her eyes heavy with fear, I knew that this part of the discussion was at its end. We would talk about it again, I was sure. But for now, we would take everything in stride, accept the information, and deal with reality.

"All right then." I exhaled the breath I held in. "What's next?"

"I think it's time we look at your books. They came to you because they had something to tell you," Gram informed us, happy to see my compliance. "Raidan, let's start with you," she gestured to him.

"Well, I don't know what's in it, but it didn't take me long to figure out the author." He pointed, lifting it for us to see.

"Mom!" I gasped, reaching over to touch the cover. She wrote in this book. It took me a moment to remember that she, too, was a witch. It was all so strange to wrap my mind around this new world. It was as if I were seeing for the first time. It was terrifying and electrifying all at once.

"Oh, Eden." Gram sighed, smiling faintly as she turned to my brother. "It only makes sense that you retrieved your mother's book, seeing as how she's the source of your newfound powers. You will do well to read it through." She smiled proudly. "As you know, she was a Medica. This book strictly contains the use of healing magic. I've read it myself many times, and I know that it is safe to read and practice on your own. Just follow her guidance." She reached across the table to pat the book.

"Can I open it?" he asked.

"You may," she allowed, and he flipped it to the first page:

This is the book of Eden Grimsbane.
After me, whoever this may find may use it as they wish, for all my knowledge is now their own. Happy healing!

My heart was heavy as we looked through the pages in amazement. Notes were scrawled all over the pages in my mother's messy handwriting. It was incredible. There were many hand-drawn illustrations of plants with blurbs next to each, undoubtedly describing their use.

"Can I open mine now?" Satyra begged, already lifting the edge of the cover. Gram let out a sigh of laughter and nodded in her direction.

"What's yours about?" I asked.

"I'm not sure," she breathed and flipped through the pages. Raidan and Gram kept looking through Mom's book, and my heart warmed at the small piece of my mother that she had left behind. I was glad that my brother received this gift. I looked back to my cousin, who had stopped abruptly, jaw dipped in fear.

"What?" I questioned. She looked like she had just seen a ghost. She looked up at me and faltered when Gram shut the book. "Satyra?" I forced her to look at me.

"The page I just read... It said necromancy," she whispered; the single word so volatile it stung.

"Like, dead people?" I gasped, horrified.

"Necromancy is one of the many gifts that witches have been given; a gift that can also be a curse. Conjuring the dead can be of great use, but only when the dead you seek to bring back is of pure intent. The dead often are the ones who grant us our seer sight," Gram said. "Nevertheless, you must be very, very careful. This is a very risky kind of magic." Satyra only nodded, staring down at the book in front of her.

"You can't be serious," Raidan stirred. "Bringing back the dead?"

"I am severely serious," our grandmother said firmly. Raidan looked like he was about to be sick.

"Like, zombies?" he prompted a little further.

"No, it's not like the movies," Gram assured us. "It's either for a brief moment, guiding the apparition of a spirit, or reviving someone back to complete health."

"Back to life, you mean," Raidan contemplated aloud. I began thinking about Mom and considered what Satyra could do with this power. Could she have brought my mother back to life? Her own parents? My grandmother's severity told me that it was a possibility, which scared me to my very core. The look on Satyra's face told me she was thinking the very same thing. My mind surfaced back to the conversation at present. Raidan was still mumbling to himself about zombie theories, and Gram just nodded, barely paying attention to his babble.

"Is that her power, then?" I asked for Satyra, cutting Raidan's rant short. "Necromancy?"

"It could be one of them." Satyra's head shot up at Gram's words.

"Could be?" I prodded.

"There's more?" Satyra gasped, looking upset. Gram sighed and placed a hand over my cousin's.

"More gifts? Yes. There are many possibilities for those with spirit affinity. As I mentioned before, you are a seer, you are full of intuition, and you have the ability to create a mental block. It seems your power comes mostly from your spiritual mind's strength. I know this book well, just as I know Raidan's well. Spirit runs strong in our family. My grandmother and mother were seers, and so were my daughters, and now, all three of my grandchildren have the spirit affinity. Satyra, my dear, you compelled a family grimoire that has existed for more than a hundred years," Gram stated. A shuddered gasp escaped from my cousin.

"You see dead people?" she shrieked.

"Not everyone has that kind of power." She shrugged. "But, yes, I do. Only if I want to. I always want to see my loved ones, and therefore, I am happy to have this gift." We looked at her in horror.

"Wait." Raidan paused. "Our whole family has the spirit affinity?" he asked, looking at Gram. "Even me?" She smiled at him reassuringly.

"Yes, my dear. That's where the healing gifts come from. You can heal the mind, body, and soul. I'm not sure if Eden was able to give you all of her power. I was only able to find the traces of Medicus in your cup."

"Why do you think I have it, Gram?" I wondered. "Spirit affinity, I mean."

"Oh, you've been using your spirit affinity your entire life. I knew you were a powerful witch from the moment you came to this Earth."

"How so?"

"You were born en caul; a veiled birth."

"What's en caul?" Raidan asked for me.

"It is when the baby is born inside the sac, still intact. It is the symbol of great power among witches," she explained. "Your sister was born for greatness."

"Okay, that is a strange occurrence, but that doesn't explain why you think I have the spirit affinity," I pushed.

"Yeah, Gram. Are you sure Shivi has it too?" Satyra questioned.

"Oh, most definitely," Gram assured us. "I've kept a close eye on all of you throughout your entire lives. Shivalri was the first to show any signs of magic. Just her birth alone was an indication, but the minute she could move on her own, be cognizant, she has been chatting with the spirit world." My back stiffened at her words. I hadn't been losing my mind all of these years. I believed in ghosts just as I believed in humans. I have always sensed a presence, sometimes eerie, but often, just a sense of company.

"I was never imagining it," I muttered. I shook my head in disbelief. "All those years... Dad never believed me. He mocked me for being scared of ghosts. Mom never once showed me that she believed, always shrugging it off as an active imagination. If Mom knew about witches, ghosts, and magic... Why did she dismiss me like that? Why wouldn't she have told me the truth about our family?"

"I think your mother thought to protect you by hiding the truth until you came of age. But I have always believed you, Shivalri. What your parents couldn't see, I could. What your mother dismissed, I took note of."

"I have goosebumps." Saty groaned, rubbing at her arms.

"I'm still a little confused," Raidan confessed. "You said that Mom had spirit affinity too. Wouldn't she have seen the ghosts? Wouldn't we all?"

"No, it doesn't work like that." Gram sighed. "An affinity is an umbrella term, meaning that there are many categories within. Just because you are gifted in a certain field does not mean you have every one of the abilities in that affinity's classification. It means that whichever ability you do have, you gather your strength from that affinity."

"Like with my healing powers?"

"Precisely." Gram nodded.

"Shivi." Satyra turned her attention to me now. "Do you have the power of necromancy?" My eyes flew wide at her question, blood frozen in place.

"I have no idea...." I swallowed hard. "I hope not."

"Why not?" Raidan questioned.

"I don't want to raise the dead!" I shrieked, not wanting to imagine it.

"Wait." Raidan stopped me. "Gram, could you raise Mom and Aunt Enya from the dead?" Raidan asked, his face as pale as snowfall. "Or Pépère and Uncle Olly?"

"No, I would not do that to their souls. I spend time with their ghosts, but only if they so choose to see me," she spoke as if this was a natural thing to say. I gulped, and my scalp became itchy from the panic. "That's what Satyra saw me doing down here... I had myself a little reunion of sorts."

"You talked to them?"

"I did," she said. "That is how I knew that your mother had passed. She came to visit me in the mausoleum. Enya showed her the way."

"That's terrifying," I whispered. "Are they here right now?" I asked. I felt goosebumps rise on my arms.

"No, they're not physically here with us at present. However, they've told me that they send you little bouts of energy whenever you're in need," she informed us. "Have you ever felt it before?" she asked. We all shook our heads in disagreement. "Well, the important thing is to know that they are with you when you need them." She smiled. I couldn't understand how she could be so at ease.

"So, you use this gift—our gift, often?" Satyra asked, still hunched over in her bubble of fear.

"Not often." She shrugged. "When I do, however, I thank my gift for allowing me such great power." She stroked Satyra's book again, then inched it over to her.

"The possibility of my having this is scaring me," Satyra confessed, slowly accepting the book.

"Me too." I grimaced.

"It does come with a price, but girls, this gift is worth it all," she said and smiled in reassurance. "I am glad that I might pass it on to you. I know you'll take great care in learning how to work with this magic," Gram said proudly, but Satyra still looked unsure. I knew I matched her worry.

"I don't think I want it," Satyra murmured. "Are you sure this is my book? Maybe Shivi knocked it down by accident."

"No, this is your book, sweetie. It's for all witches with spirit affinity. You don't necessarily have the power of necromancy. This book simply covers every spiritual power that exists."

"I hope I don't have that particular power...." She sniffed. Tears started to form as her lips trembled. I wanted so badly to take this hurt away from her. She had been so excited about being a witch up until now. Raidan touched her hand, and she immediately stopped crying. Laughing, she blew a big breath. "Thanks, Cuz." She sniffled again, wiping her face. It surprised me to see him use his power again and so effortlessly.

"Already learning from Mom, I see," I said in amazement.

"It comes in handy," he replied and ran his fingers through his hair.

"In *hand*-y," I retorted, forcing the group of us to laugh at my ridiculously cheesy pun.

"This is a grave matter at *hand*," Satyra replied with a light laugh on her tongue.

"Ouch." Raidan chuckled. "The puns just keep coming. Badly," he teased.

"Okay, okay. I get it. We're bad. It's enough." Satyra snickered. "Are you going to open your book now?" she asked, directing her attention to me. I looked at Gram in question.

"Am I?" I asked nervously.

"You are."

20

———

THE RIPPLE

The book felt thick in my hands. I let it balance for a moment, weighing it and contemplating its contents. Carefully, I lifted it to my face and blew atop the cover. Flecks of dust drifted into the air, flitting above our heads. I wiped the remaining dust from its surface to reveal the title in bold: *Prophetiae.*

"Oh my," Gram exclaimed, grabbing the book from my hands. "Oh my, oh my," she trailed.

"Hey," I exclaimed. "Give it back! I want to see what's in it, too," I said frustratedly.

"Patience," she ordered with the wave of a hand.

"Gram?" I questioned, trying to take the book back from her. She opened it quickly, skimming the pages. She used her finger to scan the words, and I peered over to see just what she was fussing about. I was becoming irritated.

"Shivalri, you said that you touched this book before I told you to search for one. Why did you do so?" she asked, not looking up from the pages. She continued to flip through rapidly.

"I don't know. I just wanted to touch it. Badly," I answered brashly. "Gram, what's going on? What's this book about?" She was still flipping through the pages, which frustrated me even more. I huffed and slammed my hand onto the book, causing her to discontinue her search. She was mute, eyes set on the volume. One by one, she pried my fingers off of the text in front of her. She looked to be in shock.

"Uh, Gram? You okay?" Raidan asked, about to reach for her.

"That's it," she uttered. "That's it. Oh, this can't be right, but it only makes sense..."

"What is it?" I probed.

"It's what I thought," she began, looking directly at me. "It's the first thing I guessed, but I wasn't sure." She searched my face, panic flitting about in her gaze. Her eyes darted back and forth, and I had the sudden sensation that she was looking past me rather than at me. She turned her focus back to the book, and I couldn't help the cold sweat that came from the feeling of worry she emitted.

"Sure about what?" I pushed. "Gram, you're scaring me. You've got to explain."

"Yeah, Gram. What's going on?" Saty added, just as confused and curious as me.

"I wasn't certain, but I had a hunch... And I surely didn't think you, or I, or anyone in our family, would've had anything to do with it. But... Oh, all of the pieces are fitting more wholly than I'd like."

"What pieces?" I shouted. I couldn't take it anymore. This obscure, frantic version of my grandmother was unraveling me most uncomfortably. I plucked at the book, but she pushed my hands away, eyes never leaving the pages. "Please, Gram. What's the book say?" I tried. "What's wrong?"

She finally caught her breath, as if her mind was working faster than her body would allow in her moment of panic.

Looking up from the tome, she considered me with somber, all-seeing eyes.

"If I am correct, and I truly believe I might be, you are in a grave amount of danger." My stomach sank in shock. I hadn't expected her to say anything of the sort.

"Danger?" I gulped. She held my gaze. I thought she was excited by my find, but her words brought me back to reality.

"Why is Shivalri in danger, Gram?" Raidan demanded. "What can we do? What can I do?" Though she did not answer him, her eyes distributed a million words.

"Gram?" I pushed, insisting that she answer. She took a long, deep breath and released it shakily. This only made me worry further. Gram was not the type to undo so easily.

"I have three questions for you," she told me. "When I ask, do not overthink. Follow your instincts and answer truthfully." Her face expressed urgency.

"Okay..." I agreed. "I'm not sure what you're trying to get at here, but I'll try."

"Just follow your instincts, like you did when compelling your tome," she suggested.

"I will," I answered, sweat intensifying all over my body at the thought of magic curling from my fingers. Would my panic unleash more unchecked power? I swallowed that thought and tried to concentrate on staying calm.

"First question," Gram said. "When I ask you to think of Heaven, what do you think of?"

"Heaven?" I asked, certainly not thinking she would ask me about such a thing. "What does that have to do with witchcraft? And my book?" I wondered.

"Everything," she replied. "Don't think about it too much." She sighed. "What do you think of when asked of Heaven?"

I considered her words and tried to concentrate on the subject. I imagined going up into the sky, flying into the night.

I pictured myself amongst the clouds and being able to reach the moon. "What first comes to mind?" Gram prodded, pulling my attention.

"The skies... The stars and moon... Flying..." I answered truthfully. "But how does that—" She cut me off.

"I am the one to ask the questions." She pointed a stern finger at me.

"Okay," I agreed, backing down. I was still so confused. What could my book, my powers, have to do with Heaven?

"Good. Now when I ask you to think of Earth, what do you think of?" she continued.

"The Earth," I answered immediately. "Simple as that. I think of planet Earth and the things that are living on Earth. Life, maybe." I shrugged.

"Good, good. Now lastly, when I ask of Hell, what do you think of?" She looked at me expectantly. I paused for a moment, and I cleared my throat to make way for my words.

"Hell makes me think of death." I swallowed hard. "Hell is death and endings." I shivered. She laughed jarringly, and I jerked away at the change in her posture. She leaned into the back of her chair and exhaled, then pushed the book forward and spun it for us to see.

"Just look at this." She was still laughing, disbelief written in her eyes. There, in the book, existed an image of moons: a crescent, a full, and another crescent attached to one another, forming a pictogram. Beneath the symbol, I read the text.

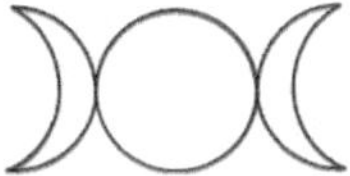

Triple Goddess – Divine Power
Goddess of the moon, the Earth, and magic.
Ruler of realms Heaven, Earth, and Hell.
The Mother, Maiden, and Crone: deities of three come together
as one.
She who ties the triple Realms.

Maiden: Magic, initiation, new beginnings, birth; youth.
Mother: Love, fulfillment, strength, power; life.
Crone: Wisdom, tranquillity, death; endings.

"Holy shit." I covered my mouth in surprise.

"Shivalri," Satyra echoed my surprise. "If you break it down, that's pretty much what you just described."

"Okay, but anyone would say something similar to that," Raidan scoffed. "Heaven; the skies. Earth; earth. Hell; the dead."

"You are missing the point, grandson," Gram replied.

"What am I missing here?"

"Her answers were uncanny. Like they are a part of her being."

"What does this mean then?" I asked, astonished as I read the words that mirrored my own.

"What do you think it means?" she questioned. I reached for the book, and Gram let me take it this time as I pulled it a little closer to my end of the table.

"Okay, so I'm related to them? Or do I have powers like them? Is that what you're trying to tell me?"

"Firstly, it's *her*, not them. Secondly, no, that's not exactly what I'm saying," Gram said. I was entirely flummoxed.

"Then what? I get that I correlated the words." I was trying to piece the puzzle together. "I have a sixth sense?"

"You are the words," she replied, rubbing her forehead. I scowled out of frustration.

"What do you mean?" Satyra asked for me.

"The Triple Goddess is of divine power. It is said that she was gifted the five elements by her maker and is in control of the realms Heaven, Earth, and even Hell. She is the guardian of the Gates," Gram explained. As if that were enough to clue me in, she stopped there in her speech.

"That explains nothing!" I yelled, irritated now more than ever. The wind whipped around me in reaction to my panic. The fire in the torches swiftly burst into a harsh white; flames stretched upward, dancing to my words.

"Calm, Shivalri," Gram warned. I took a deep breath, and it all came to a stop. I closed my eyes, my thoughts racing in my mind.

"Gram," I began cautiously. I reined in my annoyance and unease. I was tired of the games and my grandmother's vagueness.

"Yes, dear?"

"Tell me now." I closed my eyes, taking a deep breath. When I opened them again, my grandmother nodded in earnest.

"You are she incarnate," she whispered, and my eyes flew wide open.

"You think I'm the Goddess?" I whispered, standing from my chair. The sconces were brighter than ever now. "Well, this is just ridiculous! I'm most definitely not. This has to be a mistake." My mind was spiraling with the never-ending questions that floated about in my head.

"It makes perfect sense, Shivalri, and you know it."

"No, it doesn't! That's ridiculous!" I spat, pushing away from the table.

"Sit back down. I am not finished with you." She spoke with such severity that my thoughts were wiped clean from my mind. I sat back in my chair, my body obliging but not feeling like my own.

"Why?" I heaved, unable to think for myself.

"Listen and listen to me well," Gram commenced. "You are important, and you are in danger. You need to understand that this is not just about you being the Triple Goddess incarnate. There is so much more that comes with your awakening that you need to understand." I shivered at the thought.

"I'm listening," I said, voice void of emotion.

"Turn the page back one," she ordered. I obliged.

The page was titled *"Prophetiae,"* just as the book's cover was. Depicted across the page was an image of a tree split down the middle. Above it, the branches folded to either side, revealing an abysmal hole where all the leaves should have been.

"*Prophetiae*," Gram bellowed. "It translates to prophecy." Horror struck me cold as my eyes landed on the text at the very bottom.

PROPHETIAE

Hear me now, Hear me loud; I am gatekeeper
  of all.
Leave me now, Mark me without; The balance
  of worlds will fall.
Mine they are, To rule so far; As Heaven, to
  Earth, through Hell.
From good evil feeds, As good makes evil bleed,
  Divided they shalt dwell.
That which is night, That who is light, She
  must mend her deed.
Born from might, She who ignites; Created for
  he to be freed.

I PUSHED the book over to my grandmother, who sat in her chair, her face stone hard.

"This prophecy has been told and told again. Taken apart and brought back together, piecing the mystery of it all," Gram said, brushing her fingers across the pages. "Never in a million years did I think I'd live to see the day it came to light." She closed the book. "Never in a million years," she continued breathlessly, "did I ever imagine my eccentric granddaughter would be the one to bring it to life." She looked at me in disbelief, shaking her head sympathetically.

"This is an ancient book, Gram." I tried rationalizing with her. "There's no way it's meant for me."

"Oh, but it is," she said earnestly. "I do not doubt it. You were destined for this, though I wish the burden didn't come with this gift."

"How is it a gift if I'm in danger?"

"It's hard to explain." She appeared to think it through. "You are a critical component in the world's viability now, my little witch. To me, you have always been important, but now, you belong to so much more."

"Let's get straight to it then," I said, stretching to crack my neck. "Explain it. I need to know what this means. Why am I in danger?" I demanded.

"We never know for certain what the specifics are, but that which I do know, you will not like." She looked at me, frowning. Satyra and Raidan remained quiet, ever fixed on the book with the prophecy.

"Not liking it doesn't make it any less real, so understanding it seems like the most responsible thing," I answered, crossing my arms. She was worrying me. I could hardly believe any of this to be true. I was not special. I was just wrong. The way that my grandmother was acting toward me forced me to pay close attention. Maybe I hadn't understood.

Perhaps I had missed something. I couldn't be a Goddess incarnate. I was far too ordinary for this kind of foresight.

"You make a fine point," Gram said. "Just because one does not like the truth, it does not mean it is any less important to learn of it." She nodded and folded her hands on top of the marble table, and I couldn't help but think she looked older at this moment. Her rigor intensified her age. "I had a feeling that something was wrong. I could feel it in my bones the moment it happened. As did you all."

"What do you mean?" I questioned, my understanding still unclear.

"As we've witnessed, you hold much power, Shivalri. I've never seen someone with such inexperience compel the magic you've released." She shook her head as if trying to grasp her thoughts. "It only makes sense that they've come to you if you are tied to this prophecy."

"How do you know that I'm tied to this prophecy?" I wondered aloud. Maybe it was still just a fluke incident.

"Yeah, Gram. How are you sure?" Saty asked.

"Because Shivalri can control the five elements, just like the Triple Goddess. Those being water, fire, earth, air, and most prominently, spirit," she informed us. Surprisingly, that didn't come as a shock to me. After experiencing my eruptions of magic, this felt relatively reasonable. What didn't sit well with me was the relation to the prophecy.

"That explains the fire," I muttered.

"And the water," Satyra added.

"Don't forget that windstorm," said Raidan.

"And your growth of flowers," Gram confirmed. "The ghosts, too. You have it all. Fire, water, air, earth, and spirit."

"Okay, but if you made flame disappear and reappear, and you have spirit affinity, what makes me different?" I asked.

"I use a spell to conjure magic that does not belong to me.

It's a rule of giving and taking. My energy is exchanged for power. You, on the other hand, did not use spells. The magic is already in you."

"Oh." I nodded. "I see." There was no point in questioning these sudden powers I had gained. It was strange and foreign, but it was unmistakably existent, and I surely hadn't used a spell. It was time for acceptance. Gram took a moment to think. Satyra and Raidan looked between us, waiting just as intensely as I did. I wondered what they were thinking. How were they taking this information? I couldn't read anything more than curiosity on their faces. After a pause and deep exhalation, Gram's frown evolved into determination.

"Your elemental powers seem to be completely controlled by your emotions at this point," she said as if to herself.

"I can agree with you on that one." I flushed, embarrassed at how little control I had over my emotions. Though there were considerable parts of this that I was reluctant even to entertain, this part made sense.

"So, you lost your mother," Gram stated, causing me to flinch and distracting me from my inner thoughts. "When you saw her, did you know, in your gut, that she was gone?"

It took me a moment to remember my feelings that day. The flashback of the scene would haunt me for the rest of my life. I remembered thinking that my mother looked lifeless. A great shiver ran through me, and I trembled in my seat. I had known in my core that my mother was dead. I knew from the minute I stepped foot outside and saw the car wreck. I just hadn't wanted to believe it.

"I— I did," I stuttered. Taking in her statement tore at an open wound.

"So, when you realized that your mother was gone, your emotions got the best of your affinities, intensifying the three severed realms. When you harness all five affinities at once, just as the Triple Goddess does, it invokes the magic in the Gates," said Gram.

"I didn't see any magic," I whispered, still feeling the heavy loss of my mother. "There was no fire or anything around me."

"I believe you besought the elements directly from their sources. They would have manifested at the core of the Earth."

"So, what does all of this mean?" I wondered, trying my best to understand.

"You've taken the realms that the Goddess created and awoken them; stirred their magic. You removed their veil," she said coolly. I choked on a cough.

"Veil?" I repeated.

"The veil between worlds."

"Oh, my Gods," Satyra murmured. "The red sky..."

"Yes, precisely," Gram agreed. "That's when I felt like something was wrong in our universe. It has never felt like a natural occurrence to me. The red skies, the loud, cracking sound like lightning at its deliverance. Shivalri, you've lifted the veil to the realms of Heaven and Hell."

All in an instant, I felt the world topple over. Spots of white flickered through my vision as I tried to focus on my surroundings. I felt my warm, damp hands clamp to the cool marble table in front of me and steadied myself in place. What was she saying? How could this be?

"What does that mean?" Raidan asked for me. I was too frozen to work my voice.

"What is usually a closed curtain is now lifted for all to see," Gram explained. "If this information gets into the wrong hands, terrible, nasty people could try their hand at truly opening the Gates." I froze in my seat, chills racing up my spine.

"I..." I choked, never finding the words. I had done this. My mishandled emotions had doomed us all, quite literally.

"It seems like the realms cannot be fully opened without your aid, regardless. At least we can take peace in knowing that it cannot be done without our knowledge. It can't be done without you."

"Can we stop this?" My voice was splintered, not feeling quite like my own. "Is there a way to fix what I've done?"

"You are the only one with the power to fix it." My grandmother flipped the book and continued scanning the page. "Well, that's not entirely true," she corrected herself.

"What?" I asked, befuddled.

"It's kind of like a riddle. Very vague, but the pieces are there." She shrugged. "It clearly states that light and dark need to work together, and you need to free whichever one you are not. It says you need to free *he*. I believe one of you must represent Heaven and one Hell."

"So..." I pondered. "I must represent Hell then because of my DNA." I quivered as another chill came rolling through my body. The hair at the back of my neck tingled as I considered my peril.

"It could be literal, as you mention. But it could also be referring to intent or physical state. In which case, I don't believe you are the symbolism of night." She crinkled her nose at the thought. "I could be wrong, but we won't know until we know," Gram thought aloud, looking over the page once more. "No one knows what the prophecy truly means, only that we've all been expecting a new Goddess to take the Triple Goddess's place."

"Great," I said shakily, looking down, drowning in my thoughts. We sat in silence for a moment, gathering our minds and trying to make sense of things. This was becoming all too much. Firstly, my grandmother informed me of my ability to wield all five elements. That was no surprise, as I couldn't get a grip on myself for even a second since the magic started stirring in me, and the elements were present during each outburst. That in itself was hard to swallow, but I could take it. Being the Triple Goddess was the cherry on top of the most absurd fate. I honestly didn't want any part of it. What kind of life would this be? Would it even be mine to walk? The prophecy laid out my destiny without my say in the matter. Whether I wanted to be a witch or not, whether I wanted to be a part of some grand prophecy or not, I was not given a choice.

"Gram?" Raidan asked. His voice surprised me, waking me from my burden.

"What, Raidan?" she answered, raising her brows in question.

"What do you mean by Shivalri opening the gate, or veil, to Heaven and Hell?" I looked up at him, finally wholly grasping what Gram had said. The total weight of the realization pressed in hard.

"Oh my Gods, wait...." I stilled, eyes wide in horror.

"I mean that Heaven and Hell can potentially be delivered on Earth. The veil is to see through, but the Gates... Well, the Gates are to walk through. Which can mean no good for any of us," Gram stated. "No good at all."

"Well, no shit!" I started to panic out loud. "I thought it was just like, some kind of window for the realms to peek through!" I shrieked. "Demons on Earth? And I'm responsible? How in the world am I supposed to fix something like that?" I could feel an anxiety attack setting itself into my nerves. I had to calm myself, but all I could think was that demons would inevitably cross my path. How had this happened? Why me?

"The veil is sort of like a curtain on a window, in that, when it is lifted, it allows the beings to look through, and sometimes, if the window itself is open wide enough, they can influence things on the other side." Gram said calmly. "The veil is like the window, whereas the gate is like a door. No one has the power to keep the physical gate open, aside from the Triple Goddess. She has pledged her entire existence to keep the Gates closed and guarded. She protects us all for the sake of humanity."

"So, what's happening right now?" Raidan questioned. "With the Gates?"

"As far as I know, the Gates are still closed. The imminent danger is that the veil is gone. Some magics are strong enough to allow another being to visit for a brief period if the veil is lifted, even if the Gates are not open."

"By some magics, you mean Shivi, don't you?" Satyra whispered.

"Only her and the former Triple Goddess." Gram nodded. "Because Shivalri, in some way, shape, or form, has been chosen to replace her."

"Oh, Gods..." I couldn't believe it.

"If the otherworldly beings haven't already found out that their veil has been lifted, they will soon." We all nodded grimly. I looked around the table at my family, my gaze landing on each of my relatives. Raidan was drenched in disbelief, sweat beading down the brow of his wide eyes. I could tell he was worried in the way his jaw hung open, not wanting to believe this could happen. Satyra was shaking in her unrecognizably pale skin. My cousin hadn't spoken during this cautionary tale, seemingly dumbfounded and genuinely unnerved. My grandmother was solemn and worn. She looked as if she were setting herself for battle. Sorrow and so much fear flooded us all. I felt the crushing pressure of my failure swallowing me whole. My family and the entire world were in danger, and I had been the cause of it.

"So, what do we do?" I trembled at the thought. I didn't even want to begin imagining what *I* had to do.

21

REPOSE

"I think we could all benefit from a good night's sleep," Gram suggested. I trembled at the thought of leaving this conversation, as it were. My body felt the desire to shut down, but my brain argued that I needed to stay up and continue learning and keep trying to understand my role in all of this. My nerves were shot after all of tonight's affairs. I wasn't sure which would win the battle; my anxiety or my need to rest.

"I don't think I could sleep right now," I said, passing my nails between my teeth to chew at them.

"Oh, come now. You will have plenty of time to worry tomorrow." My grandmother took my hand from my mouth, but I tore it from her grip and continued chewing. She clicked her tongue at me.

"That's not going to help your situation," she said. "You need rest. We all do." I spat my chewed-up nail to the ground and stomped on it.

"To hell with sleep. I need more answers," I grumbled, mushing my foot into the ground.

"You will get them in the morning," she insisted.

"I'm not opposed to sleeping right now, actually, Shiv," Satyra said before stepping away. I looked at her in disbelief.

"Raidan?" I asked, looking for him to see my point in staying up.

"Sleep sounds good. We should probably also try giving Dad a call," he supposed. My nerves unspooled at the mention of our father.

"Oh, my Gods. I forgot all about Dad."

"Oh, don't worry," Gram interjected. "I called him during your outburst of fire."

"What?" I asked, perplexed. How had she found the time? More intriguingly, how had she done so?

"When I went to grab you a sweater, I took a brief moment to call your father. I do have a cell phone for emergencies, you know."

"Since when do you have a working phone?" I asked. Satyra snickered.

"It's always off. She even removes the SIM card," she told us. "Bad energies." She laughed, sarcastically mimicking our grandmother's ominous tone. Gram jokily smacked her upside the head.

"Hey!" Saty groaned, rubbing at her skull.

"You'd do better to listen to your silly grandmother. Have I not proven myself to know more than most?" She winked and gestured to the cave we still stood in.

"Good point," she said, patting down the hairs that she'd fussed.

"Was Dad angry with us?" I asked, bringing back the subject. "Did he get the note we left for him?"

"He was not angry." Gram sighed. "He was in an uproar but entirely out of worry for you both. He was glad to hear that you are safe and has agreed to your stay here."

"He didn't argue?" Raidan wondered aloud.

"I don't think he had the energy to argue. He was distraught," Gram told us. I sighed in relief, then felt guilty for putting him through the worry. Then I remembered why we left in the first place and decided that my guilt was unnecessary as long as everyone was all right. Satyra turned to me and gave me a look of sympathy. She pointed to the stairs and waited for a sign of surrender. I sighed.

"Fine, we'll sleep."

"Let's go," she insisted, and I followed her up the stairs, Raidan and our grandmother following behind.

At the top of the stairs, I smelled the odor of incineration again and stifled a small sneeze. Gram took out her keys and locked the door behind us.

"Do you still have to lock it even after we've been down there?" Raidan asked, disappointed.

"It's not just you that I kept from this basement, Raidan. You can never trust that you're safe."

"You're scared of burglars?" he sneered.

"I take precautions because they are necessary. And no, I am most certainly not scared of burglars," she answered, squaring her shoulders.

"Then who?" he asked.

"You never know when evil may be lurking about," Gram divulged, voice low. "These woods are full of creatures dying to get their hands on my most prized possessions." My cousin gave me a wide-eyed look that mirrored my own as we turned to look at our grandmother.

"Creatures?" we said in unison.

"Jinx!" we said together and giggled. Gram's face was stone hard, bringing our attention back to the gravity of her statement.

"We are not alone in these woods; therefore, I've placed a spell to protect my house. A strong, robust spell." She lifted her finger to her temple, and then her face turned from pleased into troubled. "Now, knowing that angels and demons could potentially roam free, the spell is almost useless against those greater beings. I'm not sure what good my spell would do to protect against them."

I had never seen my grandmother so rattled. It was hard to wrap my mind around this fiction-turned-reality. I had always believed in ghosts, but creatures lurking in the woods felt ridiculous. Even worse, angels and demons. All I could think was that I had brought this horror upon everyone. I'd opened the veil and inadvertently invited terror to strike. I had endangered the world—I had compromised my family.

"I'm going to fix this," I proclaimed. I didn't feel confident in saying so, but I knew that it needed to be said. It was what my family needed to hear.

"And we will help you," Gram added. Satyra and Raidan nodded in agreement, but I could see the fear quickening behind their eyes.

"Okay," I mumbled, primarily to myself. Raidan put a hand on my shoulder in comfort.

"We'll get through this, Shivi," he swore. "We've got your back." I nodded, trying my best not to flinch at the thought of involving them in my endangerment.

"First order of business; sleep," Gram announced. "Off to your rooms."

"You got it," Raidan said as Gram yawned, spinning to find her bedroom. My poor old grandmother looked so worn. She had always carried a pep to her. She had a liveliness like no other elder I'd ever seen. This disaster weighed on her heavily, and it was unusual to see it in her appearance.

"Come on, Cuz. You'll sleep in my room with me, and we'll give Rai the spare room next to Gram's," Satyra suggested. "That way, we can all sleep on the top floor." Though there were many bedrooms in this house, I liked the thought of staying close to everyone. After tonight, chills of terror were ravaging my nerves. I didn't want to be alone.

"Good idea," I said as I exhaled, trying to release some of the pressure of this evening's events. Satyra nodded, linking our arms together like back when we were children.

"A sleepover!" She smiled at me. "It's been a while, huh, Shiv?"

"Not long enough," I groaned, remembering Saty's sleeping problems.

"Hey, it'll be fun! I'm not that bad," she grumbled. "I've gotten better at sleeping through the night."

"Whatever you say." I laughed. "But you'd best believe I'm creating a wall of pillows between us." I snickered when she scoffed at me in disbelief.

"As usual," she answered and huffed a big sigh.

"Listen, you're freaky when you sleep!" I held firm, remembering all the previous sleepovers.

"Not my fault!" She snorted and started flitting her eyes to look possessed.

"Stop it!" I screamed, half-afraid and half-amused. "Your eyes will get stuck like that one of these days!" She raised her arms and pretended to be a monster in response.

"I want to eat your brains..." she growled low. It was an amusing attempt at a scary voice. With a voice as chirpy as hers, she sounded like Tinkerbell with a scratchy throat.

"You're unreal," Raidan said, rolling his eyes. "Go to sleep."

"He's right, you know," Gram said from her doorway. "Go on, you two. Off to bed." Gram laughed and walked out of view.

22

NIGHTMARE

Crimson skies and murky clouds loomed above my head. As it started to rain, I could taste a copper stain in the air. It filled me, enthralling all of my senses at once, concealing me from my logic. The clouds, flourishing, cried out blood. I followed them as they moved ahead, my nose raised to the sky.

Trees appeared before my very eyes, making my gaze leave the clouds to look in front of me. I was in the forest, though not the typical kind, as the trees grew in all directions, twisting as if the branches had minds of their own. It was nighttime; my surroundings were dark and weathered. I was relaxed, taking in the environment.

A raven cawed, captivating my attention as I looked for its position. In the tree, the bird perched above my head and cawed at me once more. It was beautiful, black, and mystifying —like a dream I recognized was a dream. It looked at me now, and I steadied my gaze, looking directly at its third eye. We blinked in time, and the world went black.

I felt a heavy pressure on my head, followed by my ribs, hips, and knees. I opened my eyes to see that I was facedown on the ground. I tried to turn, but my muscles would not obey. At last, I succumbed to the ground and lay still as ever. I heard the sound of slithering all around me and tried tilting my head, but to no avail; I still could not move. I stayed calm.

From the corner of my eye, I saw the tendrils—blackened roots from the bird's tree enveloping me. They slithered across my back and wrapped around my every limb. They stung my skin, spreading pain all over. I closed my eyes.

Suddenly, the ground beneath me was gone, and I was suspended in the sky, being held by nothing but feeble roots that wrapped around me. A rumble of thudding arose, and my ears rang a piercing sound. The roots became brittle, my body lowering with every snap of tendril. The rumbling grew louder. And then I fell, my gut slamming into my ribcage. I blinked, and the sky turned from red sun to blue moon, beautiful in contrast with the night. The crescent in front of me lit my hair that whipped in the free-fall.

"It's a nightmare..." a deep, dark whisper of a voice breezed past my ear.

"It's a nightmare...." I repeated, searching for the voice in the wind. Warmth brushed my cheek, and I closed my eyes to soak it in. Even now, falling from the sky with no ground to be seen below me, I felt safe as I plummeted to my death.

The sound of pounding woke me with a start. My heart was beating so fast; my blood pressure spiked in tune with the deafening thuds that rang in my head. Not again.

"Saty." I hissed, opening my eyes. There sat Satyra against the bed's headboard, slamming her head into the wall repeatedly. I sat upright and pulled the covers off my legs. I took one of my neatly stacked pillows and timed the moment I could slide it under her neck. There was no waking Satyra when she had these fits, no matter how hard one tried. I was used to seeing her do this. She'd taken up the habit early in childhood. The first time I saw her do it, I screamed so loud Gram came running into the room with her broom in hand, prepared to fight off my enemies.

I managed to slip the pillow under her, and the banging yielded. Still, she shook the bed. I took my side of the blankets and created a makeshift cocoon around her, and the shaking ceased almost instantly. Finally, I lay back down in my spot and curled up into myself, thankful to have the extra-large hoodie for warmth. I didn't know if I could fall asleep again. That nightmare had felt so real. It didn't help that Saty's pounding had made the sounds in my dream come to life. An impending and unavoidable headache would surely greet me in the morning. I touched my forehead and shivered at the contact. I recoiled at the touch as my cheeks became ice, missing the warmth of the dream's night breeze.

23

GROUNDWORK

hen the sun rose to shine through the window, I sprung out of bed in a hurry, last night's events whirling through my memory. I steadied myself from the dizzying I triggered and blinked out my moment of vertigo.

"Woah, what's the rush?" Satyra spoke from the corner of the room. Her voice pinched in my ears, and the early set of a migraine pressed in. My cousin was already up and dressed, brushing her hair at her makeup station. She was always one to make sure she was pretty and prepped for her day, never once stepping out unprepared.

Her makeup desk was an antique that belonged to our grandfather's mother who lived in Canada. Pépère, our grandfather, had told us that his mother, Edmée, had used it as a sewing table when he was a boy. When his mother, my great-grandmother, passed away, having lived a beautiful ninety-three years, the table was left to my grandfather. He turned it into a desk by adding drawers on each side, and it's been in Saty's designated room in the Grimsbane house since she was born; eventually, she turned it into her makeup area once she permanently moved here. There were bottles upon bottles of fragrance sprays that stood in front of the begrimed mirror. Her hair tools took up one side, and the rest of the desk had all sorts of makeup scattered atop its surface. I watched her do her hair in silence, engraving the image in my mind. It was a relief to see her doing her usual morning routine. It was a sign that what gave me a tremendous headache didn't seem to faze her in the slightest.

"Did yesterday happen?" I asked, clearing my throat. I was half hoping that it did happen just for proof that I wasn't losing my mind, but frankly, I was mostly hoping that it was all a bad dream, something my mind had made up. She looked at me through the reflection of her mirror, confusion framing her eyes.

"What do you mean? Nothing happened last night." She twisted a curl, unconcerned. She continued combing through her hair as if nothing was out of the ordinary. I rubbed my eyes and squinted.

"What?" I grabbed my glasses that were sitting on the nightstand. "You don't remember what happened yesterday?"

"Oh, you mean how we found out we're witches, you basically set the house on fire, Gram has a secret underground cave in the house, and you've quite possibly unleashed angels and demons on Earth?" She paused, flipping her hair. "Yeah, that happened." She set her hair comb down and grabbed her flat iron to smooth her bangs. The sunlight from the window cast a golden beam through her auburn hair, revealing the red coloration that we had both inherited. She looked at me and rolled her eyes. I groaned as the heaviness of it all crashed over me yet again.

"Fantastic." I plopped back onto the bed and let out a complaint into the mattress. How could this be happening? How had this become my life? My mouth tasted sour at

Satyra's mention of angels and demons roaming the Earth. I could only imagine the damage that would cause. What was I going to do?

AFTER GETTING DRESSED, Satyra and I descended the stairs. As we reached the kitchen, she turned to me astutely.

"I think we were destined for a lifetime of adventure," she said. I sighed heavily.

"I know we are."

Raidan slouched at the counter in the kitchen, half-awake and eating some corn flakes. I grabbed one of Gram's fancy china bowls and poured some cereal for myself. We almost exclusively ate on her fancy china. She had always said there was no point in passing things down if you do not use them. It destroys its sentimental potential. We must treasure these things and not fret about wear and tear. It means the next in line will have a piece of us, knowing we used it well before them.

The cereal was bland and tasted mostly of milk, which I despised. As the last few bits sank to the bottom, I clunked my spoon aside and dumped the soggy waste into the garburator. Satyra did the same.

"Soggy cereal?"

"Yup," she said. Gram walked in then, grabbing a seat next to Raidan. Raidan looked up from his bowl and blinked the sleep away.

"I think everyone's feeling a little nervous about what's to come today," Gram spoke, considering our faces. Her words forced my back straight.

"What's to come?" She raised her shoulders at me.

"Who knows?" Gram got up and started to walk away when Satyra stopped her in her tracks.

"I think I might know..." she said nervously.

"What do you mean?" I asked. Gram clasped her hands and waited for a reply.

"Well, it's just that I had a night terror last night, and I can't help but think that my dream might have had a deeper meaning," Satyra said, her eyes widening and frantically fiddling with her fingers as she spoke. "What I saw was something that I don't think I have the ability to make up. Plus, it felt like it meant something, like something about it tugged at me to pay attention," she explained. I couldn't help but recollect the nightmare I had had, too, and shuddered at the images that came from my mind.

"Go on," Gram nudged her. My cousin took a moment to gather her thoughts.

"Well, remember I told you that sometimes, I have dreams where this stranger comes to me and shows me stories? And they come true?" We nodded. "It's like a silhouette I can slip into. I can't see their face, and they doesn't even speak to me. They only show me images, like a movie, for my own personal viewing."

"Oh! I have heard of such a thing." Gram appeared surprised. "When I was a young girl, my mother had a friend who would see-walk into the minds of others," Gram explained. "They cannot physically touch you, cannot speak, but can project their visions for you to see. Some allow you into their bodies to inhabit them as they show you their surroundings."

"So, like voluntary mind-reading," said Raidan, considering the ability. "How cool would it be to have powers like that?"

"Not quite mind-reading. It's more akin to mind-showing. It's a gift that many seers have. It is used among like-powered individuals. It can be a handy tool, so long as you refrain from doing so without the receiver's permission," Gram warned.

"So Saty can receive these images because she's also a seer?" I asked.

"I believe so," said Gram. "This stranger is crossing boundaries that should not be crossed." She creased her forehead at the intrusion.

"They've never shown me anything bad before. Usually, it's just things related to the weather. And then they come true. I thought I was just predicting the weather in my dreams," Satyra told us. I was about to ask what kind of dreams, but she cut my thoughts short. "The visions only started appearing to me this month. The stranger would come once or twice, here and there. Now though, they come every night." She looked so suddenly solemn, and it made me worry for her. Not only did my cousin have to deal with her newfound foretelling dreams, but she was also being visited by a stranger who was invading her mind while she slept.

"What do they show you?" I asked her.

"More importantly, what did they show you last night?" Gram interjected. Saty paled. I wanted to know everything she'd seen, but I knew that Gram was right in specifying last night's occurrence. Something about the way Satyra's face contorted made me feel uneasy—like something was going terribly wrong in that mind of hers. Saty took a deep breath and rolled her shoulders, concentrating on a memory.

"I couldn't make out the images at first," she stuttered. "They were all muddied together. When I saw what they were doing with the animals, I realized what was happening." She gulped, wincing at the thought.

"Animals?" Raidan asked.

"There were people, extremely creepy-looking people, outside in a forest. They were all holding a bunch of black animals, petting them, kissing them...."

"What did they do with the animals?" Gram asked, pushing for more. When Saty looked up at me, my stomach curled in on itself. She looked unwell.

"Saty?" I regarded her. Her lips tightened in a thin line.

"They ripped their heads off," she spat, and I gasped in horror. She flinched at the sound.

"Oh, my Gods, that's messed up!" I cried.

"That's not the worst part," she started and looked away.

"What could be worse than ripping the head off of an animal?" I asked, appalled. She looked at me now, full of fear.

"They squeezed the animals' blood down each other's throats, swilled the blood, and spat it on the ground. Then, the blood caught fire." She stopped, shook her head, and looked me dead in the eye. "Shivalri, they were chanting your name." My knees buckled under me, my body going numb. Gram was off-color, back stiff as a board.

"It was a sacrificial spell. Those animals were their familiars," Gram barked.

"Their pets?" Raidan gawked.

"Sacrificial?" I couldn't move.

"Come. Let's go down to the basement. We'll continue this conversation in a more secure location," Gram insisted, forcing me to make my legs work.

"Do you think people are listening in?" Raidan asked in horror.

"There are ears everywhere, whether you see them or not," she replied. Without another word, we followed her into the basement. An icy heat crept over me as I pictured dozens of eyes peering through the windows, listening in on our conversation.

The cave felt protective and grounding. I was glad to be back down here. The books we had chosen, or rather, the ones that had picked us, were still sitting atop the marble slab at the center of the cavern.

"Good," Gram spoke first. "Now that we're settled in the Grimsbane sanctuary, I am able to speak freely." I sank into my chair, metal and wood piercing my spine and tailbone after this morning's painful fiasco. My rheumatism was going to hate me.

"Gram, this is the first time I have seen something so horrible. Is it accurate? What did my dream mean? What did I, or they, predict?" Satyra begged for an answer. I could see that even she herself did not fully understand what she saw. Our grandmother sighed and straightened her posture.

"I'm not sure that I believe it was a prediction."

"But—" Gram cut her off.

"Satyra, allow me to question. I am not calling you a liar. I simply require all the facts." She grabbed for the book *Prophetiae* and flipped through the pages.

"What are you looking for?" I asked. Satyra's nightmare had involved me, and now Gram was flipping through my chosen tome. I couldn't help but worry that I was the primary source of the problem, especially after last night.

"Was Saty's dream in the prophecy, Gram?" Raidan queried. She shushed us all and flipped the pages until she landed on the one with the tree we saw yesterday. I stared down at the image, cringing at the sight of the crack down its middle.

"What does this have to do with my dream? Vision, I mean," Satyra corrected, pointing to the page.

"This is the image that portrays Shivalri's actions. The splitting of realms." Gram flipped to the next page. "Here is the image of the summoning spell." She spun the book so we could all see clearly. It was the same tree, though the splitting of realms was replaced by flame. There were strange figures drawn around the tree; their feet wrapped around in its roots. I flushed at the sight.

"Gram," I started.

"It's the same tree," she said, pointing to the two images as she flipped through.

"Yes, I know," I stopped her. "That's not what I was going to say."

"What is it?" She looked confused. I flattened the pages and pointed to the image, shivering at the touch of my print on the page.

"I dreamt of that tree last night," I said, then pointed to the ground beneath the creatures. "See those roots? The ones wrapping around their feet?" I asked. Gram nodded, eyes leaden.

"I do." Satyra grabbed the corner of the book and pulled it closer to her and Raidan. She blew a sharp breath.

"That's what muddied my dream," she said, indicating the roots. "They were all over the scene, trying to cover up what I saw."

"Those roots were wrapped around me last night," I said, remembering the sting of their grip. Gram took the book and closed it tightly, dust flying out into the air.

"What?" Saty gasped, mouth jutting open.

"You have prophetic dreams, too, Shiv?" Raidan asked, face gaunt.

"I don't think so," I mumbled, confused by the interpretation.

"I was right to question the prediction," Gram spoke, voice serious in tone. "Saty, I do not believe that your seer gift is that of foretelling of the future."

"Of course, that's my power," she resounded. "I've been doing it for weeks!"

"Isn't that what a seer does?" Raidan asked.

"Not all of them," said Gram.

"But I do!" Saty whined, lip trembling. She looked to be so worried at this loss of ability. "You don't think I can tell the future?"

"No, my sweet. I don't think you can. I believe this stranger, whomever it may be, was showing you the scene directly from the source. They were there to show you it was happening. This was a warning," she told us. "The first part of the sacrificial spell has begun."

"Begun?" I repeated. My cousin noticeably shuddered and cringed away. I thought she might cry at this moment. "It happened, didn't it?" I asked, voice devoid of emotion. "The dream was real, somehow, wasn't it?" I shook my head, trying to decipher reality versus dream. "When I woke up in the middle of the night, the pain from the roots still stung. I thought it was my arthritis at first. I thought maybe I had slept wrong and tried to suppress my suspicions. But it was real. The dream happened."

"I believe so," Gram said. She looked at my cousin now, who wore her nerves on her exterior. "I also believe that the other see-walks you've experienced, Satyra, were warnings about Shivalri's outburst. It seems that her elemental power is strongly connected to the weather. You were not predicting the weather; rather, the stranger showed you the weather as Shivalri was creating it. It makes sense now, seeing as how storms usually travel from west to east. They were trying to warn you, warn us, of Shivalri's manifestation of powers."

"Are you sure I can't predict the future?" Saty asked, voice quiet.

"You are a seer, Satyra. You could potentially develop the

ability," she supposed. "Seers have a more profound spiritual guidance. Usually, a seer possesses intuitive powers, like gut feelings. Those with very strong abilities can see into the future, but that kind of power is scarce."

"I swear, I felt like I could see the future, Gram," Saty tried to explain. "I thought that's what I was doing."

"I'm sorry to be the bearer of bad news." Our grandmother sighed. "I would love for you to be able to predict the future, Satyra, truly. If you say you want that power, I want you to have it. But you simply don't."

"But you said I did..." my cousin pressed, complaining. I felt unsure of what to say as I watched her sulk. She had wanted this. She had wanted to be a witch—and a powerful one at that.

"You have the spirit affinity. Spirit runs through your veins, just as it does for me. My grandmother could see into the future, but she could only do so with the help of other seers before her. She worked with the ghosts of spirit."

"It's not fair...." Saty whispered, looking down at the book.

"I understand that you were excited, and I'm sorry for the disappointment. Nevertheless, the gifts you do possess have been such an immense help. Be grateful for your strengths."

"Yes, thank you, Saty," I said, trying to reassure her now. It was true that she had been helpful. Though it was only messages from another seer, they were vital.

"The important thing is that we have this intel," Gram said, now speaking to all of us. "The summoning spell was done at the tree where Hell meets Earth," Gram explained. We were all silent, utterly focused on her words. "The summoning spell is used to summon a demon, a Greater demon, and drag him from Hell and onto Earth." My stomach lurched into my throat, skin crawling with prickles of sweat.

"That can't be," I stammered.

"That means someone else knows about Shivi's prophecy," Raidan ground out, jaw set hard. "How did this happen? How did someone find out?"

"Anyone who knows of magic would've turned their concentration to finding the cause of the reddening skies," Gram remarked. "It was only a matter of time, and we are lucky that they did not figure it out before we got a chance to discover it."

"We've known for twenty-four hours. What good does that do us?" Raidan spat.

"We know, and that is what matters," said Gram. Raidan curled his fists and slumped in his chair.

"Do you think that the people from the dream already know that we know?" Saty whispered. A shot like ice froze my spine. I hadn't thought of that. I didn't believe for one second that the others would have the same vantage as us.

"I don't believe so," Gram supposed, which surprised me.

"How come?" I wondered.

"I can't be sure, but I think your friend the see-walker has been keeping their appearances a secret," she said. "It seems they are on the inside, showing us what is happening without the other's knowledge. I don't believe they would do so if the group knew that we were onto them. It would be too risky."

"So, the see-walker is a spy," said Raidan.

"A helpful one, at that." Gram nodded.

"Why did they show me the summoning spell, Gram?" Satyra asked, playing with the dust that coated the marble table.

"Why did they all chant my name?" I added, feeling the tremble of my panic on my tongue.

"As I said before, this was a warning," Gram stated. I was starting to understand. "And as for you, Shivalri, someone out there knows that you are tied to the prophecy. I believe they were praying to you during their summoning spell," she answered. "You're now in the place of the Triple Goddess."

"So, what?" Raidan interjected. "She's, like, a cult leader now?"

"Hell no!" I snapped.

"No, that's not what I mean." Gram sighed.

"What do you mean?" he asked.

"Either we have bad people on our side, or we've made ourselves some new enemies. I'm betting it's the second of the two." Gram grimaced.

"Who are they? How did they find out that I'm the one responsible?" The prick of last night's dream enveloped me, and I shrank away from memory, swallowing hard. I could taste the fear on my tongue.

"That's what we're going to find out. Right, Satyra?" Gram shot her a look of pride.

"Uh... Right," Saty answered. "How exactly?"

"First of all, I'd like you to try to focus on any upcoming images you receive, whether they are messages from the stranger or simply a hunch of your own. Tell us everything you remember."

"I can do that." She nodded.

"Good."

"Thanks, Saty," I murmured. "I imagine that that vision was hard to watch."

"It felt wrong," she answered.

"It was wrong," Raidan said, crossing his arms. "What they did to their animals was fucking cruel." I shivered in agreement.

"What's the other thing we're going to do, Gram?" I asked, remembering that she hadn't finished her list of demands. She bowed her head in thanks for the focus.

"Thank you for reminding me," she said, finger to her temple.

"I'm almost scared to find out." Satyra blew out a breath.

"If it has anything to do with summoning spells, count me out," Raidan said sternly, shoulders back.

"I would never dream of it," she answered.

"Okay. What's next, Gram?" I asked, directing her back to the point of the conversation.

"Right," Gram began. "I think this entire situation has gotten us all in over our heads. We shouldn't have to battle this alone." She held her hands in her lap.

"Do you know other witches?" I asked excitedly. Maybe we weren't doomed after all.

"I do," she said. "I am going to arrange a meeting with the High Council."

24

SOVEREIGN

Gram hung up her phone and immediately took its back off, removing the SIM card and placing it in the baggy she'd been using to keep her phone safe.

"There," she breathed. "It's been settled. I was able to request a meeting with the elders without giving out too much information, and they've agreed to meet at their building in Salem."

"Salem?"

"They have many meeting sites across the world. Thankfully, the one closest to us is not very far away," Gram answered.

"When do we go?" Raidan asked.

"Tomorrow afternoon. It won't take long to drive there. We'll just leave early in the morning." Raidan groaned at Gram's words, and I gave him a dirty look. He could deal with one measly early morning.

"Now gather round, little witches," Gram chimed, making her way to the foyer. She lighted the woodstove, and the room smelled like a fresh campfire. The house was massive; ceilings doubled in height. The heat hardly warmed the place, but this room was toasty and comforting.

After dinner, we all made ourselves a comfy spot to sit and sip on the homemade tea Gram stewed for us. Satyra and I sat on the loveseat and reclined with our legs out. Raidan sat on the chaise, and Gram took up a spot in her favorite rocking chair. She had never looked old a day in her life, aside from when she sat there.

"All right, Gram. Give us the details," I said, stretching out on the couch.

"First of all, I should explain to you the importance of the people we will see," she began, the rocking of her chair slowed to a crawl.

"You called them the council, so does that mean they're in charge?" Raidan asked.

"They are not just any council," she corrected him. "They are the High Council."

"So, like the big bosses," he replied with a smirk.

"You can't begin to imagine." She chuckled.

"So, tell us about them, Gram," I prodded.

"Who are they?" Satyra wondered. She curled both hands around her mug and drank deeply, steam emanating and fogging her glasses. She took her glasses off and wiped them on her shirt before putting them back. I laughed and took a sip from my tea, steam replicating the same on my glasses. I watched as the vapor slowly cleared from my vision.

"The High Council is made up of extremely gifted witches and warlocks, which we, as witches, must hold in high respects. They are in charge of global ruling and rarely appear to those who are lesser in prestige. My connection to them derives from the time my grandmother worked closely to their rankings. The power of her classification was considered an extension to the Grimsbane lineage."

"Wow..." I gawked, trying to imagine who my great, great grandmother was.

"So, are we like royalty?" Satyra asked with excitement dancing in her eyes.

"We are far from royalty by membership, but now knowing of Shivalri's prophecy, I do wonder if perhaps we may have a kind of royal blood running through our veins." Gram smiled at me, and I shuddered at the thought of what blood ran through me. I started imagining what the Goddess might have looked like when she was first created. Did she look like me? Did she have a natural red hue that flowed through her hair? Was she full-figured, with wide hips like mine? I wondered if she had any ailments like me. Did she feel anxious too? Were her bones achy and sore? No, of course not. She was divine. Gods didn't feel pain.

"Being royalty would be so cool," Satyra replied, twirling her hair. Her excitement shook me from my thoughts. She had always loved fairy tales. Unlike me, Satyra didn't seem to realize that this one might not have a happy ending like the ones she so treasured.

"So, what makes the High Council so powerful?" Raidan asked.

"Yeah, how'd they get to the top of supremacy? I'd love to know how all of that works," Satyra pushed further.

"The High Council is set to have five superior members, each representing one of the five elements," Gram said. "These are the members that we must have you learn by name, as they are most important to impress."

"Wait a minute... Are you saying they each only have one elemental gift? Last night, you told me that I have all five."

"And what a burden it has been," she quipped. It was true that discovering my possession of all five elemental powers had felt like a burden. I eased the tension in my shoulders, trying to make sense of things.

"I'm just saying if I have all of their powers combined, shouldn't they be worried about impressing me, not the other way around? Not that I would want that. People should treat each other as equals. I'm having a hard time getting past these shortcomings in their classification. Surely there must be others who have more than one elemental ability."

"Firstly, people do not treat each other as equals in our world," she stated. *Our world.* What a foreign world it was. "And you, my dear, are quite the exception. It is incredibly uncommon for a witch to have more than one affinity. Having even two affinities within one's nature is exceptional. Generally, witches will have just one, and some may have none. To work with all of the affinities, one must use spells to conjure the magics, and even at that, they are incredibly limited in their capabilities," she explained. "All five are a part of you, constantly coursing through your veins. You are a rarity, indeed."

"Lucky," Saty muttered, and my face flushed uncomfortably. I slumped back into the couch and felt my cousin's eye on me. I heated at the tension in the room. Saty wanted this. She wanted power; she wanted a world more extensive than the ordinary. Satyra should've gotten all of these affinities. She would've done better with them.

"I must tell you of the leaders now if you are ready to learn," Gram said. I nodded, and she dipped her head in understanding. "The eldest and most prestigious of the five is none other than Moira Darkmore," Gram told us. Her voice was soft as if simply speaking her name would call her to us.

"Darkmore? Can you be any more obvious?" Raidan sneered, rolling his eyes. I nodded in agreement.

"It was meant to be obvious," Gram explained. "The name

is thousands of years old, dating back to the beginnings of our creation."

"Like from when there were angels and demons on Earth?" I was stunned as I considered that period.

"Precisely."

"Creepy," Saty mumbled to herself, wrapping a fuzzy blanket around her for comfort.

"The name Darkmore means exactly what it sounds like— More Darkness," Gram informed. "Moira, along with her family, is full of spiritual powers inherited and passed down from generation to generation."

"Isn't spirit supposed to be a good thing?" I thought aloud.

"With the right person and the right intent, it can be used for good," Gram allowed. "Lord Darkmore, however, was given his gift during times of grief and chaos. Legend says he used the spirit of the Dead to conquer his battles." I shivered at the thought.

"Does Moira use it for good?" Satyra wondered. At her words, I realized that my cousin could potentially do just as Lord Darkmore had. With her likely power for necromancy, Satyra could raise the dead. I pictured it now, corpses rising from the ground. The thought of my cousin doing anything of the sort was outrageous. She was the kindest and most positive person I knew. I could hardly imagine a time when Saty might try something like that.

"She is the leader of the High Council. She must only ever use her power for good," Gram replied, answering Satyra.

"All right. That's one member. Who else is part of the five in charge?" I asked.

"Well, there's Sora Fujin; air affinity," our grandmother told us, counting off on her fingers. "Ember Blackwood; ruler of fire."

"Do you think the person showing me those visions is a witch?" Satyra asked. I had forgotten all about them.

"Most likely," she said.

"What do you mean?" I asked. "Aren't we all witches if we have powers?"

"Most, yes, but there are some other creatures who possess power."

"That's weird," Raidan thought aloud. I cringed at the mention of creatures.

"Wouldn't you say this is all just a little bit weird?" Gram grinned, wrapping her hands tightly around her mug.

"More than a little," he spoke. "Are there other male witches on the board?"

"Yes. There is he who yields water; Damek Lagunov."

"That makes four," I reported, mentally checking off each element. "Who's the fifth?"

"Lastly, and most recently, they welcomed Nesrin of the family Mehra. She inherited the gift of earth affinity from her father, Baaz. She took his place as a member of the superiors after his recent death, therefore making her the youngest and newest member of the Council."

"How old is she?" Satyra asked.

"She's just a mere child. Only twenty years old." She tutted her tongue in disbelief. "She has been with them just short of a year... I imagine it has been very challenging for her."

"Twenty isn't that young," Satyra interjected. "I mean, Rai, Shivi, and I are basically just a year or so away from twenty." She gestured to me. It was true. The three of us were all born close in age. Saty and I were born the same year; her birthday was in the summer, and mine was on the last day of the year. Raidan was born in November, the year after me, making us both the same age for one month. He was always sure to tease me about it for the entirety of December. "I know I'd be happy to join the Council," Satyra added.

"Not me," I countered.

"It is arduous work, Satyra. Sometimes, very dark work," Gram said. "Besides, you are forbidden to live anywhere other than their *Domum*. You can no longer live with family once you become a member. We would miss you far too much," Gram confessed, giving her a small smile.

"Oh..." Saty thought for a moment. "The castle would be cool, but I suppose that would be hard, living away from family."

"That and much more," said Gram.

"So, when do we get to meet the five?" Raidan asked.

"You will not. Perhaps in the future, though it is doubtful that you will ever be formally introduced," Gram informed us. "They do not mingle with those beneath them."

"That's so strange," I considered. "I hadn't even thought about that. I just assumed that we'd be going to them directly. When you told us that we would meet at the House of Enchantment, I thought it was implied."

"What's the point of learning about them if we aren't going to see them?" Satyra asked grumpily.

"Oh, you'll see them," Gram said. "You just won't be meeting them."

"So, they are coming to Salem?" I asked, trying to make sense of Gram's explanation.

"No. In Salem, we will meet with a group of elite emissaries to explain our situation. They are the ones I called earlier to request their presence," she clarified. "From there, the emissaries will decide whether or not to bring this message up with the High Council. If it is established as imperative, we will be flying to the Council's *Domum* to testify in front of them."

I nodded, trying to understand the process. This new world was going to take some getting used to. These customs were strange.

"They're going to choose to bring it to the High Council, though, right?" I asked, snapping out of my inner deliberations. We didn't know what to do, and our need for their guidance was unquestionable. Every part of our plan depended on their helping us.

"I do not doubt it. Once they hear our story, they will have no choice but to carry the message over," Gram confirmed. She seemed assured, but I had a pit of doubt growing in the back of my mind. What if this plan fell through? What were we going to do if we couldn't rely on the High Council to help us find a resolution?

"My question is, how are we going to convince them that any of this is true? We're going to sound like a pack of liars," Raidan reputed, voicing his concerns. I had to agree. Who in their right mind would believe that I, an eighteen-year-old nobody, was capable of lifting the veil? It was hard to imagine that I was responsible for the world potentially coming to an end.

"How can we make them believe us?" I wondered aloud. "Who would believe that I'd have all of these abilities? I can't prove it. I have no control over my powers." I shrank in my seat, feeling discouraged. Gram nodded and rolled up her sleeves.

"When we meet with them, we will all prick our fingers on a charmed pin. They will then ask us to squeeze a droplet of blood into a chalice, to which we will oblige." She held her finger up, making the motions.

"No, we will not!" I gasped. "I've read enough books in my day to know that blood magic is the worst of its kind. I'm not messing around with that," I told her firmly.

"It is the High Council's magic. The most trustworthy of all," Gram assured us as if that was supposed to be comforting.

"Have you done it before?" Raidan asked, catching me off guard.

"Yeah, do you know if it's safe for sure?" Satyra added. Were my brother and cousin seriously contemplating a blood charm?

"I have, once. And look at me—I am excellent." She smiled, and I gawked at her response.

"You willingly did blood magic?" My head felt dizzy and hot. "Gram, that can't be safe."

"It is perfectly safe if done correctly. You have nothing to fear."

"I have everything to fear," I spat.

"Trust me," she pled. "Please, Shivalri. You have to go with the flow. I understand that it all seems outlandish, but for us witches, this is standard."

"You have to appreciate how tough it is for me to wrap my head around any of this, Gram. I'm trying to understand, really, I am," I strained, bringing my legs up into me. My hands felt shaky from the dread, and I watched the remainder of my tea swish from side to side at the bottom of my mug. Saty reached out a hand and took my cup, placing it on the table beside her.

"It's going to be okay, Cuz," she supposed, sympathy in her eyes.

"Take comfort in knowing that I have done this magic before," said Gram. "And I will be with you when it's your turn to do so." She gave me a look I hadn't seen since I was a child. It was that of comfort during my night terrors, that of love when I needed it most. I watched her in her rocking chair, composed yet grim. I needed to have courage. My family was willing to put themselves at risk to help me fix something that

I had done. I had put them in this mess. I had to buck up and push through it. I owed it to them. I took a deep breath and settled on that thought.

"If you trust it, and you'll be there, then I guess that's good enough for me," I wavered and immersed myself in my reflections. "Hold on..." I stilled. Gram met my worried gaze.

"Yes, I do trust them," Gram said, trying to comfort me. I stopped her.

"Gram, a chalice is a cup, right?" I gulped audibly. My throat was instantly dry.

"Yes, it is." She wrinkled her brow in confusion. Instant worry crept up over me.

"Why does our blood go into a cup?"

"There is a binding elixir that goes into the cup first. Then, your blood, pricked by the truth charm, is added and mixed with the elixir. It forces us to tell the truth." My muscles relaxed at her words.

"Oh, good." I let out a sigh of relief. "For a second there, I thought they were going to drink our blood," I tittered anxiously.

"No, they won't be drinking our blood," she answered, looking at me. "*We* will." Her words triggered my revulsion, and I almost gagged.

"That's disgusting!" Satyra said. "There's no way I'm doing that."

"Yeah, I'm not doing that either. That's essentially like eating ourselves," Raidan added; anger spewed from his mouth.

"Some witches are known to do such things, Raidan. But we are not going to eat each other, nor is it outright blood that we will be drinking," Gram remarked, trying to calm us.

"That makes no sense," my brother countered. "You just

plainly told us that is what we will be doing." I watched him fume on the chaise.

"The blood evaporates when it hits the elixir," she tried rationalizing. "Just don't think of it like blood. Think of it as a potion."

"It's sick," he answered her, sitting upright. "I won't do it."

"Then you won't come," Gram snapped. This was the first act of severity I'd seen from my grandmother all day. She had been tiptoeing around our feelings and trying to be patient. I hadn't expected the harshness of her answer. I also hadn't realized that Raidan had a choice in coming or not.

"I am going," he argued, never backing down. I found it an odd reaction. I would've thought he'd be glad to step away from the problem. After all, it was not his mess to fix. He had always been a protective brother, and I had always reciprocated. I wondered, however, if I would do the same for him now if the roles were reversed. I couldn't honestly say. I shook the negativity off and turned to look at my grandmother. Her set jaw displayed the inflexibility of the matter.

"There's absolutely no way around it?" I asked, fretting.

"No," she said bluntly. We looked around at each other in disgust. My cousin was sickened, still wrapped in her fuzzy blanket. My brother was in a rage, angry for both his lack of choice and for what I thought might be fear of the outcome.

"I'll do it," I caved. Satyra looked at me and gulped.

"If it's to save the world, I guess I can handle it," she joined, pushing her glasses up the bridge of her nose.

"It's still sick," Raidan said. His posture didn't falter.

"Raidan, just pretend it's a potion. As Gram said, it evaporates." Saty tried reasoning.

"It is a potion. With blood," he refuted.

"We're saving the world," Satyra reminded him. He flung himself onto his back and groaned, leaning into the chaise.

"Fine," he agreed, grumbling into the arm of the cushion. "But I never want to be reminded of it after the fact. Once it's done, we're never speaking of this again. And we can't tell anyone."

"Our lips are sealed," Gram said.

25

NIGHTLIGHT

Satyra's room was dark and blue. Our grandmother had very odd opinions on electricity and modern technology. Her kitchen and bathrooms had all the technological modifications you could imagine, but the rest of the house remained like the olden days. Satyra had one single electrical outlet next to her makeup station. She mostly had candles to light the room, aside from the two fake battery-operated lightbulbs she had hung above her nightstand. Her makeup mirror had tiny fairy lights strung across it, but they hardly emanated anything worth using during the night.

While my cousin was in the washroom, I took this time to get into my comfy hoodie and a pair of leggings. I wanted to be warm and cozy, and the hoodie and legging combination was just how I liked it. I slid some fluffy socks on and hopped into bed, assembling the wall of pillows to my right. I made sure they were stacked neatly, dividing my side of the bed from Saty's, where she often threw nighttime tantrums. I tugged on the plastic chain and clicked the lightbulbs off, leaving just the illumination of candles glowing up to the ceiling.

Childhood memories of living here with my grandparents flooded my mind. The memories of hiding under the blankets and holding my breath so as not to alert the monsters of my presence crept into my thoughts. I was grown, and still, I was afraid of what lurked in the dark. The nighttime always gave me the creeps. The candles didn't help the matter.

The door creaked open, and Satyra came in, stepping lightly like a sleuth.

"I'm not asleep," I whispered to her. She straightened her crouch and began walking ordinarily, blowing out the candles as she made her way to the bed. When she noticed the partition that I had so graciously fashioned, she scowled at me.

"Seriously?" she scoffed, punching the pillows. "The wall of shame," she grunted and flopped onto her side, pulling the covers up to her neck.

"Hey, I'm not the one who acts all possessed in the night," I said, plumping the pillows she'd deformed with her fist. I arranged them neatly again.

"I'm only hurting myself, not you," she retorted, voice muffled by the blanket she held.

"You give me nightmares," I said jokingly. Satyra went stiff beside me.

"That's not funny." Her words sank in.

"Right," I remembered. "Somehow, I forgot about last night," I said, rubbing my hand along my arm, thinking of the sharp roots that held me the night before.

"Did it hurt?" she asked. I winced at the thought.

"It did," I answered honestly. "It felt so real. It was real...." She was quiet for a moment, and I became more and more aware of the darkness in the room.

"What did it feel like?" she whispered, interrupting my spiraling thoughts. I cringed at the flashback of tendrils all over my body and shuddered. I didn't have to think about it long to remember the feel of the experience.

"It felt like constricted ropes, squeezing me hard and stinging me. Kind of like a jellyfish with a good grip." I tried to laugh it off and curled into myself for security. My cousin let out one single chuckled breath, and I sighed. We couldn't force lightheartedness right now.

"I'm sorry you had to go through that," she told me. "It was bad enough seeing them... I can't imagine what I would've done if I had felt them."

"Let's just hope I never have to feel them again," I said, trying to shake the image.

"You won't," she said. "That's why we're going to this Council group Gram called. We're going to fix everything."

"I don't want to get my hopes up...." I trailed.

"Shivi, all we have is hope. Don't let go of it."

"When did you become so wise?" I teased.

"When you live this long with Gram, she rubs off on you," she replied. I thought about that for a moment.

"I remember what it was like when I lived here," I told her.

"I liked it when you were here with me," she said softly. "I don't know what I would've done without you." Her voice hitched, and my throat tightened.

"You're stronger than you think," I said, remembering her heartbreak over losing her parents. Having lost my mom, I had a whole new understanding of it.

"Now, who's the wise one?" she asked. I could hear her grin.

"I guess we're both wise women."

"Cunning," she said.

"Witches."

SALEM

I was nervous getting into the car this morning, knowing what I had to face today. The unpredictability of the situation agitated my remaining control. I could feel the tension my family emitted as we sat in the car, all still feeling the apprehension from a poor night's sleep.

"Has everyone fastened their seat belt?" Gram asked, looking at us through the rearview mirror.

"Just did," I said, clicking it into place.

"Buckled," Satyra added. Raidan mumbled in agreement, still groggy from sleep.

"Off we go, then." Our grandmother turned the ignition on and stepped on the gas.

Driving down the road in the Grimsbane woods gave me a chill reminiscent of that from two nights ago when Gram gave Raidan and me a scare. At nine in the morning, the mist was still hovering atop the gravel. The sun had just begun making an appearance through the trees, making the air soupy and dim. I could see that Gram was fixated on the haze through the rearview mirror ahead, her eyes squinting and creasing her face.

"Do you want me to drive, Gram?" I offered. Her driving made me nervous in general. When the weather was like this, I was even more on edge.

"Oh, no. That's quite all right, Shivalri."

"Can you see the road?" I asked though the answer was evident.

"It will clear."

"If you say so." I looked out the window, observing the fog. The trees seemed closer together in the gray. I didn't see any animals skirt the edge of the forest, and there were no birds cawing at their rouse. Aside from our car crushing gravel beneath its tires, there seemed to be no activity. As I watched the Grimsbane woods go by, I couldn't help but wonder if the unnatural quiet was an omen.

As we neared the end of the very long driveway, the haze lifted, and the sun lit the sky, swapping smog for red clarity. The sound of my brother snoring in the front seat made Satyra giggle and take her phone out to snap a picture.

"Road trip memories," she whispered and showed me her snapshot. Her aim was off, and his nostrils took up most of the frame.

"Looking for bats?" I asked when she realized she had missed her target. She leaned forward, extending her arm to get a better angle. A bump in the road caused her to sway, and she smacked him in the nose. Raidan snorted ogre-like and turned toward his window.

"Crap," she groaned and pulled away. I watched her hold in her laughter, causing her cheeks to puff out. Just looking at her initiated my snicker, and I had to snuff the sound by covering my mouth. "So much for that," she muttered, grinning from ear to ear. This was my favorite side of Satyra. She clung to childhood like the wildling she's always been. She loved to capture every moment, deeming every memory as one to treasure.

"Well, at least you got something before you hit him in the face," I supposed, unable to hide my own grin. She agreed, worshipping her wily photo.

"Gold," she said, smirk still apparent.

I could tell we were no longer in the Essex area due to the four lanes of traffic heading in one direction and four opposing. The MA-22 South was busy and full of cars, and the transport trucks that zoomed by sprayed water at us from the residual mist-filled puddles.

From the corner of my eye, I saw a darkened stain gliding through the skies ahead of us. As it flew closer toward us, the bird stretched its wings as if to land right in the middle of the highway.

"Do you see that?" I asked Satyra, pointing at the figure.

"See what?" She looked toward the windshield.

"That bird's going to die," I whispered, worry cutting my voice. I tensed my muscles in preparation for the impact.

"What bird?" she asked as it sprung its claws from its body. I panicked and clung to the door for support. Satyra studied me, grabbing my hand. "There's no bird, Shivalri." A hole in the road hugged our tires, causing Gram to swerve into the oncoming traffic. She continued driving toward the opposing lane, and I swallowed a gasp.

"Gram!" I clung to the back of her seat and shook her headrest. She maneuvered the car back into its lane and let out a strangled cry, waking Raidan from his nap.

"What's wrong?" he screeched.

"It's okay...." Gram breathed, shaking her head. "I'm not sure why I did that."

"Were you falling asleep?" Raidan asked, shaking off the mixture of grogginess and panic.

"No, I wasn't falling asleep. I just didn't realize that I was in the wrong lane." She adjusted her mirror and gripped the steering wheel with force. "I must say, I am feeling a little shaky. It must have been the bump we hit."

"Do you want to pull over? I can drive the rest of the way," I proposed. She adjusted herself in her seat and took a deep breath, exhaling slowly.

"Thank you, but we are only a few minutes away," she said, pointing to a road sign. It indicated the use of a left lane for MA-1A South. "You see?"

"Half a mile left," Satyra said. That made my nerves clatter in the pit of my stomach.

"Half a mile," I repeated aloud. As if she could sense my worry, Gram started humming. I recognized the song when Satyra began singing.

"Worry not, little child. You are beautiful and wild," she sang. I couldn't help but join in the song Gram had made up for us when we were scared, little kids.

"Don't you see? All is well when you're with me," I rejoiced, then everyone joined in.

"Take a breath. Hold it in, and sing!" Laughing with one another, we cleaned out the anxiety in the warmth of the love we shared as a family.

That song used to be my nightly anthem. Even after moving out of Gram's house, whenever I got scared or faced hardship, it was like an impulse reaction to hum its melody. My grandmother had always felt like my protector in childhood. She was the adult I turned to for everything. After my parents moved Raidan and me out of the Grimsbane manor, I was left with a strange feeling. It was like having a small hole in my chest where a valuable piece of me was gone. Being here with Gram now, hearing her sing our protector's song seemed to fill the empty well. It was warm, and it was home.

Gram took the exit for Salem and made her way through the town. Before heading to our main destination, she pulled into the nearest gas station for a short rest stop.

"If you need to use the restroom or get yourselves a snack of sorts, you have a bit of time," she told us.

"What time is it now?" Raidan asked her.

"Almost ten, and we are supposed to meet at the House of Enchantment at eleven. We made good time, considering the morning traffic of Massachusetts."

"The traffic more than doubled the time," I thought, calculating in my head. I stepped out of the car, meeting Satyra at her door.

"We made perfect time, considering it's the busiest day of the year here in Salem," Satyra pointed out. "You should see how it is when my boss sends me here for supplies during the lunch hour." She rolled her eyes as we walked into the store. "It's very similar to this, but it's not as heavy as this Halloween traffic."

"Why do you go all the way to Salem for supplies?" I wondered.

"The boutique at the dock sells many touristy items from here. It's the only place in Essex that sells so much of Salem's witchy souvenirs."

"I thought you co-managed a boat rental shop."

"I do." She laughed. "Apparently, fish and broomstick keychains are all the rage."

"Noted." I shrugged, grabbing a water bottle from the cooler as I walked by. I wasn't hungry, but I knew I needed something in my system. Water would do the trick for now and hopefully help with the queasiness that came from my anxiety.

We were all finished in the store within ten minutes and

met back at the car in the parking lot. Gram was already seated in the driver's seat, waiting for us.

"Gram, you finished up fast. I didn't even see you inside."

"Time weaver. Remember?" She winked at me and took a bite out of her pre-packaged egg salad sandwich. The smell of it wafted in the car. Something about egg sandwiches didn't make any sense to me. It smelled so bad, like rotten garbage. It was still somehow my favorite kind, and I salivated at the thought of its taste. Gram tilted a brow at me and chuckled. At her facial expression, my stomach grumbled discernably. "Hungry?" Gram asked, handing over half of her sandwich. I caved and took it, grinning sheepishly.

"I guess I am," I said and took a big bite. After chewing a few bites of the food, I started to think about what Gram had said. I wondered how her time weaving worked. What were the possibilities, if not endless? I took a swig of my water and turned to Gram. "I have a question about your time weaving," I mumbled, wiping the water from my mouth.

"Yes?" she replied, mid-bite.

"Can you take other people with you? When you time travel, I mean."

"I do not truly time travel, dear. I only manipulate time and space. To answer your question, I'm not sure. I've never tried taking someone with me. I didn't even think it to be a possibility." She considered this for a moment.

"Could you try?" Satyra asked, joining in. I jumped at her words, having forgotten that she was sitting next to me. She was so quiet, just eating her food, that it startled me.

"I wouldn't know where to begin," Gram answered her, brows raised.

"Do you know anyone else who has your gift?" I wondered.

"No, not that I know of. I've never met anyone else with my abilities, and I've never heard tell of stories like my own."

"Not that you know of. So, it is possible; to bring someone with you. You've just never heard of it."

"I suppose it could be. That doesn't do any good to me if I don't know who might be able to help me, though," said Gram.

"True." I nodded. "I can't help but think of the potential you have. Your abilities could become very useful, I imagine."

"I've always looked at my time weaving as second nature. It has never felt like a power, like with my affinity for spirit. Necromancy takes concentration and duteous devotion. Time weaving comes naturally to me," she explained. "I never thought to learn more about it, as I could do it without difficulty."

"What about one of your books at home, Gram?" Satyra asked. "You don't have anything on time weaving?" Gram paused for a moment and laughed nonsensically.

"I don't," she said. "I feel foolish." Gram let out a chuckle and brushed it off. I couldn't help but think that had it been me with those powers, I'd have learned everything I could. I would do everything and anything I could to get my hand on as many books as possible. I'd want to become so familiar with my abilities that I could easily recite the texts.

"Is there somewhere we might find a book with this information?" I wondered aloud.

"Oh, yes, actually," Gram remarked. "There is a library in the Salem House of Enchantment." My heart was racing at the thought of going to this foreign library. I imagined the hundreds of books lined on sturdy bookshelves, and a thrill coursed through my veins. "Perhaps we should look through their volumes before the meeting."

"Where is the library located?" I asked, not able to help the smile forming on my lips.

"It is found in the same building; in fact, it is at the

entrance of the House of Enchantment. We have to pass through there anyhow," she told us. "If there were to be any books with that kind of information, I would believe it to be in their collection."

"So, we're going then," Raidan said, huffing a long breath. He knew how wrapped up I could get in browsing collections from the many times he'd endured my book shopping.

"That would be a dream," I said excitedly. "More books..."

"Lots and lots, old and new." Gram smiled at me.

"I can't wait." I sighed wistfully, imagining all the beautiful books I could get my hands on. I loved reading. I've read everything from world history, mythology, and even some romance. I loved a good Young Adult book with determined and passionate heroes. I would never say no to flipping through the pages of another world.

"Then it's settled. We won't wait any longer."

27

WARD

When Gram parked on the side of an old dirt road, Raidan, Satyra, and I looked at each other in confusion.

"What are we doing here?" I asked, looking out of my window. The path was relatively narrow, and I couldn't picture a car fitting down its trail.

"This is where we stop," Gram said and removed the keys from the ignition.

"On the side of an abandoned road," Raidan commented, unbuckling himself from his seat. "This doesn't scream danger at all."

It was still daylight, so the wooded area didn't seem bad. There was no ominous presence, but it still made me weary. I wasn't used to walking around the woods, but I knew Gram was fond of it. She was always prowling the Grimsbane woods looking for berries and plucking mushrooms off tree stumps. Though this was an odd venture for her three grandchildren, this was just an ordinary day to her.

"The House of Enchantment hides beyond these woods," Gram informed us. "It is so as not to let others know that it exists here. An enchanted ward prohibits the human eye from seeing it, even if they go for a walk down this trail. However, just in case, it is hidden deep in the woods."

"How does the ward work?" Satyra asked, leaning forward. Any talk of magic had her in an enthrallment.

"It's magic," Gram said.

"Yes, well, I know that." My cousin rolled her eyes. "I meant, what exactly does it entail? Will we be able to see it? Will we even be able to get past it?" I wondered this too. If there were wards in place, were they not to keep us out as well?

"As we have magic in our veins, it will not harm us in any way. You'll see it when we get there. It is indescribable," Gram told us, stepping out of the car. My cousin and I unbuckled our seat belts, and we all followed suit, meeting her in the ditch near the narrow road.

"What are we supposed to expect?" Raidan asked. "Are we looking for booby traps? Should I keep an eye out for electric fences?" I started at that thought.

"No, no, there are no electric fences," Gram assured us. "No traps either."

"What should we look out for?" I asked, the unpredictability keeping me in place.

"Just stick with me, little witches. I will keep you out of harm's way."

As we made our way down the path, the car became further and further away, and I could barely make out its shape anymore. We crossed a large field full of tall grass that tickled my legs as we walked across. When we came to a little covered bridge, I finally noticed the water. I hadn't heard it before getting here, but the river was loud and clear once I was standing on the bridge. The stream was steady, and it flowed faster than I would have imagined a little brook to go.

The covered bridge seemed as though it had been built a long time ago. The floorboards were rickety, but they still felt sturdy enough to walk across. There were square holes along the walls of the sheltered area, making for a window-like setting. I stepped up on the ledge and put my arms through one of the squares to look over into the river. There were large rocks, slippery from the slime that coated them. I imagined stepping on them and feeling the goo glide between my toes.

"Be very careful not to fall," Gram called to me. The sheltered passage made her voice echo through the cover.

"I will," I assured her, making sure not to put my weight on any loose boards below my feet.

"Is it pretty?" Saty asked, coming to join me. A ghastly break cracked in the floorboards at Saty's approach, and my heart lurched in my throat. When she took another step closer, I could feel the tension in the boards beneath me, strength faltering with every second that passed.

"Saty, back up. Now," I commanded, holding my breath. She did without hesitation, eyes wide. I blew out a single breath, nervous from the thought that the slightest movement could weaken the wood.

"Get down very carefully," Gram demanded. "One step at a time. And stay away from the ledges from now on." I took a deep breath and tiptoed down, putting the lightest conceivable pressure on the floorboards, ensuring they could hold my weight. Thankfully, the broken board was one of only a few rotten pieces, and I was fine to continue walking. The wood beneath my feet held firm, and I carefully made my way over to Saty, who was watching me on high alert.

"That was intense," she blew out, looking me over. "You all right?"

"Fine," I said, relaxing my shoulders.

"What a way to start our adventure." She shook her head at my folly. I couldn't help but give her a leer.

"Though I admire your benevolence, Satyra, I'd prefer that, in the future, you refrain from so freely giving me such adventures."

"No promises." She smirked.

"Of course not."

A particularly thick forest wall lay on the other side of the covered bridge. It was lined with trees of every kind.

"There's no more trail to follow," Raidan noted.

"No, there is no trail," Gram acknowledged. "Nevertheless, we will continue our walk. It is elementary, you see. We simply have to keep going north. We will find our way through without any problems."

"Whatever you say," he replied and started for the trees. Gram grabbed his wrist and pulled him to her.

"Allow me to go first," she offered and waded through the sea of trees. She pushed aside some of the brush and made her way through as we walked.

Tree branches of all sorts stuck out all around us, and we had to carefully grab hold of them and slide them under our fingers so as not to have the branch whack the person behind us in the face. We had learned that the hard way after Raidan's first slip-up. Gram did the maneuver, and he didn't pay attention enough to realize that he had to mimic it, leaving me to find a branch eager to strike my face.

"Ow," I grumbled, brushing the pine needles out of my hair. They all laughed at me, and I wallowed in my self-pity. "Not funny. You could have poked my eye out," I scoffed.

"Oh, Shivi. You're just too clumsy," Satyra poked fun at me.

"Oh, yeah? You want to bet?" I pulled one of the branches like a slingshot and prepared to fling it her way. She dodged it just before the branch's thwack, which missed her by an inch.

"Hey, no need to do that! I want to keep my eyeballs in place, thanks," she grunted.

"Well, don't you think I feel the same way?" Gram turned to look at us in disapproval.

"When you pass through the branches, please hold on to them and pass them to the person behind you," she explained, trudging through the trees.

"Got it," Raidan said. "Don't smack my sister in the face. It shouldn't be a problem." I punched him in the back, and he let out a whine.

"That's for the tree branch," I jeered and cleaned my hands off on my jeans.

"Hey, your fate is in my hands right now. Are you in the mood for another tree branch to the nose?" he offered; one brow quirked up in mocking.

"Just keep walking," I huffed, pushing him forward.

There was a lot to see in the woods. Every so often, a little squirrel would run in front of us. Before we could get too close to it, it would make its way back up into the trees. We could hear leaves crunching all around us, and Gram told us that it was just little birds and bunnies. She assured us that it was nothing to be worried about. I looked all around us, watching and listening to my surroundings. I spotted all of the colorful mushrooms that sprang from the ground in various random patches. I had never seen so many colors. When I thought of mushrooms, I thought of grays and browns. This was a whole other world: yellows and reds and beautiful deep purples. We walked by shrubs full of tiny red fruit the size of a pearl and just as shiny. Raidan stopped to pick some off, but Gram blocked him quickly before he got the chance to toss them in his mouth.

"You cannot eat those," Gram decreed. "They are very poisonous."

"What?" he shouted and threw them to the ground.

"They're called holly berries," Gram said. "They look delicious, but they come with toxicity. It's called saponin and essentially, if eaten, will have you running for a toilet within seconds."

"That would have been nice to know before I got to them," Raidan scoffed, eyes narrow.

"Oh, yes, but you were too quick for your old Gram to see," she defended. "I did stop you before you ate them, didn't I?" She pointed to the berries that lay at his feet now.

"Thank God," he said.

"Yes, thank the Gods," Gram answered. "Now, keep your hands away from anything you do not already know of. As you might have noticed, there are no toilets for you to run to." I laughed at that, imagining the horror.

"You got it," my brother answered, and we continued on our hike. I couldn't help but glance back at the bush of berries. I noticed now that they were not only in the shrubs, but also grew up into the trees. Some of them must have been fifty feet tall. They were towering and deadly. They looked perfectly fine to me. I was glad that our grandmother knew the forest and the things we'd find. Otherwise, we might not have been so lucky.

When we got to the clearing, and Gram stopped, I felt a weakness growing in my knees.

"There's more walking to do?" I grumbled, rubbing at my legs. My fingers were slightly swollen now from the elevation and movement.

"Oh, no, no," Gram said. "We are here."

"Here?" Satyra repeated, her confusion just as evident as mine.

"You brought us to an empty field," Raidan indicated, taking in the place. "I thought we were going to the House of Enchantment."

"We are at the House of Enchantment, my dear grandson," Gram told him. "You just cannot see it yet. Come." She beckoned us forward. After walking a few paces into the field, I started to see an inexplicable fuzzy luminance. It was a bizarre collection of undulations—a phenomenon's refraction. It was like seeing heat waves after a hot day.

"Strange," I considered the vision, reaching out to touch it. To my surprise, my fingertips slowed in the air as if I was passing them through a shield of water. "Woah..."

"What are you doing, Shiv?" Raidan asked in puzzlement. He looked at me now like I had three heads.

"It feels weird," I mumbled, whirling my hand through the bizarre. "It's as if my hand is dragging through something." He crumpled his face in confusion and made his way toward me, sticking his hand out beside mine. I watched as amazement grew on his face.

"I feel it, too," he beamed. "Saty, come here! You've got to come and try this."

"Is it safe?" she warily asked Gram.

"It is the effects of the ward," she told us. "It is perfectly safe for witches. Come; follow me," Gram insisted, and with that, she took her first step through the ward and into nothing.

"Oh, my Gods, where did she go?" I stammered, panicking as I looked around for her. One minute she was beside us, and the next, she had disappeared.

"I don't see her anywhere." Satyra gulped, looking around the field.

"I think she went through," Raidan rationalized and started to put his hand a bit further through the ward. At that movement, his hand disappeared, leaving the end of his arm bare. The further he put his arm through, the less of him we saw.

"This is freaky," I marveled, watching him. With a swift movement, my brother was yanked across the other side, disappearing entirely before our eyes. My cousin and I looked at each other in horror.

"Is he okay?" Satyra cried out. My heart hammered in my chest.

"I don't know," I said and suddenly felt a hand grip me from the other side too. I was swept through the haze of the ward, and my heart nearly stopped. I didn't have time to blink, and I was glad. Otherwise, I would have missed the array of rainbow colors that I passed through. It was something of a dream. It was like swirls of colors, all mixed in an electrifying current. In a split second, I was out on the other side. Gram and Raidan met me there, hooting in pleasure.

"You scared the shit out of me!" I exclaimed, holding a hand to my heart. When I finally caught my breath, I let out a bellowing laugh at my wonder. I stared at the other side of the invisible wall and realized that we could see through to where we once were. Once we stepped through the ward, it no longer held the illusion of an empty field.

Gram, Raidan, and I stood patiently waiting for Satyra to walk through. We expected Satyra to come around on her own, but it didn't look like she was about to do that anytime soon. Excitedly, I put my hand through the ward and reached out to her. We could see the outside from inside the ward, but it was not the same for Satyra. I watched as my cousin looked at my hand, singularly floating around her. She looked around as if contemplating another choice. I stuck my head through now, and she screamed.

"Shivalri, what the hell?" Her eyes bulged from their seams.

"Come on, Cuz! It won't hurt you." I couldn't help but laugh at the face she wore. "Take my hand," I insisted. The look she gave me was purely horrified, fear eating her alive.

"If I die, I'm coming back to haunt your ass." She sneered.

"Sounds about right." I smirked, and she took my hand. As I pulled her through to the other side, the colors met us. I could see the awe written on her face now, and I knew it was mirrored in mine.

"That was so weird," she remarked.

"Weird indeed." Gram nodded, and we all looked at her now. Behind her, our destination awaited. "Welcome to the House of Enchantment."

28

HOUSE OF ENCHANTMENT

I didn't know what I had expected to see when we arrived at the House of Enchantment. Old castle-like walls, dungeons, and moats, maybe. None of that lay ahead of us as we strode down the perfectly groomed walkway adorned by walls of crisp, white roses. The roses continued around the grounds, acting as a barrier between the forest's wards we'd walked through to get here and the tall fortress that stood in our path. It looked like a castle, but that of a modern-day fairy tale. Someone had switched out the typical stained-glass for high, tinted windows. It looked pristine, like it had never seen a bad day.

"*Domus de Incantatio*," Gram spoke. "This is the House of Enchantment." I lifted a hand to touch a rose, but a tug at my sleeve stopped me in my tracks. I turned to see my grandmother glaring at me, nostrils flared.

"What?" I stammered.

"You were just about to prick your finger on an unforgiving bush of roses," she snarled. "Do not touch a single thing unless I tell you it is safe."

"Sorry," I muttered, rolling my eyes. Her anger bore through me, and I cringed.

"Yes, Shivalri, you would've been sorry had I let you learn from error." She flicked me upside the head, and I rubbed at the sting. "Once your blood hits the soil here, your soul is bound to this place, never to leave again. Do not scowl at me, little witch, and do not touch what isn't yours."

"Holy shit!" I crossed my arms and hid my hands. "Way to warn me!" I glared at her.

"That's messed up," Raidan said from behind me, examining the roses that framed our sides. "Why would someone do that?"

"They, the council, use beauty to stay in the lead in every way they can. Not only for their personal gain but for protection. They use splendor to lure their enemies into thinking they've struck gold, only to find they've struck a bargain with the devil himself."

My eyes widened in horror.

"The devil?" Satyra repeated, hushed and withered.

"Or so they say," Gram whispered and winked at me. "Are you in the mood to play with your luck, my dear?" I shook my head in refusal.

"Hell no." At the thought of my almost striking a deal with the devil, I couldn't help but wonder what other tricks and traps awaited us here at the House of Enchantment. Blood magic seemed to be their go-to method, and something about that rubbed me the wrong way. My stomach sank at the remembrance of our upcoming meeting with a chalice, and queasiness immediately left me flushed.

"Can we go in now?" Raidan asked, frustrated by what he deemed to be nonsense.

"After you," I nudged him, and for a split second, he teetered on his heels, his bravery wavering, and panic flashed on his face. But the fear left his eyes instantly, and he marched along the path to the big double doors. They stood over double my brother's height, making them easily twelve feet. He drove to grab the door handle, but the doors glided open the minute he stepped foot on the tread.

"Woah…" he muttered, peering in. "It's enormous."

"Can we go in?" Satyra asked, dancing in place. Gram chuckled.

"All witches are welcome." She smiled at my cousin, who was already stepping into the building. "Go ahead, my sweet." I turned to my grandmother, worry in my throat.

"I'm scared," I confessed, shrinking into myself. Stepping foot into this building meant many things to me. I was about to face the consequences of my unintentional transgressions. Once I strode in, there was no turning back. "I don't know if I'm ready to do this, Gram."

"Oh, Pumpkin." She sighed. "If I were in your hat, I don't believe I would be either," she admitted. "But I'd try." She was right. I sucked my teeth and inhaled deeply.

"Here's to trying," I said softly, and she took my hand in hers as we both stepped into the Salem House of Enchantment.

Everything was white and spotless. No furniture, no décor, only walls and walls of white stretched all around.

"It's so bare," I noted. Gram mumbled in agreement.

"When I was a very young girl, it didn't look so new. The updates are certainly interesting."

"Just say it." I grinned. "It's not your style."

"Oh, hush," she shushed and pinched my side. I perked up and turned to her, suddenly remembering the books that I had been promised.

"Gram! Where's the library?"

"Up," she replied, pointing toward the ceiling. I was utterly floored. Four rounded staircases lined the structure in each corner. Books were lined as far as the eye could see, flanking the walls across from the railings. It was a vision of art. I had never seen so many books before. I'd been surprised when Gram revealed her secret library in the basement. I reveled in the sweet knowledge that I could go there with Gram to read all of those books. I had been astounded by the number of them. But here, in the House of Enchantment, I couldn't believe my eyes.

"Do we have time to go look at them all?" Gram smiled at my enthusiasm.

"I don't think I could stop you from looking at the books if I tried." She laughed. "Go on ahead. I will go up with you in just a moment. But please, Shivalri—look; don't touch."

At that, I stalked up one of the spiral staircases and made my ascent. As I climbed the massive, never-ending flight, the building seemed taller than it was wide. The ceilings were incredibly high; it was probably about forty feet of endless height. I wondered how people managed to remove the books from the shelves so high in the air. I looked around for a ladder of sorts but didn't find anything of use. The books were neatly organized; row upon row of clean book-lined shelving stretched as far as the eye could see. I marveled at the sight. Had this new venture not been so troubling, I might have been entirely happy to come here. I might have called this my heaven.

There weren't many aisles in the library since it had been built colossally tall. It went skyward, circling the main lobby. I walked along the guardrail that wrapped around the building and tilted my head back in an attempt to see the collection. When I looked up at the ceiling, there were carvings in the molding above the bookshelves, which told me that the volumes were divided into sections. Each one had a small aisle made up of two racks. In company with the carvings, cherubs brushed along the tops, making for a beautiful scene. It almost reminded me of my high school theater, but this was something far more spectacular. People would pay considerably to see something like this. It was almost as if the statues carved in place were taken straight from the Vatican itself. Beautiful and godly; ethereal in true form.

I didn't know which way to start first. I decided to go down to the section closest to my left; I couldn't waste any precious time. I was determined to visit all of these aisles and each unit before it was time to meet with the emissaries. I was surprised to see that the gallery closest to me was full of maps. Some rolled up and sat in cubbies, but most were in glass frames, all lined neatly. Instead of having the names of the countries listed to sort them out, I realized that numbers, dates, and years classified the documents. It was strange seeing maps from before my time. I had seen an old map once in my history class, but it was only maybe one hundred years old. These maps were ancient.

Nothing before me was written in English. Most of the texts were made up of symbols. I recognized some to be like hieroglyphics. The collections in this library come from all over the world. I brushed my fingertips along the edge of the shelf and marveled at the thought of my privilege. The very fact that my fingers and my eyes could touch any one of these maps was astounding. Though I would listen to Gram and refrain from touching the books, I was still in a place of honor.

I continued walking through the compact aisle and made my way to the back wall that connected the room. At first, I scanned the books and maps neatly stacked on the shelves level to my height. There were so many. When I looked up at the ceiling, I marked my section. It read IX.X.CCC AD. I couldn't fathom how anything from before Christ could be here at the House of Enchantment.

There were so many maps and volumes, and I couldn't even begin to imagine how these kinds of records still existed in our world. How was it that they had been preserved for so long? When I started to look back down, scanning the shelves, my eyes dragged and fastened onto one of the books on the shelf, third from the highest. I felt that magnetic pull, that pulsing energy thrum through my fingertips like in the Grimsbane sanctuary. I felt the whisper of this book beckoning me through a chill breeze.

"Goddess of three...," it crooned, desperate for my attention. I could feel it in my bones—I needed to see this book. I closed my eyes for a moment, grounded myself, and took a deep breath. When I looked back up, I raised my hand and started to urge the book forward, attempting to make it flow to me.

"Watch where you're going," a stranger said, startling me from my observational posture. The thrum in my bones fizzled out, and the book high above grew silent.

"Oh my gosh, I'm so sorry. I didn't even see you there," I stammered. The old lady smiled and lifted her glasses to the bridge of her nose.

"Don't worry about it. I tend to be quiet when I'm here so as not to disturb anyone who may want to read." I looked around to see if there was anyone else she could be referring to, but the space was empty.

"Do you come here often?" I asked, concentrating on the soundless stranger who snuck up on me.

"I come here just about every day," she said. "I am a librarian of sorts." At that, I beamed.

"Well, that might just be my dream job," I said. Her frown lines sank when she returned my smile.

"Oh, it's a lovely place to be, but it's time-consuming and tedious," she granted.

"I can imagine," I answered, again looking at the books. "It must be challenging to keep all of this in order. There are so many volumes." I looked back up the third-highest shelf, trying to find the book I had been drawn to. It didn't take me long to see it, the pull sending a wave of goosebumps over my arms.

"There are hundreds of thousands of books here in the House of Enchantment, and believe it or not, I've read them all thrice."

"Thrice?" I questioned. She shushed me at my brash exclamation.

"I may not seem it, but I am quite old." She chuckled to herself.

"You must be ancient to have been able to read all of these. More than once, at that." Realizing that I might have just insulted her, the blood in my chest crept up to my face in chagrin.

"Something like that." She grinned. Gram came up behind me and put a hand on my shoulder, startling me out of my skin.

"Come along, Shivalri. Leave the sprite to her book tending." I spun around on Gram to look at her now.

"What?" I blurted. I turned back to look at the old librarian, and she giggled.

"You're quite new to all of this, aren't you?" She raised a brow, and I shook my head.

"You have no idea." I gave Gram a sharp look. I still couldn't believe that she had hidden all of this away. My family had kept this big, significant part of who I was a secret for so long, and I was ignorant for it. When Gram and I made for walking away, the sprite hesitated, then stopped us.

"Was there a particular book you were looking for?" she questioned.

"No," Gram answered. "Thank you."

"She has a wandering eye, this one. A curious, curious thing," the lady told Gram as we walked away.

"It was nice meeting you," I chimed, and the little lady waved us away and headed back to her cart of books. I wondered if she had noticed what I was doing. Better yet, I wondered if she, too, heard the voice of books calling to her. "Sprite?" I elbowed Gram now that the stranger was far enough away that she wouldn't overhear.

"I told you that there are many creatures you do not know of."

"Yes, you did, but I hardly believed you," I admitted. "What's a sprite? And how is it here in the Earth realm with us?"

"Sprites are household spirits. They, too, have partial human lineage; therefore, their souls reside here till death."

"What can they do?" I asked.

"They are shapeshifters, strong and quick in speed and wit. Usually helpful and kind, but happy to turn to mischief if given the opportunity," she explained. "I told you all of the stories are true." She looked at me knowingly.

"Next time, please tell me before I accidentally bump into a vampire and get on their bad side." I laughed. She halted and gave me a stern look.

"Shivalri, dear, you'd better hope you don't run into a dræpyr, or vampire, as you so call it. You are far too sweet to resist." I went cold at her words.

"What's a dræpyr?" I choked. My grandmother didn't so much as look at me during my questioning.

"Dræpyr are demons born with a craving for blood." At her words, I instantly felt my skin drain of warmth. "They age as they please, breathe as they please, and drink from as many as they like."

"So, vampires are real too." I shuddered.

"And so much more."

"Unreal," I mumbled. She watched me now, a curious look on her face.

"What's so hard to believe?" she probed. "How are you able to wrap your mind around being a witch? You didn't question having the power to control all five elements," she considered. "I tell you that you are the reason behind the veil lifting, and you do not so much as blink. I tell you that there are vampires, and you grow squeamish. What am I to do with you?" I shook my head at her.

"I have no explanation, Gram. No suggestions, either." She patted my back as we made for the stairs where Satyra and Raidan were waiting for us at the bottom.

"They didn't go look at any books?" I asked.

"They're not readers like you and me," she supposed. "Stories call to us."

"Did you end up finding anything on time weaving?" I asked.

"I did," she beamed, shoulders shrinking as if she held a secret. She pulled a small booklet from her coat pocket and waved it at me. "Don't tell the sprite." She smirked. I couldn't help but snigger as she shoved it back into her coat and straightened it out. Who was this woman, and what had she done with my grandmother?

As we neared the bottom of the stairs, I turned back to marvel at the books.

"I can't help but feel like Saty right now," I thought aloud.

"How so?"

"She finds the fairy tale in everything, and this, to me, all of these books full of infinite knowledge, is my fairy tale calling my name...." I whispered, envisioning my Princess Belle moment. As if right on cue, a dark-cloaked figure came storming down the stairs, his robe trailing behind him in his gale. Where there is a beauty, a beast must follow suit.

At the sight of the man, Raidan and Satyra quickly and quietly made their way over to Gram and me and stood on either side of us. My cousin to my right, Gram, followed by my brother to my left. As the man neared the bottom of the stairs, Gram's hand grew frozen in mine. Her grip bruised at my knuckles as three more figures made their way to us from the main chamber halls.

"Gram," Satyra whispered, but there was no answer to her call. Now, all four cloaked people stood before us, forming a line parallel to ours. I stared up at the man who stood face-to-face with me, unflinching. He hadn't moved his eyes from mine since coming down the stairs. Dark obsidian features devoured me. Deliberately, he looked me up and down, and I abruptly felt far more exposed than I was. He smirked at my reaction, pushing a loose dreadlock out of his face. He pulled at his hood and let it down, and as he drew misplaced hair back into his bun, he revealed the burnt flesh that lined his jaw and up his ear. I saw the scars creating a pattern in his undercut as he twisted his head, moving his attention from me to my grandmother. He was quite handsome, but his confining presence, and that of the others, distracted me from that.

"Welcome," he boomed, his rich voice echoing up into the building. He moved his fist to his heart, and the other three cloaked figures followed suit in sync. Gram put her fist to her chest and dipped her head.

"Thank you, High Council," she managed to choke out. A hot flash nipped my shoulders. I could feel Satyra and Raidan's tension spike as we all came to realize who stood before us. This was the High Council.

"We've been waiting on your arrival," the woman ahead of Gram spoke. She was tall and thin, with her hair pulled back in a tight ponytail. Her voice was poised, clean, and sharp in an Oxford English cadence. "Had we known you would be roaming at a human pace, we would've begun our travel much later." The woman raised her chin, and the male across from Raidan scoffed in agreement. Raidan stood his ground.

"We—" Raidan was cut off.

"Do not speak," spat the fair-haired, muscular male in front of him, "unless you are spoken to." The way he spoke with such severity was unnerving.

As I surveyed the faces of the strangers and heard each of them speak, I wondered how they had come to gather. I hadn't fully measured the large scale of the magical world. How far did it stretch to gift witches their affinities? Gram had said there were meeting sites all over the world. Considering it all was extraordinary. All of these different people had come together for the sake of ruling magic and safety. It was evident that they'd grown accustomed to their power and reign together. They all wore determined, mighty looks, which had me feeling small in many ways. There was no doubting their influence.

"Does that count?" Raidan countered, testing his limits. In this moment, I wished so badly for my brother to put away his natural defiance. The man bared his teeth, and the woman in front of Gram grinned at Raidan. Our grandmother gave him a stern look that said everything she couldn't.

"I like this one," the stately woman purred to the cloaks, predatorial eyes burning a hole where my brother stood. The man in front of Raidan whipped his head to the woman and hissed his disapproval. Possessiveness stained his scowl.

"Oh hush, Mr. Lagunov," the woman snapped. "It is only banter." She grinned slowly, and he stiffened at her sly look.

"Yes, Miss Darkmore." He nodded, face flat.

"Please, Damek. These are very special guests," the woman said, scanning our faces. When she looked at me, I kept still. Under her fiery gaze, I wasn't sure what to do. Remembering how Gram greeted them, I built up the courage and fisted my right hand over my heart. I could see pure entertainment dancing in the woman's eyes. I wondered if I had done the wrong thing.

"Call me Moira," she insisted, seemingly content with my gesture.

"Thank you for meeting with us, Moira," Gram spoke up. "I must admit, we were not expecting to see you here. To meet with you is an honor and privilege." Moira turned to face my grandmother, who looked far frailer compared to her, and clasped her hands together.

"We heard through the grapevine that you've found yourselves in a bit of a situation. We decided it was a matter of urgent business. One in which we had to involve ourselves," said Moira. The man in front of me winked in my direction, and aversion pooled in my gut. This group of people oozed confidence, and I wasn't sure whether to look away from it or take notes and learn from it.

"We've heard so much about you, Shivalri Gray," he said, smiling wide. His teeth glimmered, pointing at the tip. I gulped, and his eyes darted to my neck. I cleared my throat, and he smirked. I immediately thought of Gram's mention of the dræpyr earlier and had to swallow down the fear of a demon possibly present in the House of Enchantment.

"I've very recently heard of you as well," I said, clearing my throat. I sought to sound assertive. "Lovely to meet you, Ember." At the mention of his name, his face ignited, then settled in an instant—a look of enthusiasm washed away in a blink. Gram's hand clutched mine even tighter than before.

"Forgive me," he blew out. "It's been eons since I've heard my name spoken with such noteworthy admiration." Moira snapped her fingers, and he stiffened yet again at the sound of her command. A shiver ran down my spine at the thought of her power, her prestige. I wondered what it would be like to be her, to hold that kind of supremacy. Moira waved a hand toward Ember, and he bowed his head.

"This is Ember Blackwood. Fourth in command," Moira began. She gestured to the man in front of Raidan, and the cloaked figure removed his hood.

"This is Damek Lagunov. My second in command." Now she pointed to the woman in front of Satyra, who bowed her head, muted.

"My third. Sora Fujin," Moira said, then stepped back from the line. The woman was silent and avoided my eye contact. Her dark almond eyes never left the floor. "As I mentioned before, you may call me Moira. I will be your director for all intents and purposes." The four of them turned on their feet and began walking toward the stairs. As my family and I followed them, the number of bodies struck me. There were five members in the High Council. Where was the fifth?

When the High Council led us into a small room sectioned off the main area, I questioned whether we were safe. I figured if Gram trusted them and had no hesitation when following them, I should probably put those restless thoughts away. I wasn't accustomed to being around this kind of influence. Gram had a lifetime of experience. I buried my troubled thoughts in the far pocket of my mind and scanned the room for Satyra. My grandmother and brother were walking ahead of me, following the High Council's heels. Satyra, on the other hand, was a step behind me. I turned my head to face her, still walking to follow the group. She had her head down, but I could see that she was worrying her lip.

"Saty, are you okay?" She looked up at me quickly as if I had startled her from thought.

"Yeah, I'm fine. I've just got the jitters," she mumbled, lip still caught in her teeth. "It's hard to believe that this is all happening. This is supposed to be make-believe."

"Tell me about it," I said. "I just met my first sprite upstairs."

"First what?" She stopped in her tracks and looked at me with utter panic in her eyes.

"You would think Gram would've warned me before I went up there." I shook my head in disbelief.

"You think?" she spluttered, eyes wide in astonishment. "What did it look like?" she marveled aloud.

"She was nice," I supposed.

"She?"

"I think so," I said. "Though I can't be sure. She looked like a little old lady. She told me that she's the librarian here and takes care of the books. She seemed harmless. But, then again, I don't know anything about sprites." I shrugged. "Gram didn't seem to be frightened, so I don't think we have anything to be afraid of," I offered.

"Well, that's nice," my cousin said under her breath.

"She also told me vampires are real." Satyra stopped midtrack; her breath hitched.

"Are you trying to give me a heart attack?"

"Sorry! That's not my intention. I just thought you should know."

"Gee, you think?" she barked sarcastically. "I was already scared about following these powerful witches into a secret room. You just had to go and tell me that other creatures are hanging around."

"Hey." I stopped her. "I said nothing about a vampire being here, just that they exist."

"That doesn't make it any better," she hissed.

"Sorry, Cuz." I laughed and nudged her forward. "We can talk about the vampires once we're out of here. I myself still have lots of questions."

"What more is there to know?" she begged.

"Let's just say that Gram didn't tell me enough to feed my curiosity. She left me with mere crumbs for information," I sneered. "The basics of vampires are understandable, but the how is bafflement. The way things work and the way that so much folklore exists in real life is beyond me."

"Me too," Satyra added. "I've never been more excited or terrified in my life. I am so happy that we have magic and that we are witches. It feels like a dream come true."

"It's terrifying."

"Maybe right now it is, but you know I've always wanted more from all the magical stories we were told as kids. I never expected bad stuff to play such a big role in it all, but we have to let the good outweigh the bad."

"That's easier said than done, Saty. Magic has repercussions. I've crafted immeasurable ruin in the few days of it waking in me. I'm a walking disaster."

"Okay, yes, you're a bit of a catastrophe as of late. But think of all the good you could do if you'd learn to harness your powers. You can repair just as well as you ruin," she said insistently. "Shivi, we're magic." I let her words sink in and soaked up their meaning.

"It's weird, isn't it?" I answered, full of thought. "Magic."

"Weirdly, it's all been proven true," she acknowledged. "It's one thing to think about, to consider that there might be another kind of world out there that we can't see."

"It's another thing to see it," I finished for her.

"Exactly. That's what makes it so odd."

"I suppose we are odd now, huh?" I thought as we caught

up to the rest of the group. She snickered and pointed ahead of us.

"They're odd."

When we got to the room, there was a big lock on the door. It was the kind that had a bolt set in place and an old turnkey. The metal groaned as they pushed the door open and welcomed us into the dark-lit room. When we entered, everything looked ancient. This was what I had pictured when Gram talked about the House of Enchantment. It looked like nothing had ever been remodeled, and I imagined that this was how Gram liked it.

Inside, a long table stretched across the room, taking up most of the space. Tall-backed chairs lined each side of the table, and one chair sat at the head. The woman who led the High Council took a seat at the head, and the rest of the cloaked group took seats on one side of the table. My grandmother followed and gestured for us to do the same, facing the others at the opposite side of the table.

"Our Emissaries have informed us of your situation," Moira Darkmore boomed. She looked royal as she sat in her chair: squared shoulders, tight jaw, and hard-hearted eyes. She was older than the rest in the group, save for perhaps her fourth in command. I couldn't quite tell Sora's age, but it seemed as though the ladies were in their forties or fifties. Damek appeared maybe twice my age, and Ember seemed even closer to it. He looked relatively young compared to his comrades. "After your phone call, the commanding foreman of sector forty-five took to calling us immediately. He was right to do so, as this is of utmost importance."

"We are so fortunate that you have taken our inquiries so seriously," Gram said. "Thank you. Thank you so much."

"Of course," Moira hummed. "It is imperative that we stay on top of these high-risk priorities. As you know, the legends of this prophecy have been told again and again, over centuries, since the dawn of time. This, what has already happened, is portentous. This will attract worldwide opprobrium. We have all been waiting and wondering if we would ever live to see the day that the prophecy comes to fruition. Fearful of it, of course," she continued. The others murmured an agreement. "We understand that this is not an easy feat to wrap your mind around, and Shivalri, we would like to extend our honored words to you. We send a promise to you in hopes that you allow us to help you and protect you." I gulped dryly and nodded.

"Thank you," I managed, voice a little shaky. She grinned.

"You are quite welcome."

"What do you foresee?" Gram spoke now. "What shall we do to prevent the knowledge of the prophecy from being spread? The veil is lifted, and the supernatural of all realms will realize it soon enough. It is only a matter of time. We cannot allow this to fall into the wrong hands. If people know that they can use Shivalri and her powers to open the gate fully, someone with the worst intentions could unleash Hell on this Earth."

"Yes," Miss Darkmore replied. "And that would not do." She looked worried. Gram's words disconcerted me as I realized what she was saying.

"What do you mean; use me?" I asked, disturbance pulsing through my veins.

"As a sacrifice," the one called Ember intoned. His eyes were stern. He did not seem empathetic, only stating facts.

"What do you mean?" Satyra asked, voice trembling. "Like, kill her?" Ember only looked at her like he was studying a case. She turned to Gram with brows lifted in what I could only assume was horror. "You never said anything about that before, Gram!" My eyes grew wide at the sound of my cousin's concern. Was that what the summoning from our dreams was about? My memory flashed back to Saty's description of the torment, and I remembered the dark tendrils ensconcing me. I wanted to vomit.

"We have reason to believe that your body would act as a key. A portal of sorts, if you will," Moira said. "With the veils lifted, someone could easily access and create a portal at the Gates of another realm at the spill of your very potent blood."

"A portal to Hell," I whispered, nerves rattling my core.

"A portal to any realm," Moira corrected.

"And we do not want that," said Damek.

"No, of course not," replied Moira. "How much control do you have over your power, Miss Grimsbane?" Moira redirected her attention to me. I found it odd that Ember had referred to me as Gray, but Moira used Grimsbane. I wondered if it was calculated or if I was just overly uneasy. When I didn't answer, Gram responded in my stead with a sigh.

"She has just begun ascendency," she admitted. "She knows nothing of magic. It's only surfaced this month."

"Am I to understand that she has no grasp on any ability?" the quiet woman, Sora, asked. I had forgotten her presence in her constant silence.

"That is correct," said Gram. "She has the affinities, but to wield them properly, controlled... She hasn't learned yet."

Moira hummed, pondering my failures. An insurgence of belittlement wrapped itself around me as I listened to the judgmental drone. I couldn't help but feel inferior. I was not enough. I wondered why it had to be me. Why was I chosen? At that thought, I cleared my throat and looked at them all. I had to know.

"Why me?" I demanded an answer. "I know about the affinities. I know about the prophecy. But why me? What makes me the problem? Why was I chosen for this?"

"It is your fate," said Moira. "Not only do you have all five elemental affinities, but you also have the blood of demon and angel running through your veins. An infrequent occurrence." Gram gasped unusually loud, looking incredibly shocked.

"This cannot be! It is impossible," she said. I watched as her eyes darted from Moira, to me, then to her fiddling hands before her. "She can't possibly have the blood of an angel in her if she's a witch. The DNA is immiscible."

"Ah, yes. That is what ancient history has taught us. However, it is true of this young girl."

"What does that mean?" I asked. "And how would you even know about my mixed DNA?" Gram's face had shock written all over it, and that only made my own shock even stronger.

"The High Council receives every record of witchling and supernatural births. We've known about your anomaly since the moment we received your blood vials. Of course, we had no idea that it had anything to do with the prophecy. We can never predict which powers will rise within a witch. That is only discovered in the ascendency."

"Gram, is this true?" I asked, looking to her for some semblance of confirmation of any of this.

"Your father must have Nephilim blood," she thought.

"Dad's a witch hunter?" Raidan gawked in astonishment. "What the hell?"

"If that were the case, you would also be a part of this prophecy." Moira pointed to my brother. "Only you are not."

"Are you sure?" Satyra asked. She and my brother bore curious expressions on their faces.

"It's possible, Miss Darkmore," Gram interjected. "Unthinkable, but possible. Most witch hunters do come from the French and Italian churches. Their father is a French man. His family lives in France."

"We have Raidan's bloodwork as well. His is that of mortal and witch," said Damek, a smug look crossing his face.

"The father is entirely irrelevant. The fact is that the blood of angel and demon is still immiscible," Moira said firmly. "If their father were Nephilim, and their mother a witch, scientifically, these two children would not exist."

"But how does this explain Shivalri?" Gram questioned. She had never looked so confused in all my days of knowing her.

"Shivalri is unlike any other. We do not have the answers. All we know is that she carries the blood of both."

"Why is the blood immiscible?" I asked, now realizing I hadn't the faintest idea. "Why can't demons and angels procreate? I thought that's what they did when they all lived together." Moira clasped her hands together, acknowledging my question with the tilt of her chin.

"Due to the separation of realms, magic was forged into all of us. It is unknown how, but it registered the moment that the three realms were created."

"Our theory is that the maker of realms did not want the supernatural mortals to procreate and become stronger than they already were," said Ember. Moira nodded.

"The idea of the split was to have our species eventually become weaker throughout our lineage. The goal was to rid Earth of magic without having to wipe out the human race completely. They relied on us to slowly grow weaker and fewer. If angel and demon blood were to mix, it would create a whole new genealogy that could potentially come with stronger magics."

"*Da,*" Damek scoffed. "Something the average mortals could not afford." Everyone nodded in agreement, some wearing frowns, others grim in the eyes.

"As you know," Moira said, looking at all of us. "When the

ordinary humans learned of witchcraft, their fear and prejudice killed our kind. They very stupidly thought they'd gotten us all... If the world knew that more than thirty percent of the population had magic, it would be catastrophic. The maker of realms knew this. They chose to let us die out quietly and peacefully rather than make us stronger and a threat. It was either our species or theirs. The maker did not want to choose. We were all grouped in as human; therefore, we are all Earthbound."

"If it's impossible, truly impossible, to have the mixed DNA, then how do I have both angel and demon blood?" I asked, voice quiet but steady.

"What does this mean?" Gram asked, brows furrowed. "Please, this is my granddaughter. Help me understand." Moira took a long, calculated breath and pointed her eyes at me.

"She is God-blessed," she stated. My grandmother's eyes flew wide in disbelief. "It is a primordial destiny. That is all we know."

"You seem surprised at this information," Ember spoke, chin raised in question.

"It was not included in the material of my family's books," Gram admitted. Gram looked ashamed at the lack of knowledge she usually took pride in having.

"Ill-prepared," Damek muttered under his breath, and Ember sneered in his direction. Moira's face stayed stagnant, searching for more from my grandmother.

"Yes, well, enough with the family drama," Ember said, now looking at me. "Let's cut to the chase. You made a big bad mistake and ripped a hole in the veil. Luckily, humans don't realize what's happening and have chalked it up to weather issues. Unfortunately, those of us who know of the supernatural will question it."

"It is time for you all to decide if you will accept our help," Moira stated.

"Of course," Gram said. "Of course, we will accept your help. We cannot thank you enough." I bit my lip, feeling dizzy. A cold sweat ran over me as my mind worried. How could my grandmother so quickly accept their aid when they hadn't even told us how they offered it?

"What if we don't?" I asked, releasing my lip from my teeth.

"Don't what?" Moira barked, jaw firm.

"What if we don't accept your help? What if I wanted to go into hiding instead?"

"You do not seem to understand, Miss Grimsbane," Moira ground out, fuming at my reservation. "If you do not accept our help to protect you, and if you do not offer your help in exchange, we will have to resort to other strategies."

"Other strategies?"

"One cannot use you if you are dead," Damek, the blond one, said grinningly. I felt my stomach drop. Gram just looked down when I looked at her for support. She said nothing.

"Gram, you can't possibly let them kill me," I buzzed, feeling faint.

"Gram, are you seriously not cutting in here?" Raidan choked. "This is ridiculous! If Shivi doesn't want to live this kind of life, why couldn't she just hide?"

"She can hide! I'll go with her," Satyra sobbed. She was crying now, face red and puffy from emotion. I watched Ember's eyes flicker to her. I saw a quick second of remorse in his gaze, but it instantly fizzled out. I looked at Moira now, her face still hard, never flinching.

"Gram?" I whispered, looking to her for any sign that she would support whichever choice I wanted to make. When she loosed her breath, shoulders hunched, I knew I had lost the battle.

"We have no choice, Shivalri. We happily accept their help, and we will gladly oblige in areas necessary to save the world." At this, the High Council looked to us, all beaming triumphantly.

"Agreed?" the leader asked, eyes pinning me. I took a long moment before making my decision. What would all of this entail? What would I have to sacrifice to put the veil back together? Whether I wanted to or not, I had no choice. I was forced to accept whatever they wanted without fully knowing what they needed from me. It was this or death. I slowly nodded my head, eyes locked on the leader of the High Council.

"Agreed."

29

CHALICE

Once we agreed to work with them, they told us we had to conduct the remainder of our business in a different chamber. I was still hesitant to follow them and accept my fate alongside them. I was meant to believe that they were good and that they were to be trusted. In truth, they were the people I was most supposed to trust. Gram told us about the High Council before coming to the House of Enchantment. My grandmother said that they were greatly esteemed and meant to be our protectors of sorts. They were the keepers of peace and regulation for our witchy world. But following our brief conversation with them, I couldn't help but question their motives after they made me feel unsafe and so incredibly inferior. They seemed particularly keen on having our agreement set in stone. It was as if they needed to feel indispensable. They were driven by power, no doubt. It made me uncomfortable, especially after having death threatened as another alternative to my cooperation.

Having no choice in the matter made everything far worse. The fact that I had to work with them or face the possibility of them ending my life was something of a nightmare. How was this acceptable? Cruelest of all, how could my own grand-mother bow down and agree to those kinds of terms? All I knew was that I was in a heap of trouble, stuck under a rock and a hard place, and I wasn't getting out of it any time soon. I had to trust that this was my path.

Trudging down the halls, I was out of breath by the time the cloaked leaders came to a halt. Halfway up the building, they stopped at a leaden door.

"Beyond this door is this House of Enchantment's sacred room," Moira began. "It is of high honor to enter and my privilege to allow you in."

"Thank you," Gram said. "We appreciate your time and trust."

"We believe you, though I hope you understand that we must abide by Witch Law and demand a valid testimony. We trust that you have prepared your grandchildren for the imminent formality?" Moira mused. Our grandmother had told us about the spell before we came—a mixture of charms and blood to drink from a chalice of truth.

"Of course, Miss Darkmore," Gram assured her, and we followed them into the room.

It was the inside of a church—old, worn, and full of wooden benches. Directly at the back of the room, a small stage with an altar stood as a central focal point. My stomach churned as I regarded the four shining chalices that gleamed in the candlelight glowing throughout the room.

"Shivalri..." Satyra whispered to me, now standing a mere inch behind me.

"Shh," Gram silenced us. We kept walking up the aisle, passing rows of timeworn pews. We moved toward the altar, where the cloaked council stood awaiting us.

"Shiv," Satyra repeated warily. I turned to look at her, and my blood froze. She was colorless. I gave her a panicked look, and she returned it.

"It's okay," I whispered over my shoulder, lying for the both of us.

"It feels wrong," she said. I had to agree. Drinking a potion, let alone our own blood, rubbed me the wrong way.

Ember Blackwood made his way to a small table that stood to the left of the altar. Damek and Sora trailed behind him, chalices in hand. Gram placed us in positions at the bottom of the step and kneeled in front of the leader, Moira. Moira took her place at the head of the altar and flipped through the book already sitting atop it. Raidan copied our grandmother.

Satyra and I exchanged a worried look and knelt on the ground. This was all happening so fast. I had assumed that the High Council would take a moment to explain the steps and help clear our fears. After all, we were young and had never experienced anything like this before. It felt like an aberration. We hadn't even been in the sacred room long enough to take note of our surroundings. I had hoped for guidance, but this new world didn't seem to come with much of that. The motions came in a blur.

"*Quaerite Verum. Tollere Libertatum,*" Moira began chanting. My attention turned to the table where the rest of the cloaks began mixing their concoction. The lot of them were scampering around the table, wiping away their sweat. They looked just as nervous as I felt. I caught Ember biting his lip in concentration as he lowered himself to the chalices for precision. Red pierced through his bottom lip and dribbled down onto the table. He quickly looked up at me and wiped away the blood that lingered. I looked down, embarrassed for having had my eyes on him, and stared at the floor.

"They are complete," said Ember, carrying a chalice over

to Moira. She examined the elixir that bubbled and fizzed and nodded in approval.

"Hand them out," she ordered, and Damek and Sora came down from the stage. Satyra was the first to receive one, as Sora was closest to her. Damek gave Gram and Raidan theirs with a satisfied grin. I felt the footsteps vibrate in my knees as Ember walked down the stairs to me. He took my chin and forced me to look up at him.

"Drink up, buttercup," he trilled. I couldn't tell if he liked me or despised me. The way he spoke to me in these few hours of being around the High Council was unexpected. He treated me as if he knew me somehow. He acted indifferent most of the time, but sometimes he would snap at me with hatred in his eyes. Sometimes he felt comfortable enough to tease me. It left me in a great deal of malaise.

"Thank you," I replied and forced a smile when he finally released his hold on me. The cloaks stood by Moira and faced us.

"My friends," Moira addressed us as we looked up at her. She was beautiful, her face thin and long with eyes a piercing blue. I hadn't noticed it earlier due to my vulnerability during their surprise entrance. I had avoided truly looking into her eyes. "I will not lie to you," she continued. "This will not feel pleasant. You will feel ill immediately after drinking; however, it will quickly subside."

"My bet is on *bolshoi* to spew," said Damek to Ember, but Ember did not reply. He kept his head forward. Raidan only grumbled.

"It's going to hurt?" Satyra whined. "You didn't tell us that." She pointed at Gram.

"You didn't think forgoing this kind of information a bit of a lie?" I questioned, angry at her slight betrayal. She very well could have told us. She should have known that we would still oblige in these circumstances.

"It was not worth the mention, as the short pain is worth the price," Gram answered simply.

"I have to agree," said Moira. "It is of utmost importance that you accept this challenge in front of you. You are not alone, as we are here to support you. Now, as you know, when you drink this elixir, you will be forced to tell the truth. This blood-binding spell will see to it." Moira arched a brow at Gram. "Set?"

"Set," Gram replied and looked at her grandchildren.

"Set," I confirmed. Raidan and Satyra nodded. Ember took my hand, and instinctually, I recoiled.

"The blood," he reminded me, removing a tiny dagger from his belt. My eyes grew wide at what he held. I had expected a tiny pinprick, not a blade with the potential to chop my fingertip clean at the knuckle.

"Oh... Right," I supposed and carefully placed my hand in his. I was putting a lot of trust in the hands of an unknown knife-wielding man.

"Don't make any sudden movements," he advised. "It's very sharp."

"Okay." I shuddered and loosed a breath. He moved his knife above my hand and quickly, deliberately sliced through my flesh just enough to expel a drop of blood from my palm. I winced at the sting, my heart leaping from my chest. I was glad to find that the pain was gone in an instant, and it was only the shock of it that caused my alarm. It was no more than a papercut. Though I had expected a small prick to the finger, the palm didn't hurt too badly.

"Here," he said, holding my hand more carefully now as he turned it over for the blood to land in my cup. I winced as it splashed and sizzled in the already ruby liquid. Ember released my hand, and I wiped it on my knee, not caring about the stain. He made his way to Satyra and did the same for her, but with a different tool. Damek pricked my brother and Gram's hands with a little too much enthusiasm for my liking.

"*Sanguis. Potio. Involucrum,*" Moira boomed and lifted her hands to the sky as we downed the potion.

I closed my eyes in anticipation of pain or a putrid taste, but nothing happened. I felt fine. When I dared to open my eyes, I was surprised to find that I could barely do so. My heart began pattering as I tried to stand up. Move. Do anything. I could not. I stared hard at my knees, willing them to get up. A muscle in my thigh twitched, and I heaved out a breath of frustration.

"Fuck!" my brother yelped, his cry rippling through the air. Satyra began crying uncontrollably. She, too, echoed through the room. Gram, at my left, only buckled in on herself, jagged breaths revealing her pain.

"What—What is this?" she managed to weep before collapsing to the floor. I tried to go to her, to comfort her, but I could not. She became a hazy blur in front of me as the room spun.

From the corner of my eye, I saw Satyra crumple to the floor. I scanned her body for injuries as she convulsed in pain. Suddenly, she went still as if she were lifeless.

"Fuck this!" Raidan screamed and tried to get up, tripping over himself. I heard a chuckle come from Damek's direction. I couldn't move my head up to look at the figures in front of us. I scanned the floor, and in my line of vision, my brother joined Satyra and Gram, lying limp.

"What have you done?" Gram choked, her mouth barely able to form her words. Moira laughed in amusement.

"We've ensured that your agreement with us is definite," she hummed.

"What?" I managed, groggy but still fighting the urge to fall.

"Devil's Breath," Gram croaked out, gasping for air. "Shivalri, run." Before I could even register her words, my head tilted into a world of darkness.

30

TRAITORS

The night enveloped me as my body thawed. My eyes were wide as if trying to open further and improve my sight. But there was nothing to see— just the empty blackness. I started to panic as I realized what had happened in the sacred room. One single comet flew past me, casting a blaze of light into the sky. With the flash of light, I used it to see my surroundings. I was floating, and there was still nothing around me. I remembered the dream I had the night before and realized it was happening again. I thrashed in the air, trying to force myself to wake, until I heard a noise.

"With haste, brute," an angry female growled nearby. My *consciousness* finally came to me, and I stilled my breathing at the touch of hands clinging to my corpse. I cracked an eyelid to look upon my environment, head pounding from the haze. Moira Darkmore stood ahead of me, trailing through the night woods with the rest of her cloaked underlings. They held torches in their hands as they made their way further and further into the trees. Ember, I realized, had been the one carrying me. Traitors.

"She is a grown-ass woman," Ember groaned, and it rumbled in his chest and up my body. "She's heavy."

"Quit complaining," Damek rebutted. "Your hands are on the ass of that grown-ass woman you have pined over for weeks."

"Enough!" Moira barked, and the two men scoffed.

"I've had just about enough," Ember snarled and sniffed my hair. What in the world was he doing? I wanted to cringe away, but I knew I had to bide my time; calculate my actions. I lay limp in his arms and allowed him to scent me.

"Remember," Moira began. She swirled around to look in our direction, and I quickly shut my half-open lid. "She is not yours to play with." I could feel his breath on me as he considered her words.

"Oh, Moira, so jealous." He sneered. A twig snapped beneath his step, and I almost let out a screech. My body tensed under the scare.

"I gave you the assignment of spying on her as a reward for being my second for so long. Do not mistake my kindness for weakness. I will gut you in an instant if you ever consider standing in the way of our mission."

"And I'll help," said Damek. I opened my eye a crack in time to see him swing at Ember, who used me as a shield so that the punch landed on my hip. I sucked a quiet breath.

"Punching the Goddess, are we?" Ember snorted. "Not so good of an impression."

"I was aiming at you." He growled and turned back to face the trees like the rest of them. I could hear their footsteps growing further and further away. Ember was trailing behind. I opened my eye a little more, only to find him looking down at me with a grin. I panicked and tightly shut my eyes like a child afraid of a monster. I was foolish to do so. He'd seen me looking at him. He leaned in closer, his lips touching my ear.

"I know you're awake, little Goddess," he whispered in my ear. I stiffened in his arms, and he squeezed me firmly.

"No, don't—" I started, but he pressed a finger to my mouth.

"Do not make a sound. Stay asleep. Do not run," he murmured for no one but me to hear. "It will only be worse if you do not cooperate." I only looked at him, trying to read his face.

"Blackwood!" Damek shouted from ahead.

"I'm coming!" he called back. "She's hefty," he finished, directing the latter at me with a sneer. I almost blushed in embarrassment, but I covered the feeling with a roll of my eyes.

"Fall in line," said Moira, without so much as a look our way.

"Listen carefully," Ember began, lifting me higher onto his chest. "I think you know who we're about to meet... For your sake and your family's sake, just comply." His voice was urgent. I couldn't answer. My voice was too hoarse from the silence I'd bathed in. I blinked up at him in answer. "Please," he mouthed. "Pretend to sleep." I closed my eyes as a sign that I would listen. With a jolt of panic, I remembered that my family had also been a part of this. I stiffened in horror.

"Where's my family?" I whispered almost inaudibly as the air scratched my throat. I had never had such a dry mouth in my life. Ember kept his face forward, never missing the moments when Damek would look back to check on us. He was careful not to alert them that I had woken, but I did not know why.

"They are still in the House of Enchantment. Unharmed," he answered quietly.

"Unharmed?" I questioned. I looked up at him, hoping for a sign that he was telling the truth.

"We left them where they were. Raidan got a kick to the abdomen from Damek, but otherwise, they are fine." I pursed my lips into a scowl when he looked to assure me.

"You poisoned us," I stated. It was not a question.

"We gave you a dried flower only made to sedate you. Besides a little dry mouth and a bit of hallucinating, Devil's Breath is harmless," he explained.

"Reassuring," I spat. He had the nerve to smirk at my reply. "Why were they in pain, and I was not?" He frowned at that.

"All you need to know is that your family will be okay. I will see to it. But you, you're going to have a lot more of a fight ahead of you. I tried to warn you, but I can't protect you from this. This is far bigger than me—far bigger than you. Just cooperate. Put on your sleeping act, and don't let anyone know you're awake. They won't hurt you as much if you don't react." I gulped at those words, my heart sinking into the pit of my stomach. My lip trembled, and I held the tears back from spilling out. Crying would do me no good. I had to prepare myself for the worst. I had to go into survival mode.

"You'll protect my family?" I asked, needing a guarantee. "You promise?" He held my gaze now as we lingered in the dark.

"I will do whatever I can, but I make no promise."

"Please," I begged. "I need to hear it." The desperation in me cracked. He exhaled noiselessly and dipped his head.

"I promise."

The rustling sounds in the woods grew louder as we approached the rest of the cloaked figures. I peeked at my surroundings to see them standing at the base of the largest tree I had ever seen—the tree I had seen in my nightmare. As more people dressed in cloaks emerged from behind bushes, I noted the difference in their facial structures, the way some were hunched and otherworldly in shape. These were the creatures of the night my grandmother warned about. The eyes and ears everywhere that had worried her. I closed my eyes, vowing never to open them again until this ordeal was over.

"Gather round, wildlings. We've waited many centuries for this night to come." Moira inhaled deeply. "Finally, it has arrived. What better timing than the eve of Samhain? A time when barriers of physical and spiritual worlds come down. A time for greeting the other realm. With only a sliver of a moment, we must make our window of time count." The murmuring in the woods grew shriller.

"How?" said an unfamiliar voice.

"How did you manage to lift the veil?" asked another. Moira laughed a wicked, long laugh.

"We did not. This young girl did." I could feel the eyes on me now more than ever. "We've been watching her for the last year now. Ever since our tracker discovered her strange magic," she hummed. "Thanks to Mr. Blackwood, we learned that the witch did not know of her powers." Laughing erupted all around me.

"A witch who does not know of her witch-hood? That is unheard of!" a figure roared.

"A witch without powers isn't a witch at all!" one boomed, and cackling followed his words. At that, the voices buzzed in agreement.

"She had been using them unknowingly," Moira declared over the noise. "Her emotions are tied to them. She had been altering the weather with her moody, broody nature," she mocked in a whining voice. A roar of laughter stung my ego.

"Can you imagine the pitiful creature?" I heard Damek's voice carry through the noise. "A little thing trudging in the rain all because she did not want to attend school." The others joined in his mocking.

"So mundane," Moira chimed. I could hear the grin in her inflection. She was reveling in my foolishness.

"How did you convince her to open the Gates?" a quieter voice questioned the leader.

"Why, we simply killed her mother." Agony struck me as Moira Darkmore uncovered the truth. Heat radiated in my body as my rage boiled over. I was about to say something when a pinch on my thigh reminded me of the position that I was in.

"Poor little Goddess lost her mama and overreacted." Damek snorted. "Ripped the skies in two!" Everyone snarled in approval.

"Mr. Blackwood learned that her brother was the most important person in her life. We tried to kill him to trigger her power, but complications forced a different scenario." The voices continued to mumble as Ember's cough shocked my core.

"Being a raven is beneficial to my espionage and an elementary way to cause a natural accident," Ember raved to the crowd as they all cheered. I stiffened at the realization. He had been the bird I'd seen so many times over. This horrible man, this thing I had so quickly trusted as he walked me to my doom, had killed my mother. I wanted to vomit, my skin curdling under his grip. He was utterly abhorrent.

"Yes, our beautiful raven played a large role in our story." Moira rolled the words on her tongue as if savoring them. "The High Council will do everything in its power to bring our maker into this world. Our Redeemer."

"To the High Council!" a man hailed. The rest of the creatures chimed in gratitude. At Moira's cheer, I suddenly remembered that Ember did not tell me whom we were set out to meet. He had said he assumed I already knew whom we were meeting. I did not. Redeemer... What horrors waited for my arrival?

"I'm sorry," Ember whispered so, so quietly. A tear made its way down my cheek, and he swiftly removed it with the sleeve of his cloak. How could this man, this murderer, feel badly for the hurt when he was the one most to blame? How could he hold me and warn me of the dangers, knowing he killed my mother—knowing that he was part of the danger?

He began abruptly walking forward, even deeper into the crowd. My skin was crawling at the thought of going nearer. As he approached the tree, I took a peek and noticed a young girl in a cloak who stood at the trunk. The closer we got, the more her tanned face turned pale. He began tilting forward to lower me down to the ground. As he laid me against the tree's roots, I heard his words again.

"Don't run," he whispered. I remembered his words and how he had prepared me for this as much as he could. I thought of the promise he had made me. He said he would protect my family, and it was unmistakably a lie. He had killed my mother. He had no mercy. He was evil and wretched, and I despised him with everything in my being. No, he would not protect my family. They very well could be dead.

"Nesrin," Moira called. The girl in the cloak placed both hands on the tree, and a hissing sound was released by her touch. I felt utter terror at this moment. My nightmare came to life as the roots of the tree grabbed hold of my limbs, pressing me into the soil. The pain and restraint unravelled my sanity as the branches tightened, scraping my skin raw. The cool soil covered my body, making me want to vomit. Was I being buried alive? What was happening? I couldn't stop the tears now as I imagined my death. Eyes closed, I worked on my breathing.

"Keep those roots tight," Damek snarled, and I felt the

unbreakable constriction intensify. Gram had told me that Nesrin's affinity was earth. I was beginning to understand her role in all of this. She hadn't been at the House of Enchantment because she was busy preparing my trap.

"With the strength which she holds in her blood, the witchling will be able to open the other realm on her own, but only for a transitory moment," Moira boomed, gesturing to me. "We do not know how long we have before her blood runs dry, but we will take assurance in knowing we have sent our prayers to the Redeemer. He will hear us."

"Will he come to us?" a stranger asked.

"He will. Sadly, he will not be able to walk freely in this Earthly realm. His blood is tied to his realm, ever binding him to its lands," Moira answered. "Do not fret, for I have dedicated my life to him and will sacrifice my life on this Earth to go with him into his realm to help open the Gates for good." The crowd cheered and thanked her for her heroics.

"How will you do it?" a tattered voice questioned.

"With the rest of you working on this Earthen side, we will work from both ends to find a way."

"You still do not know how?" The creature prodded.

"Enough!" Moira snarled, and the creature yelped in pain. I heard a loud thud, like a body dropping to the nearby ground.

"It is time, Miss Darkmore," said Damek.

Crunchy leaves broke to dust under the crushing weight of feet as she made her way to me. I couldn't hold it any longer. When I felt her hot breath hovering over my face, I broke the façade of sleep. A cold, sharp lance froze me in place. Moira grinned, and I felt complete terror as she tilted the dagger's end at my throat.

"What would you offer me in exchange for your life?" she

crooned. I scowled at her, never moving, never talking. "Not a word? Not anything at all?"

"She has nothing," an older voice crowed.

"A pity... I would've liked to watch you beg." At this, I looked her square in the eye and collected the saliva from my dry mouth. When I spat into the monster's face, she didn't think so much as to blink.

"*Cyka!*" Damek growled in a complaint, but Moira shot out a hand, halting him in his spot. "Little bitch defiles you," he protested. Moira let out a dry laugh.

"It is nothing compared to the agony we shall bring unto her." In a quick motion, she grabbed my hand, and my back seized against the slicing of my palm. I gritted my teeth through the sting, then heaved out a breath as she released my hand. Still, I refused to give her the satisfaction of my words. I would not beg. The pain seared, pulsing as my blood spilled to the ground. My other hand met the same fate. I knew it was only about to worsen as I felt a hand grip my ankle and hold my foot steady. A chill ran through me as I imagined the feel of a knife to my sole. Moira ripped my boots off just before an agonizing pain throbbed at the arch of my foot as she sliced the tender flesh. I had never felt such a piercing pain before. It ran up a nerve, coursing through my leg and all the way into my chest.

As I braced for the other to burn, I tried to calm myself. I needed to focus. I didn't trust Ember or his advice, but I trusted that I could not fight against all these people who were evidently pitted against me. Perhaps lying here, trying not to react, was my greatest advantage for escape. My life depended on my focus and strength.

"*Immolationis hic animae. Apertus inferi porta,*" Moira boomed, pulling my attention to her. Growing up with Gram allowed me the bit of understanding I needed to comprehend her words. *Inferi* was Hell, and I was about to be sacrificed to it. The flock followed her lead, chanting her invocation.

"Open the Gates," they all intoned. *"Apertus inferi porta."*

The ground beneath me rumbled as an Earth-shattering cry escaped my lips. The roots in which I rested detained me at once. They twisted now, pulling at my limbs. It felt as if they were trying to rip me in half. The stretching burned and itched all over as the ground beneath gave way. I started to sink, leaving only my chest and head above ground. Thick, perverse roots from my nightmares infolded me. Still screaming, my throat was ablaze.

The Earth that covered my body turned to ash, and the roots blistered and sparked around my wrists and feet. The sound of lightning struck and pierced through my entire body, leaving only a deafening ringing in my ears. Dizzily, I looked up at the tree I was rooted to as it cracked in half. It snapped around me thunderously. A pit of fire burst through the bark and flung around the cloaks that stood watching tentatively. Some ducked and panicked, hiding behind the brush. Others simply gawked in shock. I turned to beg the cloaked girl who had summoned the roots for release, but she had vanished from the scene.

The tree splintered and tore, and the fire made its way up and up until I couldn't see any further. The smoke and ash that fluttered around me filled my lungs, and I coughed on the scream that tore at my throat. Hands tipped in long, sharp claws burst through the trunk and tore their way forward— tore their way to me. Strapping arms, glowing and pulsing, followed through, pulling the rest of the naked, glinting figure forward. Behind the massive build of his body, a set of dark feathered wings lifted above his head. Though the smoke permeated the air, I could see him clearly. He was the most astonishing, terrifying thing I had ever seen. He stood atop me, legs wide and revealing. The pain I felt from the trees eased as he bent to rip the roots from my body.

"Get up," he boomed as I stared in horror. His voice was deep and rattling. "Get. Up," he repeated. The roots around me turned to dust from the eruption. Slowly, achingly, I pulled myself out of the dirt, which had covered most of my body. My hands slipped in what I could only assume was my own blood, but I managed to swallow that fear in my greater panic. I stood to my feet, wincing at the pain still fresh under my arches.

"Welcome, Redeemer," Moira choked, tears streaming down her face in awe. He did not reply, never removing his gaze from me. I shivered in place.

"Goddess, you have released me." His voice was other-worldly. The frightening male scanned my face as I blinked away the pain, the terror.

"We, the High Council, your worshippers, have released you, oh prevailing Redeemer," Moira boasted and knelt before him. The creatures that skittered around us instantly dropped to the ground. Some even laid their arms flat on the dirt in high respect. The Redeemer kept his eyes on me, then twisted to wrap his hand around my waist, catching me off-guard. My skin singed and warped at his touch. The claws that stretched around my waist scraped at my navel under my sweater.

"I have been anticipating this evening for thousands of lifetimes," he began. His voice was guttural, impaling to my core. "I have great plans." The creatures surrounding us resounded in answer. With the fire lighting the forest, I could finally see the figures surrounding me. People of all shapes and sizes, dressed in cloaks of all kinds, spanned my view encircling me. There were warped noses among a group with gray-looking skin. I noted that many of them had pointed ears, and most had pointed teeth. I thought back to Ember and wondered if he was like them too. Were there other shapeshifters among us? What kinds of monsters lurked in this wild?

It didn't matter. It had never mattered what kind of creatures lived among the trees. All that was important was their motive. They were here to sacrifice me, and I had stupidly let them. I hadn't fought. I hadn't so much as said a word. Now I stood, faint from the blood loss, blood still flowing from my palms to the ground. Ember must be happy with himself; his plan had worked. All he had to do was promise to keep my most treasured thing safe. He vowed to protect my family, and I fell into his trap.

"We are here at your command," said Moira, still grounded on her knees and head bowed low. She looked weak and pathetic in this position, like a disgusting, insignificant rodent.

"I do not require your service," the voice gleamed.

"What?" Moira said and snapped her head to gaze upon him. She scurried forward like the rat she was. He tightened his grip on me, and I winced at the harshness.

"You, Goddess," he said, towering over me. "I need you," he growled and scooped me up in his arms. I panicked and tried to push off him, but he only gripped me tighter. I was weak, barely able to hold my head up at this point, but the wrath in me fumed, blood red-hot. The madness encompassed me. In the dizzy haze, I saw red and nothing but conflagration. I tilted my head back and let out a scream so fierce the fire within me lit us both. Flame upon flame whooshed around us, toiling my vision. The cuts in my palms sizzled to a close, and I shrieked at the sheer agony. It scorched me all over, and I honestly didn't care. The fire could take me as long as it took him too. He scintillated.

"Impressive," he whirred and closed in on me, dark hair flowing to the front of his face. He opened his beautifully terrifying mouth, released his tongue, and licked me from jaw to ear. The wetness of his mouth sizzled against my flame, and my fire went out in dejection. I was stunned and instantaneously outraged.

"No," I started, looking around me. My flames were gone. My perfect flames and the power within me sputtered out.

"I am built of fire, Goddess. It does not impair me," he seethed, licking his lips. "Cinnamon…" My body recoiled, and I shifted my weight away from him. As I did, I noticed that his body was rigid, as if he were stuck in place. I tried to move aside, tried to gain some traction, but the minute I did, he pulled me in closer. "My divine, mischievous Goddess… You are going to bring me so much pleasure."

"Wait—" Moira started, but the Redeemer slammed a wall of fire into the ground to guard us. "She is of no use to you! She was meant to die. A sacrifice for you!"

"A gift," he rumbled, flame dancing all around us. He turned us around and faced the towering tree that splintered and blazed before us. My heart lurched when he held me over the base of the tree. The ground had disappeared, a sky forming below our feet. I had to get away; I had to get out of his hold.

"Don't hurt her!" I heard Ember shout from behind the barrier of fire. The monster was going to drop me into thin air.

"Don't!" I lashed as he relished in my struggle.

"Come home with me," he ordered and lunged for the tree of my nightmares.

Osbuvïa
Orsimm Cave
Varakane Grotto
Palace
Emorïa
Castle Fortress
Under

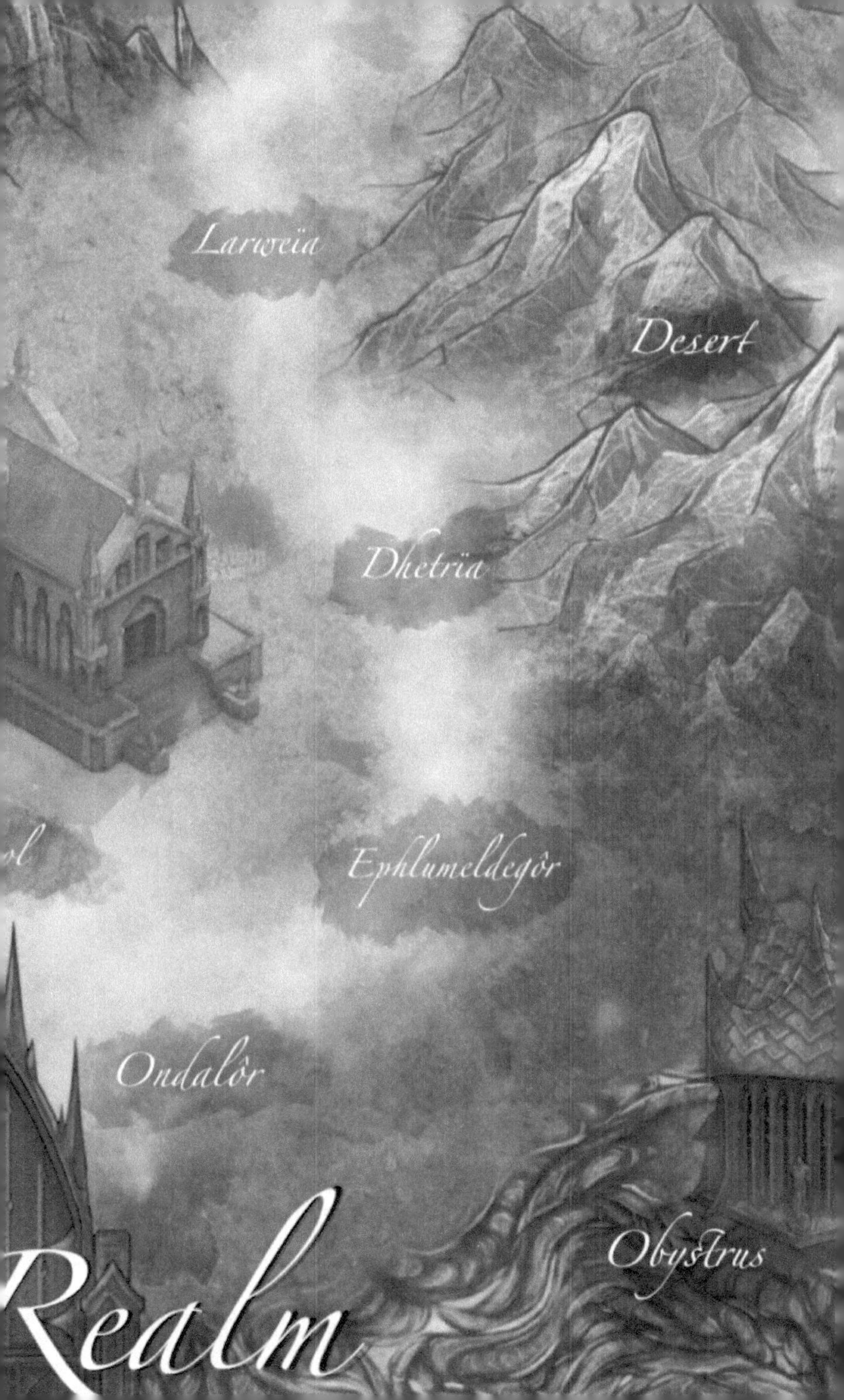

Larweïa
Desert
Dhetrïa
Ephlumeldegôr
Ondalòr
Obystrus
Realm

31

INFERNO

Hell. I was descending into Hell.

"Be still," the monster of a man commanded.

"Let go of me!" I yelled and punched at him for emphasis. He didn't seem at all disturbed.

"Letting go would not be to your benefit," he sneered. The anger I felt kept me from rationality as I looked down below at the parched, molten lands. We must have been hundreds of feet in the air as the dark-winged fiend flew us across the vast unknown.

"I'd rather die," I decided. He laughed, and it rippled through me.

"Please. You are thousands of years old," he retorted. "You cannot die." I froze.

"What? No, I'm almost nineteen," I disputed, only now realizing that I would die before the new year's birthday I had been waiting for.

"Nineteen... In this new skin." A crack like thunder erupted around us. Sparks flew above our heads as I watched the threshold of Earth close. I had been forsaken.

"Why did you take me? You must know I'm not actually

the Goddess, right?" I was unmistakably losing my mind. Who was I speaking to now, so freely, so carelessly? Absurdity spun me into folly, and I shook in his grasp. I hadn't thought about who he was, let alone why he needed me, until now—why he stole me away. I knew what the High Council had intended to do with me. I was carved and bled as a sacrifice to open the Gates when the veil was lifted. I was supposed to die so that Moira could walk through. The winged man who tore from the portal hadn't accepted their blood sacrifice, deciding to pocket me instead. "The High Council tried to kill me just now," I spat. "Are you going to try to sacrifice me too?"

"Sacrifice?" he pondered. "Tempting, though perhaps not." He stopped mid-air, sauntering in place. "I have much finer plans for you." At those words, he blasted downward, and the wind struck my skin raw.

I shrieked, and he laughed, bellowing as we plunged. I braced myself for impact when he came to a stop, falling into rocks and decay. He was solid, and neither of us faltered, save for the hair that whipped around me. I huffed out a howl, feeling delusional.

"Welcome home," he said, and I blinked away the dust from the rubble. We were standing on a castle balcony fit for the devil himself. Skulls and bones lined the balcony edge, and I turned just in time to vomit over its ledge. I was going to die here. I heaved and heaved until nothing was left to expel. I wiped at my mouth and stared at where my bile had landed. My eyes grew wide at the sight. Now that I was no longer in the air and I could see the grounds below, I thought I might be hallucinating. We were in a lone castle, floating in a desert. The building was wrapped by a narrow trench filled with magma and carcasses. I turned to my captor and squinted my eyes, tears welling to the brim.

"Bring me back," I demanded. "Bring me back now." I was

shaking. This couldn't be real. I couldn't have gone into the other realm.

"Bring you back? Why would I do such a thing?" he asked. "We were having such a lovely time."

"No, no, no. This is all wrong!" I shouted. My body caved in on itself. My terror was crashing in and sweeping me over.

"I have been waiting for this moment for ages," he alleged pragmatically. "You are precisely where you are meant to be."

"No!" I screamed. "No, please. My family," I cried. "I have to get back to them. You have to get me out of here!"

"I will do no such thing," he growled.

"I'll do whatever you want. Just take me back," I pleaded. A small crack in my voice expressed my desperation, and his face lit at my words.

"Anything?" he growled, broadening his wings. I wiped at my tears, trying to get a hold of myself amid this horror.

"What's the price?" I coughed. He had brought me here for a reason. There was something he wanted.

"Wed me," he thundered and folded his wings into himself. The blue-black feathers around him settled, and I stuttered wordlessly. Marry him?

"You want me as your bride?" I couldn't hold it in any longer. I let out a laugh so hard I almost fell back over the ledge. He snarled at me, and I wiped at my tears.

"Do you think me a fool, Goddess?" His voice dropped deadly low. I cleared my throat and forced my laugh down.

"No, no. I just... I don't understand," I told him, shoulders raised. I thought I might be losing my mind.

"No, of course, you would not," he snapped. "Allow me to clarify."

Fire ejected from the palms of his hands, and heat swept over me in a flash. The flames were so close; had I moved an inch, I'd have been turned to ash. Looking down, I realized I had been standing in a star-shaped symbol made of coal, trapping me in place. I looked up at him, and he grinned.

"So predictable." He scowled. "Spewing your feast with feet insnare." The fire was getting hotter, and the smell of burnt clothes swirled up into my nose. The blaze tore the air from my lungs, depriving me of oxygen.

"What is this?" I screamed, fighting through my tears to speak.

"My proposal," he spat, and the walls behind him started shifting. Disregarding the fire, I shivered in place as the castle's blackened coloring began to stir, revealing repulsive serpentine creatures. I had lost my glasses between being at the House of Enchantment and being dragged out into the woods, which didn't help my nearsightedness. Now, up close, I could tell that what I thought were tarnished, broken brick fortifications had been a storm of beasts in camouflage forming a wall. They crowded onto the balcony, hissing and biting at my feet.

"Please!" I yelled over the blaze. This was the worst death I could imagine. His eyes glowed red, and he turned away from me. The creatures covered in blackened scales cackled as the fire around me began to sputter.

"Put her in the oubliette," my imprisoner ordered. The creatures slid from the ground and onto their hind legs, sinister in their bodies of a serpent and human combined. Their creepy, rotting smiles grew wide as they waited for the flames to cease. Their bony, lumbering bodies stood tall in comparison to my frame. I cringed away as their crooked clutches clawed at my arms. As they forced their hands over my body, a jade substance smelted onto my bare skin. I let out a shriek at the blistering of my flesh, the matter moving as if it breathed. The fear in my blood immobilized me. I fought to keep my awareness from going under as their poison slinked up and around my neck. Still screaming, the slime crept into my mouth, cutting off the cries as the paralysis of their venom took over.

They dragged me through halls where shadows lurked in the darkness. Barely conscious, I noted the fortifications made of broken boulder-stone, grimy and ancient. I tried kicking my feet at the mass, but my efforts barely made a dent. When the group of reptilian beasts came to a halt, I could hardly lift my head to see where we stood. When they dragged me further into the eerie space, my heart sank as my feet dangled above a hole so deep that I had to believe it was bottomless.

"In you go," hissed the creature to my left, voice sour in sound. He and another held me above the pit. The drop was dizzying to look at.

"You can't be serious!" I exclaimed. I could barely feel my tongue. Bile rose to my mouth as the poison fought against my immune system.

"Try not to lose your head," he replied. The scaly creatures screeched in pleasure at my apparent terror. Goose bumps covered my entirety.

"I'll die!" I choked, jaw still tight from paralysis. "Isn't it enough that you've poisoned me?" The oozing slime slipped through the cracks of my teeth. The inside of my mouth was numb, but I felt it dribbling down my chin.

"Oh, Goddess..." he hissed slowly. "The pythrants have only just begun knowing the great Goddess of the universe. What is the fun in a poison death?" He beamed at me and shook me provokingly over the black hole. My unresponsive body twitched at the thought of the fall. I was dangling over a pit, unable to move. My body was lifeless, and there was nothing I could do.

In an instant, the claws released me, and I fell hard and fast into the black hole beneath me. The wind whipped me in all directions, and my clothes tore on rocks that stuck out of the walls. I couldn't feel the ripping of my skin as it snagged on jagged pieces of the trap, but I knew the damage was there with every slam my body took. I wanted it to stop. I couldn't even lift an arm in an attempt to grab onto something— anything that could slow the drop. The venom had fully seeped in, and it felt like I had been falling for an eternity, frozen in time. With a forceful crash, my body struck the ground, and I croaked at the crunching sound of the impact.

32

THE STARS

Darkness tightened around my mind as I went under.

"Get me out of here!" I sobbed, but nobody answered. My head felt like it was underwater. "Please, help me," I wept into my palms. Searing pain stabbed at my temple. As I looked up to find its cause, I could barely see a thing. In the blink of an eye, I spotted fire-plagued wings that supported the bloodcurdling monster in front of me. He scraped a nail on my head and dragged it across my face. The cut along my cheekbone throbbed at the incision.

"You deserve worse than this," he told me, though I couldn't see his lips. The light from his flames was too bright to make out his face. "You deserve a million lifetimes of torture and torment for the mockery you dared display." My body trembled at the might of this beast that stood before me.

"Please..." I begged, tears trailing down my chin. I tried to stop the shaking, but my body wouldn't listen.

"Get up," he boomed. "Get. Up." My legs wouldn't budge.

"I can't..." I felt defeated.

"Get up," he said again. "Get up!" His fist met my face with a thud. My nose cracked at the touch of his wrath.

"I can't!" I cried, weeping into my hands again. Blood pooled into my palms.

"Get up!" he roared. "Get up! Get up!" He was screaming now. Over and over, his voice reverberated in my ears.

A warm gust blew into my hair, familiar and kind. I stopped breathing at the touch.

"You are here...." That *voice*. It hovered quietly around my thoughts. The words molded slowly, and I shuddered at the formation. My breath quivered at the warmth, and I cried even harder. The beast in front of me continued his command.

"Get up!" he demanded, and a sudden sting lashed me from all sides. It burned like a whip dipped in poison. I remained lying on the ground, hands in my face.

"Tell me where you are." The voice brushed past the barrier in my mind, lucid and desperate. "Tell me how to find you." Another strike from the beast's whip came crashing down, but the wind around me hindered its landing.

"Who..." I tried, but my panting cries got the best of me.

"Tell me his name." The voice in my head grew frantic. "Tell me, and I will avenge you. Tell me, and I will take your pain." The voice was dark now, shielding me.

"I," I sniffed. "I don't know his name," I cried. The wind caressed me again.

"Show him to me," it said. "Open your eyes and show me his true face."

"He will hurt me!" I sobbed. The breeze whipped around me in response to my fear.

"You are dreaming... I do not know who you are, but I know your dreams. I promise," it whispered past the barrage in my mind. "This is your nightmare. Open your eyes."

When I removed my hands from my face, I appreciated

that I could see again. Barely, but I could see. A flash of the monster's smile stabbed at my wounds, and he disappeared instantaneously. I couldn't materialize his face. I had forgotten what he looked like. He was gone, though, and for that, I was relieved.

The skies around me danced, and the stars flew faster than light, causing the entire picture to glow around me. I was floating again, as I had been in my dreams for a while now. The warm breeze lifted me higher and higher into the skies, and I swam in a veil of clouds. The ache had vanished, but my nerves were wrought. I closed my eyes, humming to myself, trying to relieve the pain.

"Worry not, little child... You are beautiful and wild...." The warmth around me caressed me in an embrace.

"Safe..." I heard the dream sigh.

"Safe..." I echoed and drank in the beautiful night sky.

33

ABYSS

When I woke, a copper tang enveloped my senses. I smelled it, and I tasted it; I bathed in it. My face and body were pinned to a hard, hot surface that made the ache in my head pulse. The agony from the drop roused me with a jolt. The terrible landing must have broken me every which way. Every part of my frame was twisted in the wrong direction. It was pitch black, and I could not see a thing, though I understood that somehow, someway, my foot was buried in my armpit. I had a quick realization that I was not dead, but I certainly should be.

The popping of bones gave me shivers as I lifted myself onto my elbows and forced myself upward. Everything was stiff. My leg strained in the crook of my arm as the muscles slowly allowed it to slip from its grasp. My knee shattered as it hit the solid ground.

"Gods!" I shrieked and shoved myself onto my ass.

"There are no Gods down here, child," an elderly voice resonated in the darkness. My eyes widened in alarm, but I saw nothing. I was not alone in this obscurity.

"Gods. Ha!" said another; their sarcastic laugh rang up and around me.

"They would not gamble," said an echo from behind. I huddled into myself and buried my head in my legs. My spine rippled, cracking from neck to tailbone at the movement.

"You cannot hide from us, little lady," said a sorrowful-sounding ricochet.

"You cannot hide from any of us." Voices flurried and bounced off the walls. Sad, weeping cries splintered my hearing. My head was about to burst.

"Stop!" I wailed, voice thrumming in my head. "Leave me alone!"

"No one is alone in the oubliette," said an elderly voice.

"Who are you?" I demanded and looked around me. Still, I saw nothing.

"We are the forgotten," she answered, and the hundreds of voices resounded throughout the abyss, dreadful in their despair. It was impossible to evade them, and my crying became inescapable. I couldn't help myself. I wept with them all.

There was immeasurable melancholy here. There was a fear I had never known before. Regret and sorrow, and exasperating chaos erupted all around me. The voices rang up through the tower of darkness, never settling. They told me of their doom, some dying from the impact, some slowly draining their blood as they waited for their life to cease. Some fought to get out, recalling the scraping of their nails against the rock walls. Each had its own story, but each did not verily exist anymore. They were forgotten, and they did not recall their lives. They were ghosts, haunted by their troubles. They could only identify their death and their regrets. Over and over, their tribulations swirled about and pealed through my head. I wondered how long it would take for me to forget my name.

My crying never ceased, nor did that of those forgotten before me. I didn't know what night or day was. I might die from this madness. I hoped that starvation would take me. I wished for my heart to rest. Hearing all of the voices and their attempts to escape eventually forced my surrender. If all these voices had never made it out, it was likely that I had met the same fate.

"Worry not, little child..." I tried, but I simply couldn't find peace.

I toyed with my mother's ring, clinging to a physical piece of my life as a reminder that I was still living. I stopped trying to escape the void of my trap and instead spent every moment trying to fall asleep, searching for the stars. There was no real escape. Only in my dreams did I find the light within the darkness. I dreamt of stars and moonlight. A tiny tether to luminosity I so desperately craved. So, I slept and slept until I could no longer tell whether I was really in a hole, haunted by its victims, or if I truly lived in the Heavens of the night sky.

34

UPHEAVAL

I woke from a dream of a glowing moon at the sound of voices hissing ahead of me. As I opened my eyes, piercing light streamed from a sliver in the crack of a barricaded door. It was dull but so bright compared to my accustomed place of confinement that I suffered for having looked at it. My eyes watered at the sting as hot, prickly tears leaked out. I hadn't known what any of my surroundings looked like until the very second the light dispersed.

I had imagined my trap being underground with no escape—but realization penetrated as I marked the door that held me in. There had been a way out. I just hadn't found it. At the sight of the towering man ahead of me, my stomach curdled. Creatures crawled on all fours behind his large wings, hissing at the opening of the door. It was a sinful display—a cruel emergence.

Everything in me ached. I was sitting on a solid slab of clay, warm and damp. It was an isolated patch of emptiness, enclosed by fully formed carcasses rotting around the circular dungeon I sat in. As the monster of my nightmares approached me, taking his time for emphasis, I raised my head to look above me. The tower of dirt and decay went up and up, the beginning of my fall nowhere in sight.

The fiend stood a mere foot away from me now, arms crossed and examining me. He was beautiful in all the worst ways.

"Not a scratch," he thought aloud. "And still alive." He raised a pointed finger to me and beckoned me to him. I wasn't sure if I could move, but I knew that this was my only chance out of this hole. As I tried my best to get up from my spot, I slipped under my weight as my shaking fingers caved. A shock of pain pealed through my forearms, but I pushed forward and held myself upright. Shakily, I got up from the ground; the muscles in my calves jerked and groaned as my body steadied under my feet. My rheumatism hit me tenfold as my muscles relied on my joints to carry my body. Nausea caught up to me, and my head swayed in dismay. The monster's hand remained outstretched, waiting to receive mine.

"Where are you taking me?" I asked, my voice barely audible. My tongue felt like sandpaper against my throat, and my mouth was harrowingly parched. Swallowing hard, I placed my shaking hand in his. The sweat from my brow curled under my cheekbone, and he wrapped his fingers firmly around mine.

"To my throne room," he replied. My hand sweltered in his clutch. Flinching, I pulled it back, and he grunted.

"You're..." I fumbled for words as my tongue stuck to my teeth. "It's hot." Wavering, I showed him my hand. Even in the dim light of the oubliette, it was reddened as if he had just steamed it.

"You will grow accustomed to it. Everything is warm in my

castle," he answered and held out his hand yet again. I took it and allowed the heat to wrap around me. It didn't hurt so much as it felt uncomfortable. As he led me out of my hell-hole, the creatures awaiting us howled in excitement. I held my breath as we passed the foul mass.

The castle was every bit as disgusting as the balcony and its dungeon. Though it was dark and depressing, I could see that the walls were slick with maggots. Skeletons were piled in heaps throughout the hallways as he led me upward. I wasn't sure whether to cower from the bugs and bones or the monster that held my hand.

As we ascended further up the towering castle, I spotted a door that filtered light from the cracks in the mold. We were headed straight for it, and the slightest bit of relief settled on my shoulders. He seemed to notice as the tension in my hand ceased.

"You... Do not like the dark," he remarked, not a question but an observation.

"The dark doesn't frighten me," I replied, gluing my eyes to the door. I tried desperately to forget the scary place I'd been dwelling. I was set on finding that light. Nothing would stop me now.

"Do not lie," he snarled, and I jerked back at the volume.

"I'm not lying." I cleared my head and looked at him. His height caught my breath, and I shook the shudder off. "I'm not afraid of the dark. I'm afraid of what I cannot see. The things that hide in the dark." I swallowed, measuring the steps I had left before finally reaching the light.

"Things that hide in the dark," he repeated my answer aloud. "You must be afraid of me," he derided. I exhaled sharply.

"I must be."

We walked up the stairs in silence. The higher we got, the less hot it became. The closer I got to the door, the more eager I was to reach it. My legs were stiff going up the stairs, but I trudged forward as the light left hope in my heart for escape. After a pressing silence, he cleared his throat, and I jumped at the sound.

"I am not a torturous daimon," he said. I choked at his words. *Demon?*

"You're a demon?" I asked hoarsely and barely twisted my head to look at him. Yes. He was indeed a demon. I hadn't had the time to process my capture nor my captor during the whirlwind of it all—the body of a striking human, jet-black hair and striking countenance, but wings, claws, and temperament of a beast.

"Of sorts, yes. I assumed you knew," he said more casually than I would have expected. He looked down at me and adjusted his features. "I am Pyre Malum, daimon of the Dead." *His name.* Something about it rang in my blood. I searched his expression for any sign of having lost my mind. He was indeed physically existent. I was having an actual conversation with a demon—a demon who kidnapped me. Suddenly remembering my capture and all that it had entailed, I realized that I had a lot of unanswered questions that I had completely forgotten about. Without thinking twice, I turned to find answers.

"Pyre... Why am I here? Why did you throw me down there, and how am I still breathing after it all?" I blew, the questions coming out like a storm. "And why did the High Council summon you in the first place?" His eyes grew wide, and he laughed out loud. "What?" He shook his head at me. I shuddered, feeling small and senseless.

"Here, in the Under Realm, it is not like on Earth. We do

not use given names and surnames. We simply are the full extent of titles."

"Oh." I flushed. I didn't want to offend him, and I certainly didn't want to piss him off. "I apologize." He considered me for a moment, and worry started to build in my gut. What was he thinking? Was I about to be reprimanded over such a slight error?

"I enjoy it," he decided. "You may call me Pyre, Goddess." At the mention of the Goddess, I stomped up the last few stairs alone. My knees protested.

"Do not walk away from me, maiden," he hollered from below.

"Stop calling me that name. I am not the Goddess, and I am not a maiden." I was getting testy, but I couldn't stop myself. It was like an inexorable reaction to him.

"Not a maiden?" he crooned. "That could hardly be true." How would he know if I were unwed and celibate? At his vexing dispute and personal intrusion, I reached for the knob on the lit door and yanked at it to open. My wrist fractured at the force as I noticed how frail my arm felt.

"Fuck!" I squealed and detached my hand from the hold. The weight of my body pulled me down as the door did not budge. Before I could tumble down the stairs, the demon caught me by the shoulders and stood me upright.

"It is as if you are challenging death," he said mockingly.

"Haven't I died already?" I asked. "If not, would it hurt to try?" I grumbled, feeling helpless and so very trapped. I rubbed at my wrist as he opened the door with the force of a thousand hurricanes and gestured for me to go in.

"It is not sealed." He crossed his arms, satisfied by his might.

"Seriously? Super strength?" I muttered to myself. "What

are the chances I make it out of here alive?" He snorted as I passed the threshold.

"Leave so soon?" he mused. "We haven't yet gotten to the good part."

"I am a human," I emphasized the last word. "I don't belong here." He came to my side in three long, easy strides.

"We shall see."

35

ELUCIDATE

The room that Pyre Malum and I stood in was bright and open, and I basked in the floodlit air. The castle was built with big, sturdy rocks and clay, and the walls in this room were lined with open windows looking out into the sunlit skies. There was no glass in any of the openings, making the tug to run and jump out of one of them hard to resist. At this moment, I physically felt hope warming my bones again as I relished in the open space. Yet the hope in my chest quickly faded as I turned to look at the intimidating male before me.

"Sit." He gestured to the throne carved of bone that sat in the middle of the mostly empty room. I hadn't even noticed it, far too enthralled by the open windows. As I looked around now, I saw that it was one of the very few pieces of furniture in the room. At the far end, directly across from the chair, I spotted an oblong table with books upon books upon books. My heart fluttered beneath my skin. What those relics might tell, I couldn't even begin to imagine. I hadn't considered that the Under Realm would have books or anything mundane in general, for that matter.

My captor watched me as I examined my new cage. He was still waiting for me to take a seat, dark-feathered wings fluttering behind him. "If you please," he insisted, motioning again. As I looked more closely at the predominating piece of furnishing, a wave of disgust rolled in the pit of my stomach.

"I'll pass," I said, grimacing at the dead remains.

"Sit, and I will explain." When I didn't move, he added, "I wish to see you seated in the hearth of my castle." Instead of walking to the throne, I lifted my head and made straight for the table, footsteps light and steady. I could hear his temper rattling in the flap of his feathered wings with each step I took.

"I don't do skeletons," I said over my shoulder and blew at the dust that covered the table and its contents.

"Skeletons can be beautiful," he answered. "Like yours, for example. Perhaps if you anger me too deeply, I will use yours as a stepping stool to my throne." My muscles clenched at his threat. I couldn't let him tear me down. I knew, deep in my gut, I couldn't afford to show him an ounce of fear. This male was soaked in complacency and dominance. I understood that he could hold it against me if I exhibited distress.

"I don't do smelly feet either," I retorted, voice graceful as I turned to look at his feet. He only huffed, and I flushed, suddenly realizing his feet were bare, along with most of the rest of him. "Speaking of which, where are your clothes?" I dared question. "You know? The kind that would cover your smelly feet and..." I choked on my words, voice hitching. I couldn't stop my eyes from trailing the length of his tall build. My gaze snagged as I found the small brief that scarcely covered his unmentionable region. "And, um... Other areas." He stiffened.

"I do not need them. I am not in battle," he replied and broadened his shoulders in confidence.

"Are you not at all concerned by my gaze?" I asked, trying

to sound as confident as he seemed. This was an unexpected territory I was unfamiliar walking.

"I invite it." He grinned, then examined me and my presumably dirty, blood-stained clothes. My attire had been burned, torn, and overly worn. I could only imagine what he saw when he looked at me. I kept my eyes on his face, ensuring I didn't look any further. This was, after all, the first semi-exposed man I had ever seen. I lay on my hip and let out a breath. I didn't know what to do with myself. He sneered, looking me up and down as if he could smell my unease.

"Fine. Wear whatever you want. Just tell me what I'm doing here," I breathed and turned back to look at the pile of filthy tomes. I toyed with the edge of a leather-bound hard-cover, trying to seem unperturbed.

"You are looking at it." I beheld the books, and uncertainty swept over me. When I looked back at him for more of an answer, he had thrown a pair of fitted trousers on, and I felt the slightest bit more relaxed. Where they'd come from, I had no clue.

"This is a pile of dirty books. Help me out here." He slammed his fist into a nearby boulder, and his nails screeched along the rock. I froze in place, the sudden outburst catching me off-guard.

"You have not any patience, Goddess," he blew out and wiped at his hands, retracting his claws.

"I told you to stop calling me—"

"I will call you whatever I please, Goddess. You are in my home." Smoke filled the air, and my limbs turned to ice—frost biting at my tongue. It was easy to speak with him as if he were just a person. I had let my guard down at his teasing, neglecting the fact that this was no mere man. His rage was so powerful and incredibly threatening to my safety. The whip of his wings threw pages out onto the floor, reminding me of his might. I had to calm him. I couldn't bear another moment in the oubliette.

"I've forgotten my place, Pyre," I spoke to him softly. "I apologize for the impoliteness."

"Truly?" he rumbled thickly, scowling his thin almond eyes at me. Smoke eddied around him in time with his temper.

"Truly," I assured him. He folded his wings neatly behind him and rubbed at his temple.

"I apologize for having kept you locked up for such a lengthy time," he confessed and brushed a pointed hand through his mangled dark hair. "I regret to admit my temper lasted the five days, but..." he trailed off, and I went entirely rigid.

"What?" I stammered.

"Goddess, I—" I cut him off with eyes like daggers.

"Five days?" I roared. "I didn't eat, speak, or see anything for five days?" I could hardly believe it. The tears poured over and gushed out around me. "You're a monster!" I shouted, losing control while the beast, the demon, simply watched. I had been wasting away, losing days and days of my life to the tower of the forgotten. I could've filled an ocean with the waves of vexatious, salted waters that surged from my orifices. It was just like at Gram's when I had had an incident in the shower. I couldn't breathe. I was going to perish in this godforsaken castle.

"Magnificent..." he murmured, and it snapped me back to reality. The water evaporated as it touched the ground at my feet. I felt brainless. Drained and exhausted, I looked up into his eyes, seething.

"Why?" I asked with little sentiment, devoid of emotion. I wiped away my tears, reality seeming false. He raised a brow, sinister and cruel. He tried to pass as innocent, but I could see his true nature written all over him.

"To see if you would live," he divulged as he strode toward me. "To test the truth of my wildest dreams. The fact that you, a woman of Earth, even survived the fall is baffling. But to starve... To be swarmed by the lost in a haunted vault..." He shook his head at me and grinned. "Outstanding." I wanted to vomit.

"Why five days?" I squeaked, barely audible in the crack of my tired throat. "Five fucking days of my life are gone because of you!"

"I needed to be certain that you truly are who I've been searching for, and your will to live needed to be tested." I gritted my teeth at him.

"I'm here," I spat. "I'm alive and well tested. Now tell me what you want and be done with it."

"You do know of my request," he simply said. I shook my head in confusion.

"You were serious?" I blinked at him as he validated my suspicions. "You want me as your wife?" A dry laugh escaped from my lips at the mere thought of it. I hated this man. I loathed him to my very core.

"That is why I brought you here."

"To Hell," I clarified, anger in my tone.

"To the eternal lands of the Under Realm. To my inferno." He beamed.

"I shouldn't be here." I shook. "I am not the Goddess that everyone claims me to be. I don't understand it completely myself, but I swear I am of no use to you. I can't even control my powers."

"But you have them," he said, gesturing to the dampened remains of clothing that clung to me. I wrapped my arms around myself, suddenly aware of the too-close-fitting ensemble.

"I do, but I'm just a human. Just Shivalri."

"Shivalri," he repeated my name. The way he said it sounded like the first spark of an autumn bonfire. Crackling and effervescent. "Shivalri..."

"Yes, exactly," I said, feeling flustered by how foreign my name sounded coming from his mouth.

"Shivalri, Darling, you have much to learn about who you truly are. What you can become." I gulped as he walked to meet me at the table I stood at. He flipped open the most prominent book that lay in front of us. I winced at the closeness we held. Shoulder to shoulder, we looked at the pages.

I knew without having to read that the book was full of dark magic. I felt the wrongness of it in my core. Everything in my body told me to run, but I firmly planted my feet. I watched as he flipped through the pages, showing me images that could only have been drawn before the world came to be. I was in utter disbelief. This one book beat out the Salem House of Enchantment library tenfold.

"I can't read any of it," I confessed, still captured by the awe. It was a language I did not quite recognize, and the writing was scarcely visible due to age. "The images aren't very clear either," I thought aloud. "What exactly am I looking at?"

"You cannot read?" he asked. I huffed a derisive laugh, considering the notion.

"Of course, I can read," I muttered. "Only, I am unable to read in this particular language. Give me English or French, and I can read all day long. It's practically the only thing I occupy myself with."

"Noted." He nodded.

"What does it say?" I scanned the page as he pushed it closer to me.

"It is an invocation," he said, pointing to the page with an image of a crowned woman hovering atop a tree. On either side of the tree knelt two people with wings: one light, one dark. "Long ago, my siblings and I lived freely in the universe."

"My grandmother told me the legends," I said, remembering my awakening in the Grimsbane sanctuary.

"Your grandmother would have told you the legends that made their way to Earth. Only I and my siblings keep this secret," he said, tapping the page.

"Secret?"

"The secret to freedom," he breathed. "You see, when we were free to fly and roam and conquer what we wanted, I ruled." He closed the book, and I shrunk at the sound of its clasp. His wings grew wide again as he walked toward his throne and made his way up the pile of skulls and broken mandibles. The crunching was unbearable.

"Do you rule this place?" I asked, hesitant. "Hell, I mean." He laughed, settling into the rattle of bones.

"Hell, as you call it, is not truly ruled by any," he scoffed. "It is governed by death."

"But you have a castle. And a throne." I pointed to the demon's mess of a seat. "You have some kind of leverage, don't you?"

"I rule the dead." He grinned and shone his pointed teeth. "I rule my empire; my kingdom."

"So, you do rule..."

"In sorts, I do, Goddess," he admitted and held my gaze. "But it is not enough. I want more," he whispered, his eyes turning a bright red I had seen once before. I gulped at the sight of him.

"What does that have to do with me?" My skin crawled with nerves.

"Everything," he replied.

"Cryptic," I scoffed, laughing subtly. He swiftly flew to me and hovered above. He smirked and placed a hand on my head, swiveling us both to look at the book he'd closed. He landed noiselessly on his feet and displayed the text we'd seen earlier. My nerves pricked from the sudden touch and proximity.

"Gaze upon this imagery. What do you see?" he beckoned.

"It's a tree," I said, calming myself. "I'm assuming to the left is a demon like you." I pointed to the image. He hummed in agreement. "To the right is an angel, correct?"

"A God."

"Oh, all right," I mumbled, considering his words. "Is that supposed to be the Goddess?" I asked with eyes fixed on the crown sewn in her hair.

"The Goddess of origin," he answered, then shut the book again. I jolted at the movement, then cleared my throat. I knew that being here was awful and damning, but at this moment, I realized that I did have an opportunity like no other. Here, I could learn everything about the origin of life straight from an original source. My captor had seen it all. The legends involved Pyre Malum in ways that I still did not understand, and I could learn from him if I urged him to educate me. That knowledge was priceless.

"My grandmother told me that the Goddess was given the position of reigning over the Gates of Heaven, Earth, and Hell," I told him. "Is that correct? Does that have to do with your taking me here?"

"Ahh," he sighed. "You do preserve knowledge on the subject." He crossed his arms behind his back and turned to walk away from me.

"Hardly," I said. "But I've been trying to learn. Trying to keep up with all of these changes," I gushed.

"Changes?" He furrowed his brows in confusion. I looked down at my feet, avoiding too much eye contact.

"I didn't know about my powers," I confessed. "I didn't even know about my family's powers or that any of this existed." The memories of my family flooded me. "Nobody told me."

"A Goddess without the knowledge of magic?" He paced back and forth. "How can this be?"

"They were trying to protect me," I defended as my mind grabbed hold of an image. It was Gram's protective eyes. I then pictured Satyra and Raidan laughing at my accidents from our first night as witches.

"What is that smell?" the demon interrupted my thoughts. I shook my head in puzzlement, and as I looked down at our feet, I let out the first smile I'd made in a while. I closed my eyes and shuddered at the feel of exultation.

"It smells like home," I said and bent over to pluck a white daffodil from the ground. When I stood, I saw that he was blatantly baffled.

"Life cannot grow here," he rumbled. His scowl surprised me. I did not understand his drawback. Had I said something to upset him?

"What?" I stammered, confused by the sudden change in him. He scraped his feet through the grass, and it sizzled beneath his feet, vanishing before my eyes. I let only one tear escape and lifted my head high.

"My kingdom is that of death," he explained. "It is of destruction and decay. It is not a place for life."

"I am alive, and I am here," I said, eyes sharpening. "You saw to that."

"Yes," Pyre Malum grumbled lowly. He stood before me and took me in. I wanted to scream, to run, to die. I wanted anything but this—this beast beholding me with hungry eyes. I wanted to go home. I had conjured a beautiful memory of my family and had grown earthen life in pleasure. He extinguished my joy without a single thought. He took no pity on me. I settled my emotions and mustered the courage to brave a gentle face for the sole fact that it could save me from his wrath.

"I don't want to fight with you," I finally managed to say, eyes locked on his fierce, ruddy gaze. His eyes scanned mine, searching.

"Nor do I, Goddess." He let out a lungful of air. "I hold you high in respect."

"Respectfully, your etiquette proves otherwise," I rebutted. He was about to dispute, but I stopped him from blasting. "It is done with. You let me out of the oubliette, and for that, I am thankful. Now I will listen to your request in hopes that we can work together. In hopes that I can go back home and smell the grass and never have to let go of my family again."

He fluttered his wings and turned to look out of a window to his left. I thought that might have been the end of our conversation when he turned his back on me. He gave me no indication as to whether he would work with me. He told me he held me in high respect, but his actions spoke much louder than his words. I watched him now as I twisted the stem of the spring narcissus in my fingers, contemplating approaching him. He looked like he was in his own world. Neither here nor there, as he looked over the ledge.

"Long ago, every being conceivable lived collectively. War upon war broke our universe apart, forcing us all to go our separate ways." I watched him settle in the cast of the reddened sky. He was looking far off as if seeing what he recalled. "I was ripped apart from my siblings. I was the only one banished to a daimon realm, sentenced to give up my freedom and forced into eternity alone. Those of us banished here were not tried nor given a chance to rebut. We were torn away from our first world and twisted into captives. I am bound here, and I want to change that."

"Can you?" I asked.

"With your help, I can," he said, then turned to me. In the light of the red sun, the monster's face was breathtakingly beautiful. His skin was almost pearlescent in the beam. He had flowing black hair that almost brushed the tops of his sculpted shoulders, golden eyes, a strong jaw, and was strapping beyond measure. He was a striking statuesque marvel of a man. I had to remind myself that it was only a shell, and evil lurked in every part of his existence.

"Pyre, I don't know if I can—" He stopped me.

"You can, and you must." His eyes flared wide. "I have been waiting eternally for this moment. For you."

"Please just tell me what you want from me." I couldn't take the obscurity any longer. "Please." He left the windowsill and made his way back to me. I stiffened at the approach of the tall, winged man. When we stood a foot apart, he knelt and threw a fist over his bare chest. He looked down for a long moment. Up close, I could see that his hair was a blend of black, dark as night, and small streaks of silver, reminding me of tourmaline. The silvery onyx mane curled over his ears and down his neck. From this angle, he seemed almost human, save for the wings that spread my width thrice.

"Wed me, Goddess," he implored, then looked up into my eyes. "I vow to defend you and give you everything your heart desires."

"I—" I was dumbfounded. My heart was beating so fast I thought it might burst from the fear.

"Wed me and fulfill the sacred invocation. Take my name embedded in your soul and share my power. Share yours with me," he insisted, scraping at his chest. His nails dug into the flesh. His words rang in my head, burying themselves into my mind.

"My power?" I whispered, lifting my fingers to my mouth in disbelief. I tried to stop my lip from quivering, but my hands shook. He wanted my power.

"Our power," he amended. "The Goddess, you, Goddess, have the right to choose a world to awaken."

"No," I stammered. "That doesn't make any sense. I am nobody. I am nothing..." I could feel myself growing light-headed from the panic.

"You are unbelievably important," he told me, still on his knee. "You are everything."

"What can I possibly do for you?" I shrilled. "Conjure tears when I'm sad? Fire when I'm angry? I have no real power. I am just a problem caught up in this centuries-old dilemma."

"You are the answer to it all," he bellowed, voice deep. "The prophecy has finally arrived. Light and dark must forge together to rule the realms. I can be that for you," he ground out.

"The prophecy..." I shuddered. Bits and pieces of what I had learned through Gram and the High Council circled in my mind. Was this what I was meant to do? Was I supposed to work with this demon to fix the veil? It couldn't be. Our motives were entirely different. "It can't be...."

"I will train you, Goddess. I will make you unthinkably powerful, as you were meant to be. We will work on growing your power together," he said determinedly. "You were born for this, forged from good and evil. It flows through your veins. Even now, you feel it in your heart. Tell me, Goddess, what is your heart telling you? Do you truly believe that you are nothing?"

His words felt like a splash of cold water to the face. I glanced around the room, genuinely looking at where I was. I, a nobody, stood before a kneeling demon in the Under Realm. I was sought after by some of the most powerful beings ever to exist. Logic told me that I was essential and that Pyre Malum needed me, but my heart was shouting at me to get out and that this was not my place to be.

"I don't know what you mean, Pyre." I fumbled for words. He looked up at me from under his brow, waiting for me to give in. "What am I to do?" I asked, shaking. This time, he seemed contented with my query—a change from his usual response to my chaotic and inquisitive mind.

"Your heart is divided between the realms that split your Earthen tree. Bind your soul with mine and allow me my freedom." His eyes ignited at his words.

"You want to open the Gates." I shuddered, realizing the intent behind his words.

"I want to be freed from the Under Realm," he refined.

"I... Can't." I stumbled, knees quaking. "That would mean destruction for my world. You said it yourself! You rule the dead. This place is of destruction and decay. I can't do that to my family or Earth. I can't just choose to open the Gates. Unleashing Hell on Earth would cause us total devastation..." Shaking, I dropped to the floor and leveled with him, meeting his scrutiny. I searched his face for any sign of sympathy, a small token of understanding. We were eye to eye, equally hot with indignation and determination. Defeat ate away at me, and I sunk into my kneeling posture when his face formed a frown. I dropped the flower I held and watched as it fell between us. His breathing worsened, the sound becoming rough as he audibly gritted his teeth. His growl was unholy.

"You will choose me." He grabbed me by the shoulders and tore me from my ground, zooming through the castle in a heartbeat. Though he held my head to his chest, my heart stopped as we crashed through a door, and metal clanged behind me as my captor left me in a new grave.

"Please," I begged, scrambling on the floor. I rushed to get up and grabbed hold of the bars caging me in. Panic rose up my skin as he turned his head from me. "Don't do this to me again." The plea was desperate. "I will die! I need food and water. Please, let me out!"

"There is no such thing in my kingdom of the dead. Nothing truly lives here. Nothing ever grows here." He locked the door in place.

"Please!" I yelled. "I will die!" He looked at me now, studying me. I could sense he felt powerful having me in this position, begging for my life. I felt entirely debased.

"You still do not understand?" he sneered. "You are immortal in this realm—as you should be. You need no sustenance. You cannot die."

"Please! What can I do?" I begged, groveling at the barred door. He came closer now, the two of us chest to chest, save for the gated door between us. The sound of our panting stretched on, mine from panic, his seemingly from rage. I didn't dare blink. Steadily, he lowered his head and, before I could react, pressed a heated kiss to the top of my hair, whispering something I couldn't make out. I stopped breathing and tightened my grip on the bars. Taking a small step back, he exhaled a hot breath that pooled all around me, smelling like smoke. His eyes burned holes in mine, and I gulped dryly. This unexpected moment of tenderness completely threw me for a loop. I was utterly confounded.

"Just say the word, and you will be freed." He smiled wickedly through the bars. "*We* will be freed."

LOCKUP

That night was the first in which I truly felt the crushing weight of my fate. I was trapped in a real-life nightmare that I could never wake from. When I was left to rot in the oubliette, reality and time ceased to exist. I bathed in the darkness, expecting never to wake. Here, aware of actuality, the desolation was inescapable.

I took in my surroundings and felt the exhaustion ripple through me. I was in a medieval-looking dungeon. There was a tiny window at the top of the room to see out into the sky. It didn't cast much light; however, I could see my environment thanks to a sliver of light cast down the dark hall. The demeaning way it felt to be flown into this gaol stung my heart. I was not an object to be used or discarded, but the more I fell into this new world of chaos, the more I felt small. I grabbed hold of the bars that held me in and tried my best to peer down the corridor. There was nothing of use to help me escape. There were no people, no items lying around, just grimy castle walls that went for miles and miles, not a thing in sight.

I knew I wasn't alone when I heard the serpentine hissing

echoing from somewhere in the tower. I backed away from the door now, steadying my stance in case of attack. My knees groaned at the thought of quick movement. Dirt scuffed and blew clouds of dried clay in front of the barred doorway as the voices grew louder. I shuddered at the sight of rough feet, claws digging into the floor and creeping my way. The hissing filled my room, engulfing me in trepidation.

"How goes the Goddess?" the tallest of the creatures asked, curling a clawed hand around a metal bar. When I didn't answer, he hissed. "Does the Goddess not hear us?" His smile grew wide, showing rows of jagged teeth. I grimaced.

"I am fine," I swallowed, taking it all in. They were wrong in every sense of the word. They had full chests, arms, and legs like a man, but a tail as thick as a torso wound behind them. Though shaped like man's, their faces had slits for a nose, and their eyes glowed yellow in the dimness of the prison. With blackened scales sunken into their skin, it was hard to look at without being a little repulsed.

"Why does the Goddess not please our Lord?" the figure crooned, tilting its head to the side. The other creatures came closer now, coming to stand alongside the tall one. They sniffed at the openings of my cell door, and I suddenly grew glad to have that barrier.

"It is not my problem if your Lord is not pleased with me," I said, gritting my teeth. The serpents hissed at my response, but I stood my ground. "I cannot do what he asks of me."

"Cannot?" one questioned.

"Will not?" asked another, who stood carefully, protective over the other. They scraped at the metal bars, and I flinched at the sound. They watched me in satisfaction as they toyed with me.

"I can't." I exhaled. "I'm not the person you think I am."

"You are the Goddess," the head creature said matter-of-factly. The one next to him shook his head in agreement. "You are whom our Lord needs." I was beginning to get frustrated with the company that stood before me—no longer seeming harmful but more of an annoyance. I huffed an audible sigh and looked at them, coming closer to the door. I almost felt daring at this moment as I easily approached the creatures. Being thrown into this new life came with a strange sense of familiarity toward the abnormal. I had to pull my mind back and remind myself that I was talking to creatures and demons... I was a witch, and I was here, in the Under Realm.

"I'm just a human," I said, pointing to myself. "See? I don't belong here." The creatures hissed at my approach.

"You smell like magic." The creature smiled. I could taste the rot sifting in its mouth through the air.

"I have magic," I acknowledged.

"Magic is all we need." They all curled their claws around the door's bars now as if to try and open it. As if to get to me.

"I do not know how to wield my magic, and even if I did, I wouldn't do anything that could cause harm to Earth."

"You would harm our realm?" the largest spat at me. I ducked away as the venom sizzled an inch from my feet. I suddenly remembered what it felt like to be under the influence of said venom. The one who stood behind the leader tugged at his arm as if to stop him from going any further.

"Be careful," the creature said to its leader. He did not turn to look at him.

"Well, Goddess?" the large one crooned.

"I would do no harm to any realm," I said firmly, looking not only at the leader but also at the others. "I would never wish detriment upon anyone. That is not who I am." I knew this to be true. Even if I had the power to destroy the Under Realm, I wouldn't do it. I knew that these evil beings were not all malevolent once, long ago. They did not all deserve punishment. I knew that war was never one-sided, and though the demons were all cast to one place, Gram said they were not all cruel. However, having met all of these creatures from Hell and experiencing their might gave me pause to reconsider that thought.

"She speaks the truth," the creature said, breaking my chain of thought. "I can smell it upon her lips." I curdled at its words, pressing a hand to my mouth.

"You can smell a lie?" I questioned, eyes wide. Now I was intrigued.

"Pythrants will always smell lies," it answered, sharing its wicked smile with the rest of its companions. "Flavors fall from your lips. Truths smell like honey, fresh from its comb."

"What do lies smell like?" I asked, curious.

"Rot." I cringed at the thought.

"What is your name?" I asked the leader.

"Alriq, my Goddess," he answered, blatantly surprised by the question.

"Why are you here, Alriq?" I asked. "Why are any of you here?" I looked upon each of them, and they skittered under my watch. At their reaction, I wondered if Pyre Malum, my captor and their Lord, had sent them here to spy on me. Better yet, I wondered if perhaps they snuck here to see me, too curious for their own good.

"We came to see the Goddess," one replied. "The one who will free us all." I almost felt sorry for them when they looked at me now. Their eyes, though otherworldly, seemed full of something akin to hope.

"I'm sorry," I started, taking a step back. "You've wasted your time in coming here. I am of no use to you." I sighed heavily, feeling weirdly dramatic, and walked to the back of the cell. I sat in a corner and curled my arms around my knees; all the while, I kept my eyes on the pythrants.

"In time, Goddess," the tallest creature replied. "In time…"

With those last words repelling off the walls, Alriq took a spot a few feet from my door. The protective one put a hand on Alriq's shoulder and gestured for the group to leave. Alriq seemed to be standing guard as the rest of the pythrants slithered away and left me to my thoughts. I had to develop a plan, a strategy, to get myself out of here. I needed to start from the beginning.

I could barely think straight after all of this. How had this happened? How was this possible, and why did Pyre Malum take me as his prisoner? Hadn't he understood by now that my powers were feeble? Did he not know that I could not help him, even if I wanted to?

His words from before rang in my head. *"Your heart is divided between the realms that split your Earthen tree. Bind your soul with mine and allow me my freedom."* The image of the tree came to the forefront of my vision, making me question whether or not I had lost my sanity.

Pyre Malum wanted what anyone wanted: freedom. When I thought of him now, it was hard to imagine him as an inhuman creature after seeing the array of emotions he displayed. He wasn't what I expected a demon to look like. I had pictured monsters from my wildest nightmares—ones with marred skin and forked tongues. The pythrants were more demon-looking than my captor. Pyre seemed to have many human qualities. Despite most of them revolving around a handsome face chock-full of anger, I could understand where he was coming from. He was trapped, just like me.

He wanted me, the Goddess, to marry him so that he could leave Hell. Something about our union would somehow bind our powers together, therefore liberating him and the Under Realm. That is what he so desperately needed. The problem was that even if I were to accept, there would be no way of it working due to my inability to use my magic correctly. That was my biggest setback. Every problem I've faced since becoming a witch has been based on the fact that I have no control over my powers. If I could convince him to teach me how to work with magic, get stronger and become more powerful, then maybe I'd have the chance to fight him off or at least escape. He seemed to know a lot about magic, and he had ancient books from a time when magic was born. I'd have to convince him that teaching me was the only way his plan would work. I had to play a game of chance with the demon of the Dead. I had to learn my magic.

37

GAME PLAN

When morning came, I felt better prepared. I didn't know what to expect from the day, only that I knew what I had to do if I wanted any chance of getting out of here and seeing my family again. I hadn't slept through the night, which made me feel a weird sense of tranquility. I had focused all of my thoughts on different scenarios in which my escape would be successful. Now that the light was streaming down the hallway again, I knew I'd be facing my plans soon.

"Good morning, Goddess," a voice called. I started at the intrusion. Pyre stood in front of the barred door, picking his teeth with a toothpick. I rubbed at my eyes, removing the sleep I hadn't had. My bones ached from having lain on the hard floor all night. I eased myself up with a grimace and dusted off my shabby clothing. I looked at my captor, and horror struck me as I realized he did not hold a toothpick but rather a tiny finger-sized bone. I cringed at the thought of what former body used to be attached to it. I shook the ick off and leaned against the corner wall I'd been sitting at. He threw the bone into the dungeon's hallway.

"Good morning, Pyre," I greeted him. He grinned and strode forward, looking intently at me.

"I could grow accustomed to hearing that name on those lips," he murmured. My heart tumbled into my guts. He was more handsome than I had remembered, which rubbed me the wrong way. I suddenly recalled yesterday's closeness and cringed. I should not be thinking of a demon as attractive. It was unthinkable. But there he was, silver-spun black hair curling down the nape of his neck. His eyes were golden now as he watched me. When my eyes landed on his lips, his smirk grew. Looking away, I got up from the ground and dusted myself off.

"Hi," I mumbled. He smiled.

"Have you rested?" he asked, looking me up and down.

"No," I replied. "I couldn't." He frowned.

"That will not do," he said and opened the door. My eyes darted to the opening.

"How did you do that?" I gestured to the door, bewildered by what I had just seen. He didn't have any keys to unlock it. He had simply opened it. He laughed and turned away from me.

"You did not think I would truly lock you up, did you?" I was shocked at his response. That was indeed what I had thought.

"What?" I asked, now examining the door. I could've sworn it was locked. Then again, I hadn't seen him lock the door in place last night. I was too busy panicking. My fury rose at the blatancy of his nonchalance.

"It was not locked to you, Goddess," he huffed.

"You didn't lock me in?"

"Technically, yes. However, it was more to lock others out. You could have opened the door as you pleased." He shrugged.

"I don't understand," I said, watching his face, looking for some form of explanation. He sighed dramatically and looked away.

"I bestowed you access," he replied, still not looking at me. "I gave you permission to walk through any of my doors with a well-crafted abjuration atop your head." My eyes grew wide, and I felt the heat creeping into my bones.

"Huh?" I stammered. He stiffened at my reaction.

"*Viværte érrentrari.* With my touch and word, I granted you free access. Only you and I can walk against the wards of my enchanted locks. A sort of protection." I blanched at his words, arms slackening to my sides. A memory flash flooded my mind as I remembered him kissing my head yesterday. He shrugged and continued down the hall. I stood in place, watching him. His wings flapped once and folded into themselves as he marched away. I was so confused, but mostly, I was angry with myself. I hadn't even tried getting out last night. I had accepted my defeat without a fight. Alriq was standing guard all throughout the night, but still, I hadn't tried.

"Where are you going?" I called to him.

"Come," he said, and I quickly and stiffly followed behind him.

As I walked down the warm, damp halls, the pythrants around us slithered and prowled. I saw Alriq, the one who had spoken to me last night, and waved a hand at him. He furrowed his brow and dipped his head in my direction. His shielding companion rounded a corner and quickly bowed to the demon beside me.

"My Lord," he said, head still lowered. Pyre only grunted, and the pythrant slipped away to meet Alriq at his side.

"Have you thought on my request, Goddess, or are you still sulking?" Pyre asked. I could hear his sneer through the question as if he were amused. I couldn't believe that he was still on this track. I took a deep breath and let out a sigh as I came up next to him. Walking side by side felt strange. His wings brushed alongside my arm, and I flinched at the touch. He quickly wrapped them back behind him, catching my shrink. "I do not wish to harm you, Goddess," he said and tilted his chin down. I looked up, meeting his eyes, and could see that he was telling the truth; whether he knew how to act on those wishes, I did not know. I didn't think he had the control to rein in his anger.

"I did think about what you asked, Pyre, and I have to say I am still not sure." He huffed at my words. "However, I think you and I can find a way to work together, nonetheless, to find some form of agreement." He raised a brow at me, pausing in place.

"An agreement?" he questioned as he squared his shoulders, making his chest more prominent in his stance.

"Yes," I blew out. "An agreement." I looked away, trying my best not to look too closely at the impossibly perfect physique of this male. As we walked forward, I noted that he was bringing me back to the room with the bone throne and the large table holding all of his books. It was weird seeing it again. Last night I had been trying to picture it, trying to remember what it had looked like, but the only image which surfaced was the rage that burned all around him when I had refused his proposal for a second time.

"An agreement," he murmured, almost inaudibly. His face wore confusion and unconcealed skepticism. I could see the mistrust in the set of his mouth, but the curiosity in him lit from within his dull gold eyes.

"You said that you want me to marry you simply because you want your freedom," I said, now entering the ample space.

"Yes," he replied. "This is true."

"Right," I said. "So even if I agreed to marry you—" He looked at me quickly, but I held out a hand to stop him. "I said *if*," I clarified. "If I agreed, it would do you no good because I still cannot wield my powers. You want me to free you, but you need my powers to work properly," I explained. "I know nothing about magic. My family kept my witchhood to themselves and never told me that I had powers. I don't know the first thing about this," I confessed. "Last night, I was thinking... You seem to have a lot of knowledge on the subject. Not only that, but you have a great collection of books on magic from the old world and books about the Goddess. So, why don't we put them to use?" I looked at him, waiting. When he didn't say anything, I continued. "You teach me what you know about magic, and then we'll see how we can get out of this." He regarded me, face hard as stone.

"Get out of this?" He repeated my words roughly. "What would you like to get out of, Goddess?" That look said everything I needed to scare me. I had worded it all wrong. I took a deep breath and remembered my plan. I had to get him on my side.

"I just mean that maybe we don't have to get married. Maybe we don't need to bind our powers together, and maybe we can just help each other out." He growled at me now, but I persisted. "Without my power, I am not able—"

"You are able," he grunted, cutting me off.

"Pyre, I get it," I said. I walked over to him and steadily took his hand in mine. He inhaled loudly, and it surprised me. The shock we wore on both of our faces was a strange sight to behold. I felt self-consciousness and awkward beneath his observation, but I held firm. "Pyre," I said, gently looking up through my lashes. I played on my innocence as best as I could, knowing that was the most prominent card I had to play. "I can't promise you anything. I can't even promise that my powers will grow to be what we need." I made sure to refer to us as a unit, playing to his wants. He looked at me now with deep resolve.

"They will."

"Maybe, and maybe not. But I can tell you that I will try. I will train as you asked. I will work on bettering my abilities." His brows furrowed.

"What changed your mind?" he asked.

"Freedom," I said, relinquishing a piece of truth. A whirl of wind blew through my hair at the thought of escape. He nodded his head in agreement.

"I cannot remember what freedom feels like," he answered. His sadness made my heart hurt. I could empathize with this demon. This beautiful, scary demon.

"I am sorry, Pyre. Truly, I am," I replied and let go of his hand. He came closer to me now as if my letting go cut a tether he enjoyed. He dipped his head to me, and my blood boiled at the nearness.

"Honey..." he murmured. I put a hand to my mouth, searching his eyes. They were a bright, sunlit gold now.

"I don't tell lies." I flushed, realizing he must be able to smell a lie too.

"We will see about that," he hummed. He tipped his head and turned on his heel, making his way toward the books. I stared at him now, watching his dark feathers flow through the slight breeze. He was so big. Terrifyingly so. He had towered over me just a moment ago, and I hadn't even noticed the height. I thought he might try to kiss me at his former closeness.

Ripping me from my thoughts, Pyre slammed his hands into the table, back rigid. I jumped, clearing my mind. I cautiously approached him and caught the flexing of his jaw.

"Are you all right?" I asked, not sure if I should approach.

He straightened himself up, though his hands held firm on the table.

"Wholly," he answered, still averting my gaze. His nostrils flared. At first, I thought he might be angry, but now I couldn't tell. I walked around the table to stand facing him. He let go of the table's edge and handed me a book.

"What's this one?" I asked, taking it from him.

"A lesson on the world's creation."

38

LE DÉBUT

"To understand magic, we will have to start from the beginning," said my captor-turned-instructor. I nodded, ready and willing to absorb everything he could teach me. I was entirely focused on the task at hand, delighted that Pyre Malum, the demon of the Under Realm, had agreed to teach me about magic. I was going to be tactical and accept every bit of information he gave me. I was more than eager to learn.

"Okay. Let's start from the beginning," I agreed. "That's when you were created, right?"

"Yes," he confirmed. "I was one of the first. One of the first of many. I do not know how much your family told you; however, I will spare you the incredibly long story and cut for the most important pieces."

"I'd like to know everything," I answered, worried he might skip something that would help my escape.

"I will tell you all you need to know," he assured me.

"Thank you," I said, not wanting to push him too much, too soon. With both of us standing at the table, I placed both hands on the hard surface and pulled myself up until I was sitting on the edge. When I settled, Pyre tilted a brow at me in what looked to be confusion or amusement. I did not know which, but he dipped his head in appreciation.

"When the world was whole and hadn't been divided as it is today, every living being existed together in harmony. There were humans, Gods, Goddesses, feïnyr, pythrants like my servants, and all the creatures you could ever imagine. Every creature had a place, but no matter the place, they were welcome. Oh, and everyone had magic of sorts."

"Even the humans?" I wondered.

"Yes, even the humans. Whether they realize it or not, humans have the power to heal themselves. A minor cut or a burn to their flesh regenerates and heals without a thought. That in itself is magic, and it all derives from Mother Earth and its nature."

"I've never thought of it like that," I said. "That's amazing."

"Yes, amazing, as you put it," Pyre answered. "Though humans were not as compelling in comparison to the Gods. Gods have the power to create life from nothing; to create everything we've ever known."

"So, the legends are true?" I asked.

"Most of them," he replied. "Some legends are spun from stories being told through generations and generations and become twisted. However, most of them derive from a truth."

"That's incredible," I remarked. Gram had told me to believe all of the stories, but hearing that from him was far more awakening. "So, how did our world come to exist?"

"There was a God placed on Earth, woven in time by the Fates. He was left here on his own, born from seed. He grew into existence with the blessing of nature on his side. Though Mother Earth blessed him, he was alone, and this was difficult. He had no one with him. No love, no source of entertainment. It was hardly something one would call a life. Therefore, that God decided to create others, and each one would come with their own power to provide such things."

"Such things as love?"

"Precisely," he said.

"So, a God created Gods?"

"Yes, you can look at it that way, but truly it is Earth and the Fates who created the first God, who created the others. We have to start there. It all comes from nature. Nature in itself is magic," Pyre explained.

"Nature is magic," I repeated in awe. I couldn't help but smile. Gram was right in so many ways. She prayed to Mother Earth, and she worshipped nature at its feet. Pyre Malum's lip quirked, observing me. "Please, continue. I have to know more." He smiled at my demand, happy for my eagerness.

"Yes, Goddess. Of course." I ignored the fact that he called me Goddess yet again and paid close attention as he readied himself to tell me more.

"I'm listening." I bit my lip, anticipation eating away at me. He grinned further, matching my tilted mouth.

"The first God created additional Gods on Earth, as I mentioned before. With other Gods came other personalities, other wants, and needs. Nothing was ever enough, and because each God was able to create, they themselves created Gods, humans, and creatures to fill what they were lacking. We must remember that the Gods created the positive, but they could also make the negative. They created Gods for destruction and jealousy just as much as kindness and healing."

"Why would they do that? Who would purposefully fill the world with hatred and misery?" I asked, frustrated.

"The question is not why; rather, what was the motivation behind it all? What drove the Gods to such carelessness?"

"Cynicism?" I laughed dryly. He huffed in what I supposed was agreement and began pacing, brows furrowed in thought.

"Some Gods grew tired and covetous," he continued. "They wanted attention. They wanted things that others had that they didn't. Because they were Gods, they believed that whatever they wanted, they should have. They did not consider the consequences because Gods do not have consequences."

"How is that possible?" I asked. Having no consequences was unfathomable, unthinkable. "The world split! That must be a form of consequence."

"The world divided, yes. That is all due to the Fates."

"What are the Fates?" I asked, confused. "I've heard of fate, but I didn't know that they were actual beings."

"They aren't corporeal beings," he corrected. "More-so sentient tethers." I peered at him, entirely befuddled. He stopped his pacing and regarded me.

"What?" He laughed at the apparent confusion on my face, then crossed his arms over his chest. I folded mine in defense. "Throw me a bone here. Explain." He quirked his lip at my reaction. It seemed a go-to response to me on his part.

"They wield *aēthre*. Think of it as a magical essence weaving strings that attach to every single thing in the world. They all play a part, and everything is connected in some manner."

"Okay, and where did the strings come from?" I questioned.

"That is uncertain. Many believe that Mother Earth created them, but some say the world began through the Fates. We do not know for certain, as we were not there during its creation, and the Fates aren't keen on revealing their conception."

"All right..." I wondered aloud. So much of this was challenging to wrap my mind around. "What do the Fates have to do with the Gods?"

"The Fates make sure everything is balanced and in order."

"So, the Gods did have consequences to a certain extent."

"There were always certain rules, certain guidelines to be followed. If a God went against them, it was as if they were trying to cut one of the strings," he said and looked at me gravely. "The Fates do not allow such things." I looked away from the tension. He was abruptly serious, and I didn't know whether to press for more information. I wondered if he had tried a game with the Fates once before, during his long life.

"Do you have any examples of this happening?" I asked.

"Absolutely."

"Would you care to elaborate? Or am I prying?" He grinned at this, and I felt a bit of the tension ease around us.

"Would you stop asking questions if I said you were prying?" He chuckled to himself as if this were an inside joke. I shook my head at him.

"No," I answered and tightened my folded arms. "Does it bother you?"

"Not in the slightest," he answered quickly, wings rustling behind him. "It is good that you are eager to learn." I warmed at his watch and loosened my arms.

"So?" I asked. "Please continue."

"As you wish." He chuckled lowly and straightened his posture. "When the Gods became too greedy and created things and beings for their self-indulgence, they did not consider how it would affect others in the world. Imagine a vengeful God creating evil abominations to do their bidding. Gods ravenous for carnal pleasure, invoking ïlincubi." My eyes grew wide at the mention of carnality.

"Sex demons?" I gulped, suddenly feeling very hot.

"Yes," he grumbled, fists tight. "They were made from corrupt spirits—a form of shadow people. One God or another created all evil. Evil did not exist before them." *Shadow people, corrupt spirits, and evil Gods... What was I getting myself into?*

"That's a lot to unload," I murmured. "It's a lot to think about. To consider that one does not become evil, rather, one creates evil, feels...."

"Wrong?" he offered.

"Unnervingly so."

"Yes, well, nevertheless, the Gods did not care about the repercussions. Once you've fallen into chaos and madness of the mind, you learn to care only for yourself. When the Gods created these evils, they were cutting tethers. When a tether is cut, the balance must be restored. In most cases, the Fates would pit Gods against each other and create war. When war came, all Hell broke loose. Evil was created, tarnishing many strings. Once the rot seeped through, it spread to others."

"That's what created the divide? Good and evil? That is what caused the war?" I was beginning to understand.

"That is the story at large," he explained. "But war is always caused by little things. Non-important things that are all gathered together, creating a greater problem."

"I can understand that well enough," I said. "We see it all the time on Earth."

"Yes, and as you may have guessed, the rot never goes away. Once a tether or being is corrupt, it continues its path of immorality and spreads." I was shocked at this revelation. I had always believed that no one was truly evil. I wholeheartedly believed that people could change.

"You don't believe that people can change? That people can choose to be better?" I questioned. He took a small step away from me and the table, and I felt a bit of his heat leave the air.

"Belief has nothing to do with it." He sighed. "It is a pure fact. That is why the Goddess, the one before you, created the split. The Fates allowed her the gift of all five elements, rendering her far more powerful than most other Gods. With her strength and purpose strung by the Fates, she decided that it was better to put corrupt people all in one place, and those who were deemed righteous or more important were placed in another. The humans and demi-divine who hadn't finished their soul path, never having chosen their side, were all placed on Earth." I could hardly imagine the circumstance. According to Pyre, the Triple Goddess had been the one to separate the realms. I wondered if she had given anyone a chance to change, to atone.

As I thought about my captor, I understood his mistreatment of me. Did he see the Goddess who had marked him as evil and sent him here when he looked at me? He knew that he needed me for the powers I was born with, but did the requirement burn him at every mention of it? To be reminded that his freedom lay in the hands of his infringer incarnate must be hard to bear. I wondered if Pyre Malum had been sent to Heaven instead of Hell, would he feel the same way?

Pyre cleared his throat, and my head whipped in his direction. He had been watching me as I thought it all over. Pyre had come back toward me now, creating less space between us than before. He was silent as I considered him and his probable hatred for me.

"Sorry," I whispered. "I was lost in thought," I confessed, looking away from his gaze.

"What were you thinking of?"

"The division of realms," I supposed.

"What of it?" he asked.

"You mentioned a third realm," I stated. "Am I to understand that there is a Heaven? A place for the righteous?" He scoffed at my words.

"If you would like to call it that, indeed. There is a Heaven or a haven of sorts," he answered, grinding his teeth. I could see this bothered him.

"What's it like?" I wondered aloud.

"I wouldn't know. It is a realm in which mighty beings live," he answered casually. "But I personally would not call them so righteous."

"What do you mean?" I looked at him, confusion set in my brow.

"I believe that the Goddess had a big heart and was able to overlook many of their wrongdoings, therefore placing them there. I often question where the Goddess drew the line. How much was too much corruption, and why did those Gods get away with enjoying their Heavenly life? Why did Gods of immorality come here into this inferno? What did I do that was worse than others?" I cut a sharp breath and looked at him quickly.

"You're a God?" I resounded. "I thought you said you were a demon!" He chuckled deep in his gut, and I felt nauseous at the sound. He took a slow, steady step, almost closing the gap between us. I held my breath and shivered.

"A daimon is a God. An exiled one," he muttered, looking down. "Not to be confused with a *demon*," he emphasized the first vowel. "Those are evil spirits."

"I am so lost," I mumbled, looking down. I was with a God. Pyre wasn't a demon; he was an exiled deity. How was this possible? How could I have missed this? "Are you sure you aren't a demon? What about the pythrants?" He laughed under his breath and sneered in my face.

"I wonder how they would feel if they knew you thought

they were demons." He lifted a dark, angular brow, seemingly trying to tease me.

"I didn't know what to think!" I blurted. "This is an extremely foreign world to me. Imagine being in my predicament. They are half-man, half-snake. They poisoned me with venom. What was I supposed to think?"

"It's understandable." He smirked. "I won't tell them if you won't." I looked at him now, studying his face. What did he think while he watched me? What was I, if anything, in comparison to him?

"You're a God," I gulped, tongue sticking to the roof of my mouth. His lashes lowered as if almost humbled by the recognition.

"I was an influential God after ascending at one and twenty. That was before they decided to clip my title. I'd only been given a few years of life as an ascended God in the first world," said Pyre. "I am the ruler of the dead. Born of a Primordial deity, one of twelve in the third generation." He sighed and looked back up to meet my eyes. Everything in me stilled as his eyes ensnared me. "Yes, I am a God. I am just not the kind of God that people wish for and pray to."

"You're..." I trembled, trying to grasp this information. "You're the God of the Dead?" His wings fluttered, and he slowly shifted to full height. He looked too young to have lived so long and with such a significant role. He was ascended at twenty-one... But how long had he been this age? My gaze followed him, my head tilting back in disbelief.

"Yes." He beamed, eyes glinting. A shiver ran up my spine at the realization that not only was I in Hell, but I was also with the God who ruled it. He had played coy about his ruling, skirted around the truth. He had told me that no singular being led the Under Realm, yet here he was, with a title so bold.

"I didn't know," I whispered, chewing at my lip. I could feel his eyes watching me. "I didn't know what you meant by daimon. I was taught that there were just demons and angels, Gods and us humans." He frowned at my mention of the beings.

"There is so much more than that," he spoke. "Daimon is just a word that the Gods decided on for those of us who are damned. It is a title for the beings who were thrown into the Under Realm. We are the exiles, condemned to suffer eternal punishment." I shook at the horror—at the truth being uncovered.

"Like the fallen angels?" I quivered, feeling a little lightheaded.

"No," he said abruptly. "Fallen Gods," he corrected. "The word angel stems from 'angelos'... It means messenger. Angels are just spirits trapped in the In-Between—the spirits of the dead who either have things left undone or unsaid, or those who were not able to choose their side. Our souls expect a message at the end of life. They are held in place if the spirit cannot carry it over." He paused, shoulders raised as he shifted his weight. "Gods live in Heaven, and many deceased spirits are placed there too. Angels simply float in nonentity."

This was all so strange. Everything I had ever believed had washed away in seconds. I felt so deflated, so hopeless.

"What happens to them? To the angels or spirits?" I whispered, suddenly feeling cold.

"They don't go to your Heaven or Hell. They are stuck in their limbo forever," he replied grimly. That startled me, suddenly bringing forth the memory of Gram's mausoleum at the Grimsbane sanctuary. It explained so much, yet still not enough. I couldn't imagine living such a haunted eternity. However, it might be better than being sent here for the rest of existence.

"That is heart-breaking," I said, solemn in thought.

"Is it?" he replied, contemplating.

"Wouldn't you be sad in that kind of situation?" I asked, looking up at him. He was sorrowful, reflecting. He put a hand beside me, leaning on the table I sat upon.

"An eternity being lost, or an eternity of damnation..." he pondered. He slowly lifted his gaze to meet mine. "Which would you choose?" Complete dread burrowed into me as I considered having to choose either. His eyes burned me, and I quickly averted my gaze, wanting to change the subject. I wanted desperately to put some space between us. I got up and walked around the other end of the table, pulling at the dust with the swipe of my index.

"My family and the High Council told me that the blood of demons and angels were immiscible. Do you know what that means? If demons are shadow people, and angels are only lost spirits?" I asked, quickly avoiding his earlier question. His shoulders went upright as if the change in subject had improved his thoughts.

"Ah, yes." He sighed. "It is true, aside from the words they used. These rules were set in place the minute the separate realms were created. They are referring to Gods. They use the term demon for those born from the blood of the Under Realm and angel for those born of celestials. The Gods and beings of the Under Realm and the Celestial Realm cannot produce children together. Nor can their semi-divine kin."

"Why?" I wondered aloud, tracing patterns in the dust that settled on the cover of his tome.

"To avoid the possibility of creating a being with too much power over more than one realm. It is to avoid new chaos." His explanation was similar to that of the High Council. Though their terminology was off, they'd been on the right track. It made sense. It felt a bit extreme, but then again, if I considered what the rules were set in place for, everything was extreme.

"You've taught me about the beginning of time, and I appreciate that. Now, will you tell me how magic works?" I asked, flipping through the book. He looked at me watchfully and furrowed his brows.

"You did not understand?" he asked. I was confused. Had he told me?

"Did you cover magic?" I asked, wondering if perhaps I had missed something. Pyre grabbed the book from my hands and flipped it to show me one of the pages. It was a photo of the large tree again, but inky splotches drew lines across the page this time—strings connecting to all things. From flowers to people, clouds to trees. Everything on the page had a string attaching itself to many other things.

"Magic comes from nature. Nature is magic. It is within you, as it is part of your biology."

"How?" I asked. "Magic and science don't exactly intermingle," I pointed out.

"Do not consider it from a scientific perspective," he answered. "You must remove that part from your mind. Think of it as feelings and intentions. Think of it as part of you. It is your magic which grows within everything," he resolved.

"Everything?"

"Everything," he confirmed. "Not everyone can use said magic, however. You must be open."

"I am open," I said reluctantly. "Scared but open," I admitted.

"That is all we need," he said and smiled. "I would like to show you something," Pyre insisted and raised an arm. It took me a moment to realize he'd done so for me to link mine.

"Where are you taking me?" I asked, nervous and excited all at once.

"I have something for you." I drew my arm into his, barely allowing my arm to rest against him, as he led me out of the training room. It was weird being connected to him like this— arm in arm, side by side. I wasn't sure what to think of it. An unsettling amount of unease came with it, but I also felt like I was taking a step in the right direction. We strode down the hallway, and within seconds, we stopped. I turned to look at him, a little bit jumbled.

"That was far," I muttered sarcastically, perplexed by the relatively short distance. He smirked and turned, making us face the door to our right.

"Here," he said and twisted the knob to open it for me. An intricate hole was carved just above this knob, which told me it would lock by skeleton key, just like Gram's basement. It was strange to see an actual doorknob for once after only seeing old, warded locks in the dungeons.

When he opened the door, I was shocked to see a bedroom set in a space with many windows. It was designed just like the throne room, only a smaller version of it. The windows were strange looking, long, and narrow. It took me a moment to realize that they were not meant to view the scenery; instead, they were set in place to make use of archers.

"What is this?" I asked, not understanding. Was he taking me to his bedroom? My gut sank at the thought.

"It is your chambers," he simply replied. I turned to look at him, unable to hide my quick smile. I was being given my own room. This was the first kindness he'd shown me since I had arrived here. I had assumed the worst, only to be given a luxury.

"I don't know what to say," I blew out. He nodded, trying to hide his grin.

"I believe a thank you would suffice."

"Thank you," I blurted. "I can't thank you enough." My back ached at the thought of the comfort that the bed offered.

The room reminded me of Gram's house in a sense. Lanterns and candelabras lined the walls, bringing back the memory of my family home. There was a proper bed in the center of the room. The pillows looked to be made of feathers, and someone had draped a gorgeous fluffy blanket atop an old-style mattress. There was a small wooden table at the back wall just to the left. A metal-looking bowl and what looked to be facecloths of sorts were sitting next to it. My heart leaped at the chance of being able to wash my face. The Gods knew I needed it. *Gods*. He was a God. I shivered in place.

"Well?" Pyre mused and gestured through the doorway. "Have a look."

Walking in was like a breath of fresh air. I had my own little space just for me. At that thought, Pyre walked in behind me, and I immediately remembered that this was not my home and that I was here as a guest. No, not a guest—a prisoner. But I was happy to be given a room, so I would not dampen the fact that I was finally offered comfort by thinking of my imprisonment.

"It's perfect," I said. "Thank you." I went over to the bed and sighed as I sat on it. I sank in without effort and felt a pang of alleviation in my joints. I cracked my neck at the relaxation it provided, and Pyre jumped at the sound.

"You are unwell?" he said, the question rhetorical.

"I am fine." I smiled and stretched my shoulders over my head. They popped and groaned, too, as I released some of the tautness. He winced again, coming closer.

"Do your bones break?" He stood beside me now, examining my shoulders.

"I have rheumatoid arthritis." I sighed. "I've had juvenile rheumatoid arthritis since I was a small child, but it's turned into a permanent thing." Pyre looked confused at that, and I considered that he might not know anything about my world's diseases and medicines. "It's inflammation in my joints and such. It's an autoimmune disease."

"A disease?" He quickly took a sizable step away from me, and I couldn't help but laugh.

"It's not contagious, Pyre." I chuckled. "Surely, a God wouldn't contract a disease, even if it were."

"You are a Goddess, and you have it," he pointed out. "If it is a God-apprehending disease, I have reason to be cautious."

"It's not something I can spread. It only affects me."

"How can this be? A Goddess contracted a disease..." he pondered.

"I have scoliosis too, but that doesn't affect my day-to-day life as it's not severe. I've been trying to tell you this from the very beginning. I am not a Goddess. I am mortal," I grunted.

"Perhaps on Earth," he said, shaking his head. "But you are immortal in the Under Realm. You should not feel this ailment."

"Well, I do," I insisted.

"I hadn't thought that you would feel pain." He looked away, his despondency clear.

"It's okay. I'm used to it. See?" I said and flexed my wrists to crack. He cringed at the visual, looking at his feet.

"The oubliette... I did not consider that you would be affected by the fall." This irritated me. He hadn't considered me at all when he had me so brusquely tossed to my doom. But I had to remove the anger from my mind. If I so much as blinked wrong, he could take this room away from me in an instant. I crossed my legs and exhaled sharply.

"Well, it is done with." He looked me in the eye, and I sensed the sting of a tear coming on. I looked away quickly, forcing the tear back. He stood there, unmoving; I could feel the heat of his gaze on me. I breathed carefully and looked back at him. He was doleful in the face but promptly changed his expression, seeming to be embarrassed by the emotion.

"The linens are clean." Pyre coughed, hastily clearing his throat. "They will continue to be cleaned, as the pythrants will see to it. They will be certain to have your chamber proper and your things replenished as needed." He walked toward the table with the bowl. "Here, you will find water, and I've given you some strips of cloth to do your cleaning. Do with it as you see fit." I relaxed my shoulders in contentment. I was finally going to be able to clean myself.

"Thank you," I said. He nodded, then stuck his finger into the pile of coals beneath the bowl. The coals turned red hot within seconds, and the water above started steaming. Seeing that heat and clean water was pure ecstasy. I made to get up, but his words caught me before moving.

"I've gotten you some new clothing," he continued. "Two dresses. I imagine you will be able to interchange them throughout your days; however, if you need another, you may ask." I looked at him in confusion.

"Where did you get the dresses?" I asked.

"Never mind where I got them," he replied. "Please, would you try them on?" My eyes grew wide in surprise.

"You want me to try them on now? With you in the room?" I could feel my face heating.

"There is a paneled partition just in the corner over there." I scoffed, and he laughed. He looked to his feet, shaking his head. His dark curls flitted across his face. "I will keep my eyes averted," he muttered. I didn't trust that.

"I think I would be more comfortable trying them on once you've left," I stated quietly.

"Nonsense," he said. "I will turn to face the arrow slit. I insist that you try them now, as I would like to make sure they fit. It is better to have you in new clothes promptly before starting our training. You couldn't possibly do any activity in your rather homely attire. It's been ripped to shreds." I burned at his words, remembering what I looked like as I looked down at myself. I hadn't seen my reflection in a long time, but with the slashes and filth all over, I showed more skin than I wanted to and smelled like a grave. Quickly, I realized it was a good idea to try on these dresses. I desperately needed new clothing.

"Where are they?" I asked with a sigh.

"They are hung behind your partition." He gestured to the folded panels. It looked to be made of bearskin or something of the sort. As I made my way to the room dividers, he headed to the window. He turned around to look at me, and I swiftly gave him a stern look.

"Please, if you will." I twirled my finger in a gesture for him to turn around. He clasped his hands behind his back and turned to face the narrow window.

When I got behind the divider, I noted that there were two dresses. Both were made of linen, and both were floor-length. One was more on the brown side, and the other a beige. They were not dresses of my time, as they looked like peasant clothing depicted from long ago. Somehow, they were plain looking, but they held a lavish touch. There was embroidery around the collar, and the sleeves had a meander-like pattern at the wrists. I wondered where he had gotten these dresses. Was there a whole world out there in this inferno? Were people or creatures spending their time doing mundane things, such as making dresses?

I grabbed the brown one and lifted it over my head. Unexpectedly, it fit me like a glove. As I slid both of my arms through each sleeve, the length was tailor-made. It was as if it were made specifically for me. The collar was cut into a sweetheart neckline, the embroidery's shimmer jutting out at the peak of my breasts. It surely wouldn't have slid on so well if the material had continued up my chest. It hugged me tightly, adhering to every inch of my skin. As the dress went down, it clung to my waist and slowly slackened as it landed on my hips and draped to the floor. The garment was beautiful, but it was not comfortable. There was absolutely no stretch to it. I thought that if I lifted my arms overhead, perhaps the seams would rip.

"Have you gotten one on?" Pyre asked from the other side of the room. I came around the corner and pulled my hair behind my shoulders, trying to look presentable.

"Yes," I said. "It fits, but I don't know how practical it will be to wear." As I turned the corner of the partition, I saw a set of dark feathered wings standing tall at the back wall. Pyre was still looking out of the window, and the light that shone through cast a brightness through his feathers, making the blue more vibrant than usual. "I am decent, Pyre. You may turn around." I let out a soft chuckle.

When he turned to look at the dress, his eyes immediately flew to my chest. There was no mistaking it as I watched his throat bob, and I felt a shiver run up my spine. I shook it off and tugged at my sleeves uncomfortably. Slowly, his eyes lifted from my chest to my neck, then to my eyes. I stared back, unflinching.

"Perfect," he said, voice gruff. It took me aback. What did he see when he looked at me? He cleared his throat. "The dress. It suits you well." I looked down at the floor to avert his gaze as he slowly walked toward me.

"Thank you," I muttered.

"You do not look as though you like it," he pointed out. I looked back up at him, scared that he might be angry. I was even more scared that I'd find him looking at me in the way he had before.

"I do like it. It's beautiful," I said, trying to reassure him. I tried to move to meet him, but a bolt of black ran through the bedroom door, catching me off guard. Unexpectedly, my foot snagged on the hem of the dress as I stumbled in my movement. "What is that?" I yelped, flinging my arms out to catch my balance. Before I could hit the floor, Pyre came to my aid, grabbing me by the waist and lifting me back into place. I knew that I was blushing from the heat in my face, completely embarrassed.

"Are you hurt?" he asked, wide-eyed. I shook my head, flustered, then suddenly remembered the mass of black I had glimpsed.

"Where'd it go?" I asked, terrified by the blaze of shadow I'd seen rushing in. "Where's the creature?" Pyre grinned, hands still holding my waist. He lifted a brow, seeming boyishly amused.

"Drakovyr?" he called, and a loud, growling noise sounded from behind me. I stiffened, unable to turn around. As the sound grew closer, goosebumps pricked my arms. "She is a guest, Drakovyr. Heal," Pyre demanded, but the creature did not falter.

"What is it?" I choked, keeping my eyes on Pyre.

"My *drædho*." He smiled, flashing his teeth.

"What?" I gasped. What the Hell was a *drædho*, and why was it coming for me?

"He's here to make sure no living humans come through to the Under Realm. It is his duty."

"But I'm a living human!" I squeaked. The growling seemed to louden at my words, and Pyre let out a low chuckle.

"He is a guard hound. So long as you leave him be, he will

not harm you. Just don't offer him the chance." At that, I felt the brush of a heated beast rub against the backside of my legs. It was tall, reaching the lower part of my back. I swallowed sharply, and Pyre let me go. Everything in me told me to run, but I had a distinct feeling I would not be able to outrun this creature. I closed my eyes with brutal force as I felt the beast come ahead of me. The growling sound was rippling, its breath hot on the air. My lungs were on fire, and I couldn't take the fear much longer. Shakily, I released the tension in my face and opened my eyes to find a large, black dog reminiscent of a Doberman. I stilled. Had that beastly sound come from this dog?

"Oh," I gasped, lungs happy to release my breath. "Hello there." The hound only looked at me, teeth bared and polished. I took a step toward it, and the hairs on the back of its neck flared to life.

"Don't approach him," Pyre warned, but I could see through this dog's front. It didn't hate me; it couldn't possibly. It was only frightened of me, not knowing whether it could trust me. I kept my eyes on the dog and lowered myself to the ground in front of it. "Goddess, don't!" Pyre boomed, but it was too late. The hound rushed at me expeditiously, a snarl ripping so loudly from its maw that it was hard to believe it was real. It was coming, fast as lightning, ready for attack. I took a calming breath and sat on my heels. Seconds before its violence, I held my hands out and allowed it to see my offer.

"Drakovyr!" Pyre cried as the dog's giant mouth widened over my arms. About to snap down, the dog released its tongue and licked my palms. The hot, wet mess offered relief, and I let out the shaky nerves, calmed myself further, and allowed the dog to sniff me.

"Hi there, boy," I whispered to it. Its nose came forward, mere inches away from mine, and it huffed a big breath. I couldn't help but let out a laugh. "You're just a big baby, aren't you?" I teased and kissed the dog's snout. "Drakovyr, huh? Have I got a fun nickname for you, or what, Mister Malfoy?" I laughed internally, comparing this beast to the blond wizard I'd grown fond of in the books I'd read as a child.

"Now, that is something I never thought I would see...." Pyre's voice was low as he walked toward me.

"What?" I laughed, petting the length of the dog's muzzle.

"You are just full of surprises, aren't you?" He observed me.

"I think he likes me," I said as the dog sprayed a sneeze all over us. Pyre scoffed and wiped at his face, and I burst into laughter.

"Are you laughing at me?" He groaned, but the smirk on his lips told me he was more amused than annoyed.

"Maybe." I shrugged, and his grin turned into a smile. He was incredibly handsome in this light. He was teasing, talking in easy conversation with me. Best of all, he had a dog. A pang of warmth flooded my heart as I thought about Diego, remembering his sweet little face. I missed him so much. I looked away from Pyre and back to the dog. "I think *you* should be the one laughing at *me*," I supposed, looking over my shoulder at him as I petted the hound. "Before I tripped, I was about to tell you that this dress is probably not the right outfit to wear for training, but my inelegance gave you a perfect example without having to tell you," I grumbled as the embarrassment sank in. He shook his head at me, a smirk still in place.

"What shall we do with you?" He exhaled and got to his feet. I gave a final pat to the dog in front of me and stood up.

"Well, firstly, I'm very thankful that you've provided me with these dresses; however, I think replacing them with a more standard wardrobe may be beneficial to both of us. I won't rip it and hurt myself, and you won't have to worry about catching me before I fall." I shrugged. He looked at me with a downhearted expression.

"I do not have anything else for you. This is the only attire I was able to procure."

"Oh, I'm sorry," I said, flushing. I hadn't meant to be demanding or rude. "What about your clothing? Do you have anything I can borrow? I don't want to put you out...." He laughed at the thought.

"You would truly wear man's clothing?"

I sneered at him. "You are very behind the times, Pyre Malum. I am happy to wear just a shirt and pants." He looked me over before shrugging his shoulders.

"Very well," he answered. "Though I am reluctant to give in, you've convinced me that it is undoubtedly the right choice, seeing as how you are the clumsiest thing I've ever come across." I rolled my eyes at his comment.

"Thank you." He grinned at my appreciation.

"I do love hearing those words come from you," he jested as he walked toward my door.

"Don't get too used to it," I called. He turned to look at me, standing in my doorway. What was I doing? Teasing a God?

"I wouldn't dare," he held. "I will have my servants send you some of my clothing."

"Thank you." I covered my mouth at my blurted appreciation. "I mean..." He laughed and shook his head at me.

"Come, Drakovyr," he commanded and turned to leave my new room. I huffed as I watched him and his giant dog go.

39

VERVE

When Pyre was gone, and I had the room to myself, I immediately ran to the water basin and threw my hands into the warm liquid. I moaned aloud as it eased the ache in my fingers. I scrubbed my dirty nails and carefully removed the grime from my mother's ring. I was glad to have this small piece of my life from Earth with me. It was a constant reminder that I was still alive. I had something to fight for, to live for.

I lowered my face to the bowl, not bothering with the scrap cloth, and splashed the water onto my face. This was bliss. When I finished washing my face, basking in the hot steam provided, I turned to find clothing piled neatly at the foot of my door. The pythrant from before rounded the corner in a hurry as if trying not to disturb me.

"Thank you, Alriq," I called to him. He stopped, tail whistling behind him.

"My pleasure, Goddess," he replied quickly. Whenever I saw the pythrants, I couldn't help myself from feeling pity. They looked on the verge of being alive—awake, going about their daily tasks, but not entirely living. There was something in the way they stood, their body language emanating a sense of worry and heedfulness. They were always on duty, seemingly on high alert with a constant guard up, and that, more than anything, made me want to reach out a hand.

"How are you?" I asked, not sure where to start. His shoulders stiffened at my words, and I thought he'd disregard my question when he surprised me by smiling.

"How are you?" he asked me the same. I blinked in surprise.

"I'm well, thank you," I reported. "But you haven't answered my question." He seemed to loosen at my prodding.

"You would truly like to know?"

"Of course," I stammered. His reaction caused my fumble. I wondered now if anyone ever asked about him. Did he have friends? Did anyone care to ask how he was doing? There was one other pythrant that seemed to be at his side most often. I wondered if perhaps he was his friend. I observed his posture, realized I had been staring, and cleared my throat. "I would like to know how you are doing. I see you every day." I shrugged. "You've become a familiar face to me."

"What do you mean by this?" he questioned aloud, eyes darting back and forth.

"I just mean that I've become used to your presence in this strange place. It's nice to see you, and I want to know how you are doing."

"Well, Goddess," he replied. "I am well."

"Good," I said, the awkwardness heavy in the room. Neither one of us moved, but I gave him a curt smile.

"Goodbye," he uttered, his tail swishing with his movements. He was out the door so quickly I didn't even have the time to blink, let alone wish him goodnight.

I was happy to see that Alriq had left me several articles to choose from. Fawn-colored garments, billowy-legged pants, and some charcoal legging-type pants too. All of the shirts were long and flowy, but the material had no stretch, similar to the dresses Pyre had me try on. The shirts were made of linen and went halfway down my thighs. A leather wrap-around belt was also left for me, and I tied it at my waist. It bunched the shirt appropriately so as not to get in the way of my legs if I needed to run. It was perfect. Far better than my tattered rags and certainly a step up from the dresses.

After choosing one of Pyre's long shirts as a nightgown, I hid behind the partition, completely undressed, and scrubbed every bit of myself down until my skin was raw. I found that the several barrels stuck in the corner were filled with clean water. I splurged and decided to dunk my whole head into one. I scrubbed at my scalp and felt the tangles loosen with each comb of my fingers. I wrung out my hair, put my new clothing on, and sank into bed. It felt unbelievably renewing to be clean again, and the comfort of the bed was extraordinary. This was going to be my first proper sleep in Hell, and I was more than content at this moment.

40

UP IN FLAME

"Tell me again why I have to run so early?" I groaned, half panted, as I jogged around the throne room. Morning's first light lighted the tower, and my eyes fought to focus on my feet. Pyre stood in the center of the room, observing my poor excuse for running.

"As I've explained on more than one occasion in the last hour, you need to build stamina. Summoning your power, using your affinities, is a draining task. You need to be able to summon all five affinities at once come time for your purpose." At Pyre's words, my heart sank to the pit of my stomach, unable to stop myself from imagining what would come of said purpose. "Knees up," Pyre barked in order. I rolled my eyes and picked up the pace, focusing on the stone walls I ran past.

"How much longer am I supposed to keep going?" I asked, counting the windows as I passed them by. Over and over, I pictured myself giving up and risking the fall.

"Until you no longer pant like Drakoyvr on duty." Had I just been compared to a dog?

From the corner of my eye, a large, orange sphere launched just ahead of me. If I had been overly lost in counting windows, I would have run right into the ball of fire.

"What the hell, Pyre?" I gasped, coming to a complete stop, only to tumble over my feet. I nosedived, narrowly avoiding the flame that smoked off the wall in front of me. "Are you trying to kill me?" I howled in incredulity, staring up at the smoking brick.

"On the contrary, Goddess. I aim to train you enough so that you might avoid such things." I looked away from the wall, and to the God, who stood wide feet apart, arms crossed over his chest, wearing a damn grin on his face.

"And throwing fire at me is the way to achieve that?" I spat, shaking my head at him. His dark wings fluttered behind him as if in reaction to his entertainment.

"Come now, Darling. It was but a spark." I looked at him in disbelief. He chuckled under his breath, and when he dipped his chin down, a black strand of hair fell forward, covering his right brow.

Wiping my hands on my thighs, I stood on questionably stable legs and cracked my neck.

"Again," Pyre demanded, lifting his head back to his habitual proud posture.

"Are you planning to join me on this run at some point?" I questioned, jutting a hip out as I rested my hand in the crook of my waist. He looked at me, amused. Pyre started walking backward, cocky in his grin as he lifted his arms, flexing in the light pooling in the center of the room. I almost let my jaw drop but remembered to limit drooling to internal thoughts only. He smiled, a beaming, teasing smile, then shook out his hair in a playful gesture. This asshole was having too much fun at my expense.

"Again, Goddess," Pyre insisted, then turned around, clasping his hands behind his back, showing me the entire expanse of black feathered wings attached to his shoulder blades. I took a dramatically deep breath, then let it go, along with all the thoughts which stirred about in my mind. This was going to be a long day.

***

"Magic is all about finding your center," Pyre told me after deciding I'd run enough for the day. He took the role of instructor very seriously, and I was both glad and annoyed by the lessons. The training had been a brutal awakening I hadn't expected this morning. I had finally had a tolerable night's sleep after washing and sleeping in a bed. Pyre had me running laps in his throne room from the moment I stepped foot through the door. I hadn't exercised in a long time, and this would take some getting used to. I still couldn't believe how he'd responded when I asked if he would join me in my run. He'd just shrugged his shoulders and then flexed his muscles—exhibiting vanity, spirit, and strength in one quick move.

"My center?" I asked, pointing to my chest, my breath heavy.

"A little lower." He moved my hand, placing it above my navel. I inhaled at the intimacy of this touch. This was a God I stood before, who spoke to me and touched me as if I weren't a mere mortal. "Think of it as a seed, deep in your core. It works best when you can find it, nurture it, and let it grow. As it grows, you will become more robust, and it will provide you with all you need."

"I think I can do that," I said, trying to concentrate. I loosed a breath and closed my eyes, wrapping my arms around my stomach. I tried to picture the seed he spoke of, imagining it settled in my core, but nothing came to mind. I was drawing a blank, which felt inevitable. I inhaled deeply and tried again with wavering confidence. I was an imaginative person. I should be able to create this image for myself. To no avail; I still felt no surge of power come forward. Ill at ease, I opened my eyes under Pyre's scrutiny and grunted.

"Hmm," he hummed, brows furrowed.

"This isn't working," I grumbled.

"You have used your powers before, Goddess. I witnessed it on more than one occasion," Pyre said firmly. "What were you thinking of then? What was your focus?"

"That's just it! I wasn't thinking at all. I was just feeling. I don't believe that my powers stem from focus. They just come to me out of nowhere," I confessed. "It's something that I can't control."

"Perfect," he answered. I looked at him, confused.

"What do you mean, perfect?" I snorted. "It doesn't make any sense. If I can't concentrate and draw from a source, I can't conjure my magic. How am I ever going to wield my powers?"

"I have an inkling." He beamed. Before I could detect his movement, the cracking of my wrist tore a scream from my throat I had not expected.

"What are you doing?" I hissed, trying to yank my arm free. He held his grip firm, digging his claws into my skin. "Let me go! That hurts." It wasn't harrowingly painful, but I didn't like this change in demeanor. It unnerved me more than anything. Pyre dipped and applied more force. Fear and anger took over my senses at the position I was in.

"Precisely," he taunted. I could feel it now, my rage boiling to the surface, looking for release.

"Stop. Now." I gritted my teeth.

"Make me," he commanded, and a guttural rumble made

its way from deep down in my gut and up my throat as I grew hotter and hotter. I couldn't stand this vulnerable position anymore. I looked at him in horror. His eyes lit in delight, and in the reflection of those eyes, I could see myself ablaze. Panicking, I started to beat at my arms, but nothing was going out. I was on fire.

"Please make it stop," I begged. The God looked at me, confused.

"Now, why would you want it to stop?" he provoked me, trying to further my anger, but my anger was gone. In its place were equal parts of irritation and fear.

"Pyre," I warned.

"You will have to learn to put it out yourself, Goddess," he told me, with his hand still on my wrist. "Until then, tell me; does it hurt?" I shook my head and took a moment to realize that the fire was not hurting me, and neither was the grip he had on me. I looked at him in disbelief.

"How is this possible? I'm literally on fire." He chuckled and released his grip.

"Because it is your fire to wield. It will not harm you if you do not wish it to. It can even protect you, creating a barrier around your skin. It will help keep you from pain if you allow it."

This entire situation was unfathomable. It was hard to believe that I had this power inside of me. I had used it before during my outburst at Gram's house. When I first met this daimon, the God of the Dead, it had also come to me, but I hadn't been fully cognisant. It was a quick reaction, and he terminated it by licking the side of my face. I shuddered at the memory of sizzling.

"How do I make it go away?" I asked. "If it's mine, I should be able to make it go away," I added, feeling uncomfortable. He shook his head, smiling.

"Why on Earth would you want it to go away? You are glowing." He smiled out of character. It was awe written all over him. I was overwhelmed by the heat of this chilling discovery. I could feel the tears welling to the brim, and to my surprise, they sizzled as they leaked down my still-hot cheek, drying before making it down my chin. I wiped at my face, then quickly realized that my hands were still on fire. This was so strange.

Laughing in incredulity, I lifted my hands to examine them now, golden flame settling all around me. It honestly didn't hurt. It was as if the flame merely surrounded me but had no physical contact with my skin. As I moved my fingers, the fire danced along with them. I was wholeheartedly amazed. I looked up at Pyre, who was standing only inches away from my face. From the look he was giving me, he was astonished too. He frowned when he marked my distancing as I took a step back.

"You will have to become more comfortable with me at a point in time, Goddess," Pyre said, clearing his throat when I moved away from him. I had done it instinctually. It was hard to think when he came this close to me. I choked back my discomfort and nodded.

"Mmhmm," I mumbled when he took a step closer. I had to look up now to see his face, the height making my neck strain.

"We will be tied to one another soon enough, so long as you are able to hone your magic," he supposed. At that, I started to think of what was to come and looked away from his gaze. I had pushed it all to the back of my mind, focusing on survival and strengthening my magic. I didn't want to marry this exiled God. I couldn't bear the thought of the catastrophe that lay ahead of me. I kept telling myself I'd be able to get out of it when the time came, but the more I spent time with Pyre, the more I grew curious about him. I was learning not only about the other realms but about him too. I was beginning to understand just how powerful he was. My chance at escaping felt further and further away as time flew by.

"What are you thinking?" he murmured. My eyes snapped back up to his, and a wave of emotion tugged at my heart.

"Your eyes..." I whispered, my hand inexplicably lifting to his face. I wanted to explore, needing to feel for proof that he was real. To prove that he, in fact, had the most beautiful eyes ever to exist. Shakily, my fingertips, still ablaze, landed just above his cheekbone, and he hitched a breath at my touch. The pigment of gold that swam in his irises seemed to brighten at my action.

"*Your* eyes," he murmured, voice guttural and cracked at the end of his speech. "So very blue," he spoke, searching my gaze. "With a ring of pure gold." At that, I snapped my hand away and took a step back. I reeled myself in, the flame around me sputtering out as I tried not to shudder from having held my breath for so long. Why was I doing this? Why had I let Pyre get so close? Most intriguingly, why had he wanted to? I couldn't help my imagination wandering as a million different scenarios ran through my mind.

"Tell me more about the binding," I fumbled, my words almost too quiet to be heard. The shock he wore was inescapable. I thought that perhaps this was the wrong question to ask, as it seemed his mind had gone to the same place as mine.

"What of it?" he asked, covered in sweat from our earlier training with flame.

"What exactly does it entail?" I swallowed hard, then forced a shrug. "When we spoke of it last, I didn't give you a chance to explain yourself fully," I admitted. He took another step closer, leaving hardly any space between us.

"You mean when you refused my proposal for the second time?" he grunted. A faint smile tugged at his lips, and I thought I almost caught a glimpse of amusement on his face. I thought that maybe, I liked to see that kind of smile from him and that it wouldn't be so bad to see it again.

"Yes, well, my emotions wreaked havoc on the opportunity to allow you the chance to explain yourself better." I smirked and watched his lip curl into a grin matching mine. I did like seeing this smile. What was happening to me?

"A habit of yours," he supposed, voice still low.

"Ha, ha," I mocked. "Are you going to tell me you're not quick to anger as well?" I thought this might stir said anger in him and create more space between us. I thought it might help me clear my thoughts because, evidently, I was not thinking straight. To my surprise, his grin grew wider at my teasing.

"A commonality." He let out a low laugh.

"Tell me now," I asserted, pulling the topic back to attention. "How does the binding work?"

"It is like a contract," he explained, finally taking a small step back. His look was more serious now as he tried for the words. "When Gods, of any kind, make a binding oath, it is a law they cannot break. The blood in our veins will intertwine, and knowing of the contract, it will meld to form a united power in us." I shivered at his words.

"It's all magic," I said quietly, pondering the world's origins.

"Of the oldest kind," he confirmed. "This particular binding only works if both Gods accept the new fate. All of the cords must align."

"What happens when they do?" I asked, trying to shove aside the actual question I had in my mind: What happens if one of the Gods does not accept?

"When the binding is complete, the pair share a lifeline. They will share in each other's magic and immortality. It will be an infinite union. The most powerful position a God can attain is a wedlock binding," he resounded. He studied me now, and I felt anxious under his gaze. I knew what he was thinking. When he looked at me, I knew that he was dreaming of the day he could combine our strengths and rule the realms. I shivered in place. "The power wielded by a coupling as strong as us could conquer any realm, face any God, and could live on forever." I gulped at the thought of being tied to the God of the Dead for eternity. Goosebumps flooded my arms from the horror.

"Why do you want a wedlock binding with me?" I wondered now. It seemed he wanted the power, but more than anything, I thought he valued the possibility of his freedom. "Why can't you just go through the Gates on your own?" A memory of Pyre Malum snatching me in the night and taking me into the Under Realm flashed through my mind. "What's stopping you from killing me and going through? You could just use my blood like the High Council did to open the Gates for you. And you could marry any God to bind your powers with." He pointed his eyes at me and scoffed in distaste.

"You truly do not value your life if you so blindly offer such things, do you?" He folded his arms across his chest, muscles flexed and glinting.

"I'm only trying to understand." I shrugged. "Why do you need me specifically?"

"I am tied to this world. If you bound your powers with mine, you would give me your ability to walk through all realms. You could give me this power."

"Yes, but as I said, you could just kill me, walk through and find someone else to marry."

"No."

"You said any two Gods. Why not?"

"It is impossible." He scowled at me.

"Why?" I searched his face for an answer.

"I cannot leave this realm and survive in another for long. Not without binding myself to you." He paused and released a breath. "You can open the Gates and live in any realm you wish. You are of all realms. If we marry, I will become of all realms." My eyes grew wide at the realization.

"Oh," I stammered, bewildered by my truth. He laughed, and it made me stumble. "What's so funny?" I asked, watching him. He shook his head at me, and I couldn't help but trace his smile with my eyes. It was a beautiful thing to witness.

"The things you do not know..." he trailed off. I clenched my fists, trying not to lose my temper, and he watched my movements.

"Listen," I started, throwing my weight on one hip. "I only know what my grandmother and the High Council told me. I'm new to this. Instead of mocking me, why don't you explain yourself?" He watched me intently, his smile slowly turning to a smirk on his lips.

"Very well, Goddess," he said. "I'm happy to teach you."

"Thank you," I huffed. He let out a low laugh, and I tried to relax my stance. He nodded, seeming to approve of me.

"I am going to assume you know the bare minimum; therefore, I will try to cover all of the bases," he began. I rolled my eyes at him, waiting. "We start with the Celestial Realm. The virtuous Gods and their children have reign over the Celestial Realm. The Gods rule in their haven, and when their semi-divine children of Earth pass on into the afterlife, they are greeted at their Gates. So long as they meet the requirements to enter, their spirits may live out their eternal deaths there. The immoral Gods and their daimon children live and rule in the Under Realm, just as the Celestial beings do. Though, there are not nearly as many here. This place is mostly occupied by souls of the dead, the damned, and a handful of beasts." *Beasts*? This was such strange territory to explore. I could hardly believe I was among Gods, the dead, and creatures of all kinds. I was definitely going to have nightmares after hearing all of Pyre's stories. Though the goal was to escape my prison, I couldn't imagine venturing outside of this castle.

"What about Earth?" I asked when I noticed he paused to watch me. His eyes did not leave me, seemingly glowing. I bit my lip, feeling unsure of myself under his gaze. His lower lip tipped open, his eyes trailing my mouth. "Pyre?" He blinked, seeming embarrassed for having been caught staring. He cleared his throat and looked away, and I was glad for the moment of reprieve. What this God's eyes could so easily do to me made me nervous. My brain knew his beauty shouldn't tempt me, but it was hard to convince my asinine core to show restraint.

"Humans are of Earth," Pyre said, interrupting my corrupt thoughts. I blinked away the shame and listened attentively. "If they do not possess the blood of the Gods of any kind, they simply cease to exist after death. You have to be semi-divine to enter another realm for an afterlife."

"You mean like me?" He looked at me with impatience, and I met him with the same face. His features settled, turning into amusement.

"You have the blood of all three realms. You are not simply semi-divine," he stated, clasping his hands behind his back. His wings tightened, their height growing with the movement. "You are made of pure Godly blood. You are the fertilized seed of two Gods, harvested and sowed into the womb of a human before the splitting of realms." Pyre moved closer now, wings widening around him. "You were born on Earth, but you are a

Goddess. You are a pure-blooded Goddess with ties to the humans, celestials, and the Under Realm, all thanks to the Triple Goddess, the Fates, and Mother Earth. A true treasure indeed."

"No," I stammered. The implication of his statement was like a punch to the gut. "That's impossible. My father is my father. My mother is my mother. I look just like her! My hair is the same color as the rest of the women in my family!" I exclaimed, pointing to my roots.

"A product of magic, *Sōrza.*"

"Magic *Sōrza*?" I blew out. "What the hell is that?" I was starting to hyperventilate.

"It's going to be all right. Just breathe. You will come to understand everything with time," he assured me. "I know it's difficult, but you must accept it." Now I *really* lost control of my breathing. How could he be so calm while delivering this information? This was life-altering. I didn't want to believe any of it.

"No, come on," I huffed, rapidly feeling lightheaded. "That's impossible."

"It's the truth," he held. He was so sure in his words. "It is the prophecy come to life."

"I don't understand," I uttered, knees going weak, falling into silence. Who I was and who I was supposed to be was inconceivable. My parents... No. This was impossible. Ridiculous! My head was pounding from the attack on my nerves. My mind was shot. This was absurd. I was becoming more and more distraught as it sunk in. My life was incomprehensible. I didn't want to believe it. I couldn't believe it. But here I stood, in the Under Realm. There he stood, Pyre Malum, the God of the Dead. He had been waiting all this time for me. I was his only chance at opening the Gates of Hell. I thought about my lineage, thought about my family, and realized that everything I had ever known was never as it seemed.

"What are you thinking?" Pyre jolted me out of my spiral.

"I don't even know...." I stuttered, feeling faint.

"Are you unwell?" he asked, concern creasing his forehead.

"I don't know that either...." I whispered. "There were so many lies... So many secrets... I don't know what to believe. Why should I believe you over my family? This can't be real. My family..." He looked at me closely, and I felt as if he were trying to absorb my thoughts straight from my head. My heart and mind joined forces, attempting implosion.

"Are you scared?" he wondered, taking a step closer to me.

"How could I not be?"

"You shouldn't be," he insisted, voice strong yet warm.

"But my family...."

"Your family will still be your family."

"They aren't my blood," I whispered, mouth trembling.

"No, they are not, and that is all right," he said. "Your blood is powerful, allowing you to walk carefully through all three realms. We have been waiting a millennium for this to occur," Pyre explained.

"What for?" I looked up through my tear-filled lashes, searching his face.

"You lifted the veil between Earth's realm and the Godly realms when your magic awoke. When the veil is lifted, we can see through to the other realms, like adding a window to a solid door."

"What use do you have for that?" I murmured, then cleared my throat. He smirked at my change in posture and took a step back.

"When the window is cracked open, we cross between those realms, but only for a brief period of time. It is like sticking your head out the window but never being able to pull your whole body through," he supposed.

I couldn't help but think of Gram using this same analogy not so long ago. My grandmother, who was somehow not my grandmother. I couldn't help but wonder if I had another grandmother out there somewhere in one of the Godly realms. Did she know about me? Who was my biological family? Did my family back home know about this too, and lie about it, just like they had with my witchhood? If I was a Goddess, was I even a witch at all? There were too many questions and not enough answers.

"Is that what you did?" I asked, trying to shake myself from the destructive thoughts rounding my mind. "You stuck your head through?" He chuckled at my words.

"It is your blood which allowed me to cross physically through the veil to retrieve you. My worshippers spilled your blood of all realms at the base of the life tree." I tried not to think of that terrifying night. It was a nightmare I did not want to relive. At the thought of Moira Darkmore slicing my skin, I imagined the hot sting of blood pooling around me. A pang of hurt ran through me as I remembered Gram telling me about my blood, my DNA. I shook the imagery away and focused on getting my information.

"Right before the High Council took me, they had told me that my DNA was mixed. Are you sure I'm not only partially a Goddess?" His eyes grew wide, lips parting. "What?" I asked, brows knitting together.

"That is the first time you've referred to yourself as anything remotely Godly," he whispered.

"Oh," I stammered. He cleared his throat as I watched him.

"I am certain that you are pure blood. It is in the prophecy. You were created by celestials, harvested by daimons, and born from a human. Your DNA is the result of magic."

"Is that why they called me the Triple Goddess reincarnate? Because of the ties to three blood types?" I asked him. "Who was she? Are there any others like me? I can't possibly be the only one." My mind was scrambling for answers.

"The Triple Goddess was a deity, like you and like me. She was called the Triple Goddess because of her ties to the three realms. Now you are called the Triple Goddess because you were chosen to take her place. It is not only about your blood, though it does play a large role. You must also have a direct link to the Triple Goddess. Whether she or a string of destiny claimed you, you were God-blessed."

"What does that mean for me?" I asked. I could still remember the feeling that washed over me as Moira declared similar information about my being God-blessed.

"Like you, she was made of all three realms, made to protect and rule over them as a guardian to the Gates. You were gifted all five elemental affinities, just as she was long ago. She has willingly passed her ability on to you. You can open the Gates as long as you're able to use your magic and call upon all affinities. You need the blood of the realms to walk them, but you also need the five affinities to open them. With both, you can safely open, pass through, and rule any of the realms," he said, observing me carefully. His eyes were intent on burning a hole in me. This was information he had been sitting on for longer than I could imagine. It was strange to take a step back and remember what this meant to him and what I meant to him. "You were destined for this, Goddess," he breathed, looking me up and down. I gulped at the intensity I bathed in. "You were hand-selected by the Fates. No other may do as you do."

"The Fates?" I gasped. "How does that work? Why only me?" I could see the impatience wearing him thin as I asked my millionth question.

"Though it pains me to admit it, I do not know all. I can only assume that the Fates allowed this. The Triple Goddess struck a bargain. Just like the Fates paved the way for your birth, they also allowed the Triple Goddess to gift you all elemental affinities." He paused to gaze out of the window nearby. "It is only you, Goddess. You are of all three realms; you have the affinities... It is you." A long pause of silence hovered around us before I finally voiced my inner thoughts.

"I wish I knew why they chose me," I mumbled, twisting a lock of my hair that came loose in front of my face. "They expect so much of me, it seems. I still don't know what to think of all of this. I'm glad to know more about it, though."

"I am pleased that you are learning," he spoke softly. I noticed that he was starting to look tired from all this talk. I felt drained too. It was a lot of information to process, and my fate was a hard pill to swallow. Though we were both tired, I still needed to know more. I was supposedly chosen to rule over the realms. The safety and livelihood of the Celestial Realm, Under Realm, and Earth was in my hands. I had to be careful. I needed more.

"Pyre, do you know how I am supposed to rule the realms?" I thought of the threat of sacrifice Ember had thrown at me and blanched. Was I supposed to sacrifice myself for this cause? Was my fate a curse?

"Harness your divinity, Goddess. I will explain further when the time comes," he answered and straightened himself up before walking away. I still had no idea what I was in for, and that was terrifying.

* * *

After conjuring fire, albeit due to blunt force, I couldn't help but smile as I washed my face in my water basin. My power had shown itself today. I had worked magic. Hope fluttered in my chest at the thought of seeing my family again, and a light breeze fluttered over me. I dunked my hands into the warm water and let them soak, easing the strain from my fingers. We had had a long day of training, and I exerted myself during the physical education. Pyre explained that it was essential to keep up my agility while using my magic. My powers needed to protect me without my mind and body working for it. I was glad to begin this kind of training. It meant that I was going to become stronger and faster. It meant that my chances of going back to Earth were far better than I had hoped for.

"What are you doing?" Pyre interrupted my thought, and I gasped at the sound of him. Water splashed around me as I drew my hands from the basin to my heart. I hadn't expected him to come into my room, as he had never come to see me during the night.

"Oh! You scared me," I said breathlessly, wiping my hands on my shirt.

"What are you doing to the grounds?" he asked. I looked at him in confusion.

"The grounds?" I repeated. "I've just been washing up." His eyes narrowed and slowly made their way to my feet. I followed his gaze only to find that I was standing in a heap of dirt with bits of weeds growing between my toes.

"Oh, my goodness." I sputtered, then burst into laughter as I wiggled my toes in the soft earthen soil.

"You've washed only to dirty yourself again," Pyre remarked, unable to stop his grin.

"I didn't intend on doing this," I admitted. "I didn't know I *could* do this again." I had only been able to summon my earth affinity twice now, and both times were unintentional, just as this incident had been. Pyre had scolded me when I had grown the daffodils in his training room, wiping away my moment of happiness.

"What were you thinking of?" he asked. I quickly hid my eyes as I realized that I had been thinking of my escape. I couldn't tell him this. I couldn't possibly relinquish this kind of information. He would lock me up again, losing my trust. I had a feeling he would no longer continue our lessons either if he had heard that I was planning to betray him. "What is it?" he pushed.

"I was thinking of my family again," I confessed, deciding to tell him one of the truths.

"You miss them," he remarked, not a question but an observation.

"More than anything," I whispered solemnly. Pyre advanced and knelt, swiping his fingers through the dirt. Some of the weeds at my feet wilted and crumbled into dust, perhaps from his touch or maybe from my sadness.

"This is impressive," he murmured. "Are you able to control it? If you think of your family, can you push further into your affinity and create more?"

"I don't know. I've never tried," I answered.

"Now is as good of a time as any." He waited. "Try."

"Okay," I said, shifting in place. "Do you have any advice?"

"Do as you were doing before I interrupted. Think about your family." I nodded and closed my eyes, concentration heavy. I needed to grow life. How hard could it be?

Gram came to the forefront of my mind, crouched to the ground in her giant garden.

"Now, Shivalri, what have I taught you?" she asked, looking back at me. I was smaller now, just under four feet tall and much slimmer and darker from the days of being out in the sun.

"No matter where I am or where I'm from, the Earth is you and me and everyone," I heard myself say.

"And that means?" she questioned further. Pépère came into view, wearing coveralls and a big straw hat. His great gray beard shone in the sun as he lowered himself to help pick berries.

"That I am never alone," Pépère and I chimed simultaneously.

"That's right." Gram chuckled. She picked a strawberry straight from the plant and handed it to me. I looked at it in the palm of my hand, the red skin of the fruit glistening under the blistering sun.

"Does the strawberry know I'm going to eat it?" I thought aloud. Pépère patted me on the head, and I looked away from the berry to my grandparents.

"The strawberry knows, and it loves its purpose." Gram laughed. Pépère winked at me and took a big bite from the one he held in his dark, tanned hands. I beamed at him and took a bite from my own.

A warm breeze flitted around me, and when I opened my eyes again, Pyre's eyes were aflame as he watched me. At first, I thought he had been frustrated, but I quickly saw that the ground was now bursting with strawberry plants when I looked around. They spanned across my entire chamber, the delicious scent of Earth wafting about. Pyre was not angry with me; he was in awe of me.

"You've done it," he said, eyes alight. His smile was so wide; I thought I had never seen so many perfectly placed teeth in my life.

"I've done it," I blew out, astonished by the view. He bent over and picked a ripened strawberry from the ground, the bright red in great contrast to the pale shade of his skin. He passed it to me, and I folded it into my hand, just like how

Gram had given me the strawberry in my memory. A moment of déjà vu disconcerted me where I stood. A sudden bark sounded from the hall, and a moment of delight pricked my heart.

"Drakovyr!" I called, unable to relax my smile. I hadn't seen Pyre's hound since I met him. A storm of black fur whooshed us by as the dog ran through the doorway and into the room. "Hi, baby," I squealed as he jumped up onto me. His two big paws slapped my chest and pushed me onto my bed.

"Drakovyr, down," Pyre boomed, rubbing a hand over his brow. He groaned audibly and stalked forward. Drakovyr didn't so much as pay him a look. He was too focused on licking me from chin to forehead. I laughed at the contact, feeling so much love from this giant guard dog of the Under Realm.

"Oh, come on, Pyre." I beamed. "He's just looking for some kisses." Drakovyr licked me again as if in reply.

"That is not your bed." Pyre groaned and lifted the giant dog off of me. I patted the dog's head, and he sat at my feet, devotedly enjoying the attention.

"He likes me." I smiled at him. I looked up at Pyre as he observed his dog and me.

"Undoubtedly." He chuckled, smirking at me. "Perhaps even more than me." At that, the dog stood from its perch and sauntered off to stand next to his ruler as if reassuring the God of his devotion. He put his big nose in the palm of Pyre's hand and received a caring pet to the snout. I decided that this was how I preferred the God of the Dead. Something about the connection he held with his dog melted a small piece of the ice guarding my heart.

"Great work," he said, tipping his head to me. He plucked another strawberry from the ground and fed it to the dog, who happily swallowed it whole. I giggled at the sight of the happy hound. "I will leave you to your nightly dues and see you first thing in the morning." I exhaled, glad to have succeeded in this lesson. To see the green, red, and beautiful chocolate brown of the soil was a wonderful feeling.

"Thank you," I answered with a smile, still holding the strawberry Pyre had given me.

"Goodnight," he said and walked off with Drakovyr at his side.

41

FAC TUA MAGICAE

"You are making good progress," Pyre praised. I was still bothered by the fact that Pyre Malum had caused me discomfort to coax the magic out yesterday, but I couldn't help admiring my newest achievement. Magic was becoming far more accessible now that I was applying myself. Still, it took much effort and even more introspection than I thought humanly possible.

"It's so weird," I said, whooshing my hands through the air as I called fire to me again. Pyre's lip curled at my wonderment, bringing me back to reality. The flames sputtered, slowly winding smoke around me until all that was left was a smell like pewter.

"You are blocking yourself from your full potential," he chided, and I rolled my eyes at his pointed insult. He was very keen on indicating my flaws.

"I'm not trying to," I managed to say, reluctant to feed his need for argument.

"Tell me, what is holding you back? What do you fear most?" I averted my eyes and dusted my hands off. Practicing magic was exhausting, and having Pyre Malum teach it was even more tiresome. When I looked back at him, hand on hip, he raised a brow at me. I wanted to say that death was my greatest fear. I wanted to say that being in Hell or being captured by a renounced God was my greatest fear. I wanted to scream it from the top of my lungs. I met his challenge and raised my own brow at him.

"What's your biggest fear?" I asked instead. He grew somber and dark, and I immediately regretted my asking.

"You cannot begin to imagine the fear I have. The fears I have faced which still haunt me." He grimaced. I felt a pang in my chest at his vulnerability. It was rare that he shared this side of himself. He was mainly impatient and often bitter. But I was starting to see a glimmer beneath his hard façade. These bouts of openness tugged at my delicate heartstrings in ways I wasn't sure were safe for me.

"I will never begin to understand how you feel. Your history is that of hardships," I supposed. "I am sorry that you went through the split."

"Do not pity me," he grated, fists clenching at his sides.

"Don't mistake my empathy for pity. I do not pity you." He eyed me carefully, hesitant to continue. I wanted him to open up to me. I needed to believe there was a shred of light in this dark God. I needed to see that he had some form of a heart under all that wound-up hate.

"It was a long time ago," he said, stirring me from my thoughts.

"It was, but it doesn't make your traumas any less valid," I offered, sitting cross-legged on the stone floor. He followed suit and sat in front of me, one knee bent and his elbow resting atop it. It was odd to see him so casual, notwithstanding the blue-tinted black wings mounted behind him.

"You did not answer my question," he said, evading my attention. "What do you fear most?" I took a minute to think about it, then took a deep breath. I had to be careful not to strike the wrong chord.

"I fear failure," I said, finally admitting my defeat. "I fear loss—the loss of time and the loss of people."

"Do not omit your fear of the dark." Pyre teased, pointing a quirked brow at me. I huffed in both annoyance and admission.

"I fear the unknown...." I trailed off.

"You have many fears," he stated. I noticed his fingers twitching in his lap, and I wondered if he was troubled by my fears or displeased by them.

"Yes, I do. I have lots and lots of fears." I exhaled. "You want to know what I think I fear most?" I laughed, shaking my head. He tensed at my change in humor and looked away.

"What?" he grunted. His hands curled into fists now.

"Myself," I supposed. I watched as his brows furrowed. My answer sank in and ignited something in him. He met my eyes again after hiding from the answer.

"As do I," he remarked. "As do I."

"Great," I muttered. "That's helpful."

"Can you create more flames?" Pyre asked; a wicked grin grew auspiciously on his face as he changed the subject. He leaned forward, and I braced myself for the fatigue I knew awaited me.

"I don't know," I said honestly. "I didn't really make it happen. I mean, I didn't try to catch fire yesterday. Today is just like yesterday. It just happened."

"I made it happen," he crooned and got to his knees. "Shall we go again?" The fear settled in as he crawled forward, like an animal closing in on its prey. He had the same look on his face that told me he was in the mood to exploit his dominance. I had procured flame today, but it wasn't enough for him. Nothing would be enough for him when it came to securing my power. I got up in a rush and began to back away. When I started to turn from him, he again grabbed my wrist. "Consume the fear, Goddess," he demanded. "Lean into the anger and use it for your defence." The scrape of his claws was a taunting pain as he ordered me to fight him. The sting was barely there but enough to rouse me.

"Pyre, please don't try this again. It's enough," I said, unable to understand his behavior. One minute he was open and sharing the deepest parts of himself, and the next, his walls were up and fortified.

"Who is to say what is enough and what isn't?" he taunted me. I could never predict his words or his actions. Why did he insist on pushing me like this? Why try to stir my magic by angering me or making me feel defenseless? I was doing what he asked of me. I was trying my best.

"I'm to say." I shrank. "I am done with this. Trying to control the flames around me... I don't want more fire right now. I don't want any of this!" I spewed. His eyes grew dark and menacing. Nothing of his vulnerability from a moment ago shone on his face. He was back to his usual self.

"You don't want any of this? You don't want any of the power that I am so willing to teach you?" He snarled at me now. "Insensible," he said challengingly, gritting his teeth. His nails dug deeper into my wrist, seeping into heat. A bead of blood dribbled down onto the floor, making me jump as it splattered. I hadn't expected him to go this far. I gasped at the sight of cruelty and tugged at my arm, urging him to let go. The playful combat felt far away as the liquid crimson oozed from my skin. I used my free hand now, trying to pry his fingers from my wrist. In one quick move, he used his strength on my moment of fright and spun me into his chest. The wind knocked out of me as my back hit muscle, and I froze.

"Please." I coughed, my plea soundless. "You're scaring me."

"I have been benevolent, Goddess. Do not take my kindness for weakness," he growled in my ear. My hair stuck to my face from the sweat. I started to panic, the air coming back into my lungs. The hyperventilation came soon after. "I know you're angry with me. I can feel your rage seeping from your skin. Erase the fear and focus on it," he said. "Pain and anger stroke your fire." I shook from the frenzy. He had me captured yet again, only this time, it was physically in his arms. I didn't like this feeling of being caught. The pain from his nails was bearable, never quite pushing me over the edge into agony. I closed my eyes, my heart beating fast, and strained all my muscles till they were sore. The wrath in me built up with no end in sight.

"Let me go," I ground out, widening my stance. He laughed down my neck, and a shiver ran up my spine.

"As I've said before, Goddess—make me." I planted my feet and tried to tear away from him, but he gripped me further, pushing my body into his own. "Good," he grumbled. "Keep trying," he huffed in my ear. "Use your weight with your strength." Everything in me wanted to make him feel how he made me feel. I wanted to hurt him, wanted so badly to be the intimidating one. I would do just that.

"You will free me," I demanded, gritting my teeth as I leaned into the anger. My left arm came loose under his grip, and I took this moment to swing it free from him. I jerked it forward, threw my elbow back, and landed a blow to his abdomen. He grunted over my shoulder, and it pleased me.

"Almost." He groaned, grabbing my elbow and forcing it

back into his grasp. He had gotten another hold on me, but I would make it this time. This time, I would free myself from his snare.

"I said, let me go!" I wrenched myself from the daimon as fast as possible, digging my heel into the ground. I swallowed the fear and screamed so loud that the rocks became rubble. I could see the fire alight in my hair, moving with my motions. I screeched, ears piercing as I watched the dust settle around us. Bits of small, loose stones tumbled from crevices in the walls and ceiling, and I wanted to sing from the power brewing inside me. Thin, jade vines came curling up from the ground and wrapped around my captor's feet. I couldn't help the grin that flourished on my face and roared in a fit of laughter. I felt it all. This was my doing. I was a force to be reckoned with, and Pyre Malum would soon come to realize it.

"So strong," he rumbled, losing his grip from a moment of surprise. His irritation shone at my fleeing from him. I ducked away from his swing when he tried to grab me again.

"Don't touch me," I said, backing away now. I felt a warm sensation dripping down my jaw, and I put my fingers to the spot—a hot splotch of blood stained my fingers. My shriek had made my ears bleed. I shivered at the sight. When I looked up again, Pyre was hovering above me; a single vine still draped around his left foot. I had never seen him look so dark. He was the pure definition of fury. His title suited him, the God of the Dead.

"You have to listen," he ordered, flapping his wings. "You will train and end the self-pity."

"I will do as I please," I said, wringing up the nerve to stand up to him. He showed his teeth, pointed into a snarl.

"Do not force my hand," he warned. "Do not make me hurt you. I do not want to."

"You already have," I spat, pointing to my wrist. My hair

fell forward, the red flame drenching the strands without ever burning me. "You don't need to hurt me to make my magic rise."

"As I said, I don't want to hurt you. Your magic is reacting to the pain. Your magic is caused by your response, by emotions." He fought, his wings booming as he landed a foot away from me now. I held my breath as he stared down at me. His black hair fell to the front of his face as I looked up, met his scrutiny, and stood my ground. "I am only trying to help you."

"I will learn to control my magic," I hissed back at him. "But mark my words, Pyre Malum, I will do this pain-free and on my terms." I straightened my shoulders and held firm. He studied me, a look of disgust marking his face.

"Don't call me that..." he growled.

"What?" He lowered his eyes, breathing heavily and hard. I found pain and embarrassment flitting in his expression. "That is your name," I held, looking up at him. A guttural noise rumbled in his chest as he looked down at me.

"*You* don't call me that," he insisted, searching my face. His eyes were still a burning red. "I don't like it." His voice was hushed.

"Well, I don't like it when you use your dominance against me. I don't like walking on eggshells around you, wondering if you're content or in the mood to play with me like I'm shatter-proof. And I hate it when you tease at pain like it's so easy for you to inflict," I rebutted. It felt good to get those words off my chest.

"You are vulnerable," he grunted, locking my gaze. My mouth fell open, dumbfounded by his response. He lifted a hand, and I flinched at the movement. I fixed myself, closing my mouth shut. I didn't want to anger him any further, and I didn't want another chance of him trapping me again. I stood still as his hand moved to me, landing atop my cheek. I stiffened as he brushed his fingers along the side of my face. "I don't want to use my force against you. Not really. I just—" He stopped, frowning down at the floor. He sighed heavily and met my gaze again. "I am trying to help you the only way I know how. This is how we Gods were taught. You exhibit the same manifestations as most all Gods. Your magic begs for motivation." He paused, looking to make sure I heard him. His finger still traced my cheek, and I couldn't for the life of me understand why. Though I wanted to shy away, I listened, wanting to hear him out. "We were trained endlessly, pushed to the breaking point and then even further. Pain is a built-in advantage—one that drives your defenses high. I want you to have protection, just as I want you to learn your magic." His eyes went from his red hue to the golden one I had only glimpsed twice before.

"Pain is not the same for me as it is for you," I held. "My bones aren't strong enough to endure the ache if you pull and push at me too hard. My skin will heal fast, as it has been while here in the Under Realm. But the ache in my joints lingers."

"You are so fragile," he murmured. He seemed to be easing himself down from the ire. I began to recognize that these changes I could find in his eyes told me how he would react to me. I could navigate his response to my words and my actions. I took it upon myself to consider this a safe moment and loosed my breath. The impact of his emotional outburst was nauseating.

"I am only human, after all," I whispered, voice shakier than I would've liked. He took a strand of my fiery golden hair in his fingers and twirled it before placing it back over my shoulder. I saw the auburn shade glint before me and realized my roots had grown considerably. A reminder that I was a prisoner here. A reminder that I was still alive.

"Born under the guise of a human; destined to be a Goddess." He looked over to the window that stood behind me. He paused now, watching the skies around us. "What a curious fate."

42

GLIMPSE

Darkness flooded my bedroom as night fell. The sconces spaced throughout the chamber were lit with lambent flames, courtesy of my frustrations circling my mind as I readied for bed. As I replayed today's events and remembered the feeling of being snuffed out by Pyre's power, it was easy to find the energy within me. With a fire-tipped finger, I lifted onto the tips of my toes and reached for the wick, lighting it with a sense of satisfaction. It took only my memory of the God's red eyes burning through me to rouse the magic.

If only the magic would come this quickly while I trained with Pyre. It would certainly make things easier for both of us. Though the God of the Dead enjoyed proving himself powerful, I could see bits and pieces of his hardened self melting away each time he inflicted pain. It was almost as if he didn't understand my humanity, then felt the guilt once it was all said and done. Perhaps being kept away from the vulnerable for so long had erased his memories of what it was like for beings with weaknesses.

It was true that while being in the Under Realm, I wasn't

entirely human. Though I hated to admit it, I was much stronger. I had magic and a lot of it, and I was also healing incredibly fast. Though my muscles ached and I sweated like a pig in the sun while training, I gradually became less fatigued after finishing the session. Cuts and bruises I'd procured mostly from falling and running into walls while hurtling past shots of fire were always gone the following day. My joints still hurt, but I was used to such things. Though it was odd that my body excluded my arthritis when healing, I was at least thankful for whatever magic relieved the other aches and pains. Though I strongly disliked the ugly of the training and all the discomfort that came with it, Pyre's explanation today ignited a new contemplation in me. He'd told me he wanted me to have protection for myself and learn my magic. It wasn't just about being powerful but also about controlling my safety. That had me questioning his motives and wondering where those words had come from. I often forgot that he'd proposed marriage to me. Perhaps, in his own way, he pictured us together at the end of everything. Maybe he wanted me to learn to protect myself because he didn't want to see me get hurt. I could only be sure of what he told me, which meant I'd just have to deal with the unrelenting vexation.

Tucked into the warm blanket of my bed, I stretched out my legs, flexing my feet forward and releasing some of the tension. I was so in over my head with everything. I was in the Under Realm, working with and against an exiled God. It felt weird to feel this cozy as I lay in bed, staring at the castle walls which held me in. I wondered what could be out there. What might I find if I wandered out of the castle and through this inferno?

I closed my eyes and let my imagination run freely, picturing the dry land beneath my feet as I ran through hills of igneous rocks and coarse sands. A heady wind smelling of a fall forest and nighttime bonfire invaded my senses. I looked around, searching for the comfort of woods and nature, but no tree was in sight. A loud growling pierced through the night, and I whirled on my heels, bolting ahead and away from the noise. Feet, thousands and thousands of heavy footfall chased me through the dark expanse, and the further I ran away from the sound, the darker and eerier the land became. Unaware of my surroundings, my feet tripped over a large, hard surface, and I plummeted to the ground. Pain shot up my legs as I reached down, feeling for what I was sure would be a broken femur. My hand stilled as the sounds around me came into focus. Claws on a hard surface, slithering beasts, and the cackling of terrors surrounded me as I lay unseeing in the middle of nowhere.

"Leave me alone," I begged, feeling the slip of my mind as my heart's heavy beating took over my body. I suffered through the tug of claws at my feet, tearing into flesh. I felt the slick snake-like bodies wrap around my arms, squeezing, unrelenting. I was being pulled in all directions, and my gut lurched as I imagined my limbs slowly being severed. There was nothing I could do. I couldn't see a damned thing, and unseen creatures took over my hands. "Pyre!" I called, remembering the God's fierce gaze; golden, warm, and surprisingly solicitous. He would help me. If I could yell loud enough for him to hear, he would make this go away. He was strong, and he was the ruler of this realm. He would take this from me. I knew it deep in my bones. "Pyre, I need you!" I screamed as a slithering serpent slid over my lips and forced itself between my teeth. The scales scraped against my tongue, and I lashed out, shaking my head from side to side as its head wiggled down my throat. Was this the end? My last words rang a hard truth as the serpent forced itself, pushing against my esophagus. A tug at a cord which bound my heart snagged, rocking as if joyfully exulting in my surrender. *I needed him.*

"Shivalri!" I heard and threw my eyes open, panting as I clutched my throat. My eyes darted as I searched the area, finding Pyre hovering over me, eyes ablaze as I knew they would be.

"Get them off of me!" I cried, scraping at my neck, still feeling the touch of claws and scales digging into my flesh. The snake was deep in my throat, heavy in my ribcage. Pyre grabbed my hands and forced them away from my neck. I tried plying them from his grasp, needing to remove the feel of the creatures from my skin. Pyre held firm, his eyes frantic as he forced me to look at him. I couldn't breathe. I tried moving my head away, needing to see behind him. Needing to make sure the beasts hadn't followed me into the room.

"You're all right," Pyre said, voice insistent. "There is nothing on you, Shivalri. There is no one in here but me." I finally let go of the notion that the creatures might have come for me in my chamber and looked to him. I felt something in my chest unlock as I found the golden eyes I'd yearned for in my time of distress. The mass pressed against my ribs was not a serpent but the fullness of what it meant to have a fate such as mine. The burning emotions haggled their way forward, bursting out of me in a wave of tears. Shock, revulsion, and genuine terror forced tremors to course through my veins. I couldn't shake the feeling of the nightmare. It had felt so real. The sentiments that came with it certainly were. Pyre pulled my hands to his chest, clinging so tightly I could burst from the consolation. He'd come for me. I'd called for him in my moment of desperation, and he'd come.

"You came," I said, trembling and unsure of what that meant.

"You called for me," he answered, voice gruff. His hands

still clung to mine like a lifeline. "I thought something had happened to you. I thought you were being attacked," he said, blowing out a sharp breath. A strand of dark hair fell forward over his brow, casting a shadow over his face. "You should know, Goddess; I will always come for you. You have my word." I nodded, feeling the thick lump in my throat slowly ease. "What did you see?" he asked quietly. I could still make out his features in the dark due to his nearness and the faint firelight throughout the room. He wore evocative concern, and his eyes were pools of gold, proving earnestness.

"They were everywhere," I gasped as a shiver of disgust filled me to my teeth. "It was so dark; I couldn't see them. But they were there. Beasts with claws and snakes... I felt every one of them. They were going to tear me apart. They were going to destroy me from the inside out." I couldn't hold it in any longer. My cries were no longer muddled. They were panic-stricken and thick as I sobbed, not caring about the mess my face had become. Pyre took me into his arms, and, for once, I didn't flinch away.

"You're safe," Pyre murmured. "I've got you. No one will ever hurt you so long as I breathe." I felt his large hand tremble as he cupped the nape of my neck, cradling me to his chest. "I've got you," he repeated, and I felt the heat of his breath atop my hair. Never in my life had I felt such whiplash from my emotions. I had never experienced a terror like this, only to be comforted and feel warm instantly afterward. He was the last person I should have wanted, yet the first my soul called to. *I've got you*, he'd said. And it was true. In so many ways, it was.

Pyre let out a heavy breath and his arms loosened around me. Panic flooded me in an intense surge, my back going rigid at the thought of him letting me go. He could protect me. He *would* protect me. I knew it now more than ever.

"Don't." I swallowed, clinging to his muscled arms, urging him to return the body-hugging hold.

"Goddess, I—" he faltered, pulling away, leaving an inch between us as he looked down at me with furrowed brows, searching my face, appearing desperate to read me. His face was strikingly sculpted, electric in the sharp composition of his bone structure. It socked me again just how beautiful he was, evidently carved by the most gifted hands to exist. There were questions in his gaze, abundant and flurried. Though I wasn't ready to rummage through any of them, I needed him to stay. The tug in my chest told me so.

"Don't go," I implored, searching his face for any sign he might flee. His jaw ticked as he bit his bottom lip. My eyes followed the movement, and a very small part of me danced in the back of my mind, enjoying how I'd affected him. "Please," I added. "Just for tonight." He stared down at me for a long moment, and I thought he would flat-out refuse me.

"Why?" he asked, his eyes hidden behind lowered lashes. His voice dipped, and I felt it reverberate. I swallowed hard, all too aware that I was treading on ice. This could complicate things. I was sure he knew I wasn't implying I wanted him to stay for the heated way he looked at me. But it did stir thoughts, dangerous ones. If my mind had skirted the edges of those thoughts, it seemed his had delved below the surface in the way his golden irises sparked in the dark. I wanted him to stay with me because it felt right to have him close. It felt good to be held, and after that horrid nightmare, I was eager to give in to my need to find solace. Consequences be damned. What did this say of me? That I sought comfort from my captor, the ruler of the Under Realm, did little to calm my nerves. But I pushed away the gnawing prudence, allowing myself this moment—just this moment, and nothing more. I cleared my throat, and he watched me tentatively.

"Because I know you'll protect me." His lips twitched, forming a light smile before his chin dipped into a nod. Without a word, Pyre lowered us onto the bed, and a very foreign nervousness tingled all over me. I watched as he took the blanket, slowly and carefully wrapping it around us. My heart hammered wildly in my chest, beating against my ribcage as I tried and failed to hold my breath as I listened to the silence between us. I felt every part of his body that touched my own. My left foot met his right; my hip rested against his arm, which lay between us. I didn't dare move, hardly dared to breathe as the tension built. Though we lay side by side, barely connecting, the weight of his presence was intoxicating. His finger suddenly moved, scarcely brushing the curve of my side, and my breath caught in my chest as I realized he was trying to soothe me. My skin tingled at the contact. I clamped my jaw, willing my head to turn just enough to catch a glimpse of him. He stared up at the ceiling, unmoving, save for the finger which caressed me still. I took a steadying breath as I let my eyes roam the planes of his face. His perfect lips were pouted, and his dark, angular brows were drawn together as if he were fighting a war within himself. His lips suddenly parted, and I might have missed the quiet words he muttered if I hadn't been staring.

"With my life...."

43

PROPAGATE

When I had agreed to learn my magic and try to work together with Pyre Malum—the daimon of the Dead, old God with cut ties; I had no idea what it would entail. All I knew was that this was the only way to get out of my situation, and even after the unexpected sleeping arrangements last night, that was still what I aimed to do. Though pieces of me were hesitant when considering leaving Pyre behind, it was ultimately my only choice and the right thing for me to do. I needed to learn how to use my magic. Learning was the only way I might have a chance at getting free. I needed the ability to fight him off and find a way to get back to Earth—back to my family.

It was strange working with the God. Each day was a new task. Learning control, focus, balance, and how to harness all of it. Each lesson ended with the same thing: Pyre got frustrated and controlled the situation by inflicting small amounts of authoritative power. No matter how many times I tried, that was always what he resorted to, whether or not we had good progress during the day. It worked, but I hated it.

"Pyre, please," I pled. "I am trying." I put my hands on my

knees, out of breath. Sweat beat down my brow as I took a moment for myself.

"It is not enough." He scowled. "Many days have passed, and you are still not capable of wielding your fire affinity without some form of torment. It is the fiercest of affinities, and you must learn to harness it with facility." I cracked my wrists in complaint.

"You haven't given me the chance to try without upsetting me," I scoffed. "I don't need your claws near my skin or for you to taunt me; I just need you to trust me." I rubbed at the soreness that rang through my bones.

"Trust?" He laughed. "This has nothing to do with trust, Goddess, and everything to do with getting what I want." I sat now, having caught my breath. He was back to having his walls up, and I didn't like this version of him. He watched me tentatively, and I exhaled shakily from exhaustion. Tentatively, I stretched my legs, pinched my toes with my fingers, and leaned into the burn. With each hard lesson, my joints were getting more swollen, and my muscles made up the backing I lacked. Not only was I wielding fire, but I was also running and deflecting Pyre's blows. I ran and forfended to the steady rhythm of my heart that was working double-time to keep up with my movements. Not once did I let his flame touch me, but it took a toll on my body.

"You'll get what you want, Pyre," I spoke with my voice muffled, head facing my lap.

"Will I?" he questioned, circling me as I sat on the floor. I was getting used to being hovered over by this dark-winged daimon. He was always trying to intimidate me, always trying to make my fire come forth. At this point, it was hard to care. I curled myself into a seated position and hugged my knees.

"I'm able to conjure the magic we're looking for. I've summoned fire and earth and even shifted the air at will.

What more do you want from me?" I asked. "I haven't had very long to learn. You've had your entire life to control your flame."

"Yes, but we do not have an entire lifetime to teach you," he pointed out.

"Do we have a deadline?" I asked rhetorically. *I* had the deadline. I wanted out of here as fast as possible. Pyre stopped his prowling and stilled in front of me. He squatted to meet my level.

"I want my freedom, Goddess," he said eerily calm. "I want my freedom now." He extended a hand, compelling me to take it. I sighed, submitting, and he lifted me from the ground. We stood face to face, ever silent. He wore a look of concern in his eyes as he looked me over. "Are you well today?" Pyre asked, unease lining his frown.

"I am, thank you," I replied as I tucked my loose hair behind my ear. I recoiled at the reminder of last eve's nightmare and pushed it to the recesses of my mind.

"And your bones?" he continued, coming closer to me now. Since I'd told him about my condition, he was more alert in how he acted physically, especially after last night. The way he'd cradled me as if I were the most delicate thing he's ever touched had me determining more of who he was on the inside. I knew the training he provided was for my own good, and he was slightly less aggressive, which I was certainly glad for. However, seeing the God of the Dead worry about my well-being was strange.

"My bones are complicated." I shrugged and hid my hands in the sleeves of my billowing shirt.

"May I?" he requested and reached for my arms. His actions startled me; I did not expect him to touch me so freely outside of a training session. Last night had changed things. *Consequences be damned...* What had I done?

"What are you doing?" I wondered as he pulled my sleeves back, rolling the material up to my elbows.

"I would like to see if you don't mind?" He took each of my hands in his, carefully, delicately, and turned them over. He looked intently at my palms, searching for some indication that my bones were unusual. He flipped them back over, seemingly eyeing my knuckles. He swiped a delicate finger over my right hand, touching my mother's ring. I flinched back instinctually, not wanting him to connect with any part of my family. That was not for him to touch. It was not his to take. He looked up at me quickly, brows creased, then steadied my hands in his again. His thumb rubbed across the lump that sat atop my right wrist, and he looked up at me. "Does this hurt?"

"No," I muttered, stunned by the change in focus. "It's uncomfortable when you apply pressure, but simply touching me doesn't hurt."

"What is this?" He rubbed his thumb again, referring to the lump.

"A rheumatoid nodule," I stammered. "They come and go with the swelling. I get them during flare-ups."

"Flare-ups?" He cocked his head to the side in intrigue.

"It's like an intense attack on my system. For me, it's always been caused by trauma." His eyes narrowed, still rubbing at my hand in wonder. My words bothered him. I could see it in the set of his jaw and the way his frown deepened.

"Did I cause this to happen?" he questioned unexpectedly, face hard. "When I grabbed your wrist, did it cause this lasting pain?" I shook my head at him in disbelief.

"Now you care?" He let go of my hands and took a step back.

"I do not wish to harm you, Goddess. I only mean to make you stronger. It is how I was taught so long ago. The discomfort that I inflict is not intended to last." He paused, looking away from me to the floor. "Your power and immortality are supposed to protect you from the long-lasting effects, but if my actions are truly causing lasting distress, then I will assuredly stop. I regret to confess that I did not see how strenuous our training has been for you," he held, shoulders rigid. I wanted to tell him that he had caused many kinds of pain to last a lifetime, but I decided against it. Though I wanted him to feel guilty, I did not want to lie to him about the nodules. He would inevitably smell the rot seeping from my mouth if I did.

"I've had those lumps since long before I arrived here, Pyre. You were not the cause." He gradually moved his eyes from the ground, looking me over in thought—discomfort rooted in his gaze.

"Why?"

"If it's all right with you, I'd rather not discuss my deformities. It's embarrassing enough that I have crooked pinkies, can't straighten my fingers, and my spine is trying to imitate the hunchback of Notre Dame. We don't need to talk about my lumps."

"I'd be delighted to discuss your lumps." He grinned, lowering his eyes to my chest.

"Funny." I coughed, heat rushing to my cheeks. Did he just outwardly flirt with me? What on Earth was going on? I immediately grew desperate to change the subject. This conversation had taken a weird turn.

"What is the hunchback of Notre Dame?" he asked, before flicking me on the nose. My eyes widened in surprise. Stunned by his teasing, I gawked at his lip-bitten smirk. I blinked several times before shaking myself from my open stare.

"It's a *who*, not a what. And it's not important," I assured him. "Let's get back to training," I mumbled. "*Without* torment," I added, straightening myself.

"That's the spirit." He clasped his hands behind his back and strode away from me. "When you conjure fire, it frequently stems from anger. It correlates to your pain. Earth comes from love and inner strength. That has been purely evident." I nodded in agreement. "When you conjure water, it is from sorrow. Sometimes from joy, but mostly from sorrow," Pyre explained. "When you conjure air, what is it that you think of?" I thought about the wind and remembered when it came to me at the Grimsbane manor. Then, it had come from desperation, a kind of hope mixed with anxiety. But here, at Pyre's castle, I'd briefly felt it whenever I thought of escaping.

"I think of freedom and hope," I resolved, quickly knowing the answer in my gut. "I think of just being." I closed my eyes at the thought. I felt a cool breeze flow around me as I imagined myself hovering in the air.

"Good. Continue," Pyre ordered from a distance. "What does *being* feel like?" he questioned further.

"Just being." I tried to find a way to describe it. "Being, without a worry; without care. Believing in all that you are, and just existing in yourself; however you want."

"Existing." He laughed. "Open your eyes." His demand confused me.

"What?" I asked as I opened my eyes and realized I was drifting above the ground.

"Holy shit! I'm flying!"

"You are hovering." He chuckled and clapped his hands.

"How do I get down?" I was still laughing from the high.

"How do you get up?" he countered, and I closed my eyes and thought of the skies. I felt myself rising now. Higher and liberated, I went. I thought that, in this bliss, if I dared open my eyes again, I might touch the castle's ceiling. I enjoyed this moment—this tiny sliver of freedom, this moment of being. I thought back to the ground and quickly started falling. My heart thundered as I anticipated the hard stone beneath my weight. I threw my arms out, attempting to slow my descent by miracle.

Before I could fall, Pyre sprinted over to me with arms wide. I was scared for a moment, as it seemed he might tear me down. I braced my arms in front of me, preparing for impact from either him or the ground. To my surprise, he grabbed me to his chest and swung me around. My mouth gaped at the absurdity, and I suddenly felt the urge to laugh from the euphoric feeling of this instant.

"What are you doing? Put me down." I giggled. He let me go and held my shoulders. I was stunned. I hadn't ever seen anything close to joy on this man's face. This whole affair was bizarre and outlandish, yet so beautiful.

"How does freedom taste?" he asked, smiling from ear to ear.

"It's exhilarating." I beamed. "Do you think I can do it again?" He grinned and let out a laugh.

"Of course, you can." He nodded. "Join me." I did.

* * *

When it came time to retire for the night, I dawdled by my water basin, taking a relatively long time to bathe. After last night's terrors, I wasn't eager to attempt to sleep. I'd scrubbed my skin raw, remembering the horrible feeling of monsters attacking me in my nightmare. Now, squeaky clean but still not wanting to test slumber, I decided to take some time to experiment with my affinity for earth. It came to me quickly and certainly more controlled than the others. The magic only required my thoughts to drift into happy memories of gardening. Happy thoughts, in general, were the source of my earth affinity; however, I found that focusing on moments in nature was a seemly way to ensure my magic came when and where I wanted it to.

I closed my eyes, remembering how Pépère stuck circular cages around the tomato plants, teaching me to be gentle when placing the tomatoes through the loops. Red, plump, and delicious, they made for a flavorsome snack, and I was in the mood for a taste of summer. I planted my feet, imagining the ground filling with soil, covering the tops of my toes in rich, damp earth. I could smell the greenery sprouting around me as I stood in my chamber. It smelled like the very end of summer. The leaves would still be vibrant in the time I pictured. The vegetables would be ready and ripe to harvest.

"I thought I smelled divinity," said the familiar voice outside my door. I'd left it open a crack, not wanting to seal myself with the creatures of my imagination.

"Pyre," I said, taking a step toward him, forgetting the soil beneath my toes. I squashed a juicy tomato and halted, slowly lowering my head in embarrassment and woe. The sound of Pyre's throaty chuckle had me blushing, and I gradually lifted my foot, watching as the peel and slime fell from my toes and thunked to the ground. Pyre strolled into the room, looking both regal and casual as he came toward me, one hand coolly rested in his pants pocket. He was shirtless, as usual, and his large, feathered wings were tucked behind him, casting shadows over his features. I observed him as he approached.

Standing a foot apart, I stared at him, defectively attempting to keep my eyes away from his brawny chest. His lips pulled up into a smirk, the kind that made the charm in my gut spring to life. Pyre started to kneel, and I almost backed away, but not before he took my filthy foot in his hand and removed the rest of the goo. He gently placed my foot back to the ground and stood from his kneel. A patch of brown now stained his knee, and I bit my lip, considering his actions. He'd removed the filth from me only to dirty himself. He wiped the gunk from his fingers onto his pants, uncaring.

"You seem to be doing much better when it comes to your earth affinity," Pyre said, shrugging as he surveyed the grounds of my bedroom.

"I think it's my favorite," I admitted, looking away from him and to the plants that now sprouted around me. The tomato plants had manifested with but a simple thought, just as I'd wanted.

"I would naturally say that fire is my favorite of all gifts," said Pyre, pulling my attention back to him. "Now, I'm not so sure."

"You like the earth affinity too?" I asked. A smile tugged at his mouth, and my own copied his gesture.

"I like that *you do*." His words stirred a flush within me, and I swore the heat between us was a tangible thing. I turned toward the nearest plant and picked the ripest from the bunch. I chewed my lip, swallowing the nerves as I lifted it to Pyre, offering him the fruit. His brows, dark in contrast to his skin, raised above his golden eyes.

"Tomato?" I offered. The magnetic pull between us was intense, causing my hand to shake. Pyre leaned forward and pressed his lips to the red fruit, taking a bite straight from my hold. The breath left my lips as my jaw fell open, unable to look away. Pyre pulled away, licked his lips, and squinted his eyes at me, daring me to say something—anything. His dreamily cut almond eyes, magical and alluring, finally fell away as his lashes lowered.

"Thank you," he said, breaking the silence. I cleared my throat, still trying to process what the hell had happened. Pyre picked the fruit from my still outstretched hand and stepped back. The moment he pulled away, I felt the air around me dull. Though it was stale, it was easier to breathe.

"Uh, you're welcome...." I managed and finally let my arm fall to my side.

"Will you be all right tonight?" he asked. I scrunched my nose, confused.

"What?"

"The nightmare..." he clarified. "Will you be all right to sleep alone tonight? I am more than happy to—"

"Oh, no," I blurted, cutting him off. As if there weren't enough of a flush in my cheeks, he had to go and offer another eve in my bed. "You're fine. I mean, I'm fine. I will be fine." I stumbled over my words and pulled at the sleeve of my shirt, feeling awkward and senseless. Pyre nodded, seeming to catch my discomfort, and backed toward the doorway.

"Very well," he replied, sparing another glance around the room. "Well done, Goddess. Now get some rest."

"Okay," I answered, squishing my toes in the soil, unsure what to say or do as he stared at me. He turned away, making to leave. "Thank you," I uttered, stammering and sounding far chirpier than I felt. I caught a glimpse of a smile tug at his lips before he left down the hall. The draw between us stretched taught as I watched him leave, tomato in hand.

44

———

MAELSTROM

The following week of training was not as arduous and far more manageable. Floating, or hovering as Pyre called it, was a non-thought. I just had to close my eyes and think of freedom. It was a breeze going through the motions. I spent a lot of time in the air, looking down at the room. Fire came to me easier now. All I had to do was think about being trapped down here, wallow in the self-pity, and I burst into flames. It was extinguishing the blaze that was harder. Settling my rage was the trick—one I hadn't quite yet conquered.

I also learned to grow flowers and plants in this dry, lifeless dwelling. Earth had quickly become my favorite affinity. Though sometimes it was hard to clear my mind from this place, the earth affinity came to me by thinking about happy memories. The power progressed if I concentrated on days of gardening with my grandparents. The first thing I grew intentionally, aside from the initial experiments, was a bitter ginger plant. I was thrilled to have worked my magic and produced my grandmother's sudsy ginger plant, which she often used as a shampoo. The feeling of washing my hair with soap was delightful on its own, but the *smell* was magnificent. The scent of spiced ginger clung to my hair throughout the day, and my skin elicited the aroma with every move I made. I'd begun twisting my hair to the front of my face just to get a whiff of the warm fragrance. It made me think of home.

Lavender grew from every corner of this castle now. Honeysuckle draped every window ledge, and vines grew up most walls. I brought to life everything that Gram had taught me about gardening. Pyre informed me that being immortal came with certain advantages, such as requiring food far less often than humans. Even though I didn't feel any hunger in this Under Realm, I planted a garden in the throne room along the wall with the windows. The once clay floor turned into soil filled with rows upon rows of vegetation. Pyre even enjoyed snacking on the beans that grew from their stalks, often sharing bites with Drakovyr, who was visibly eager to receive them. It was weird to see him do something considerably mundane. It was even stranger comparing him to my younger self, who used to steal Gram's beans straight from the stalk as a child.

Pyre's servants also took from the plants when they thought I wasn't looking. I had told Alriq, the leader of the pythrants, that they were free to have what they wanted. He quickly thanked me; still, I did not know if he had told the others. Though Pyre and the pythrants did not need fruits and vegetables for sustenance, they appeared glad for the treat. I mostly enjoyed the berries. I had forgotten how lovely a strawberry tasted and how wonderfully fresh fruit smelled. I ate my fill of fruits and vegetables while I could produce them and thoroughly appreciated them.

I enjoyed this earth affinity, but I had to be meticulous. Seeing the life in this palace typically made me happy, but sometimes it triggered my anger. When upset, it took but one touch to the floras for the rage to take root, turning it all to ash. Then I had to regenerate the development. This problem would happen every so often. Something would upset me every couple of days, and I would combust. There would be no warning and no flame retardant in sight—just me, enclosed in the fire.

For the most part, I was able to control everything, which made me feel much better about my progress. It solidified the possibility of my escape. Pyre seemed happier with each day that passed, his mood lighter than usual. I counted the days as they went since being out of the oubliette. Eleven, to be exact. Almost two weeks of learning magic and my entire life depending on it. I thought about my grandmother, brother, cousin, and Dad. I thought of everyone I left back on Earth and often wondered what they were doing—curious and hopeful that they were well.

I had to take them out of my mind because I lost hope if I thought about them for too long. When I thought about Gram, Raidan, and Satyra, I imagined them in the house. I pictured them huddled up together, sitting on lounge chaises and drinking tea. I had to envision them smiling and healthy. The imagery of them lying limp on the floor at the House of Enchantment gave me shivers. I was stolen away from them, unsure if they were dead or alive. They had to be all right. They were everything to me.

As day seventeen of my being here in the Under Realm would approach come morning, I found that time grew a little faster with each passing day. As I learned and trained, my magic became stronger. It was more controlled and built the confidence I didn't know I had. I had spent all this time under the care of the God of the Dead, and it was everything except boring. It was terrifying and exciting all in one. On the one hand, I knew he was supposed to be the classification of evil, but on the other, it was amusing seeing his different sides of him. It was becoming easier to play to those different sides. I had to bring myself back to reality most of the time and remember that this wasn't a dream. It felt like an out-of-body experience. Unrealistic. It was the strangest thing I had ever experienced, and I had never imagined something like this could be real. I still had to wrap my head around magic, never mind that my birthday would be coming up soon, and I would be spending it in Pyre Malum's inferno.

Pyre didn't discuss the days. He wouldn't tell me about weekdays or the specifics of the calendar. When I asked once, he told me they were for humans and that time was elusive and insignificant in the Under Realm. So, I began counting from the day I got out of the oubliette. The God had told me that I had stayed in the tower for five days, having survived the fall, famine, and the dark. I still couldn't believe I had lost such time wasting away. Since then, the eleven days I'd counted had passed, making the over two-week stay a long and challenging one.

After the night Pyre had stayed to comfort me after a nightmare, he began checking on me before bed after the end of each day, lingering in the doorway. It was almost as if he were waiting for me to invite him in again. The thought of how close I'd allowed myself to get to him sent goosebumps up my arms. Something very wrong was stirring between us. There had been a shift, a cosmic pull I couldn't shake. I was delighted to be nearing the end of this quest. Even happier to see my powers manifesting. I would get out of this soon enough. I would have to. Meanwhile, I'd take advantage of the time I had here by learning my magic and entertaining myself with the God of the Dead.

"Will you teach me to really fly?" I looked at Pyre, who stood near his books, waiting for him to deny me. I sat on the windowsill, and I knew he observed me when I looked out the windows. I knew he could tell that I often wished to leap out at the first chance. Though all I'd been able to see was an extensive expanse of desert and what seemed to be a river made of lava that ran the space of the land, I would still love the chance to get out of this castle.

"Teach you to fly, you say?" He put a finger to his chin in thought. "Where would you like to go?" He gave a stern look and threw his eyes to the window behind me. I shrugged, dangling my feet below.

"Wherever you're willing to take me," I supposed.

"We cannot leave the castle," he stated. His face was firm, and his fists clenched at his sides. I knew that that would be his answer, but it didn't mean he couldn't still teach me to fly.

"Fly me through the castle," I said. "This place is big enough for an adventure on its own, and you fly around the halls all the time."

"Yes, I do. It is my preferred method of travel." I smiled at that.

"I noticed." He met me with a wicked grin and quirked his head.

"You've been watching me?"

"Purely for educational purposes, of course." I winked, emboldened by his mischievous smile. He laughed out loud, clutching a hand to his chest, amazement marking his face. Something in my gut curled in excitement at his laugh, and I thought I might squeal at the sound. I had managed to make this miserable God a little brighter in my days of working with him.

"Did you just wink at me?" He grinned, white, pointed teeth glinting in the sunlight.

"Perhaps." I giggled, feeling the flush burn my cheeks. He sighed with a smirk, approving me.

"You've convinced me, Goddess. I shall teach you to fly. Be warned, in any case. It takes great effort to fly as gracefully as I. It will take time to get you flying properly, as you do not have wings like me." My eyes landed on his dark, black-blue wings, and I found myself marveling at them yet again. They looked so soft, a shade of black so like the night with a shimmer of indigo I'd grown to admire. I had never feared that part of who he was. The wings felt like a good presence. It was like a piece of the greatness he once was. When I watched him fly, I thought that so long as those wings remained on his body, perhaps the good would remain a part of him, too, whether he realized it or not. When I looked back to meet his eyes, they bore humility. It seemed a recognition of self as if he, too, found his wings to be the best part of him. As if they were a reminder of the good times so long ago.

"Teach me to fly," I insisted. "Please. I'm practically begging here." I kicked my feet out in front of me, clinging to the ledge of the window. He laughed lowly and extended a hand.

"Do not tease me with the idea of your begging," he taunted, and I took his hand, coming down from the ledge. I blushed at his wry grin, imagining where his thoughts had landed. Even more intriguing was where my mind had gone.

"Okay, Pyre. Show me your magic and teach me your ways," I said mockingly, feigning a bow. He dipped his head in return.

"We start by first getting you into the air."

"I can manage that." I smiled. He released my hand and allowed me space to focus. Hovering came contentedly to me as I spent much of my time here thinking about my freedom. It was a dominant need I had; therefore, I could tap into it almost effortlessly. I found it interesting to see the progress I'd made when tapping into affinities. Strange that in such a short time, I'd become an entirely different person.

I closed my eyes and took a deep breath in, filling my lungs with air. The wind flitted through my hair, and I welcomed the familiar breeze I had come to know. It was my own production of air. It smelled of musky-sweet leaves and flowers in bloom. I released my breath, and with a gush, I opened my eyes, knowing well that I was in the air, floating an entire foot above Pyre. He smiled up at me, beaming in what looked to be pride.

"Well done," he said and spread his wings. He was instantly high above me, relishing in his flight.

"Hey, not fair!" I yelled up to him as he swooped high and low. The wind whooshed around me as his wings flapped nearby. He came to a halt directly in front of me and let out a bellow.

"Care to join me, Goddess?" He fluttered in place, stretching his arms out wide. I rolled my eyes.

"A little help," I demanded, pointing to myself set in place. It was my turn to reach out a hand to him. He quirked a brow at me, amused by my boldness. Instead of accepting, he flew around to my back, and I tried to turn my head to follow him.

"Pay no mind to me," he said. "Look straight ahead. Focus on your path." He came up behind me and wrapped both of his arms around my waist.

"What are you doing?" I batted at his hands, suddenly too aware of my stomach beneath his touch.

"Allow me to help you." He squeezed a little tighter, making sure he had a firm hold of me. My belly folded under the constriction of his hands, forcing me to huff a breath. He loosened his grip, chuckling unswervingly in my ear. It tingled a little, and that pushed me off-balance.

"Fine," I jeered, clinging to his arm for support.

"Always so eager to protest," he said quietly.

"Always so eager to prevail," I retorted. He let out a breath, and it traveled down my neck.

"So sensitive." He pressed himself into me, and I gasped at the nearness. I had never been so close to anyone before. I could smell the scent of earthy grounds drifting over my body. The smell of fresh soil and sweet-smelling woods had always been a favorite of mine, though I'd never experienced its carnality until now. My hands felt instantly clammy, and I wiped them on my shirt.

"Where are you taking me?" I wondered, breath a little shaky.

"We will ease into the flight," he explained. "It's going to feel like I am carrying you at first, as I will be handling the drag you cause until you are used to pulling your weight against the wind."

"Are you calling me heavy?" I nudged with my elbow to poke him in the chest.

"Perfectly so," he replied. I was glad to be facing away from him now. Otherwise, I would have been embarrassed for him to see me redden.

"Let's go," I said, finding my voice.

"Gladly."

Pyre flew us around the castle for what seemed to be hours. I was the most content I'd ever been while being here. We flew across the entire expanse of the castle, and I took in the building. I was both using this time to memorize its patterns for a better chance at escape but also enjoying the view it afforded. The Under Realm was unlike anything I had ever seen before. Pyre didn't venture away from the castle, but we went outside briefly as we flew over a rickety bridge connected to the second half of the building. After taking one look at the passage, I was thankful to be in the air and not at the mercy of the broken tangle of ropes and wood. Being outside provided an even greater sense of freedom. I felt feather-light, a weightless breeze in Pyre's arms.

"Are you all right?" he asked me through the soft wind which played with my hair.

"More than all right." I breathed, relishing the moment. Pyre's grip loosened a bit, allowing me to find my own footing in the air. He made to release me, and my stomach fell to my throat at the thought of falling. I gripped his arm, which held my waist, tensing until he curled more snugly into my back.

"I will not let you fall," he told me. A brief caress of his thumb against my side took me by surprise, and I eased into the touch. I secretly smiled into the breeze, finding that I believed him. Somehow, unbeknownst to me, I'd grown to trust him. Not entirely, never wholeheartedly. But at this moment, I trusted him to carry me through the skies, feeling safe in his embrace.

"I know," I said to him. I felt his head lower to my shoulder, and a small part of my soul melted at his gentle, reassuring actions.

"And so, Goddess... Do you enjoy flying?" I looked around me, pulling away from the lingering thoughts of Pyre's nearness, and really took in my surroundings.

"It's wonderful," I replied, and I truly meant it.

Seeing everything from up high brought a new light to the place. I was pleased to see color from the plants I had grown all over the building. The best part of it all was the feeling of liberation. Though I was wrapped in the God of the Dead's arms, I was exhilarated by the wind whirling around me. I played with the air, dancing in its aura. In this moment of bliss, I wanted to pause, to make it last forever. Pyre held me strong as we flew, guiding my every move.

When we decided to take a break, we made for the throne room, and he slowly released me so that I could hover in place on my own. He held out a hand, and when my fingers slipped in his, he steadied us parallel to his throne of bones. He held me soundly, and I didn't let him let go.

"Pyre," I said, quieting my voice. He looked at me intently as if trying to read my face. "Have you ever felt happy like this?" He furrowed his brows.

"You believe me happy?" he questioned.

"Yes," I declared. "You've been smiling. Truly smiling. I'd say that makes you look happy." He smirked at that mention, hunching closer to me now. I had to tilt my head back to meet his gaze. He was so much taller than my five-foot-five frame. I felt the heat under his watch. It settled in me like wildfire.

"Are you happy?" he asked. My smile quickly turned to a frown, and he lightly tilted my chin, forcing me to *really* look at him. "Do not hide from me." He searched for my reply. I had been holding my breath at his touch. I didn't think I had an answer, and if I did, it was probably the wrong one.

"I'm not sure," I answered simply, many thoughts within me at war with each other. We were standing in front of the table amassed with old manuscripts, and it held me in place. I couldn't escape his inspection. When Pyre stepped nearer, I met the edge of the slab with the back of my thighs. I hadn't expected this proximity while facing him, and I quickly became disordered. He pinned me there and simply watched, waiting for clarification.

"Hmm..." he hummed, and it reverberated in my chest.

"Honestly, I don't know, Pyre," I said nervously. His muscled legs touched mine now, and I could feel his eagerness pressing into my thin breeches. What was happening? A tingling sensation ran through me at the thought of the intimacy that came from this closeness. Aside from fleeting moments with Pyre, I had never felt anything remotely close to this before. I had no interest in men, no interest in anyone. I thought about the butterflies I felt at Nathan's kindness, and the first time I saw Gladys O'Donnell's eyes. That was only admiration. Nothing compared to this passion. This stirring deep in my core was absolute lust, and it tasted delicious. Here, with this Godly being staring down at me so close that I could taste his breath, I wondered what it would be like to let go of my restraint and fulfill this yearning. At that thought, his eyes called to mine; his were radiant with a raw ferocity. He groaned, and I felt his hands leave the table's ledge to grip my hips. I inhaled sharply at the unexpected touch. With that single piercing breath, the scent of redolent woods came over me, turning my insides hot. I was breathless. I should stop him, I thought, but I was utterly immobile. He had a hold on me, and I'd only be lying to myself if I said I didn't like it. He grinned now as if reading my thoughts.

"I would like to make you happy, Goddess." He leered. The points of his teeth both scared me and thrilled me all at once. His two hands seized my hips, and I gasped in response. He laughed lowly as if savoring the sound that flew from my mouth. I stared at his lips, entirely entranced. "What would make you happy?"

"Freedom," I whispered, and with that, he let me go. I hitched my breath at the sense of his release, missing his heat. He took a step back, beholding me as I sat on the table, books on either side.

"I see." He grimaced. I started to worry that I might have hurt him. I almost read embarrassment on his face but then chalked it up to antipathy.

"Isn't that what you want?" I stuttered, finally building up the courage to speak. He had caught me so off guard I couldn't think straight. Our day of careless flying and thoughtless nearness had awoken a darker part of me that had swelled deep within for some time now. I saw that it stirred in him too.

"Yes," he ground out, gritting his teeth.

"Good," I said. "So, we will work on getting you that." His hands formed into fists at his sides, and I watched as the muscles ticked in his forearms. "Did I say something wrong?" I examined, scared to find the answer. He returned to me now, and I felt all that heat rushing back like a frenzy.

"This is all wrong," he said. "This was supposed to be easy."

"Easy?" I breathed, a strange tingle of hope festering in me as I contemplated that one word's esoteric meaning.

"Easy. With no complications," the God confirmed and lifted a finger to my mouth. It lingered there, feather-light atop my lips. They parted at the touch of rapture. I felt a shiver run down my spine from the pressure that grew in me. I thought of elsewhere my lips might land if I grew so bold. "You've become a complication," he said brusquely.

"I'm sorry," I stammered; not a genuine apology—just a response.

"Are you?" he susurrated. His finger slipped from my lips and burned down my neck, slowly curving around the back of my head. Lightly, he tangled his fingers into my hair and tilted my head to meet his face. We were so close. The anticipation was killing me. It seemed this proximity had the same effect on him. Pyre's breathing was controlled, but I could see his shoulders tensing, his jaw tightening. He was trying to control himself.

"Pyre," I let out in a shudder. His legs ground into me at the sound.

"I want my freedom, Goddess," he let out in a breathy declaration. Something like disappointment dropped within me. He looked at my lips now, contemplative. I went still, fully aware of his stare. "But when I hear that appellation on your lips, freedom becomes only one of many desires," he said roughly. Revelation ignited as I watched him. Slowly, Pyre made his way back up to my eyes. They were burning. I swallowed dryly, and his fingers wrang tighter in response.

"What else do you desire?" I rasped, almost panting now. The heat was too much, yet not nearly enough.

"*You*," Pyre groaned; a low, guttural sound came from his throat. With that admission, he met my lips with rapturous force, compelling a gasp out of me. This only seemed to rile him more and gave him the push to further the kiss. When I eagerly returned it, he flung his wings out wide, wrapping me in his darkness.

His tongue met mine, and a quiver ran through me from head to toe. This was passion. I didn't know what to do with myself. I had never kissed anyone before, let alone a God. As if he understood my inexperience, he pulled away quickly, staring at the mess he had made of my lips. It was exhilarating seeing the look on his face—that look of raw desire—for me.

"What?" I exhaled, catching my breath. I touched my fingers to my lips now, trembling. Down in my core, I felt the heat gather, intensifying. Pyre snarled, showing his teeth in a wicked, sinful grin. His chest rose quickly, and he let out a grumble—a grumble that told me he was not yet satiated.

"More?" he ground out.

"More," I answered, and in one swift movement, he grabbed me at the waist and held me to him. My legs instantly knew to wrap at his abdomen as he gripped my ass. The thrill provoked me even further; this moment of being craved. I grabbed onto his bare, muscled shoulders, deepening his kiss. This man's raging passion for me boiled my blood in the best way possible.

He began kissing down my neck, his teeth grazing my skin. I had never felt so alive. It was strange to feel alive in the Under Realm. Though I was immortal here, I had typically felt lifeless; defeated. A wave of emotion flowed through me as his mouth met mine again. As his lips made their way down my collarbone and onto the top of my breasts, I had never been more thankful for my abundance of curves. Usually causing me to strain from carrying their weight, in this blissful moment, they elicited pleasure. I never knew this skin could be so sensitive. I hungered for more, but Pyre pulled away in a haze. His breath was hot all around me.

"Tell me you want this," he implored, and when he said so, reality came crashing down. I blinked and started to panic. What was I thinking? This was not just a man. This was a forsaken God. The daimon standing before me had trapped me here, toyed with me, and used me for my power without considering my wants or needs. I knew that. And I was *kissing* him. I was *enjoying* his touch. Alarm sank in with a heavy thud. Pyre Malum didn't feel any genuine affection toward me. More importantly, I didn't care for him in this way. I couldn't possibly allow myself to care for him in this way, and I didn't want to do this with someone I wasn't in love with. My actions dripped with salacity.

"I can't do this." I trembled, gasping for air. I started to feel faint. The room was spinning around me. His body went rigid, and I felt the pulsing of his heartbeat. In an instant, his eyes went from sparkling embers of gold to a lifeless, dull bronze. I knew this moment of weakness had gotten me in trouble. Even more, I knew that it was over.

He cleared his throat and set me down. My knees were weak, and I wobbled, trying to stay up. I could feel the embarrassment set in. The worry slinked blearily to my mind.

"All right." He looked away from me. He fixed himself and brought his wings back behind him.

"I'm sorry," I spilled. He walked away, body rigid.

"You say that quite frequently."

45

TRANCE

When I woke the next morning, I awakened to a tangle of white roses surrounding my entire body. It was like I had caged myself in, creating my very own fortress while I slept. I had had a horrible dream, a vision of wrath as Pyre held me captive. I was a firestorm, and he bellowed as he watched me burn. The nightmare didn't last too long. After such exhaustion, the terror became tranquility.

When it turned from a nightmare to a calm dream, I felt protected and safe, lying beneath the stars and watching the moon glow. I was still in the castle, still seeing the training room I'd been accustomed to, but the dream lifted the roof like a weight off my shoulders. The dream was a gift of peace. That peace was quickly interrupted when I woke from shooting pain in my foot. The roses had grown quite close to me as I slept, and a thorn pricked the sole of my heel, jolting me awake. It was surprising and lovely waking up to the sight of life. I loved that I had this power. This one was my favorite of them all.

I knew that Pyre had been in my room this morning when

I looked at the water basin. My heart made a funny little jump at the recognition of his gesture. Perhaps he did care for me in his own way. Since moving into my chamber, he had come to burn the coal to warm my water in the morning. It was a kindness. He didn't have to do this for me. I could produce fire, too; however, it took more effort for me to achieve it. At first, I found it uncomfortable that Pyre did it. It meant that he had been coming into my room while I slept, and it felt strange to imagine him in here while I was unconscious. I wondered if he thought about the night we'd spent together, lying side by side in the quiet dark. I couldn't remove the memory from my mind, no matter how much I tried to after closing my eyes to rest.

Though it was bizarre being aware of his creeping presence, after using the warm water to clean myself, I grew not to care about his being in here while I slept, as I would much prefer that he continued. I was, however, surprised that he had still come this morning after our fight last night. There had been a moment of passion, a flicker of recklessness, and I had tipped him over the edge.

As I started to get up from my bed, I took a moment to appreciate the white roses, taking a mental picture of the sight and memorizing its smell. The magic was beautiful. Nature was beautiful. Then, recalling yesterday's awkward and chilling confrontation, my mood quickly turned from admiration to acidity. Pyre Malum had kissed me, and worse, I had kissed him back. I frowned at the memory, distaste coating my tongue. I'd gone too far.

I touched a petal closest to my nose and watched as the flowers wilted, crumbling to dust—a fitting vision to match my guilt and embarrassment. Looking down at the pile of ash was overwhelming and eye-opening. It reminded me that I was a dangerous thing and needed to be vigilant in training myself. As quickly as I could create life, I could end it with a simple touch. The flowers crumpled on the floor of my bed: gray, black, and a darkened carmine closest to me. Funny, I hadn't remembered seeing any red roses. My head was murky from the nightmare, and I felt woozy getting up. When I stepped over the dead flowers and started toward my new belongings, I tried my best to be mindful of my surroundings. After washing my face with the water and cloth provided, lavishing in the warm, ginger scent, I changed into training trousers and a loose-fitted top. When I was ready and fully awake, I made my way toward the door—another day of training, another day toward my freedom.

When I left my room, Alriq was standing guard at my door. I noticed a few other pythrants slithering through the halls at the far end of the building.

"Good morning, Alriq," I said, almost glad to see a familiar face. He had grown more comfortable with me over the last few days. Passing by him in the halls most often solicited a nod in my direction and sometimes a greeting with a small smile. I rarely had time to speak with him as he seemed busy leading the pythrants and ordering them about. I, on the other hand, spent every waking minute in the training room with Pyre. Today I noticed that the pythrant did not look at me when I greeted him, which was strange behavior. "Alriq, how are you doing this morning?" He looked up at me now, blinking in confusion.

"Good morning, Goddess," he stuttered, shaking his head. I giggled.

"Were you sleeping just now?" I asked, brows raised. His eyes grew wide in panic, tail rattling, unnerved.

"Please, Goddess. Do not tell my Lord," he pleaded. "It was a mistake, I swear it." I smiled calmly, comfortingly.

"Of course," I assured him. "Your secret is safe with me."

Though I had assured him I wouldn't say a word, his shoulders didn't relax from their stress, and his tail hadn't settled either.

"Is the Goddess well?" he asked, looking me over. He took both of my arms, to my surprise, lifting and examining them. I scrunched my face at him.

"What's gotten into you?" I swatted him away.

"I must keep watch over the Goddess," he replied, finding nothing absurd about his behavior. "I must confirm your safety."

"I am fine, thank you," I told him. "Just on my way to training for the day."

"Very well, Goddess," he replied and gestured to the door.

"Get some sleep, Alriq," I demanded. "I think you're in need." He dipped his head and turned away.

Walking from my chambers to the training room gave me only a minute to contemplate retreating to my room. I walked begrudgingly, cautiously, toward what I assumed would be a very uncomfortable training day. I wondered how Pyre would act toward me. I tried to imagine how I would feel and act toward him too. Would he forget about yesterday and act as if nothing had happened, or was I about to step into a room full of discomfort? I could only hope for things to turn back as they used to be. Training with Pyre had been painful and daunting at the beginning of my stay. I had finally gotten him to lighten up and show a bit of empathy. Then, in a moment of fiery desire, I had washed it all away.

It was hard to think that Pyre Malum, a literal God, one of the strongest ever to exist, had lustful feelings toward me. How it could be remotely possible for this to occur, I could not fathom. I had given him nothing but trouble, and I couldn't provide what he stole me for in the first place. The God of the Dead had ripped me from Earth and dragged me to Hell, only to learn that the Goddess he had been waiting for was raised a lowly human, born into power she did not know how to wield. How he could even look at me without thinking solely of disappointment, I did not understand. But to have him pining over me, to have the heat entangle us in a mutual passion I had never experienced before, left me in disbelief. A God from the Under Realm had kissed me. Had *wanted* to kiss me.

When I entered the training room, I was surprised to see Pyre sitting on his throne made of skeletons. It took me by surprise, as he rarely sat in it. It seemed as though it was there purely for decoration. I worried that yesterday's affair had produced a new temperament in him. Before I could ask him what he was doing, the door behind me slammed shut, eliciting a yelp from me. The wind whooshed through my hair, tangling my vision. When I looked at him now, I saw that he was seething. He was holding a white flower in the palm of his hand. Had he been in my room?

"What's wrong?" I asked. He growled at me like a violent animal.

"Do you expect me to entertain the thought of you not knowing, Goddess?" His voice was guttural.

"I think so..." I was dumbfounded. I had no idea what he was referring to. Was he still upset over the kiss? "Pyre," I started, but his roar interjected.

"Stop," he boomed. "I do not trust the words that come from your deceitful lips."

"I don't understand," I professed. "We were at such a good place. What did I do? Where did we go wrong?" I started to walk toward him and watched as his hands gripped the sides of his seat and crushed each skull bone that held it aloft. The remnants' dust settled at his feet. "If this is about the kiss, just forget it! We don't ever have to talk about it again. Just please, don't be angry with me."

"Angry does not even begin to describe what I feel, Goddess." His storm of words cut me like a knife. This kind of temper was lethal. "Do you know how I felt?" He ground his teeth.

"I—" He cut me off.

"Imagine the surprise, the horror that struck when I entered your chamber this morning to find you were lying in your bed full of roses, but all I could smell...." He laughed dangerously. "Well, I did not smell roses."

"You're mad about the roses?" I stuttered cautiously. "I didn't grow them on purpose, Pyre. When I woke up, they were wrapped around me. I think my nightmare stirred them out of me."

"This is not about the roses, maiden," he scoffed. I faltered, feeling the weight of the belittling title.

"What's the problem?" I wondered, eyes fixed, trying to find what he was trying to say.

"I smell something else on you." His eyes turned to slits. "You have a new scent on you, and it is not a fitting smell."

"A smell?" I asked. "You mean like with lies?"

"No," he boomed. "Not like the lies. A smell like somebody else has been around you." I stumbled at his words.

"No one's been around me," I assured him. "Only you. I haven't even seen the pythrants in the last few days. I saw Alriq this morning, but other than that, it's just been you." Panic rose within me. Was there someone else here in Pyre's castle? Could they help me? He grumbled as if he could sense my train of thought.

"You cannot fool me," he spat. "I have a rather rare olfactory gift."

"I'm not lying, Pyre," I tried to no avail.

"I can smell all lies, and though you have never lied to me before, I now wonder if you've managed to trick me."

His eyes narrowed, nose crumpling into a snarl of distaste.

"No, I haven't tricked you! I haven't lied to you before, and I am telling you the truth at this moment too." He was starting to get on my nerves. He was accusing me of lying, something I rarely ever did. I took pride in being an honest person, and this was burning me.

"Perhaps you have not lied outright. Perhaps you have found a way around my gift," he pondered, voice low and growling. I considered my hopes of escaping and wondered if he had caught on to my wishes. I swallowed the thought down hard, never flinching.

"I haven't. I swear." I stood my ground. He observed me, contemplating. It was killing me, trying to hold my ground when genuine fear rattled my bones. I had to play my cards right. I had to be careful how I spoke to him.

"There is another God present," he murmured, almost silently. If looks could kill, I'd be dead. My mind was scrambling for an answer. I was trying to understand.

"A God?" I tested, unsure if I had heard correctly. "I've never met another God, Pyre. I am new to all of this, having been veiled from the truth of my identity. You know this. As of now, you are the only God I've ever met. I swear. There were no Gods on Earth, and I've never left here. You locked me in here, and I quite literally cannot leave." I gestured to the door behind me. "You've made sure of that."

He spat on the ground. "How did you contact him?" he demanded, completely disregarding my discourse. "No one else was supposed to know you are here." He looked down into his hands, staring at the flower he still clung to.

"Contact who?" I was starting to get upset. He was accusing me of something impossible. He was dangling a false hope over me, and I did not like it.

"The God! Who else?" he argued. Smoke tendrils lifted from his shoulders, filtering the air. If I could have contacted another God, let alone anyone from any realm, I would've done it quickly and with pleasure.

"As I said before, I haven't been around anyone. I've been here. We can go over this as long as you would like. My answer will remain the same," I stated tersely, and infuriatingly, he huffed at me.

"Lies," he hissed.

"No," I rebutted. "And you would know that if you came closer," I suggested. "You can smell lies, right? Am I lying?" I threw my arms in the air in frustration. "Come on, Pyre. Ask me outright."

He took a moment, observing me. He stood from his throne in a rush of wind, wings beating a tempest. The rubble crumbled under his feet when he stepped off his seat. I winced at the thought of the smashed skulls. I could feel the heat emanating off of him—this rage. He stalked toward me, eyes fixed.

"Tell me, Goddess, have you been with anyone else?" His voice was calm but deadly. "Have you seen anyone other than myself or my servants?" he ground out, teeth scraping against teeth.

"No," I said, assertive in tone and posture. I had done nothing wrong and had no reason to be afraid. He continued skulking forward.

"Hmm..." he rumbled, dark wings fluttering.

"Well?" I asked. "Am I lying?" He came closer now, a foot taller than me, hovering over me. Dipping his head low, he searched my eyes, darting back and forth, before closing his and inhaling intensely.

"I— I smell honey," he trailed, voice throaty. I observed him, unmoving. Confusion knit his brows as he concentrated.

His throat bobbed as he slowly opened his eyes and met mine. They seared with a golden intensity.

"Honey," I whispered. "You can smell my honey." I was practically holding my breath from being so cautious of his nearness.

"I smell your honesty, *Sōrza*," he amended, now lowering his eyes to my lips. My core heated as I recalled the touch of his against mine. He exhaled deeply and quickly pinned his muscled arms on either side of my head. He leaned on the door behind me, his breath wafting smoke around us. "I smell your sweet honey, just as plainly as I've smelled your desire each time you've thought about me so lecherously." My breath hitched at his words.

"You smelled my...." I couldn't think to say the word. An unfathomably sultry laugh escaped his lips.

"I can smell your desire now, Goddess. Tell me, why do you find it necessary to distract me so?" He growled, his mouth hovering just over mine. I couldn't help but hold my breath. He lifted a hand to my cheek and brushed the flower he held against my skin. I shivered at the contact. When his hand lowered, my stomach grew butterflies. He was not carrying a white rose. He was holding the daffodil I had produced several weeks ago. My eyes widened at its sight, and in an instant, he pulled away, and I felt the cold rushing back to me.

"I'm sorry." I hesitated, eyes still on his hand that held the white bloom. "I don't mean to...."

"I can smell him on you." He turned away, growling. I blinked in confusion.

"Who?" I pushed, his words waking me from the fervor. "Who do you smell on me, and how is that possible? I haven't seen anyone." I swore. I wanted to say that he had been the only one on me, but I refrained from remarking. I watched him wallow in frustration, and I couldn't take it anymore. "Look at me," I demanded, and to my surprise, he submitted. He studied me carefully, though never meeting my eyes. I could see the worry and anger battling to overrule in his frown. I inhaled sharply at his watch and released my breath, along with the tension. I closed the space between us, and I saw the small flinching in the tiny misstep of his foot.

"What?" he murmured.

"Look at me," I insisted. He didn't have a choice now as I stood before him. A little, yet still very prominent, part of me wanted to run as fast as possible to find this other God, to rid me of my problems. My mind told me to run now that I had the chance. But a very loud part of me that grew harder to ignore with each passing minute wanted to comfort this man. Almost everything in me wanted to take away his burden and give him all he wanted. He watched me, perplexed by my fixed closeness, breath controlled but full. I looked up into his eyes, and reaching out, I cupped his face with both of my hands. A thousand and one emotions rattled my bones as I drowned in this man's eyes. Enmity, resentment, empathy, and lust. Far more lust than I should allow and all the curiosity in the world. I had begun caring for him, and it was dangerous territory. The enchanted cord between us tugged delightedly.

"Shivalri," he began. The way he said my name tore down all the walls between us. A muscle ticked in his jaw as he watched me. I had never seen him so staggered, so openly astonished. I knew what he needed from me. He coveted trust. He wanted to depend on me and my word, something I suspected he had not done in a mournfully long time. He'd relied on his gifts for so long. He'd never had to trust anyone because he could always tell whether or not they were being honest with him. But I had been honest with him. My entire time in the Under Realm, I had told him the truth. Whether I wanted to be here or not, I had never lied about who I was or what I was thinking. I was going to make him understand this. I was going to prove myself to him, and maybe one day, he would learn to trust me without his magic at play. Why I wanted his trust was disturbingly close to treason against my beliefs, my world. But it was right.

I took a steadying breath, feeling lightheaded from the heat of the moment, and bore into his gaze.

"I will never lie to you, Pyre," I whispered, quiet but firm. "I promise, I have not seen another damn soul." He said nothing for a long moment, then swallowed hard. I felt the movement of his jaw beneath my palms.

"I am sorry," he said as he released the tension in his shoulders. "I believe you. You haven't seen anyone, but he has seen you." That shook my nerves, forcing my hands to slip from his face.

"Someone else has seen me?" I questioned, feeling the unease slink up into me.

"Yes," he breathed. "When I went to light your charcoal, I smelled him immediately. I tried to wake you, tried to remove you from the room, but you wouldn't wake. Instead, you grew thorns and roses around your bed," he ranted, shoulders stiff and jaw clenched. "When I tried to pull you through, you bled at my feet. I couldn't move you." He ran a hand through his dark, tangled hair. "I couldn't move you without hurting you." He stalked toward his window and looked out into the reddened horizon. He looked as if he were searching for something. I felt cold as I stood in the middle of the throne room. Castle walls encased me, but the frigidity of my surroundings froze me in place. There was so much I did not understand.

"What is it, Pyre?" I examined his viewpoint. An electric current of both worries and hope leaped in my chest. I observed from my spot as the God, who usually appeared resilient and assertive, grew weary as the sky around us illuminated. "What are you looking for?"

"My brother," he thundered.

"How is your brother here?" I asked, completely dumbfounded by this new information. "I thought you said that you were the only one of your siblings that were sent to the Under Realm. How did he get here?" Pyre clenched his fists, trying to hold back his temper.

"I don't know," he growled.

"What do you mean you don't know?" I pushed—none of this made sense. I could feel myself falling into a spiral, anxiety rushing through my veins and pulsing at my temples. "Did I do this?" I wondered. It had to have been me. I was responsible for guarding the Gates. If anything had gotten through, if anyone had traveled past it, it was my fault.

"I don't know how he got here, but he is here. Even if an entire millennium passed me by, I would still remember his scent," he spat. "He was in your room... With you." He shook his head as he paced back and forth. I surveyed the gust he concocted as it carried his feathered wings up above him.

"How did he find me?" I asked, still watching his storm of fury. "How is any of this possible? Did I slip up?" I looked to him for some form of reassurance, but he had none to give me. "Pyre, please, stop pacing," I begged, unsettled by his worry.

"I cannot," he boomed. "If my brother is here, you have no idea what kind of trouble we are in." I felt the heat escape my body at his words. If the God of the Dead was scared, I was sure to be petrified.

"Did I open the window?" I whispered, barely audible.

"What?" he asked, stopping in his tracks. His black hair fell into his eyes as they widened now. As if, finally, he was catching on to my train of thought.

"When you came through to Earth... When you took

me...." I looked down, not meeting his eyes. "Did someone else slip through the cracks?"

"No..." he stammered. "How would they have known? How would he, in the Celestial Realm, have known?"

"Because of the veil, Pyre," I said, finding his eyes. "The veil is gone."

"They can see through." He gulped. I had never seen him so visibly afraid. "The Gods know."

46

THUNDERSTRUCK

Slithering erupted all around me as the pythrants banded the entire expanse of the castle. There would be no stone left unturned. Pyre Malum was on high alert, scouring the palace. In his neurotic screening, he ordered me to the prison at once. I tried reasoning with him, begging him to stay in my chamber, but he wouldn't budge. Someone had managed to get in my chamber unnoticed; therefore, he deemed it too risky.

"Thank you," I managed to say as Pyre's servants came in and out of my prison, carrying some of my belongings.

"We are here to serve," one of the pythrants replied lowly.

"Where is Alriq?" I asked, but he did not answer. Instead, the pythrant left my room to retrieve another piece from my chamber. I didn't like being back in this prison, but I was thankful to have small comforts brought to me.

"Your clothes are in this basket, Goddess," said a pythrant who startled me as he entered.

"Thank you, um...," I blanked, trying to find his name. I had seen him a few times, often following just behind Alriq when on duty.

"Nor," he stated, eyes to the floor. "I am called Nor."

"Thank you, Nor," I said and offered him a hand. Instead of shaking it, he handed me the basket he held, and I smiled. "Not one for handshakes?"

"I would not dare to touch my Lord's Goddess," he said, head low so as not to reveal his face.

"I do not belong to anyone," I said firmly. "And if I offer you my hand, you most certainly are allowed to take it." I held out my free hand again, and he hesitated before taking mine. He offered a small smile, and his eyes flitted like a snake's.

"I will not forget this kindness," he stated. I shook his hand firmly.

"Happy to formally meet you, Nor."

"And you, I," he replied. "We have been waiting for the Goddess for so long. It is divine to make your acquaintance." I let the odd praise slip and smiled at him. I could only imagine what Pyre had taught the pythrants about the prophecy. Though I was sure they knew I had become more of an obstacle than a benefit, I figured it would be best not to question his admiration. I quickly turned to set the basket atop the small table that his companion had left me and faced him once more.

"Nor?" I started. He looked at me, eyes wide.

"Yes, Goddess?"

"Do you happen to know where Alriq is?" I asked. "It's just that, you see, usually I'm guarded by him. I've gotten used to seeing him around, is all. Not that having you in replacement is bad. I just wonder, is there a more pressing matter he may be dealing with? Is he looking for Pyre's brother?" Nor's eyes grew solemn, and my gut instantly told me there was trouble.

"My consort is no longer on duty," he answered, regret upon his face.

"Consort?" I asked.

"My mated consort, Goddess," he clarified.

"Oh, I'm sorry. I didn't know he was with someone."

"You would not, as he rarely speaks." He laughed, but his eyes were still wary.

"What's wrong?" I asked gently.

"I fear my consort has been banished from serving our Lord...." His face formed a dejected look.

"Not serving Pyre anymore... That's unusual."

"Not entirely, Goddess," the pythrant said, lowering his gaze from mine. "He failed his duty last eve. He did not protect the Goddess."

Understanding lit my mind.

"He fell asleep," I whispered, alarm striking a chord. I remembered this morning all too well. I had laughed at his hiccup, thinking it silly to find a guard asleep at his post. I had felt bad for him, knowing well that he was tired and needed rest. I hadn't thought anything of it other than to tell him to go to sleep.

"I am afraid for his life, Goddess." Nor looked up to me quickly, as if he had to get the words out fast. "My consort was born and bred for this life. He knows nothing else. I fear he will not listen to our Lord and will fight to stay."

"What happens if he does?" I blanched, considering the idea of anyone defying the God of the Dead. It didn't take much effort to remember how he had acted toward me during our first encounter.

"If Alriq rejects his banishing, refusing to leave the castle as an exile, he will be executed immediately on site." I gasped incredulously.

"No, that can't happen... Pyre wouldn't do that. He couldn't. It wasn't Alriq's fault! I mean, he's always on duty. He never gets a break," I stuttered. "I will fight for him if it comes to it, Nor. I swear it. I will tell Pyre that Alriq was overworked.

He will understand. He will have to." I chewed at my finger-nails, contemplating how that conversation with Pyre might go. "Execution is far too dramatic for something as trivial as falling asleep."

"I am afraid you are far more benevolent than he, Goddess. You give him too much credit where it is not due." He hissed, then took my hand, throat bobbing. "You did not hear my words." His tail swished behind him in unease. I quickly understood that not only Alriq was in danger of losing his life. If Pyre Malum had heard his servant belittling him, I had a feeling Nor wouldn't have much of a chance either. It was clear in the way Nor's fear shown. Any act of defiance or defamation of their Lord's name was an act of treason. I wondered if that was why the pythrants hadn't spoken more than a word to me while I had been here in their castle. I wondered if they were not just shy or intimidated by me. Perhaps it had nothing to do with me and everything to do with the possibility of slipping up. They could unintentionally say or do the wrong thing, but the repercussions would come, nevertheless.

"I am not your enemy," I said, voice sure and kind.

"Thank you, Goddess."

"It's Shivalri," I told him.

"Shivalri, you are everything we could have hoped for. For protecting my mate, I owe you my life."

After Nor left my prison room, the rest of the pythrants set several pillows in the room for me to sit on. I had a set of new clothes, and a servant had folded my blanket neatly on top of the pillow. Unfortunately for me, my bed was too big to fit in this cell. I sat in the corner of the prison I had happily forgotten, and I sulked. There was nothing I could do but oblige. I watched as a strong-armed pythrant hammered away at a protruding spike in front of my door, sealing me in. Though I still had the power to open any of Pyre's doors, I was caged with no escape in sight. I was reminded that it was to keep others out, not keep me in. I had told him that it felt all the same.

All the light from the day had ceased to exist, and the castle became a dungeon once more. Though we were surrounded by desert, magma, and the epitome of death, the air around me was cold. I could see my breath as I breathed, teeth chittering from the frigidity. Pyre had extinguished every torch in sight, making the darkness my refuge. It was odd behavior, making me think of the human world. It was weirdly familiar as I imagined myself shutting off all the lights so that when unwanted company arrived, they would assume I wasn't home. Was this what he planned to do? Would he pretend he wasn't home?

I couldn't help but wonder about this new God. Pyre Malum's brother. Who was he? More importantly, what was he doing here? I shivered at the thought of Pyre's last words he shared before ordering me to my chambers. I swore to him that I hadn't been conspiring with anyone and hadn't seen anyone but him. *You haven't seen anyone, but he has seen you*, he had said. What did that mean? Was there someone lurking about the castle? Had someone been watching me sleep? I quivered at the thought of my exposure. I had grown too comfortable in this hellhole, and it showed.

Thunder erupted all around me, turning the night sky vivid in light. I watched as the lightning zigzagged across the clouds, illuminating the dark red sky. The scene struck me as beautiful. Having that spark of light lifted the ominous feeling. During its brief moments of illumination, I felt a second of haven. Being trapped here, alone in the dark, was lonely.

I didn't like the dark. I never had. I wondered if I should have kept my fears to myself. I remembered telling Pyre, upon my retrieval, that I was afraid of what lurked in the dark. I frowned at the memory of giving away that critical part of myself. Was he using this to his advantage? Did he know that the darkness would keep me at bay? I wondered if he was happy with himself, picturing me huddled in my corner, legs wrapped in my arms and blanket cradling me. Was he pleased by my terror? Or would he try to comfort me after seeing me so helpless? I remembered the way he held me to him while I sobbed against his chest after a horrid nightmare. The way his hand shook as he dared caress and comfort me. Where was he now while I sat in the dark, reminiscing, perplexed and frightened?

I hadn't seen the reproved God all day or evening, but I knew he was looming about the castle. I heard it through the whispers of the pythrants that crawled up the walls. The slithering of their tails sluiced in the night, and their hissing echoed wherever they strode. Did they know who this other God was? Were they prepared for his arrival? I had overheard some of the serpentine men worrying about this drawback. I could feel the fear in their voices among the shrill of their tongues. It seemed as though his presence was unexpected. There were guards posted at my door, making sure I stayed in my room. I tried asking them what was going on, but they didn't so much as look at me, let alone reply. I was left to ponder on my own, and my brain kept going to the worst possibilities. Fear crept up and swallowed me whole. If the God of the Dead had such a bad reaction to his brother's arrival, did this mean that we were in danger? If his scent was on me, was I the target?

While being here, the focus was trying to find my way out. I hadn't thought much about the Under Realm as a whole. I hadn't wasted time thinking about what else I might discover outside of the God of the Dead's castle. Now, I couldn't help but wonder who might be out there. How far would I have to travel to meet someone new? It wouldn't be safe to venture out into the Under Realm. I knew that. During our lessons, Pyre Malum had told me of this realm's inhabitants. Not only was this a place for the cruel-intentioned and deceased, but there were also daimons—malevolent and renounced Gods just like Pyre, and maybe worse. From my captor's wording, I knew there were people and creatures here who were not entirely immoral. He explained that the Triple Goddess had decided who would dwell in each realm. Pyre had seemed perplexed and frustrated by the line she drew, not understanding what was morally acceptable enough to forgive.

A crack of thunder had me shuddering away from my thoughts. It had to be well after midnight. I had been in my room for hours. Annoyed, I threw my blanket over my head and willed my mind to rest. Instead, a spark of flame burst from my fingertip. I had just enough time to stick it out of the blanket before catching my surroundings on fire. Great. This was going to be yet another long night. I tried calming my thoughts, focusing on my breathing. Deep breath in, smooth exhale out. A deep breath in, like the ones I took under the spell of Pyre's gaze, a shaky exhale out when I pictured him coming closer, kissing me. The memory of electric pleasure pulled me under as my eyes fought to close. *That damn kiss.* I couldn't remove it from my mind. It had changed me irrevocably so. I had kissed the God of the Dead, and though the guilt gnawed at my nerves, I had enjoyed it.

A sinking feeling stirred my dreams as my consciousness fought to come through. My body rolled, pulling me from my side and onto my stomach. I groaned, tugging at the blanket and fisting it under my chin. A featherlight touch on my cheek made the fog clear away, and I realized I wasn't alone anymore. I opened my eyes, barely able to see in the night. I had drifted off, but I mustn't have slept too long, as the skies were still dark.

Removing my face from its stuffy position on the pillow, I blinked up at the form sitting beside me on the bed.

"I woke you," Pyre noted, his voice but a low murmur. Groggily, I pushed up on my elbow and pulled myself back on my side, too sleepy to concern myself with the proximity of the God I'd been dreaming of. Pyre smiled, then bowed his head. His lips broke the smile, turning into a look of anguish.

"What's wrong?" I asked, yawning midway through the question. He shook his head, his black hair covering his eyes. His dark and looming wings curled around him, shielding his face from sight. I pulled myself up, concern flooding my system. "Hey," I spoke, soft and reassuring. My hand fluttered toward him, finding purchase on his firm thigh. "Pyre, you can tell me. What's wrong?" He sighed heavily, leaning into my touch.

"I'm sorry." I sat up straighter, peering around the massive wings that hid him. I had to do a double take, staggered by how I found him. He was solemn, and sincerity garbed his features.

"For?" I questioned, sitting with my back against the wall, cradling the blanket to my chest.

"Does it matter in the end?" he questioned. His grimace was the most prominent feature on his face.

"It does to me," I dared say, watching him attentively. I pulled the blankets over my chin, feeling the fabric against my lips as the apprehension took over. Was he about to apologize to me? For taking me from Earth and shattering my life?

He turned to me, face hard, but eyes a liquid pool of gold.

"I want you to know that I did not intend to place you in more danger," he said, voice somber. He looked down, seemingly angry with himself. "With my brother knowing where you are, him being so close, I've put you at a great risk, and I'm sorry for that." So, he wasn't sorry for taking me captive. I didn't need Pyre to feel sorry for his brother's involvement. I wanted him to feel remorseful for the things I wanted him to regret. But he wasn't sorry for the oubliette or for inflicting pain as a means of teaching. *That* was what I needed him to apologize for.

I was in danger whether this new, unwelcome God had found me here or not. My life was not my own, created by the Fates who'd planned out every detail of my being. I was destined to face danger. It wasn't because of Pyre that I was at risk of being taken by another God. I was in trouble no matter where I went or with whom. I was the key to this ancient-old prophecy, a weapon all hands wished to wield.

"If you didn't personally invite him here, then there's no need to apologize for his involvement," I said blandly. The words tasted sour, knowing I wanted to say far more than that.

"You don't understand," he blew. His fists curled in his lap, and in the darkness, he looked helpless. A tiny seed of pity fermented in my gut as I watched him, waiting for him to say more. His wings fluttered, tightening behind him as he looked up at me. His lips parted, and I knew he wanted to say more, but he closed them before the words could leave his tongue. My heart sputtered. I had so many mixed emotions when it came to this man. I wanted to strangle him and hug him all in one moment.

"I'm listening, Pyre," I said. My lips brushed against the blanket I held up to my face. I wanted to convince him that he could speak to me freely. I tried to pry his thoughts from his mind; I wanted to know what made him suffer internally. He gave me a poor attempt at a smile and blew out a long breath. Lifting a hand, he gently tugged the blanket from my grasp, then held my chin between his fingers. The heat of his skin felt nice on mine.

"Get some rest, Goddess." Pyre let go and stood from the bed, making my legs spring on the mattress. "I'll be close by." I held my breath as I watched him go, magically locking the door behind him. I knew by observing that he'd put a new spell on the doors, ensuring no one could get in and I couldn't get out.

***

A few nights passed as I stayed locked away in my prison. I busied myself with growing flowers and watering them with my tears. I wasn't sad. I was past that point. It was misery being left alone with my thoughts. Pyre had come to check on me throughout the day but was otherwise preoccupied with taking extra precautions to keep us safe inside the castle. He'd been scouring the place, according to the whispered talk of the pythrants who guarded my door at every waking hour.

As the sky dimmed, obscuring the things I'd collected in my room, I grew increasingly tired of playing this waiting game. What was going on? Was Pyre's brother truly here, or was this all a ruse?

Expunging that thought, the door to my room opened, and Pyre stepped inside, quietly surveying the area.

"I'm still awake," I grunted, sitting cross-legged on the makeshift bed. I knew he'd be visiting around this time. As soon as the skies went dark, I could count on him to show face, checking to see if I was still safely trapped in my cell.

"Are you well?" he asked, coming forward. I grunted, throwing myself backward to lay in the heap of tumbled blankets beneath me.

"Fine." I heard his steps falter and lifted onto my elbows, eying him. He quirked a brow inquisitively.

"So you say," he answered wryly. I cast an exasperated breath, daring him to make light of the situation. "Please understand that you are being kept here for your safety."

"What makes this room safer than the others? What makes you think I'm safer in here, alone, rather than out there with you?"

"Here, you are guarded, and there is an enchanted ward that not even my brother can break. So long as you are in here, you are safe."

"But what if I don't want to—" a loud bang cut my words, and the two of us shot up. Panic flooded my chest as my pulse thundered beneath my skin. "What was that?" Pyre didn't take a moment to answer. He was lifted in the air, wings high, and out the door instantly.

Wrapping the blanket from my bed around my shoulders, I hugged it close to me. I got up off the bedding, the floor cold as I tiptoed barefoot across the floor, jumping at each step. I made to follow Pyre, but the guards posted outside my door slammed it shut before I could leave. I decided to try to pry answers from the pythrants at their station. I needed to know what was happening.

"Are you guys ever going to let me out of here?" I asked. They did not reply. I made to grab for the door's bars, but one of the pythrants hissed at my movement. I pulled away quickly and moved my hand back into my blanket. "Do you know what's going on?" I asked. "What was that loud noise?"

"We are here to guard you," the one called Nor answered me now. His voice was sharp, uninterested. I could tell by his attitude that he was trying to cover the fact that we had spoken before. I was content to play along for the benefit of his safety, remembering the conversation we'd had.

"Why?" I asked.

"We were stationed at this post," he replied. I was going to have to be more specific.

Sir," I said, trying to reason with him. "Please. You have to give me something. Why am I being guarded? Where did Pyre go? Do you know his brother?" Nor's tail coiled behind him at the mention of the Gods. Narrowing his eyes, he approached the other side of my barred door.

"Do you know his brother?" he asked accusingly. I shook my head in confusion.

"No. What would make you think that?" One of the others snorted at my reply yet still did not say a word. "Nor, come on. I'm trapped here. You know this. There's no way for me to get out. I have never met anyone else. I only know you guys. I only know Pyre." I noticed the pythrants stirring at my words. Nor's face wore alarm as I realized that the others were looking at him in distrust at the slip of his name.

"The Goddess has been trying to escape this whole time," he said challengingly. "We know your plot." I scoffed.

"I don't have any plans."

"Lies!" he hissed and spat his venom through to burn my prison wall. I moved away, my heart beating fast. I hadn't expected him to show any kind of violence. "You want to leave, no? I smell it on you." The others hissed in agreement.

"The rot festers in your cell," one rustled.

"Okay, I want to leave, yes. But I haven't acted upon any plans, so you have nothing to accuse me of," I spoke.

"You mean to tell us that you are not conspiring with our Lord's brother?" he questioned.

"No," I said. "I swear." He pointed his eyes at me and then nodded, seeming to accept my answer for what it was—the truth.

"You have caused so many troubles, little Goddess," he told me.

"I didn't mean to," I said softly, accepting my defeat. "I never wanted any—"

A loud boom interrupted, similar to the last, reverberating through the palace. The walls shuddered, and the pythrants chased the sound, immediately leaving their posts at my door. Nor stayed a moment behind, and to my surprise, he swung the door open, nearly ripping it from its hinges.

"The God of Nightmares has arrived," Nor said under his breath. "You will protect Alriq," he insisted. My eyes grew wide. Was this an out? Was he helping me get away? What about the enchantment keeping the door in its place? Pyre must not have had the time to place to spell again when he left the room. He'd gone in such a hurry; it must have slipped his mind.

"If it comes to it, and I am present, I will fight with my life," I swore.

"Run, my Goddess." Alarmed by the noise and total disbelief, I hesitated before opening the door, but I knew this was my only chance of getting out. Nor squeezed my hand, and we both started running; he, toward the noise of slithering brethren, me to my hopeful escape.

To the beat of my heart, my feet flew atop the cobblestone floors of this dungeon. The blanket I still held around me sailed at the speed of my flight. It was incredibly dark, and I could barely see ahead of me. I had an arm outstretched to further my senses, hoping that I wouldn't bump into anything. Another boom collided with the castle, making my knees buckle under the quake.

"Damn it." I skidded, pausing to get a hold of myself. "You can do this. You can get out," I assured myself. I continued until I found a bit of light ahead of me. It was a forked path, leaving me to decide which chance I'd take. Both routes would be tricky. I knew that I would have to choose between going left or right once I got to the end of that hallway. To the right, I would have to cross the bridge which connected two significant parts of the castle, but I knew that the bridge barely held, and it was thousands of feet in the air. I shook at the thought of a free fall. The only other option was to go left down the tower's oubliette. My nightmare made a reality. I had spent five days with the tortured souls down there. I was left to be forgotten in the dark, my mind going senseless. Though it had been a while since Pyre let me out, the feeling of emptiness was fresh in the hollow of my bones. It was the last place I wanted to go, but I knew it was my best shot at achieving an escape. The bridge wouldn't hold, but the oubliette tower might have another way down. A flash of memory came to the forefront of my mind as I remembered Pyre and his servants opening the door at the bottom of the oubliette, where I thought I had been left to die.

A slight pang of indecision rolled over me, and I steadied my mind. I wanted desperately to escape, but there was something more in Pyre I still had not discovered. He was awful in many ways, but his were learned behaviors, and he seemed to be warming up to me, especially after that kiss. It was like a declaration. Nevertheless, leaving him would have to be the right choice. Though the strings which tied us together wept, my mind told me that it was the right choice. I released the blanket from around me, dropping it to the floor, and did not hesitate when I got to the end of the hall. I knew that the tower was my only option. When I got to the rounded room, I looked down at the dark hole, remembering the empty feeling in my stomach from when the pythrants had held me over it. My stomach went into my throat as I recalled the feeling of dangling in midair as the poison seeped into my blood.

"I can do this," I muttered. I scanned the rounded room, looking for clues, trying to find a staircase or door to get to the bottom of the tower. I felt the cobbled bricks, desperate to find an escape. Around I went, feeling more and more frantic as I searched the same places thrice. The room was spinning, my head pounding, lungs aching for breath. It was no use. There was no other way down from here.

I knew that there was a door at the bottom of the oubliette —a door that would lead to the main floor, indicating my exit. I stood on the ledge now, knees wavering as I contemplated the plummet. I survived it once before; I could survive it again, especially now that I could hover. But if I couldn't control my descent, how long would it take me to come back from consciousness after I splattered to the ground?

It did not matter. I did not have another choice. A stone beneath my feet grumbled and protested at my weight. Tiny pebbles skidded over the ledge, and I waited to hear their landing. A minute went by before I caught the quiet scattering down below. What was I thinking? I could never escape. Pyre would find me before I would have the chance to get out. The door would most likely be locked, trapping me down there, whether Pyre found me or not. This was not a good idea.

I leaped off the ledge and back onto the floor, panting. Was I really just about to jump down there? A clamor halted my thoughts, and I inhaled a sharp breath, catching my surroundings. There was little to no light. I could scarcely discern shadows taking form around me. Cackling reverberated, bouncing from ceiling to floor.

"Did you miss your little friends down there?" a voice spoke derisively. It was Alriq. His muscles rippled with his slithering. I rarely saw the pythrants use their full snake potential. It was unusual to see him on all fours and using his tail to glide toward me rather than his long, bony legs. Something about it left a sour taste in my mouth. His glowing yellow eyes pierced the darkness. Slowly, deliberately, he lifted the dirtied blanket he'd carried behind him. "Thanks for the trail marker," he sneered and stood to his full height. *Damn it.* I was so damn careless for having left it in the halls. I hadn't thought that it would be an indicator of my location. It had been in the way, making my escape more difficult, and I had shrugged it off without a second thought.

It took a mere instant for a swarm of pythrants to surround me, turning their shadows into something corporal. They circled me, some hissing and some crowing. Enclosed in their snare, I had no getaway. I turned to look back at the oubliette that was just a step behind me and considered making a run for it, but I knew better. The minute I jumped in, they would make their way down the castle and retrieve me. I would be unconscious and unable to do anything about it. As if knowing my loss, Alriq grabbed me by the arm and took me for a walk. I inhaled at the touch of his scaled hands.

"Let's go," he hissed.

"Please don't hurt me," I begged.

"That is not for me to decide, little Goddess." He gripped me harder, and I obliged, following him into the night.

"I know that you've been banished, Alriq," I stammered, trying to find the right thing to say to persuade him to let me go. "I know you're angry, but please, do not take it out on me. I will protect you!" I cried, mustering the courage to show him just how. I let a spark of flame combust in my fist.

"Your magic is too weak, I'm afraid," he said, solemn but stern. "No one can save me but myself."

"I can help," I gushed, trying to convince him otherwise.

"You can and you will, Goddess," he hissed. "When I bring you back to my Lord, I will have redeemed myself. My success in this conquest of retrieval will have him disremember my failures, and my Lord will pardon me." At that, I stopped squirming away and decided to walk along with him. What was the point of fighting this? Though I didn't want to admit it, he was right to take me. He was only doing his duty, and by doing so, it just might save his life. I didn't want anyone to die, whether they were unkind or not.

No. Screw that!

I couldn't allow myself to think that way. I shoved away from the guilt and turned to survival mode. I didn't want anyone to die, but my life was just as important. I couldn't accept defeat so easily. I had made it this far in the Under Realm, conning the God of the Dead into teaching me magic. I was stronger now. I would play to my strengths with every minute I had left.

"Take me, then, Alriq," I spat. "But you must live with the knowledge that you've chosen my death over yours." He gripped my arm even tighter.

"For the cause, I will do this," he hissed. "And I do not fret for you, my Goddess. You are his salvation."

"What would Nor think of this?" I snapped, accentuating his consort's name. He whipped around with pure fury in his eyes.

"Nor will not know of this. He has abandoned me in this chaos, as he does not want me to refuse the banishment."

"For good reason," I retorted. "He doesn't want you killed! Neither do I." He grimaced at that.

"My Goddess is too generous with our kind," he said, voice low. "We serve you as we serve our Lord, Goddess. But he is our ruler, therefore, the priority. Know that I do not wish harm to you."

"His rage could see to my death, and you know it." I was fuming and desolate. I needed to get through to Alriq. I needed him on my side. "When Pyre finds out that I tried to leave, he will kill me. And if that doesn't work, whatever other God is out there will try next."

"Kill? My Lord would not risk it. The other God, perhaps. But my Lord needs the Goddess. Persecute you; he might... But you will not die."

"Sometimes I think I should...."

47

REPRIEVE

The closer we got to the training room, the more the floor rumbled, and lightning flogged the sky. I could see much better now as it illuminated my surroundings in the castle hall. I'd never seen a storm so fierce. My brain was on high alert as I approached the room. A throne room, where I had spent weeks training and honing my magic with the God of the Dead. Would the daimon be waiting for me on the other side of the door?

Before I could reach the latch, the door ripped off its hinges from the inside. As Pyre threw it behind him, the clash of the iron crashed all around us. His eyes flared a bright crimson. I felt the prick of tears in my eyes as I beheld his malevolence.

"You," he snarled, looking past me to Alriq. In an instant, the pythrant closed in and grabbed hold of me from behind, using me as a shield. His claws protracted, gouging my skin, and I watched as he drew blood from my bicep. A rumble from deep within Pyre's chest had me looking up at him, and I found pure wrath in his eyes as he beheld us. "Hand her to me!" Pyre boomed and launched himself at Alriq. The pythrant hissed and, at the last minute, let me go. It was just in time for Pyre to grab me at the waist and fling me across the throne room. The wind whipped at my face, and I didn't have time to grasp what was happening as I crashed onto his throne. The bones crumbled under me at the impact. My own bones splintered in places I had never felt pain before, ribs stinging to the point of agony.

"Goddess!" Alriq and Pyre hissed at once as they both ran to recover me.

"Gods damn it!" I screamed, wincing at the pain roiling in my body. Through teary eyes, I saw that Alriq was merely a foot away from me, but Pyre flew past him before the pythrant could get a hold of me again. The God of the Dead grabbed my face, his eyes wild as if he couldn't believe what he'd just done.

"Shivalri," he breathed, his chest heaving. "I'm so sorry." From the corner of my eye, I saw that Alriq had made it to the mess of bones I sat in. He approached cautiously, reaching out as if to touch me. Pyre roared, showing all his teeth.

"Do not touch her!" Pyre boomed. "Do not ever touch her!"

"I found her for you to keep her safe!"

"Something you should have done in the first place!" Pyre snarled. "Something that might have prevented all of this from happening." He scoffed, and a growl reverberated in his chest. Smoke seeped from the tips of his claws as he seethed in place.

"But—"

"Do not speak back to me, worthless, shameful coward." Pyre's fire lit the room, slamming into the pythrant at full force. "You cowered behind her, drew blood from her flesh. For that on its own, you deserve no mercy." Alriq scampered back, his screams echoing as he tried to run free. He flailed his arms, shrieking unintelligibly, panicking in the fire. I was struck silent, horrified beyond belief, and I could feel the tears burning my cheeks. Pyre turned to me, and I truly wished to die in this moment of torment.

"You will not run away," he thundered. "Do you know what's out there? Who could've gotten hold of you? You are mine! Do you understand me?" I just blinked at him, tears still pouring from my face. He shook me, and my entire body dipped in his clutch.

"Gods!" I screeched as my bones swelled from their aching. His eyes welled with startling tears, and he took my hand shakily, placing it on his chest. I watched a tear fall down his cheek, and irreversibly felt the crushing weight of Pyre Malum's fragile heart thudding beneath my palm.

"Please. You have to be mine," he whispered.

"I cannot be," I cried. At my words, he took me into his arms with more care, holding me so that I was pinned between him and the wall. I reached for the spot at the back of my skull that warmed to a sting. When I moved my hand before me, the blood that soaked my fingers made me sick. My hands were trembling, blatantly displaying my fright. I shifted my eyes back to the beast who had caused the mess. Panic flared in his eyes as if he was now truly understanding the depths of pain he'd bequeathed. "Are you happy, Pyre Malum?" I shook.

"I—" he faltered, hands slackening around my waist.

"Let me go," I demanded, my lips quivering in my attempt to hide the raw sting in my chest. Not only were my bones aching and my skin so incredibly sore, but the fact that he would hurt me like this, intending to or not, disillusioned me strongly.

"I can't. Not until you accept your fate," he said, and I spit in his face. Blood tainted the spill, and he wiped it away.

"What do you want?" I gritted my teeth, anger and panic rattling in my head.

"I want you to listen very carefully, Goddess, and listen well." I looked at him, waiting. "I did not mean to hurt you. I meant to toss Alriq away to get him off of you. I understand why you fear me, but my *sōrza*, I am nothing to fear compared to my brother. You spit on my name and hate on my existence, but you have known nothing of hatred and fear until you've met this God."

"I have a pretty good idea." I glared, mouth still hard. My legs quaked, betraying me. Pyre brought his hips closer, holding me in place. I knew it was to help me stand, but it felt like a cage.

"He sent this storm to shake me." Pyre laughed and spat on the floor. "To entice me. He wants me to know that he is here."

"Why?" I asked, never averting my eyes. He ground his teeth.

"He is marking his claim on you," he gritted out. My eyes searched his, trying to understand.

"I don't know what you mean." I shook. "Make this make sense." He smashed a fist through the stone, and I winced at the sound.

"I'm sorry," he blew out, frustration written all over his face. He removed his hand from the wall, and I shuddered at his effort. "Are you hurt any further? Should I examine you?" Though my head was throbbing, I shook my head, sucked in a breath, and unstably let it go. "He knows you are here and has come to take you away from me, to use you as he pleases. I will not let him take you away from me," he avowed, fuming. I quivered under his wrath.

Lightning struck rapidly, blasting a hole through the wall nearest the window I often looked through. Just like that, it was suddenly gone. I had often thought about jumping out of that window, thought about the freedom of flying away. Even if I did know how to hover on my own, I knew full well that Pyre could fly and trap me again if I ever took the chance. Seeing the window and wall destroyed released my desperation, and I so badly wanted to flee. I had been pushing the desire down for so long now.

Pyre roared at the sight of his beloved throne room broken to pieces. A dark shadow cast over the room at his roar, and I stared in reverence as the figure landed in the center of the throne room. Shadows flurried all around him like a mist. His dark bat-like wings spread out behind him, power coating his build. This was darkness.

Pyre's taut body kept me in place. His back stiffened, his wings thrashing behind him in a show of might.

"Please stay," he ordered and turned to face the creature. I couldn't make myself look at it, this new, otherworldly being that unmistakably demanded attention.

"Cousin," the dark one crooned. His voice was smooth like velvet. Something about it invited me to swim in the sound. It was like peace in the form of a potion. Pyre growled and took a defensive stance in front of me.

"Ombrose," said Pyre. I could hear the gritting of his sharp teeth. "To what do I owe the pleasure?"

"Just traveling by," he said, nonchalant.

"Where's my brother?" Pyre snarled at him. I didn't understand. If this wasn't his brother, then who was he? What was he doing here?

"I do not know." He shrugged. "I haven't seen any of your siblings in ages."

"Impossible!" The God of the Dead was furious in his bearings. "I smell him on you," he growled. I heard the creature laugh lowly, and Pyre's snarl rumbled further in his throat.

"Harboring a mortal, I see," the creature mused, switching the subject over to me. At the wave of his arm, I instinctively watched his movements as he gestured to me.

"She is not a concern of yours," Pyre ground out.

"You mean to tell me you've found the audacity in your ridiculous arrogance to keep this woman here when she so clearly does not belong?" he questioned.

This was it. This was my way out. He was defending me and trying to save me. I could feel the hope fluttering in my chest as I tore my eyes from his shadows and marked the strength of his body. Tall, dark, and exceedingly muscled. I could tell that he was very different in comparison to Pyre Malum. Where the God of the Dead bore light features enveloped by dark hair and wings, this man was rich night. My hope of escape swelled at the sight of his golden umber skin dipped in browns. He looked strong. He looked able to rip his enemy to shreds.

My hope was quickly disconnected when my eyes met his, and I noted that somehow, unbelievingly so, his were almost completely black. There were no whites, just a glowing ring of lightning blue where the iris might be. What was this creature? When he locked my gaze, I felt an enigmatic tug, as if my soul was telling me to look further and not to avert my stare. His mouth gawked as an electrical current passed over me.

"What is this?" he demanded as the God of the Dead blocked his view. I couldn't see the blackened eyes anymore. Something snapped in me at that wound—a longing for my escape.

"None of your concern," Pyre snarled. The shadowy one approached, his wings spread high above his head. The dark haze rose all around us.

"She is a Goddess," he snarled back at Pyre. "You've been torturing a Goddess?" He was angry now, screaming, lightning crashing all around us. I jumped, my heart leaping out of my chest. He didn't know who I was.

"What do you know of the Goddess?" Pyre barked. "Oh, that's right," he said now, flames erupting around him. "You and my brother have been hunting her." He growled deep in his chest. "I detected his scent on her, just like I can smell it on you now." Pyre's cousin hovered above us now, ominous in form. He looked like night enveloped in a storm.

"She is a Goddess..." he said again in disbelief.

"A Goddess you've been torturing with your nightmares, I presume," Pyre spat, and the fire roared, seeping up from the ground.

"The God of Nightmares," I whispered, trembling. They both whipped their heads toward me at the sound of my words. I pulled a hand over my mouth and watched in shock as the two terrifying Gods beat my skin with their eyes. The God of Nightmares surveyed me with a look akin to shock written across his face. When I looked away from him to Pyre Malum, I staunched my breathing. Quickly, he shot his hands out at me, and a burst of fire fled a hairsbreadth from my body. I screeched in anguish as I realized that his flame was not like my fire. This one *burned*. Had I moved even an inch, I'd have been scorched to ash.

"Stop," the dark-eyed God demanded. His wisps of night surged forward for me. Pyre held me to the wall with his barricade of flame and demanded my attention. I thought I might be bubbling under the heat.

"You called for him," Pyre accused.

"I didn't," I screamed, heaving. Bile rioted in my throat, and I hurled at my feet. This heat was all too much.

"You knew his name!" he roared, flames growing hotter.

"The pythrants told me," I cried, wiping at my mouth. "The pythrants told me the God of Nightmares was here." At this proclamation, the flames lowered ever-slightly, allowing the tendrils of darkness to slip their way around Pyre and wrap around my frame, extinguishing the blaze. I immediately felt the cool sensation healing my hot flesh. Pyre flung out a hand behind him, and I watched as the God of Nightmares was heaved across the room. I trembled at the sight. My hope of escaping crumbled to dust in an instant. Pyre was stronger. I was overwhelmed, in shock from all of this. I needed a getaway.

Pyre's gaze landed on his cousin now. With his attention elsewhere, I considered my options carefully. If I stayed in place, I was sure to die at the hands of a God. If I tried to find a way out of the castle through its many halls and towers, the pythrants would capture me and return me to the throne room. There was only one option in which the outcome may be a successful escape. I had minimal experience with flying, but if I could not fly, I could unquestionably hover. I could jump out of the busted wall and gradually lower myself onto the ground if I focused on manipulating the air correctly.

Building up the courage, I took a chance and made a run for it. There was no turning back now. I ran as fast as I could to the edge of the castle wall. My ankles buckled, never having to withstand such force and so quickly. I ignored the pain, forced my fears down, and landed in front of the vast hole where a window used to be. I had no time to think. It was now or never. When I made to bound off the ledge, a gust of heat knocked me against the brick, and I thought that Pyre had shot his fire at me.

Instead, a swift, torrid flame spread up to where the wall used to be, forming a barricade. Hot and blazing, my steps faltered. The flame rendered me motionless, stopping me from my descent, and caging me in once again. At this, my sanity tipped over the edge. Everything in me boiled over, and I exploded in indignation. All of my might, all of my power burst from my core and ensconced the palace.

"Let me go!" I shrieked an ear-piercing command. The entire castle shook at my wrath. I screamed and screamed until my lungs tasted of blood. Copper tang invaded my senses, the ringing in my ears deafening to the point of bliss as it drowned all other thoughts. I submerged myself in madness; a wicked laugh, not sounding like my own, tore from my lips in anguish. I tasted the blood that dripped down from my nose and into my mouth, savoring the force of my power. Because that's what this was—my power. I would bow to no one. I would not leave here, but I would not let the daimon of the Dead or his cousin take my life. If they wanted to kill me, if anyone wanted me dead, they would come crashing down with me.

Beneath my bare feet, a crack appeared on the cold stone floor. Before I could move away from the break, the castle floor tore beneath my footing, creating a deathly crater that split the room in half.

"Fuck!" Pyre thundered. "Hold on!" I clawed at the jagged rocks and held on for dear life. Suspended only by my grip on a boulder, I looked below to the hissing waters awaiting my descent. I couldn't lose this battle now. I was not finished.

"Goddess," the God of Nightmares called to me.

"Do not speak to her," Pyre snarled, closing in on his cousin. I could do nothing but watch as I tried to find a better hold. Shadows burst from the God of Nightmares in wisps of cool air. I felt the tug of a tendril around my arms, and my strain lessened as it tried to help me over the edge. Fire burst from Pyre's palms, and the heat turned the shadow into nothing in the blink of an eye. I felt the force of my weight pull at my shoulders, and my fingers begged me to let go.

"You would let her fall?" the other rasped, shaking off his cousin's attack.

"Where is my brother, Ombrose?" the God of the Dead boomed.

"Pyre..." I sobbed, barely audible. He didn't even look at me, too focused on the threat of the other God present in his throne room. Too worried that his brother was nearby.

Slithering flooded the castle walls, and suddenly, my hands strained even further under the stress of gravity. It wasn't enough that I was stuck at the mercy of two angry Gods, and I couldn't get myself up from the edge of the fall. Naturally, the pythrant army came to defend their Lord. A hard lump formed in my throat as I swung from the rocks, limbs achingly heavy. At this moment, I knew that I was going to go down without a fight, and this was the last thing I would see before perishing. A broken castle, flames so bright they were glaring, with the creatures of the Under Realm taking space in every corner of the room—a mess of fire and shadow battling before my very eyes.

"Leave her be, my Lord," a pythrant boomed. "Let her go with the God of Nightmares." I whipped my head in the direction of the voice, entirely baffled by the claim on my safety. It was Nor.

"Nor, don't!" I trembled, hanging on for dear life. He would die for this defiance.

"I will not allow you to harm our Goddess," Nor shouted for all to hear. The pythrants hissed in agreement. I couldn't believe it. These creatures who barely ever looked at me were here to guard me instead of their God. "We defend in her honor. We serve her."

"We serve her!" the rest chanted. Pyre roared at the insolence.

"You would hand her over? Betraying me?" His flames grew higher, the air lessening in the process.

"Our Goddess shows no prejudice against our kind. She is benevolence and mercy. She is hope, and she is our salvation," he raved, fangs releasing from his secretions. Though I had done nothing to gain their loyalty, these creatures of the Under Realm stood for me in my weakest moment. When Nor looked at me, his face told me everything. Like his last words to me, he wanted me to run, to fight for my life.

"You conspire with my cousin." Pyre spat. "You knew that the God of Nightmares was here, yet you failed to report this to me."

"Ombrose will take her where she belongs," Nor said, voice soft, still looking at me.

"He will do no such thing," Pyre thundered, and my heart begged me to implode. The pythrants were helping me. The God of Nightmares wanted to take me home, and Nor knew this. Nor had helped him into my room. I thought of that morning when I woke, remembering the barricade of thorn-filled roses that caged me in bed. Pyre had said that he had tried to remove me, but he couldn't. The thorns had prevented his endeavor. Had this new God attempted the same thing, failing to do so?

Pyre stalked over now, standing before me, centuries of rage blazing all around him. I flinched at the sound of his boots crushing the rocks near my hands. The pythrants slithered around, cautious not to get too close to the fire and careful not to fall into my abyss. I could do nothing but watch as I waited to see what my captor would do.

"I'm sorry," he said with his face hard, for only me to hear. Would he not help me up? Would he force my fall? Pyre smiled at my fright and lifted his foot. I watched in horror as he slowly crunched my fingers, eliciting a screech of pain. "Hold tight."

"Please!" I rasped. I was entirely at his mercy. His aggression kindled as he pressed further into the step. Bone crunched at the weight of his punishment as he basked in his cruelty. The God of Nightmares stood behind me on the other side of the barrier, dark wings flapping, sending a breeze of cool, black tendrils my way. I looked into his depthless eyes and recoiled at the sight.

"Help her up, cousin!" he hissed at Pyre.

"With you here?" he barked. "The minute the Goddess stands again, she will run or die trying." He twisted the sole of his foot into my right hand as he turned to face his cousin. Blood-curdling pain rippled through me, and I thought I might pass out.

"Stop!" I begged, wailing at the top of my lungs. At this point, I imagined there was nothing left of my bones. Only Pyre's foot held me from falling.

"If you will not help her, I will," Nor sibilated.

"Try," Pyre dared. His dirty, black hair whipped around him, catching in the sweat that lined his smile.

Before I could stop them, dozens of pythrants leaped from their perches and sprung forward. Fire roared to life, the flame loud and glinting. Pyre stood his ground as heavy arms, and thick tails slashed away at him. A rock beneath my left hand broke from the ledge, and I lost my grip. My body swung right, ribs crashing into the rock as Pyre's foot kept my right hand in place. My wrist twisted at the pull as I watched the bone remove itself from its socket.

"Help me!" I screamed, but no one tried to hear me. I clenched my teeth and swung myself left, pushing through the pain in my right arm until I finally caught the ledge again with my other hand.

Pyre didn't move from his place as he fought off the creatures that continued throwing blows, striking where they could when they had the chance. I could do nothing but watch as, one after the other, the pythrants fell down the hole I was suspended in.

"No!" I cried as I watched them perish in a matter of seconds. Nor was getting closer now, fighting his way through spheres of fire that hurled past him.

"Nor, stop it this instant!" a familiar voice boomed from the doorway. To my revulsion, Alriq stood in the frame; his skin scorched from Pyre's attack. I watched as Nor began to recognize his consort.

"Alriq?" he croaked, then fell to his knees.

"Move away from the Goddess," Alriq ordered him. Pyre snarled in agreement.

"Listen to your mate, Nor," the daimon warned. "Or the next body I toss will be yours." But Nor didn't back away. He was still on his knees, closer to me than ever. I watched as a single tear fell down his cheek.

"Goddess," a voice coiled around me, smooth like velvet. I whipped my head around, trying to find the sound. "I cannot get to you while his touch is on you." I wept in confusion, sweeping the room.

"What do you mean?" I wheezed; my voice was raspy from the screaming.

"Shh... All will be well. You have to trust me." The God of Nightmares locked me in a gaze. The ring of blue lightning burned so brightly in contrast to the black in his eyes.

"Who are you?" I trembled at the sight.

"Let go of the ledge," he boomed over the chaos erupting

around me. I whimpered as Pyre let a rippling snarl escape from his clenched teeth.

"Her immortality will cease to exist at the touch of the steaming waters," he gnashed. "It is the Ondalôr, the River of Pain. Without proper passage, she will drown in her own boiling flesh."

"No." I sobbed, forcing my fingers to tighten, one hand free and one under the pressure of Pyre's foot.

"Look at me," the dark one pleaded. "Do you trust me?" His eyes were never-ending. I looked back to the daimon of the Dead, and he laughed at my despair.

"She does not know the meaning of trust," he spat. When I saw he had no mercy for me, my heart shattered. Gone was the man I'd thought him to be beneath his hard surface. It hadn't been a façade. He hadn't been a secretly tender-hearted God. No matter how much good we made of our time during training, no matter the empathy and kindness I bestowed upon him, it meant nothing when it came down to it. Though he needed me to fulfill the prophecy, his rage was more potent than his judgment.

Nor came up from his crouch and started to walk toward me again. Pyre snarled as he held me in place with his foot. I could barely feel my hand now as it crumbled to dust.

"Please, my Lord," Nor began. His voice was calm, his face a match. "End this now. Help her up and let her walk. She does not belong here."

"You know nothing of what you speak," Pyre ground out, shaking his head with frustration. "Stand down," he ordered, wings flapping in the smoke of his fire. Though Pyre commanded him, Nor did not look to the God of the Dead. As Alriq stalked forward to retrieve his mated consort, Nor did not move.

"I love you," he mouthed, barely a whisper on his tongue.

Alriq's serpentine eyes grew wide in panic. He was running now, panting in the heat of the fire.

"No," he screamed. "No!" Nor looked at me now, his face wet with tears.

"For the Goddess," he said, and with a giant leap, he plunged into the abysmal fault and slammed into my back, knocking the wind out of me.

"Nor!" I yelled, the weight crushing my spine as he clung to my sides. Shadows wove themselves all around us.

"Let go, Goddess," Nor whispered in my ear.

"I can't." I sobbed.

"You can. For freedom. For hope."

"Remove yourself from her!" Pyre boomed. Lightning erupted all around us. "You'll make her fall!"

"Alriq, you have to help us!" I screamed, frantically forcing my blurry eyes to find him. "Help us up!"

"No, Goddess," Nor quietly said as we watched his mate bolting for us. He was outrageous! I had to get him off of me. I had to get us out of this mess. My arms burned at the strain of my muscles, feeling as if they were about to snap off.

"Pyre, please," I begged. I could barely speak the words. My throat was raw from screaming. "You once told me that no one would ever hurt me so long as you breathe. Yet here we are, and you've gone back on your word. Did that not apply to you too?" Pyre stared at me with openly glowing eyes.

"I will save you, and only you," he swore, eyes a bright red. The gold seeped through like sparks in a fire. He hissed as he looked around at all the creatures, the men who were trying to save me. "Stand down, pythrants! I will deal with you all when I am finished with my cousin. When he is locked in the bowels of Obystrus, I shall send you to your judgment."

"No, please," I squeaked, voice cracking from the pain. "Don't do this...."

"Let go," the smooth voice beckoned.

"I can't," I cried. "Nor will die. I will die." I sobbed.

"No, my Goddess," Nor whispered. "You will finally live."

"What about you?" I started, and he kissed my cheek.

"I am already lost." And with that, the pythrant released me and plummeted into the abyss.

"Nor!" Alriq roared, making it to the ledge only seconds too late. "What have you done?" he boomed. In the seconds it took Alriq to make his decision, Drakovyr came blasting through the doorway, making the pythrant his target. As Alriq charged for Pyre, the hound bounded forward faster than the speed of light.

"Now, Goddess," the voice soothed. I looked down at my doom, awaiting my embrace. When Alriq's body slammed into Pyre's with a blade in hand, I did what I thought I couldn't and let go.

48

RETRIBUTION

PYRE MALUM

Being stabbed repeatedly was the least of my worries. I had lived a thousand lives, and not once had my chest ached in this manner. The knife wounds had nothing to do with the tightness pooling in my ribcage. All I had strived toward, all that Shivalri and I had worked for, had vanished before my very eyes. I had seen it then, the look of betrayal and hurt she'd bored into me. I needed her to stay put. Nearly begged her, yet she was still defiant and ever looking for an escape... An escape from me.

I cannot blame her for choosing death over being forced to stay here with me. I am cruel to a fault none other than my own. Though I was taught to be malevolent, I had never once attempted changing my bearings. Not until her. I was who I was made to be. An unwanted God, exiled to rule over this eternal Hell.

I am a fair ruler and give what I can where it is due. Shivalri would not know this of me, though, as I was sure to keep her at arm's length when it came to information on my past and ruling. I didn't want to sway her opinion of me. That was one thing I would give her. I would give her the freedom to decide for herself what she thought of me. I had assumed her guard was coming down over the last weeks, but it was I who had let my guard down. The minute she was given an escape route, she tumbled over the damnable cliffs of her own making.

I still saw the final moment—her screams ringing in my head. I had no choice but to attempt inattention to her while Ombrose was present. He was working for my brother; this I knew. If my brother were to discover her true importance to me, whether she was essential or not, he would want to rip her from me. I could not allow such a thing. So, I stood by, still feeling the crunching of her delicate bones under the soles of my feet, dying to ease the pain I caused her. I had to choose between letting her go or showing my hand to a player who was desperate to conquer all. I could find her again. I *would* find her again. I had promised her just that. Whether she saw it as a promise or a threat, I could not tell from the way she watched me; doe-eyed and beautiful as ever. I had screamed her name and promised to retrieve her, but she did not call back to me from Ombrose's arms.

I would find her. I had gotten her into this mess and turned this into more chaos than intended. Though she was still necessary in my plans, I would not allow her another moment of strife. She did not deserve this torment. I would make things right for her.

A cold ache emanated through my tired form as I willed my eyes to flit open. I instantly recoiled at the feel of the hard floor beneath me.

"Shivalri…" I called, remembering the High Council's deceit. I made to move, examining the room now where I led my grandkids, my little witches, to drink a cup full of drugs. Raidan and Satyra lie unconscious on the floor next to me.

"Raidan?" I said, voice slightly withered from having been asleep. My mouth was parched. "Saty, sweetie?" A stitch pricked me as I tried to reach my two grandchildren. On trembling legs, I lifted my head, scanning the room. The High Council was gone. As I looked at the floor, a pair of golden-framed eyeglasses lay broken where Shivalri once sat.

"Oh, Shivi…" I murmured, bending over to pocket them. Hobbling over to Raidan and Satyra, I was hasty yet fearful to examine them. My lineage was bound for greatness, I knew, but right now, the feeling of loss was far more prominent than the recognition of our power.

"No, no, no," I whispered, voice dry. "Please, get up," I urged. They didn't make so much as a move. I had to get them all out of the House of Enchantment. I had to protect them. Pushing them closer to one another, I tucked the unruly white strands of hair out of my way and used all my strength to get them as close as possible. Wrapping my arms around their limp bodies, I commanded my power to rise.

"Gods of the greater realm, hear my plea," I began, using all my might. "You have given me this gift of weaving, and I have never once asked for your help wielding it. Help me now. Allow me to use it for good." I closed my eyes, muscles tensing at the ripple of power I produced. *"Auxilium! Deos, precor!"* I bellowed, my voice echoing through the dimly lit church room. "Help me, Gods. I pray..."

It was no use. I did not have the strength to bring my grandchildren with me.

A small, hard object poked at my side as I leaned over Raidan and Satyra.

"The book," I wheezed, removing the small booklet from my coat pocket. I had forgotten that I'd taken it from the library earlier. "There must be something in here," I said with a rasp, flipping through the pages. My old fingers trembled, fighting to hold the book steady. "Come on," I begged.

Landing on a page that read *"Portare plures,"* I jolted with faith. "Oh, yes! Thank you, Gods." I beamed, tilting my head to the ceiling. I'd never been more thankful for my knowledge of Latin until this moment. *"Portare plures!* Aid me in carrying more than myself. Assist me in carrying my grandchildren as I weave our time."

Everything around us started to slow. My motions grew heavy and calculated as I pressed across time. I could see the strings glowing a bright red. Tugging and twisting, I untangled the mess we were in. It was harder, far more strenuous, to wrestle not one but three people's life-strings in one spell. I had never done such a thing, never thought to attempt it. I knew what to do when weaving myself, but playing with my grandchildren's fates was a risky game. Still, I pushed through, taking one step at a time, being sure not to cause disorder in their lives and in the timeline.

In an instant, we were back in the safety of my Grimsbane manor. What should have taken us half an hour only took me a mere second to arrive by car. I'd zipped through traffic, knowing where each vehicle would be before catching up to them. The others would not see me as I moved faster than the speed of light. With great strength and intense concentration, I followed the glowing strings that pointed to my family home.

It was the dead of night when we appeared in the foyer. I let my grandkids rest, affording me a moment to search the basement for clues as to where the High Council might have taken my granddaughter. I, Raidan, and Satyra were safe, but Shivalri was not.

"Why did they fool me?" I questioned, rummaging through my tomes which were scattered all over the table. "Their actions were supposed to be for the greater good. Drugging me? Drugging my grandchildren? That was never a part of the plan... What am I ever going to do?" The High Council was sworn in as magical law enforcement, the patriarchy of witches. Instead of helping make the world safe and keeping their fellow witches protected, they were the cause of chaos. This was dark magic at play.

When the creak of the basement door sounded, I lit the torches along the cavern walls to allow Raidan and Satyra a better chance at coming down the stairs.

"Gram?" Satyra called.

"Down here, my sweet," I replied. "Come quickly." Their footsteps pattered down the stairs, and I met them at the bottom. They were white as sheets, drained of all energies.

Satyra's lip quivered when she made it to the last step. Raidan rubbed at his eyes and snuffed his cry.

"Where's my sister?" he asked, barely audible. It was hard for me to look at my grandkids in this light. Not only had they suffered the loss of parents at far too young of an age, but they were also forced into a new world full of trepidation. They had been obligated to accept their fates, drugged by powerful strangers, and Shivalri had been kidnapped before their very eyes.

"The High Council has taken her," I answered solemnly, showing sadness in how I spoke. The pair of them looked at each other and then back to me. As their elder, they clung to my every movement, waiting for me to solve all of their problems. As a crone, I felt the weight of the world on my shoulders as my two grandkids looked at me like this. "We will get her back," I said. "I swear it on my life."